Sir David Brewster

Letters on Natural Magic

Sir David Brewster

Letters on Natural Magic

ISBN/EAN: 9783744765398

Printed in Europe, USA, Canada, Australia, Japan

Cover: Foto ©Andreas Hilbeck / pixelio.de

More available books at **www.hansebooks.com**

LETTERS ON NATURAL MAGIC

BY

SIR DAVID BREWSTER, M.A. D.C.L.

WITH

CHAPTERS ON THE BEING & FACULTIES OF MAN, AND
ADDITIONAL PHENOMENA OF NATURAL MAGIC

By J. A. SMITH

A NEW EDITION, WITH ILLUSTRATIONS

London
CHATTO & WINDUS, PICCADILLY
1883

Ballantyne Press
BALLANTYNE, HANSON AND CO., EDINBURGH
CHANDOS STREET, LONDON

PREFACE TO THE PRESENT EDITION.

ɪɴᴄᴇ the 24th of April, 1832, when the last of the accom-
nying Letters by Sir David Brewster to Sir Walter
:ott was written, many circumstances have occurred to
:tend the importance of that wide and comprehensive
bject which Sir David nas embraced under the name of
atural Magic; for though education, intelligence, and
ientific discovery have been advancing with rapid strides,
edulity has not been, and does not seem ever likely to
wholly eradicated by their means, while the ingenious
ɪvе been armed with immense and varied additional
ements to favour deception if they shall choose to employ
om for that purpose. It has appeared to the editor of
ɪe present edition, therefore, of the highest importance
give the work the benefit of that profounder interest
hich must arise from a consideration of the physical and
etaphysical existence or being of man—the union of
ɪese two conditions of his being in their action, through
:e faculties or powers of human perception and verifica-
ɔn, and also from a consideration of the range of natural
ɔssibility; for by a proper knowledge of these mankind
ill be better aware of the extent of their liability to be
ɪceived, and of the means of verification and correction
their command, as well as of the mode in which their
ɪbility to deception ought to be guarded against or

protected from the influence of imposture, and verification applied in defeating or exposing delusion.

Much of the ease with which we are deceived by the phenomena of natural magic arises from our want of previous preparation, and our deficient knowledge, for the moment, of the laws within which the true explanation of these phenomena may be found. Hence, very much in proportion to our ready knowledge or intelligence we are either credulous or sceptical—the words are used in a philosophic sense merely; and history has shown that men are often quite as far from the truth in the extremity of their scepticism as they are in the extreme of credulity itself. Mere scepticism has in fact been a great barrier and enemy to the progress of science ; and though the credulous have often sunk into superstition and become intolerant, they have more generally recognized than ignored those temporarily incomprehensible facts which the advent of calm science has satisfactorily explained. Indeed, but for this slight difference, these two extremes only too often meet ; for the extreme of scepticism is credulity, and the extreme of credulity, or superstition, is scepticism. Both distrust truth ; both trust their own prejudices and impressions rather than truth ; both misrepresent and persecute it ; both obstruct the progress of its intelligible development. Even in this day many facts of science are, in consequence, left, without examination, in the hands of charlatans whose function always is to render them odious by exaggeration and therefore repugnant to scientific study and explanation ; for the scientific mind ever recoils from the wares of the quack, and—too hastily ignoring the small grain of genuine and philosophic truth which is necessary and almost in every case present to sustain any enduring pretension—considers the whole elements involved to be as much matters of imposture as the individual by whom they are employed.   This is barely excusable in a thinking age, and it is most certainly not the way to disarm imposture or to put it down. If the thinking and intelligent will not examine and explain what is used to deceive, how can the unthinking and the ignorant be but deceived, and continuously deceived, by it? Nay, we all know the experience of human weakness in this respect to be such that the person whose credulity has given way to deception in one case does not always, where it has been rescued by explanation, resort to greater caution and scepticism for the future, but, on the contrary, that the idiosyncrasy of many individuals is to be deceived in every instance in which competent explanation is wanting. Nor, even when caution and scepticism are produced by detection of imposture, are these the great results which philosophy and truth would desire to achieve. Intelligence is the only bulwark of the human mind, and it is in presence of this great and necessary adjunct to the integrity of our normal being that the additions here made to Sir David Brewster's excellent and popular work are now offered to the public; for the liability to be deceived, from which we all more or less suffer, ought to be, not a ground for scepticism, but only a stronger incentive to obey that divine injunction: "GET KNOWLEDGE, GET WISDOM, AND, WITH ALL THY GETTING, GET UNDERSTANDING." .

From the nature of the case, as will be readily understood, the eminent author's Letters have in themselves been left intact, as an essential feature of their authenticity, and the new matter has been introduced in the preliminary and additional chapters.

From what is explained in the succeeding chapters, it will be observed that *comparison* is the great means by which we are enabled to assure ourselves, according to the existing organization of our being, of the truth or falsehood of any phenomenon, and that this comparison extends not only to the evidence of one faculty as compared with another, but to the comparison afforded by different points of examination in the use of the same faculty, so that we may reasonably assume, where such verification is unfairly excluded, that we are entitled to suspend our judgment in all cases in which immediate decision is not absolutely necessary. But it is a singular fact in connection with this subject that almost all animals are made with duplicates of each of their faculties, as if to supply by comparison a check to the inaccuracy of the faculty *within itself.* Thus we have duplicate brains as well as duplicate eyes; and while a man with two eyes sees with both, and would detect imperfection in one eye by means of the accuracy of the other, so we have reason to believe that a man thinks in duplicate, or with both lobes of the brain, although from the co-operation of the organs only one single train of thought is apparent; just as by the use of both eyes one subject is alone presented in consequence of the co-operation of both organs of vision : for it has been found that where one of the lobes of the brain has been so injured as to be incapable of action, a perfectly sane and healthy power of mind has been maintained in the individual by the sound action of the other lobe of the brain only, just as accurate vision may be experienced by a person having only one eye, or shutting the other. The explanation of this power is not referrible to the physical, but to the metaphysical part of our being, as will be better understood by what we have introduced on the subject of Consciousness; for there is just as much a duplicate of thought produced in employing both lobes of the brain as there are two physical images when both eyes are used— the unity experienced in each case existing in the combining power of the Consciousness only.

J. A S.

Sept. 1868.

CONTENTS.

THE BEING AND FACULTIES OF MAN IN REFERENCE
TO NATURAL MAGIC.

CHAPTER I.

CHAPTER II.

CHAPTER III.

CHAPTER IV.

CHAPTER V.

LETTER I.

LETTER II.

LETTER VI.

LETTER VII.

LETTER VIII.

LETTER IX.

LETTER X.

LETTER XI.

LETTER XII.

LETTER XIII.

ADDITIONAL PHENOMENA OF NATURAL MAGIC.

THE BEING AND FACULTIES OF MAN

NATURAL MAGIC.

CHAPTER I.

*Material and immaterial nature of man — Body — Mind — Life—
Feeling—External matter—Touch—Separation and connection
of all these—Plato and the soul—Electricity—Epicurus—Bishop
Berkeley—David Hume—Consciousness and matter—Conscious-
ness and the immaterial—Reciprocal contact—Man's primary
perceptive power—Its contact with and knowledge of matter
and the immaterial—Its proximity to the infinite—Cause of the
Epicurean error—Berkeley's blunder the other way—Cause of
Hume's error—Self-deception in philosophy—Fallacy in a
Syllogism.*

MAN is a being with two natures, one of which is physical
and material, the other immaterial, or *metaphysical* as it
is called, and both are intimately but mysteriously and
incomprehensibly united in all that is known of actual
and practicable human existence and action. The
physical portion of man's being we may examine by the
light of science, and perfectly and accurately know; but
the metaphysical or immaterial portions of his being, com-
prehending the three widely distinct and separate though
co-operating and co-acting departments of MIND, LIFE,
and FEELING, are subject to no law of science with which
we are acquainted, and are in their elementary composi-

B

tion entirely beyond the range of scientific or philosophic investigation. It is true that profound and ponderous metaphysical works have been written on departments of this subject; for the phenomena of mind are not wholly beyond the range of study and contemplation; but it would only vex and annoy the reader of a popular work like the present to pile up before him the heavy speculations of that crude department of Philosophy usually called METAPHYSICS comprehensively, and PSYCHOLOGY and ONTOLOGY distinctively, with its special and embarrassing nomenclature and definition of terms, and we prefer for every practical purpose here a simpler and a clearer course, and one which the most general reader may follow with immediate ease through language used in its most ordinary acceptation, and the whole signification of which is decided at once by the obvious aim of the context in which it appears.

Man, then, consists of two natures, divided into four parts: a material Body, an immaterial Life, an immaterial Mind, and immaterial Feeling. Three-fourths of his whole being therefore is metaphysical or *immaterial*, and only one-fourth, and that the least essential portion of it—his body—physical or material. To prove that Mind, Life, and Feeling, though co-operating in human existence, are essentially distinct in themselves, it is only necessary to show that they are each capable of distinct and independent existence. Thus, in the vegetable world, we have Life without Mind or Feeling; among the inferior animals we have Life and Feeling without Mind; and in man the latter is added to the others. It is of importance, however, to observe, that while Mind may exist without Feeling, neither Mind nor Feeling can exist without Life. On the other hand, Matter may exist without being associated with Life, Mind, or Feeling; as it is observable that all the chemical or Material elements of the human body may be found in a state of separation from these, and that when Life, Mind, and Feeling are withdrawn from man the whole Material elements of the human body remain; and it is hence reciprocally inferrible that Life, Mind, and Feeling may all exist in a state of separation from Matter, and that the soul of man, or his whole metaphysical being, may exist apart from his body.   It is not intended by this deduction to say anything in favour of Plato's theory of the Immortality of the Soul.   Those who conclude that he proved the immortality of the soul rush hastily to an unwarrantable assumption.   The immortality of the soul is a conditional and subjective fact of the Divine Will, ascertainable only by revelation of that will; it is not an inherent power or quality of the soul itself.* Plato's argument was, that because the soul does exist it must have always existed, and must always continue to exist.   But this argument is fallacious by analogy, and utterly inconsistent with human experience; for on the same principle, and by parity of reasoning, Consciousness exists, and it must therefore have existed from all eternity, and must always continue to exist.   But notoriously, in the experience of every man, our consciousness did not exist from all eternity, and within the limits of

* Plato in one passage appears fully to admit this, but the admission is not easily reconcileable with his other reasoning, which, however, was early found to be unsatisfactory and unconvincing on the subject. Cicero felt it to be beautiful, but not impressive. The passage in which he makes the admission referred to also goes, unfortunately, too far, and asserts that the Divine intelligence *has given* the human soul the right of immortality. But Plato does not base this assertion on its only possible foundation—a known revelation of the Divine Will, and nowhere shows that he knew of any such revelation, though it has been suggested, but not established, that he may have got some of his knowledge from the Hebrews. The intrinsic evidence is certainly against this supposition, as his doctrines on the subject of immortality are too Pythagorean for any conceivable Hebrew source.

our present experience it does not always continue to
exist, for it may be and is frequently in a state of absolute
suspension.   It is not therefore true, on any principle
either of direct or analogous reasoning, that because a thing
exists it must have always existed, or must always continue to exist.*   The very converse is the rule of human
experience, and it is a rule which admits of no demon
strable exception ; for even matter did not always exist to
human consciousness : hence the eternal endurance, or in-
destructibility of matter is not demonstrable by so limited
and finite a being as man.   He can no more tell or demonstrate what shall be after him than he can prove or
demonstrate what from all eternity has been before him ;
and he is no more warranted in assuming that matter is
indestructible, simply because he cannot destroy it, than
he would be in assuming that the moon and planets are
incombustible because he cannot set them on fire.   Man's
ordinary and too popular inference, therefore, that matter
is indestructible is an impotent conclusion, founded
entirely on the assumption that his own small and limited
powers are the boundary of all physical possibility and all
knowledge, and not on any complete and absolute acquaintance with the whole laws and possible conditions of
matter.   This defective knowledge of man may be proved
by facts recently observed which are exceptions to all
the chemical laws and conditions of matter with which
human science is acquainted :—Biela's Comet, a small
nucleus comet without a tail which moves round the sun in
a short orbit, which it traverses every six years and a half,
was in 1846, without any ascertainable cause, observed to
divide into two parts, which have since continued in a state

* Plato's reasoning, even in his own hands, results in the conclusion, not so much that the human soul is immortal, as that soul
must have existed from all eternity · in other words, there must have
been a *Living First Cause*

of complete separation, demonstrating the fact that there are conditions in which matter may not be possessed either of cohesion or concentric attraction—a circumstance which no known law of chemistry or other science can explain; and yet we are compelled to recognize this fact, on the authority of astronomy, as being quite as authentic as any with which that great science, or any other, science, has made us acquainted; and other facts might be cited. All that we can venture, on the basis of human experience, therefore, to say is, that man cannot destroy matter, but that we are not sufficiently acquainted with its laws to assert that it absolutely cannot be destroyed.

But another and a nearer fact which we must equally believe, though we cannot explain it, is that Life, and Mind, and Feeling are introduced into, contained within, or withdrawn from Matter, such as our material bodies, without changing, increasing, or diminishing the physical character or amount, or adding to or deducting from the bulk or weight of their Matter. How electricity is contained or operates on and within bodies we may acquire some knowledge of, but electricity is a material element, capable by its application of expanding and contracting bodies, as electrolysis has shown, while Mind, Life, and Feeling thrill and float along our nerves and tissues, or flush into the wide region of imaginary existence and action by a mysterious power and range of volition to which we have no key—a fact before which logic is dumb. Electricity is not Life, however fondly some have sought, in eager haste, to call it so. True, it has wondrous powers. Dead men have been made to move by it—their eyes have opened, and the cold and rigid features have changed and varied with a ghastly counterfeit of the expressions of life. Nay, the stomach has, under its influence, been made after death in some degree to perform the function of digestion. But no application of this great agent has ever, even in one instance, restored Life absolutely departed, or arrested in the dead the slow but certain progress of decay. The physical and metaphysical portions.of our body, once really separated, cannot be reunited by this or any other physical agency.

Life, Mind, and Feeling are thus obviously not inherent in electricity, nor in any other Material element of which nature is composed. The question hence has frequently been asked, what can we know of the external world, seeing that our minds cannot properly know what they are not in actual and tangible contact with? This question has been much complicated by the controversial mode in which it has been stated and dealt with, and also by the unwarrantable but unchecked assumptions which have from time to time formed, and still in a large measure form, part of the propositions laid down and admitted on both sides by those who canvass such questions. The Greek-physicist laid down the proposition, that *nothing but matter can touch or be touched;** and from this aphorism, too hastily assumed as an axiom on the mere faith of its own plausibility, it was fallaciously inferred that everything must be material. When Bishop Berkeley laid down the counter-proposition—that *feeling, or the sense of touch, is not an attribute of matter*, because, as must be apparent, it nowhere exists inherently or inseparably in matter—he confronted the previous proposition with an aphorism equally plausible, and, from the reason just given in support of it, more unquestionably axiomatic; but then, so fallible is human reasoning, and so eager is man to rush at ultimata and premature conclusions, that Berkeley at once felt himself warranted in drawing this inference:—As feeling is not material, and as we can know nothing but what we feel or experience, *therefore* the existence of matter cannot be proved, and we are warranted in concluding that there is no such demonstrable

* This proposition is the basis of the philosophy of Epicurus.

thing as Matter. Hume's philosophy was founded on this basis, and was rendered further preposterous and extravagant by his plunging at once into the dark, as far as scepticism could possibly go, with the wild and spectral inference that :—Because the existence of Matter could not be demonstrated, *therefore* the existence of no Reality could be demonstrated, and *hence* there is no such thing as Reality. Now if human reasoning leads men of intellect to conclusions like these, leaving the disciples of the physicists, on the one hand, with the proposition that there is nothing but Matter as their creed; and, on the other, arrays the metaphysicians round the counter-proposition, that Matter cannot be demonstrated, and hence there is no such thing as Matter, and the sceptics at the back of these to draw their wild and wide conclusion from both sides of the controversy, and, if they have a mind, state it in a syllogistic . negative thus : *As nothing but matter can touch or be touched, and the existence of matter cannot be demonstrated, there can be no other tangible reality than matter, and the existence of no tangible reality can be demonstrated—* the result is surely disastrous only to man's intelligence.

It is melancholy to find men of thought and unquestionable power contented thus to pervert the great qualities of Godlike intellect, and, in deference to their own pet and favourite theories, leave the grand questions of eternal truth in this state. It is so easy in such directions to reason a little way above the average intellectual energy of mankind, that it becomes just the more deeply and indelibly reprehensible to stir up mere sediment into the fountain of truth, and leave the common mind to grope in the darkness of its muddled and inky waters. And yet such is the condition in which partizan philosophy has left this noble department of inquiry and thought.

In the preceding summary we have condensed this subject, and stated its substance rather than its detail, that we might not embarrass the general reader with tediously protracted sophistries, nor foul his free and healthy mind with subordinate and disingenuous controversies intensely unworthy of his attention. Truth is not so dark when candour comes to deal with it as these subtle and merely technical philosophers would make it; for the whole truth of their philosophy depends, not upon the facts, but on the accuracy or inaccuracy of the terms or language in which they have expressed themselves; and it is only necessary to state their propositions in detail to show in how many parts the chain of logic is broken and fragmentary, and the reasoning inconsecutive, because they have assumed their language to be perfect!

Let us take then the proposition, 'nothing but matter can touch or be touched,' and, following it, the proposition by which it is so obviously refuted, that 'feeling, or the sense or consciousness of touch, is not material, nor an attribute of matter.' From this latter proposition, which is obviously correct and irrefutable, the next proposition is said to be drawn, that as our feelings or sensations are not material, and as it is from these feelings or sensations that all our knowledge of what is external to us is derived, and we are conscious of nothing but them, therefore we have no knowledge of matter or external nature, and the existence of matter is not, and cannot be demonstrated. This inference is certainly very plausible, but it is not warranted by the antecedent proposition on which it professes to be based, and without which it has no foundation. An intermediate link of the logical chain has been dropped in arriving at it, and when that link is replaced it will be found fatal to this last over-drawn inference, for it does not bridge the leap between it and its antecedent, but carries the current of deduction and truth off in a totally different direction. While it is quite true that feeling, or the sense or consciousness of touch, is not material, nor an attribute of matter, it is not true that feeling, or the sense of touch, as is hastily assumed by the succeeding inference we have stated, does *not* touch; for it could not be a sense or *consciousness of touch, without touching*. The missing link in the chain, therefore, is the proposition that *the sense of touch does touch*, and is a *consciousness of touching*. It is, in fact, the point of contact between Matter and the Immaterial or Metaphysical, and but for the fact that the sense, or consciousness of touch *touches* the first proposition, that nothing but matter can touch, or be touched, would not be disproved by the other proposition, that feeling, the *sense of touch*, is not an attribute of matter; for it is only because the sense of touch *touches* that we are enabled to demonstrate the inaccuracy of the first proposition, and say that something else than matter can touch or be touched—that *our consciousness of touch*, which is not material, *can touch Matter*, and that Matter can, reciprocally, touch our Consciousness. Hence our consciousness of touch is *an actual contact with* that which we call *Matter*, and is a demonstration to us of the *existence of that Matter*. What then becomes of the wild inference that the existence of Matter cannot be demonstrated? And what of Hume's wilder and wider leap into the chaos of metaphysical intangibility, that Reality is incapable of demonstration?

The result of this correction is that the proposition—

1st. That 'nothing but matter can touch or be touched' is untrue, for

2nd. Feeling, the sense or consciousness of touch, is not material, and

3rd. Feeling, or the sense of touch, *touches and is consciousness of touching Matter*, and, consequently,

4th. Matter and the immaterial or metaphysical may be, and are, mutually capable of touching, and are in actual contact when the consciousness of touch is occasioned, and

5th. By this positive and actual contact *the existence of the physical* or material world is, *by contact, known and demonstrated to the immaterial and metaphysical.* Hence

The inferences that the existence of Matter and of Reality cannot be demonstrated are reduced to absurdity, for

First. Consciousness, though not material, is a REALITY and is the great primary perceptive faculty of man.

Note. As such it claims the primary place in the preceding table occupied by the false proposition, that ' nothing but matter can touch or be touched ;' the remaining four propositions of the table following it in logical sequence, and demonstrating that,

6th. *The primary reality of Consciousness is capable of knowing and demonstrating to itself the existence of Matter by touch, as well as its own metaphysical or immaterial existence and reality by its Consciousness of such existence and reality.*

Hence Epicurus, Bishop Berkeley, David Hume, and their respective disciples are all in error, though it must be borne in mind that to Bishop Berkeley is due the honour of refuting the materialists and laying down the second proposition in the preceding table, which forms the groundwork of their refutation; but it is the third proposition of that table, founded on the second, which really contains the refutation expressly of their proposition by demonstrating that something besides matter can touch and be touched, and that *consciousness of touch* is the actual *contact* of the physical and metaphysical.

But now let us consider some further facts connected with Consciousness—this great primary perceptive faculty of our being; for all our physical senses and faculties are mere vehicles and channels of its action, and without it the eye, however perfect, is blind, the ear deaf, the touch, smell and taste all alike powerless and incapable of vital action; for it is only when our Consciousness is present in any of these faculties that they perceive, or are capable of perceiving. While Consciousness, then, is a reality, and is our primary perceptive faculty, the following propositions are true in regard to it, and follow each other as consequences and experiences from it.

1. Each man has only one faculty of Consciousness, and that Consciousness constitutes his primary identity to himself, for in the course of life his body and other points of temporary identity change from childhood to age and lose all the features of literal identification.

2. This faculty of Consciousness is not capable of doing two things at a time, or receiving two or more simultaneous sensations, but its acts and sensations are successive, one following another: thus when the consciousness of hearing is in action the consciousness of seeing, or anything else, is for the moment suspended.

3. This faculty of Consciousness, though not forming any part of our bodies, nor inherent in the matter of them, does, while we live in this world, reside for the time being within our bodies and within and in actual contact with the Matter of them, though not within any particular portion of our bodies or of their material components; for,

4. The faculty of Consciousness is capable of pervading every part of our body in the most rapid succession, changing from head to foot, from hand to hand, from eye to ear, from taste to smell or touch, and from any point of touch to another over the whole surface of our bodies, and all this with such celerity and ease as sometimes to deceive us into the idea that we have received simultaneous instead of merely rapid successive impressions or sensations.

5. The faculty of Consciousness is therefore, and as they are successively exercised in conjunction with it, *in actual contact with the impressions of all our faculties*, and can consequently place itself in actual though metaphysical contact with every physical impression which our physical

faculties are capable of receiving or being affected by, as well as with every other kind of impression, not necessarily physical, by which they are affected. Thus, when we indulge the imagination or memory, or when we dream, the physical faculties, engaged for the time in any of those occupations, are impressed or affected by the metaphysical influences of imagination, of memory, or of dreaming, and the amount of Consciousness exerted for the time is in contact with these physical faculties, and, through them, perceives the metaphysical influences by which they are affected ; and hence it follows that,

6. The metaphysical faculty of Consciousness is capable of actual contact with all the physical faculties of our nature, and with all the other realities, or influences of other realities, whether physical or metaphysical, by which these physical faculties may be impressed or affected.

7. It follows from the preceding that one metaphysical fact or influence, such as imagination, memory, or dreaming, may come into contact with another metaphysical fact, our Consciousness, by using a physical and material faculty as its intermediate channel or vehicle of operation in doing so. Thus the physical faculty standing between may be in contact with, and acted upon by, the metaphysical on both sides, and hence we reach the hitherto unapproached conclusion—

8. That other metaphysical powers and influences besides consciousness of touch may come into actual contact with Matter and with material faculties, and positively act upon and impress, and cause action in, the Matter of these faculties just as really as a physical body may penetrate and stir water.

But may we not go a step further, and, strictly within the limits of logical deduction, place ourselves on the boundary of a greater and a still higher truth, and prove from the following premises, viz.: It is not the eye that sees, but the faculty of consciousness when in the eye; it is not the ear that hears, but only the faculty of consciousness when using the ear; and so of all our other physical senses—it is not they that perceive, but consciousness that perceives by them. But consciousness is not a special organization adapted specifically to seeing or hearing: it is *a metaphysical perceptive power*, capable of realising in living experience and knowledge any or all of the impressions of our physical faculties, and more—it is capable of using these impressions and its knowledge of them as elements of new creations, and new combinations, and climbing the steps of logic and the heights of imagination and memory with them into regions apart from matter, illimitable, and all its own. The eye as an actual faculty, bearing upon the outer world, is to the consciousness nothing more than a mere camera with an image in it portrayed on the retina; but the retina, without the vital presence of consciousness, is no more capable of seeing the image portrayed upon it than a piece of photographic paper or a plain mirror are capable of seeing because they have images upon them. The retina merely mirrors the image; it is the Consciousness which perceives the image portrayed, and consequently,

9. The same faculty of Consciousness which is capable of perceiving with all its details the illuminated surface of the retina, or mirror of the eye, and the picture upon it, must be equally capable of perceiving the images on any other mirroring surface, or the details of any actual surface whatever, were that faculty of Consciousness equally free to come in contact with such mirroring or other surface, and hence the present factitious, but not inherent limitation of the faculty of Consciousness to our physical and organic nature and its faculties is a restriction rather than a full development of its perceptive powers. And tho'

10. Such a fact lands this great primary perceptive faculty of our being fairly and fully on the margin of the infinite, and proves it to be capable of being enabled to perceive all reality, physical or. metaphysical, beyond the range of our present experience, were it only allowed to come into competent contact with such reality ?

It will be observed that the argument here is not for the immortality of the soul, but for its highest powers of perception or knowing, and of acting. The immortality, or *durability*, of our consciousness is, as we have said, dependent, not on anything inherent in itself; for it did not exist from all eternity; but on the Great Will and Power by which it was called into existence and continues to exist, and no one can prove what that Will is but by the revelation of it, so that a proof of the immortality of the soul on any other ground is impossible.

From this point let us—omitting the third proposition, p. 9, now stated, and all that follows upon it—look back for a moment to the condition of human philosophy displayed down to the present time by the state of these questions, and what it reveals of man's mental power of self-deception.

When Epicurus based his philosophy on the aphorism, nothing but matter can touch or be touched, he was guided by one faculty, the eye only, in arriving at the conclusion to which he came; for had he been guided by the sense of touch itself, in addition, he must have become aware of the fact that FEELING *touched* as well as MATTER. His blunder, therefore, was that he reasoned from partial and defective premises. Indeed, caustic though the remark may seem, it is more than doubtful whether a blind man would have fallen into the same ditch, for a blind man does not so readily perceive the contact of matter with matter, and is more impressed with the contact of *consciousness* with *matter*. Aristotle and Plato accused the materialists of refusing to believe in anything they could not handle with their hands ; but this is even more than what was true of their philosophy, and less than discriminative in judging it. They evidently did not believe or allow for feeling or consciousness in the hand, but falsely assumed that the whole of the hand's function or consciousness of touch was material and apparent, and nothing more than what they saw of the hand with their eyes. But while they saw physical contact with the hand, they never saw feeling or the consciousness of touch in it, and they therefore drew a conclusion as to touch at variance with the sense of touch itself, and with the evidence of every other faculty of man but his eyesight.

Berkeley, on the other hand, refuted their proposition not absolutely or directly, but only by implication and without really perceiving what was necessary to do it. His proposition that *the sense of touch is not material* implies the refutation, but this element of his proposition he himself expelled from it by gratuitously assuming that the existence of matter could not be demonstrated, and that there was, therefore, *nothing for the sense to touch.* From want of logical discrimination to state the third proposition (p. 9, *ante*), he not only did not refute the Epicureans, but left himself without a correct basis for further logical progress, and went off into all the errors of his subsequent fallacious and inconsecutive philosophy. Had he perceived that the sense of touch, though not material, touches—*is a sense of touch, and must therefore have something to touch before it is sensible of touching*— he would not only have refuted the Epicureans in direct terms by showing that something besides matter can touch and be touched, but he would also have avoided the blunder that matter is intangible and cannot be demonstrated, and all the errors he, and Hume after him, crowded on the back of that fallacy. Berkeley confesses to a desire to defeat the materialist philosophy by a sweeping conclusion against the whole basis of their arguments—the existence of matter—and he lost his impartiality in the eagerness of his zeal. "Matter," he says, "being once expelled out of Nature drags with it many sceptical notions * * * * without it your Epicureans, Hobbists, and the like have not even the shadow of a pretence, but become the most cheap and easy triumph in the world." He fell, therefore, into the weakness and error of seeking to destroy a reality for the purpose of confounding those who perverted it. How little the cause of truth is capable of being so served or promoted is conspicuously illustrated by the fact that the very means employed in achieving his object laid the foundation of just as much evil as it sought to cure, and reared up Hume instead of Hobbes, and something more than even absolute Egomism* in the place of Epicurus. For it is painfully evident that, if Bishop Berkeley had not sacrificed his candour to his zeal, he would have made it much more difficult, if not impossible, for David Hume to have been an infidel.

The power of self-deception, it will be found, from the preceding remarks, is by no means impaired by the study and pursuits of philosophy. Let us hope that candour, and an inflexible love of truth for its own sake, are able to steer clear of those subtle shallows on which theory and speculation have so often foundered and gone to ruin. Many eminently wise men have lived and died without being a whit the more foolish from not knowing much of metaphysics. Is it impossible to believe that these great minds have perceived, altogether outside of metaphysical science, that the great primary perceptive faculty,

* The denial of everything but one's own existence. Hume denied even the reality of his own existence

human consciousness, possessed a power of touch or contact with physical nature, without their finding it necessary, as a step in the logical progress of their intelligence, to lay down that fact among the abstract sequences of dialectics, and that they have not erred the more in all the practice and nobler aims of life from neglecting to do so? Fortunately, practical human life is not conducted under the light of dialectics, but men have to judge very much on the impulse and necessity of the occasion in most things, and were it not for their power to do so few would be able competently to meet the responsibilities of existence.

It may now form an amusement for such of our readers as care for the exercise of logical analysis to turn back to the syllogism stated at page 7, of the preceding remarks, which contains the whole concentrated force of David Hume's philosophy, and satisfy themselves how much sophistry there may be, after all, even in so solemn a formula as a syllogism, and how utterly false it may be in every member of it; for in that instance it will be found that the first blunder is a double one in the major proposition. For those who would like to follow the subject of Metaphysics still further, reference is made to the learned and discriminating article, " Metaphysics," in the Encyclopædia Britannica, and the first dissertation prefixed to that work, which will show what a muddle has hiherto, in all ages, been made of this great department of thought, and in what a disgraceful condition it has been left to the present day from want of a little consecutive directness and unbiased simplicity of thought.

But the primary perceptive power or Consciousness of man, its actual contact with, and knowledge of, Matter and the Immaterial, and its proximity to the Infinite, having been so far indicated, let us now deal with the physical faculties in connection with it. as forming its existing channels of operation, and with a few features of their structure and action, which Sir David Brewster has not in his Letters brought forward, but which, in some instances, tend to throw considerable explanatory light on many of the phenomena of Natural Magic he has set forth.

CHAPTER II.

Consciousness as the primary perceptive faculty of our Being—Its contact with reality and with all our impressions and sensations of reality—Eye and Ear more subject to influence from simulated impressions than the other senses—Touch and Taste possess more positive powers and means of accuracy—Smell intermediate in point of power—Bishop Berkeley and the Eye—Not the Eye that requires education from experience, but the Consciousness—The Eye perfect from the first—Difference between the Consciousness of man and of other animals—Difference between instinct and reason— The Seat of Sensation—Misapprehensions as to it—Consciousness moves through our bodies—Capable of extension on surfaces— Consciousness of space—Action of the senses not necessary to Consciousness in them—Power of Consciousness over the faculties —Pleasure and Pain—Attention—Thought—Memory.

IN the preceding chapter let us venture to hope it has been proved to the satisfaction of even the most general reader, who is at all a thinker, that CONSCIOUSNESS, the great primary perceptive power and faculty of our Being, is actually in contact not only with all we know—with all the impressions with which external nature or reality affects us—but also with all the channels, senses, powers, or faculties, material or immaterial, organic or inorganic, with which we are endowed as means of knowing or receiving impressions, real or imaginary, *at all times when we are conscious of those impressions :* and also that whenever touch, or actual contact with anything, is necessary to the sensation with which we are impressed by it, our consciousness is present in the act of contact, and, as such, is the only means by which we are aware of that contact, or receive any impression or sensation from it

Whenever we receive impressions without actual contact with the objects or causes which produce them, our consciousness comes in contact with the impressions so produced, and not with the objects or causes themselves; and this applies especially to what is seen and heard by us, for in these cases the impression produced on the eye or the ear is all that our consciousness comes in contact with by seeing or hearing. And as hearing and vision are thus faculties, or powers of perception, which do not come into actual contact with the objects or causes from which their impressions proceed, but only with the impressions proceeding from those objects, it follows that the eye and the ear must be much more subject to influences which simulate their real impressions, and must therefore be more liable to deception than the other senses are. And the experiences detailed by natural magic show this to be strictly true. The senses of taste, touch, and smell, are rarely deceived in comparison with the senses of seeing and hearing, and the means of deceiving the former are much more limited in number than those which may be brought to bear upon the two latter faculties. This will be better understood from the following analytical comparison of the powers of the various senses.

Pleasure and pain—the agreeable and disagreeable—are more or less common sensations of all the faculties; but two of our senses, Feeling and Taste, involve touch, or actual contact, and the perception of temperature in their exercise. Two others, Sight and Hearing, do not involve touch, or actual contact, neither do they involve as a sensation the perception of temperature. The fifth sense, Smell, occupies an intermediate position between the four others which are thus arranged into two sets, and partakes, and in part does not partake, of the powers of each set; for the sense of Smell, or the olfactory organization, does not as a rule come into actual contact with the object from which the sensations by which it is affected proceed, but only comes in contact as a sense with special atoms or particles of what that object emits. This may be said to be partly contact, and partly not. The olfactory organization is also capable of perceiving extreme variations of temperature as a sensation, though it is not very sensitive to the impressions of common temperatures. Extreme heat will consciously affect it, as well as extreme cold; the latter causing the convulsive action of sneezing in it. It will be thus perceived that the two senses of Feeling and Taste have actual contact and the perception of temperature, and the sense of Smell partial contact and partial perception of temperature, in addition to their respective and distinctive perceptions of feeling, taste, and smell, to protect them from deception, more than the Eye and the Ear, which only see and hear, have.

Let us now consider the great primary perceptive faculty of Consciousness as it operates through these various Senses as they are called, or, more properly, channels of its action. If the senses be organically perfect in their structure they must operate with perfect accuracy from the first dawn of our experience. Bishop Berkeley, who has been highly complimented by Professor Dugald Stewart on the merits of his work upon the Eye, speaks of the eye being educated by experience. However unpleasant it may be to damage a literary compliment, truth requires it to be said here that Berkeley is altogether wrong when he so speaks of the eye. That organ is a mere reflecting telescope mounted by nature for us, and is as perfect at the beginning of our existence as it is to the last. The image portrayed on its retina or speculum must, if the optical structure of the eye be organically perfect in childhood, be as accurate in receiving and detailing the first object it is impressed by as any subsequent object or image. It is not the accuracy of this

image, or its details, that is ever improved by experience
in any healthy eye, but it is the great perceptive faculty
of Consciousness that improves by experience in its knowledge and appreciation of the eye's images. It is not
therefore the EYE, but the CONSCIOUSNESS, that is educated
by experience. A few analogous facts of comparative
science will render this very clear. Some animals are
endued with perfect sight from their first contact with
light. The sight of a chicken is perfect as soon as it
chips the shell. But we have no reason to know or believe
that the eye of a chicken is more organically matured or
perfect at that age than the eye of a new-born child. Its
anatomical structure is in nothing that we can perceive
more efficient or more complete. The retina in a child is
a perfect mirror, and all perfect mirrors give at all times
perfect images. But then a chicken's consciousness is
given it to perceive and act; a child's consciousness is
given it to perceive and reflect; and an acting consciousness is more easily educated than a reflecting consciousness. Hence the difference between instinct and thought.
A chicken's perceptions are enough for its guidance. A
child is guided by its reflections, and hence its reflections
have to be educated and allied to its perceptions, for its
guiding power is not in, but separate and apart from
its perceptions. A chicken's consciousness is perfect at
once within the whole range of its faculties, for its consciousness is merely perceptive, and all its faculties are
perfect in their impressions. A child's consciousness is
reflective, and is not perfect at once, from want of elements
of knowledge to enable it to reflect, and it therefore grows
by means of knowledge and experience. Hence the
superiority, in point of immediate accuracy, of instinct
over reason. A chicken will not run into water unless
it be of the aquatic species, because it is conscious of
danger; a duckling, though hatched by a hen, will, because

it is conscious of safety. A chicken, or a duckling, will not run into fire, because it is conscious of danger ; a child will, because it is unconscious of danger until it has learned it, not by instinctive perception but by experience. We have not here spoken of animals born blind, for the obvious reason that these cases are not within the analogy we are discussing. In such cases the eye is not perfect or fully matured till it is opened at a period after birth, such as in dogs and kittens. In the latter the development of the eye's organic maturity is slow, and the full opening of the visual faculty gradual ; but children are not born blind, and we are aware of no gradual maturing of their visual organs after birth as in the case of kittens. Berkeley alludes to the fact that a human being suddenly endowed with sight would not be immediately able to see, but would require experience to enable him to use the faculty ; and the assertion is apt to be employed against the evidence of miracles and their possibility, though that would be contrary to Berkeley's intention in making the remark. To prevent this abuse of it, and also to correct the remark itself to some extent, we have only to ask what is to prevent a man from being instantaneously endowed with the power of perfect sight, just as much as a chicken, by the same source from which both derive vision? Nothing therefore can be founded on this remark of Berkeley's against our Saviour and his apostles giving instantaneously miraculous sight to the blind. It is not at conflict even with experienced natural analogy.

We have now shown, let us trust, that it is the CONSCIOUS-NESS, and not the PHYSICAL SENSE of man, that requires to be educated by experience. It is of some importance therefore that we should endeavour to know as much as possible of this great primary faculty and ultimate perceptive power, Consciousness—how it operates in conjunction with the physical faculties, and where it resides in our being, because a good deal of language with which we have become familiar from childhood is apt to give false impressions on this subject. Thus we hear frequently of the SEAT OF SENSATION, and we would naturally like to know precisely what it means. An idea has been created by the use of this expression that our Consciousness resides fixedly at some great centre of our physical organization, toward which all our nerves tend, and where they enter into subtle combination, forming a cumulative basis for its highest powers of comparative perception and action. But this must not be taken as an implicitly concluded axiom because a certain amount of countenance is given to it by our anatomical structure. It is true there are nervous regions and nervous centres of our physical being, but it is not necessarily true that these are the only Seats of Sensation, or that Consciousness fixedly resides there. It appears much more probable to our experience, and judging from it, that when the sense of touch is exercised the seat of sensation for the time being is at the point of contact, and that the Consciousness is there also and shares in the contact. In like manner, of seeing, the seat of sensation is in the eye; of hearing, in the ear; of taste and smell, in the organs of taste and smell; and that the Consciousness does not reside fixedly anywhere, but travels from one sense and one point of touch to another along the nerves, and that a nervous centre is necessary only to enable it to do so, and to connect all the ways and means of its passage for that purpose. And from hence it would follow that Sensation does not travel along our nerves to any seat or centre of Sensation, as has been supposed, but that our Consciousness travels along our nerves in passing from one point of perception or impression to another, and that this is the reason why we are incapable of simultaneous, and only capable of successive impressions. Another peculiarity of our Consciousness is, that it must be capable not only of travelling along our nerves, but must also be capable of extension upon certain surfaces of them; because in the eye and in the sense of touch, more especially, it is capable of perceiving the extension of length and breadth not as a successive detail merely, but also as a united and present whole in the combination of the many qualities which constitute *form*. Consciousness therefore, whatever it may be, is something more, and of greater dimensions, than a mere point—if indeed such a circumscribed amount of surface as a point can be said to exist, for there is no point that we can conceive of so minute that it may not be subdivided—for a point, however small, must have a circumference, and that circumference must have a centre with a still smaller circumference; and there seems no reason to doubt of infinitesimal divisibility and diminution if we had means and powers sufficiently fine to perceive them. So that, however small the surface of concentrated consciousness of touch may be, it must be something more than a point. But if Consciousness be thus capable of extension on surfaces of our nerves and tissues, why not also on any other physical surface separate from them if free to reach it? It certainly appears to be the fact that when the touch is extended over any such surface the consciousness present in the touch is also extended over and in contact with that surface in the sense of touch. But while these facts appear to justify us in ascribing extension of surface to Consciousness, they do not afford us the slightest means of ascertaining that Consciousness has any definite form. We may be enabled to say that its size or extension of surface is as great at least, and fully commensurate with the size of any surface it is capable of appreciating by actual contact, but that does not enable us to say that Consciousness is of the shape of that surface, or that it is not still larger than that surface, and capable of indefinite expansion.

It has been said we have but one faculty of Consciousness, and that it is capable of only successive, but not of simultaneous sensations. It is not, however, correct to draw this last conclusion quite so far without giving a qualified effect to many considerations bearing on the subject in our experience. Thus, if we lay the open hand down flat on a table or other surface we feel the sense of touch over the general surface of the open hand, but if we raise the hollow of the hand, leaving only the points of the fingers and the part toward the wrist in contact, there will be touch, and consciousness of it, only in two parts of the surface which was generally conscious of touch before, and the sense of touch will be suspended in the intermediate portion of the hand. But this division of the sense of touch does not create two faculties of consciousness for us, it merely occasions one consciousness of touch in two portions of surface. In like manner our volition is capable of double action : thus we may will to raise both hands and bring them by mutual and simultaneous motion in contact with any external object or with each other, yet there is but one volition exercised though two members of the body are simultaneously impelled and controlled by it. Indeed, in the experiment with the hand touching a table, just mentioned, it is more strictly true that the Consciousness is extended over the points of contact and also over the part of the hand intermediate between them, and that it is only the *contact* that is suspended in the intermediate part, but *not the Consciousness*, and that this may be looked upon as a case of *the extension of Consciousness to and between simultaneous points of contact;* and a more extended illustration of the same thing may be exemplified by the use of both hands in touching an object, in which case the extension of the Consciousness is as great as the distance between the two hands, even to the extremest point of their possible separation from each other. Thus both hands may bo used simultancously to touch an object at two points more than a yard and a half distant from each other upon its surface, and though the intermediate surface of our own bodies between the hands is not in contact with any object, yet Consciousness, though without contact, will exist over the whole length of that intermediate portion of our bodies when touch is so exercised. This would seem to show that Consciousness may be exerted simultaneously over the whole physical range of our sense of touch, and that, as the whole luminous range of the retina may, by the presence of extended Consciousness, simultaneously see, so the whole physical range of touch may, in like manner, simultaneously feel. But actual contact is not necessary to Consciousness in the faculty of touch. When a blind man raises his two hands before him, and separates them horizontally to a distance greater than the width of his own body without coming in contact with any object, he satisfies himself by Consciousness in the faculty of touch, but without any actual touch or contact, that there is sufficient space before him to allow him to advance his body forward without interruption from any object; and in this case it is by simultaneous consciousness in both hands, and simultaneous consciousness also of the whole distance between them, that he satisfies himself he may proceed. *Actual touch is, therefore, not necessary to Consciousness in the faculty of touch;* and hence Consciousness, that perceptive power of our being by which we become aware of all things we know, does not absolutely require contact with matter to enable it to discover the existence of reality. It can discover and prove to itself the existence and the reality of space, even though that space were absolutely void of matter. True, it may be said that by extending the hands in space as we have mentioned the blind man uses his hands as a material means of measurement in gauging space, and this qualification is fully admitted. But when the student in a narrow room, with narrow and visible walls of solid matter all around him, shutters closed, and all external light excluded, darts away by an act of thought from the midnight lamp before him, and in one bound of free and outward bursting will contemplates in imagination the remotest cluster of coloured stars that gem the distant sapphire of the night, and plunges into and peoples with his fancy the wide and ever-expanding infinitude beyond them, it is not the real or material that is or ever can be to him a practicable gauge of that vast and traversed region of his mental will, but it is the abstract power of his Consciousness alone, and its inherent contact with and appreciation of the possible—its divinely endowed intelligence—that makes him aware of space which no physical perception can reveal, and no expanded power of material optics ever measure or exhaustively explore. It is here and in similar instances that he finds his metaphysical powers to be superior in their capacity to all his physical capabilities, and that his Consciousness is shown to be aware of space to a degree far beyond all that mere physics can know or reveal. Another characteristic of man's Consciousness, therefore, is that *it is capable of action beyond the range of all known physical agency.*

But as actual contact is not necessary to consciousness in the faculty of touch, so neither is actual seeing necessary to consciousness in the eye, actual hearing to consciousness in the ear, nor actual taste nor smell necessary to consciousness, or the presence of consciousness, in these organs. Consciousness may be present in any or all of them without their being actually in exercise in a physical sense. Further, Consciousness may excite them into artificial action, and influence them with, and make them the medium of hypothetical and imaginary impressions; and this fact forms *the physical basis for the mental constructive power of our being*, which may be said to be the distinguishing power of man over other animals. Their greatest power is the *power of their faculties and impressions over their consciousness*, and the physical perfection of these impressions in producing correct instinctive action and choice. Man's greatest power, reversely, is the *power of his Consciousness over his faculties*, and his means of operating upon them so as not only to perceive correctly what is, but to prove what is not, but is possible or impossible. But even when our Consciousness uses our physical faculties in the discussion of hypothetical impressions, the initiative and directing power is not in the faculties, but in the Consciousness. So that the will and the power to create and dispose of those hypotheses is not in, or a part of the physical faculties engaged, but is entirely in the Consciousness and its power of volition and abstract perception ; and as this power is generally exercised with an aim which, though distinct and fixed, is not immediately capable of being reached in every instance, this fact proves our Consciousness *to be possessed of the power of forecasting, anticipation and predetermination of purpose*, which is a power superior to the physical faculties or their action. Over many artificial and hypothetical impressions with which our physical faculties are capable of being exercised, our Consciousness uses therefore special and predetermined anticipation as well as supervising selection and control, and the faculties are merely passive under such direction, so that it does not reside in them, but in influences apart from them.

Let us now consider the impressions of Pleasure and Pain, which are also sensations perceived by our Consciousness and not by our physical nature ; for anæsthesia has clearly proved to us that the physical nature may be violated, even to the hazard of life, without producing the slightest sensation of pain. as shown by surgical operations performed under the influence of anæsthetic agents, by means of which the Consciousness has been rendered dormant for the time. What we call physical pain is, however, produced by injury or violence to the physical system, and is only felt by the Consciousness in connection with the affected part of that system. Yet physical pain is not in the physical system, nor in the injury done to it: neither is it in the Consciousness apart from the physical system. Pain must therefore be an injury done to the Consciousness itself when present in the portion of the physical system which is injured. It has been already stated that Consciousness is present in the sensation of touch, when that sensation is experienced, and is in actual contact in our physical touch with the object touched. Let us suppose that in the act of touching we receive a cut, as in touching accidentally a sharp razor. The part, or rather surface of touch, is here severed. But are we not entitled to say the Consciousness is also partially severed, and that this is what constitutes pain in the Consciousness by a cut? In like manner, when a burn or scald is experienced by touching, is not the Consciousness present in the touch burnt or scalded, for it is really the Consciousness that perceives the pain of cutting, scalding, or burning, where these are felt, and not the physical parts affected, to which we by indiscriminate language usually ascribe the sensation? When anæsthesia separates the Consciousness from the part to be operated upon, no sensation of pain is felt, though all the physical parts are treated in precisely the same way as if there had been all the usual sensations of pain attending the operation. And this fact would seem to suggest that if the Consciousness were rendered dormant by anæsthesia, when attracted to the extremity of a limb which in that state was amputated, the amputation of the limb, while the Consciousness was in its extremity dormant, might possibly even sever the

Consciousness from the rest of the system along with the severed limb, and produce death. Surgeons have experienced unaccountable instances of death under operations which ought not of themselves to have been fatal, and some of these cases this might possibly aid to explain; and it might admit of being proved by such an experiment as amputating the diseased limb of some inferior animal under anæsthesia, the extremity of the limb being tickled to draw the consciousness of the animal to it while the anæsthetic agent was being applied. The failure of anæsthesia in some instances in securing entire freedom from pain might also admit of some explanation from the fact that the previous pain in the injured part rendered the Consciousness more resident in it, and enabled only dormancy, but not absence of Consciousness, to be produced by the anæsthesia. But while these remarks are by no means insisted in, save as suggesting a line of inquiry, the limits of which, whatever they may be, it is desirable to know, there can be no doubt about the fact that physical pleasure and pain are purely sensations of our Consciousness derived from its contact with the particular arrangements or derangements of our physical nature calculated to excite them, and it shows that the Consciousness abstractly is capable of being both gratified and injured. This is further proved by those sensations of pleasure and pain which are not physical, but purely peculiar to the Consciousness itself, such as sorrow, remorse, regret, fear, anxiety, longing, anger, love, mental joy, hope, confidence or trust, generosity, gratitude, truthfulness, which are attributes, sensations, or capabilities of our Consciousness, apart from physical pleasure or pain, and not capable of being ascribed to any physical faculty. For if what we usually call physical pain be not, as we have shown, really physical, nor correctly described as such, much less are these other sensations

physical ; and it would hence follow that separation from
the body does not necessarily, and of itself, separate us
from the sensations of either pleasure or pain ; for, as will
be rendered still more apparent in dealing with the
Consciousness in connection with the physical faculties,
and their structure and operation, in the succeeding
chapter, it will be found that Consciousness possesses in
itself *alone* all the attributes, powers, and sensibilities which
we usually ascribe to it only in connection with the present
physical arrangement of its existence, and that we are
thus enabled to prove the separate capability of the
existence, though not of the immortality of the Soul, or of
conscious Being.

But though we have said that Consciousness is capable
of extension over the sense of touch, to the degree of
perceiving a large amount of surface, and also of perceiving
simultaneously different surfaces or parts of a surface, this
fact does not essentially qualify what is meant when we
say that the Consciousness is capable only of successive
and not of simultaneous sensations or impressions. The
meaning of this last statement is not that the Consciousness may not receive a larger or a smaller amount of
simultaneous impressions through any one sense—not
that we may not, for example, see simultaneously both a
horse and his rider, or hear both a trumpet tone and the
note of a violin, &c., for either of these instances is but the
perception of one sense or faculty—but that we cannot
direct the Consciousness simultaneously to the impressions
of two different senses ; that its attention must be successively applied where more than one sense or faculty is
exercised ; that, in fact, there is but one faculty of Consciousness, and but one power of attention in that Consciousness.

This power of *attention* is also another source of difficulty, and we have preferred not to use the expression

hitherto on account of the tendency to mislead which is involved in it, preferring the more comprehensive expression *Consciousness* itself. For though it is difficult to show that attention is only one of the powers of Consciousness, and that Consciousness is not always, in our common acceptation, attention—because it is certain that Consciousness is never exercised as a faculty or perceptive power without attention being simultaneously and coextensively exercised upon the same subject on which the Consciousness is engaged—we have no means of showing how far Consciousness and attention are identical with and how far they differ from each other. We might, for example, say that attention does not think, it merely perceives. But then we might say the same thing of Consciousness—it merely perceives, but does not think : but this is just another of those plausibilities which, like the Epicurean proposition as to matter and touch, has more the aspect of obviousness in it than the qualities of intrinsic truth; for Consciousness perceives thought, and attention perceives thought, and these alone, if they be one and the same—unitedly if they be twain—form the only means by which we do perceive thought. The difficulty hence is to conceive that the only power by which we perceive thought is not our thinking power. We know of no other thinking power we possess but that power by which we perceive thought. The touch, the taste, the smell, sight, or hearing, cannot think, neither can they even *perceive* thought. Nay, the brain itself cannot think, though it may receive impression and motion under the operation of thinking. All these faculties possess merely the power of mechanical, and some of them also, in a limited degree, of chemical action; and we know of no other power we possess to which the metaphysical energy of thinking can be ascribed—that power of reading the records and impressions of the brain

D

and senses, and of stimulating and controlling their action—
than the Consciousness and (or ?) Attention. But it must
be obvious that the word attention is not commonly used
with the full and comprehensive meaning which these
facts ascribe to it, and indeed show to be inherent in it;
and that though the word Consciousness is, after all,
nothing more than attention, and attention nothing less
than Consciousness, when intrinsic analysis and definition
are attempted, the expression Consciousness, in common
and conventional acceptation, carries more of the meaning
we seek to convey than the word Attention would do.

The power of memory is perhaps one of the most
difficult mental qualities under the control of our Consciousness for the metaphysician to comprehend. Memory
may be said to be the store of all our education and experience, but how or where is it preserved, and in what
manner does it write down the records of life, so that the
garrulous octogenarian, dead to the present, and incapable
of identifying the most familiar features of friendship
and kindred around him, wanders back with a vivid
delight to the long-departed and forgotten regions of the
past, and blends in his narrative old age—the reality of
his second childhood—with the phantoms of the first?
Does the Consciousness treasure recollections by some
abstract metaphysical power, which at last so peoples it
with visions that the view of reality is excluded by the
thickly-crowded strata of memory's spectral years? Or
does some dusty volume of the physical cerebrum, long
crowded over and hidden beneath the cares of life, reopen
its parchment pages when the over-tension has been at
length snapt, and the superincumbent pressure removed?
And if so, in what hieroglyphic caligraphy are its pages
penned, that they are thus enabled so intensely to flit in mimic
life before us?   It is a strange region of Natural Magic,
that wild jumble of the living and the dead; and yet it is

from the nearer margin of this same phantom-peopled
region that we have to take the quickening elements for
hourly thought and daily action—the elements of all that
speculation, fancy, or purpose would achieve. Is it then
physical, or partially physical, or wholly metaphysical
in its character? Are the senses, or the brain, or any
portion of the physical organization impressed with the
images or the facts to which memory enables the Consciousness to recur? If the senses were so impressed, it
is difficult to conceive that these permanent impressions
upon them would not impede their further action and
obstruct their power to receive the ever-new and succeeding impressions to which we find them open. If the
brain were permanently impressed, it is equally difficult to
understand how the thought, or memory, should continue
to be, as we find it, a volition, and how it could avoid
becoming a fixity and a necessity as the region of the
past. But the images of memory do not possess the
character of retained or perpetuated physical impressions;
they are too deficient in the exactness of their printing, too
wanting in the uniformity of stereotype in their reproduction by the Consciousness for that. They do not
always read the same way, and the aspect of a recollected
image or event is never quite or exactly the same. It has
a conjured-up and shadowy aspect, which is tremulous,
shifting, and uncertain in the light of thought, so that
even the spectra of a dream are more vivid and distinct
than the imagery of a recollection. And from this we
are led to infer that, as the figures seen in a dream are not
real impressions on the eye, but fictions which simulate
reality, so in a much less degree are recollections the
results of retained and permanent physical impressions,
otherwise their imagery would be at least as distinct, if
not more vivid than the fictitious visions of sleep.
Everything rather tends to show that the Consciousness,

as a metaphysical essence of reality, is capable of being permanently impressed by its perceptions, just as, in distinguishing between instinct and reason, we have shown that it is capable of being educated to the use of the physical faculties.

NOTE.—From what is remarked subsequently at p. 42 in the next Chapter, it will be still more apparent that when images are physically impressed they present a different appearance and excite very different sensations.

CHAPTER III.

Th₃ senses the physical media of the Consciousness—The evidence of the senses of touch and taste—Its impartiality—Its positiveness—Evidence of the eye and ear comparative and relative—Co-operation of the senses without collusion—Distinctive perceptions or impressions of the senses—The current of ideas—How stimulated—Its importance—Our relative perception of hardness, size, weight, colour, pitch of sound, &c.—Our positive perception of form—Standards of comparison—Size differently seen by different individuals — Erect vision and the inversion of images on the retina—Neither the true size nor true position of objects presented to us by the eye—Accuracy of the eye—Its superiority over photography—A defect of photography—How caused—Further remarks on comparison—Mirrors and mode of vision.

WITH regard to the application of Consciousness to the faculties in their structure and operation, it will be apparent, after what has been already said, that it is our Consciousness which possesses all the powers of feeling, seeing, hearing, tasting, and smelling; that the touch, organs of taste and smell, eye and ear, are only the places where and mechanical channels or physical media by which it perceives these sensations; and that it possesses, in addition to these powers of perception, sensibilities which no physical matter, however applied or organized, is, or by any known law of nature can be, indued with, as an inherent and material attribute of, or coexisting identity with, matter.

Let us now consider the structure and action of the physical senses themselves, for we must still call them by that name though strictly they are only physical channels

of Consciousness, and are not senses in any meaning by·
which *sense or physical consciousness* of the impressions
upon them is implied.   Now a little attention to the
distinctive peculiarities of the five senses will make us
aware that, instead of any ground having ever existed for
Berkeley's theory of the non-demonstrability of matter, the
experience of the various senses is so distinguished and
arranged as to give us every kind of evidence necessary to
demonstrate the existence and all the externally obvious
and immediately appreciable peculiarities of matter.
Thus touch is necessary and able to perceive the actuality
of matter as well as whether it be soft or hard, and what
is its general temperature as compared with that of the
sense of touch itself—whether or not it be warmer or
colder than the sense of touch.   Taste is able also to
perceive the actuality of matter, for it, too, is touch, though
of a different kind ; and the Consciousness has thus the
testimony of two distinct and separate witnesses for the
actuality of matter, and two witnesses between which
there can be no collusion ; for they cannot, even if they
would, give the same testimony.   Their evidence is
distinct, separate, and different in character, and its only
point of agreement is, not one of identity, but of *corroboration.*   Taste cannot give the evidence of touch, nor touch
the evidence of taste; but Consciousness is equally impressed with them both.   Taste discovers to our Consciousness, not merely by actual contact like touch, that
matter is and has temperature, but also whether it has
certain immediately excitable chemical actions, or chemical
qualities, in addition to those which touch is capable of
perceiving.   It is, in fact, a more sensitively endowed and
discriminating kind of touch, and exactly that more acute
and skilful sort of witness we should wish to test a
matter of fact further for us, after an ordinary witness,
on whom we commonly relied, had first reported and

testified of its existence. These two witnesses therefore, Touch and Taste, give evidence to us, by actual contact in which our Consciousness partakes, of external matter, its actuality and certain of its qualities; and, of these, its temperature more especially. Their perception of this last quality being corroborative evidence, but distinctive while it is so; for what is warm to the touch may be, and at ordinary temperatures generally is, cold, or not so warm to the taste—the taste being warmer than the touch, as we find by applying the hand to the tongue: so that an object which the hand would not melt, or warm by contact with it, the tongue may; and thus these two senses confirm each other even while they differ, and may be called the positive senses, while the eye and the ear are only capable of being ranked as abstract senses, whose function is not to prove the reality of matter, but, after its reality has been proved by these two other senses, to aid in revealing its comparative relation to other material objects and its points of difference and distinctive identity. Thus neither the eye nor the ear comes into actual contact with objects. The eye perceives only the form and character of surface, and the relative size, position and colour of objects; and all of these but colour the sense of touch can ordinarily corroborate and confirm, or rather positively ascertain for us without the eye, where objects are within reach; so that colour may be said to be all that the eye distinctively perceives of objects more than the touch. But while the eye perceives many qualities of objects in common with touch, and only colour distinctively and by itself, the ear perceives hearing or sound by itself exclusively, but does not perceive anything in common with the other faculties. Yet even in this distinctiveness the ear is not so entirely separated from the corroboration of the other faculties as the eye is in its perception of colour; for while no other faculty but the eye can perceive colour or can, undirected by the eye, be consciously employed in producing it, the action of the touch can produce sound, and the eye may guide the action of the touch in its production. So that the hearing may be fully corroborated by the action of the touch under or without the guidance of the eye; while the perception of colour can be corroborated by no separate sense, but rests on the testimony of the eye alone. Under the expression colour it will be readily understood that light in all its varieties of white, blue, yellow, red, and intermediate tints is comprehended. Darkness the eye can hardly be said to *perceive*, since blind men are conscious of that without eyes: darkness to man being, in strict parlance, absence of optical sensation or impression.

But it is in the sensations of pleasure and pain that all the faculties are distinctive in the highest degree and most widely separated in their experience and the character of their perceptions from each other. On a common or average level of ordinary experiences they coincide with and corroborate each other in many particulars, but away from that they each and all widely differ, though their difference is not of the nature of contradiction or disagreement. The sensations of pleasure or pain are in no two senses the same, or even similar, except in the one common quality of being liked or disliked by our Consciousness. A painful object to the eye has no analogy to what is painful or disagreeable to the touch, taste, smell, or hearing; and a pleasant landscape is equally inappreciable by the hand, tongue, nose, or ear. Its reality we may prove by testing some of its details with the other senses, but its beauty, and the pleasure its beauty gives, we can recognise and enjoy only by one. "The eye," but the eye only, "loveth light." The other senses perceive it not. And so the ear, but the ear only, appreciates the pleasures of sound or music: the smell only appreciates the pleasures of fragrance: the touch, or Consciousness in it, only the pleasures of warmth or coolness: and the taste, only the pleasures of sweetness, pungency, &c.

All these rest on the bare testimony of each respective sense so completely that, though we may test by the other senses to some degree how these sensations arise, we cannot so prove them as to show that they are necessary consequences of the causes from which they spring, or indeed that they are consequences at all, save to the respective senses which alone perceive them to be so. But though thus resting only on the single testimony of each respective sense, these impressions of pleasure or pain so powerfully impress the Consciousness as to bring it vividly into positive contact with them, and therefore enable it, without other evidence, to judge in the most positive manner for itself. Such strong impressions may be said to compel the conviction of our Consciousness by their self-demonstrative power. And while ordinarily our Consciousness controls our faculties, here the strength of the impression in the faculty controls for the moment and commands the full recognition of the Consciousness, just as in cases of sudden start or alarm. Besides, such impressions are so allied to the ordinary, but neither pleasurable nor painful impressions of the same faculties, that they are all capable of proof by relation or analogy. There are many instances, however, in which the Consciousness is semi-dormant, or so passive as to be controlled by the faculties. The current of ideas and impressions continually passing through the mind and senses when we are quietly led by, rather than directing the powers of thought, is to a large degree, if not altogether, occasioned by the continuous progress of time and change, and the external actions and influences of reality around us; and the continual succession of impressions occasioned in our senses by these is compounded no doubt with previously-formed mental associations, and a strong instinctive and perfectly natural tendency to view and study all things with some reference more or less to ourselves; just as by our eye we so readily measure every sudden appearance with reference to our personal safety, and always protectively assume danger where there is no time to judge. That this tendency teaches us beneficially to know, and keeps us in a lively present Consciousness of our dependence upon, our connection with, and our obligations to events, can hardly be doubted; and therefore the fact that the EGO dominates very much throughout these currents of thought is not so reprehensible as we might blushingly be inclined to admit were our day-dreams open to the contemplation of other eyes. While therefore the illusions sometimes produced upon the senses—such as Sir Walter Scott describes in his "Demonology and Witchcraft" (Letter I., the "case of an eminent Scottish lawyer, deceased"), and that referred to by Sir David Brewster in the present Work (Letter III., "Spectral illusions, recent and interesting case of Mrs. A.," and which Sir David has admirably explained by the impressibility of the retina with permanent images by overstraining, as exemplified in the case of Sir Isaac Newton and the phantasm of the sun, Letter II.)—may be nothing more than the over-intensifying of a power natural to the whole senses as much as to the eye, the phenomena they have described and referred to are scarcely so wonderful as the fact that most of our ordinary human life is passed in a state of fiction, or romance, in connection with the current of our ideas and our day-dreams, while the proportion of our existence which is real and passed in contact with actual events and facts is a mere fragment of our history in comparison. That the imaginings of the current of ideas, and the pictures they present to us, do not intensify them-

selves more strongly, and render themselves more permanent impressions of the senses, is due not so much
to the want of power in the faculties so to record them,
otherwise they never would exist at all, as to the activity
of the mind, the rapidity of the current of thought, and
its continual change as well as the continuity of external
motion around us, by which the Consciousness is being
continually attracted, influenced, and supplied with new
elements and impulses of thought; for it is a singular fact
that sudden and absolute silence has been known to stop the
whole train of ideas, and produce an almost total suspension
for the moment of the power to think—a fact due
doubtless to the circumstance that we are less accustomed
to absolute want of sound than to absolute darkness or
want of light, and that the continual operation of noises
on the ear has a suggestive and stimulating influence on
the current of ideas, the total absence of which we are
not accustomed to, and cannot all at once dispense with.
Our mental activity, therefore, may be said to have the
continual custom established, in connection with its
normal action, of being influenced and impelled to day-
dreaming and picture-making by the most trivial and
indirect as well as by the faintest suggestions; so that
it is not at all surprising superstitious minds under
cloud of night, and under all the disadvantages of imperfect vision, should create spectral appearances out of
the most unlikely objects, and indulge in mental exaggera-
tions of the most improbable appearances; for superstition
disarms the judgment just as much as darkness disarms
the eye; but neither prevents the current of ideas, nor
stops, but rather stimulates the suggestive powers to create
*not more unreal, but only more alarming images with reference
to ourselves under the consciousness that we are not so fully
protected as in ordinary light.*

But the uncertainty of the senses is further very much

increased under such circumstances by our being deprived of the immediate power of comparison, for comparison is one of the most important and indispensable means of accuracy our nature is possessed of. Indeed, so important is it that we can hardly be said to know anything positively, but only comparatively; and that even what things we do know positively have all their most important attributes and qualities so dependent on our power to compare and distinguish by difference that these qualities can only be accurately ascertained by us through the medium of comparison. Thus hardness, size, colour, weight, distance, sweetness, acidity, acridity, flavour, temperature, toughness, pitch of sound, elasticity, are all comparative qualities of matter only, and not positive qualities; so that without means of comparison at command we can never ascertain to what degree or extent these qualities are present in matter. Mathematical forms, however, are positive and absolute. Circular, square, triangular, or other forms of surface are not relative to other forms or bodies, or liable to be affected by comparison; but beyond knowing that an object is, and that it has a particular form, we cannot be said, without calling in the aid of comparison, and the means by which comparison is achieved, to know anything about it.

Our most common standard of comparison is generally some quality or sense which we carry about with ourselves, unless where men are engaged in some occupation which requires the habitual use of a fixed measure, weight, or other standard on which they acquire the custom of conventionally relying. For example, hardness is ascribed usually to anything not impressible by our sense of touch, and in such a case the strength of our touch is made the standard of hardness; but were we to go to the Mint and see a sheet of gold rolled out and then punched into sovereigns, or rhodium our hardest, or iridium .

our heaviest known metal, struck into medallions by means of a powerful lever and die, we would conclude that if a pair of human fingers were as strong and as hard as such a lever and its die, we would cease to call these metals hard to such hands. But we cannot make the strength or hardness of our hands an absolute or a general standard, for no two pairs of hands are exactly alike in strength. Therefore we must for general purposes resort to some conventional and generally agreed on standard. If we take metal, the standard will be very little more reliable than the human hand, for no single metal we may adopt can be found of uniform purity and hardness everywhere, even with the same tempering and under the same temperature; so that a fixed standard of hardness is perhaps one of the most difficult of all conventional standards to establish. And after all it would, when fixed, only enable us to say that bodies to which it was applied were so much harder or softer than it, but not that they had an abstract and positive hardness, independent of comparison; for to some bodies they would still be relatively soft, and to others relatively hard.

In like manner size is perhaps not seen exactly alike by any two pairs of human eyes, for eyes differ just as much as faces, and that in many particulars too minute to be mentioned here. The retina of a large eye must portray a larger image of objects than the retina of a small eye. For the accuracy of the eye does not depend on its seeing objects as they really are in point of dimensions, but only on its seeing them as they appear to be in comparison with each other; so that a small bird whose eye is no larger than a cabbage seed sees the relative sizes of objects to each other, and to any part of its own body under its range of vision, as accurately as an ox whose eye is more than twice the diameter of a man's; and yet the details in the image of a landscape of thirty miles in

extent portrayed on the retina of the bird could not be
distinctly traced by us without the aid of the most powerful microscope, though all distinctly seen by the bird
itself without any such aid; and the same image on the
retina of the ox, though many thousand times larger than
that presented to the consciousness of the bird, could not
be traced by us in many of its most prominent details without having again recourse to optical science. On the retina
of the eye of the bird, a railway train passing over twenty
miles of distance in the remote horizon of such a landscape will not describe a line longer than the breadth of a
hair, and yet it will be as distinctly and as accurately seen by
a bird as by a man, because the relative sizes and distances
of all the objects seen will be maintained, though their
true dimensions are not given by the eye either of the
man or the bird. But this question will be more fully
understood by referring also to the subject of erect vision
as it is called, or why, notwithstanding the fact that all

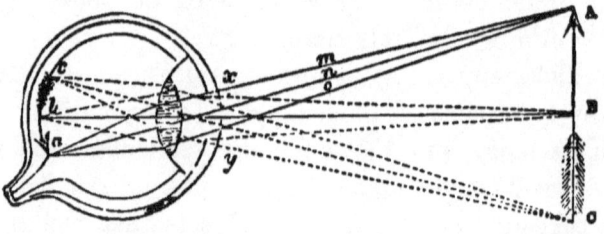

images are inverted on the retina, we nevertheless see
them in their proper and erect position. Thus an arrow
placed with the point upwards before the eye, A B C,
would, as shown in the above figure, be inverted on the
retina at c b a, or portrayed with the point downward,
because the rays m n o, and indeed all the rays proceeding from the arrow between the extremities of it, A C, and
proceeding to the convex surface of the eye, x y, would

cross each other, as delineated in the figure, both before and after passing into the eye.

Yet we are not conscious that the image is inverted, but see it as if it were erect, and the reason for this is that we see the position and direction of objects only relatively to what we see of our own bodies ; and as our bodies, and all portions of our own bodies seen by us, have their images inverted on the retina as well as the images of other objects, the relative appearance and position of our own bodies is in the image maintained by this inversion to the relative appearance and position of other objects, so that when we move our hand from one place to another, as from the point to the feather of the arrow in the figure, our hand would undoubtedly move downward, but its inverted image on the retina would move upward ; so that the hand would not in consequence afford us any means by such a motion of discovering that the image was inverted. In fact, every object external to the surface of the eye, as must be apparent from a study of the figure, is inverted, so that if the edge of the upper eyelid were seen at x, its image would be presented along the lower side of the retina at a, and hence we have no standard external to the eye itself by which we can detect inversion as a matter of experience ; for every conceivable standard external to the eye could only be presented to our vision by means of its inverted image in the eye, and hence before it could become visible to us it would have suffered inversion itself as much as any object whose inversion we meant to test by it. The explanation thus given of the inversion of images, and our inability to detect their inversion in our experience, is capable of being proved even to strict mathematical demonstration. It will thus be found on reflection, that neither the true sizes nor the true positions of objects are presented to us by the eye, but only their relative sizes and their relative positions.

But as the relative positions and relative sizes of our hands, feet, or any portions we see of our own bodies, are correctly given along with the sizes and positions of other objects, we are not conscious of any inconvenience from this fact. Another peculiarity of the eye, which has given a good deal of perplexity and discussion to philosophers, is what some have called the " outness " of vision, or that power of sight by which we perceive solidness in objects and perspective in space. Some have endeavoured to maintain that the retina was so constructed as to allow images to penetrate its surface to some extent, and therefore show one part of an object a little further back than another. But this explanation is absurd; for a common mirror or polished metallic surface gives the perspective of images portrayed or reflected on it as correctly as the retina of the eye does, and more correctly than is yet done by photography, for a reason which will presently be explained. And the true solution of the difficulty as to what is called outness of vision is really that images are just as correctly portrayed on the retina of the eye as they are on any ordinary mirroring surface, and that it is not the retina that perceives the perspective so given, but our Consciousness in contact with the surface of the retina, as already mentioned. But as has just been said, a common mirror, and the retina of the eye as well, will give the images and the perspective of objects more correctly than the photographic process yet does; and the reason for this fact is that in photography a certain amount of distortion and contraction takes place from the circumference to the centre of the image in consequence of the sensitized plate of the photographer being not a concave mirror, like the retina, but a flat surface. This will be in part, but not wholly understood, by referring again to the figure, p. 46, ante, and observing what would be the effect if the retina, instead of being concave, as there shown, were represented by a straight line from *c* to *a*. The result would evidently be that the image of the arrow upon it would be shortened by the difference between the arc of a circle and the chord of the arc. This arrangement of the eye, as compared with that of the photographer—who is necessarily, for printing, reproducing, framing, &c., confined to the use of a flat surface—is of great importance when it is remembered that visible space is a concave spherical area of which the spectator's point of observation forms the centre, and that the concave retina is obviously an optical adaptation of the eye to this natural fact for reproducing concavely to the beholder all that part of this concave space which admits of being simultaneously comprehended within the limits of correct vision, and for which no flat surface interposed instead of the retina could form an effective substitute, or one by which the consciousness could be so correctly brought in contact with the faculty. The difference between the accuracy of an ordinary mirror (omitting horizontal inversion) and a photograph is that, as a spectator advances to or recedes from the mirror, not only do the rays from the entire area imaged converge at different angles to him and in varying (increasing or diminishing) relative distance from each other, but they also proceed from different parts of the mirror's surface at each change of distance—all but the one ray in the line of which the observer is moving. A photograph, from the fixity of its parts, can thus obviously be correct only at one point of distance from it as compared with a mirror, even assuming it to be absolutely correct there. Indeed, in contemplating both photographs and pictures, the eye by long habit acquires almost insensibly a new power of adjusting itself, but only to a certain extent, so as to enable it to see these objects in relief, such as the stereoscope gives more fully, which owes its most important merits to an adjusted and fixed

E

point of view. Until this power is acquired all pictures appear perfectly flat surfaces, while mirrored images never do so. But the above will show how very accurate and perfect the eye is, even with all its peculiarities, none of which affects its efficiency or impairs its perfect fidelity and trustworthiness, under real and ordinary circumstances, even though in addition to all these singularities of structure and effect we have no fixed and absolute standard of measurement, lineal, superficial, or solid, to apply or trust to, and are compelled to resort to and adopt conventional ones, such as lineal and square and cubic inches, feet, and yards, &c., or to the relative size of our own hands, or other members, in reference to other objects where these conventional standards are wanting; the last being a very defective standard indeed, and utterly unsuitable for conventional purposes, on account of the great differences in the size of human hands : so that we may conceive how much inconvenience and uncertainty the ancients were under if they relied on the natural cubit, consisting of the forearm and extended hand, until they had reduced it to an average or fixed limit which excluded variation. With regard to weight, again, we are in exactly the same difficulty as we have just observed with regard to measure. We have no positive and abstract standard of the weight of bodies. Their weight is matter of comparison only, and relative to themselves *inter se* or to us. What feels heavy to us is the primary standard, but is incapable of being made a conventional one, from the difference between each man's strength and that of his neighbour. And here, again, for general purposes we are compelled to adopt a conventional standard on which all are agreed, such as ounces, pounds, or the cubic foot of water as unity, &c.; and even these do not afford us a uniformly fixed accuracy, for every kind of weight varies according to its altitude or distance from

the earth's centre, and the surface of the earth is not at a
uniform distance from its centre; so that slight fractional
variations take place with every trifling change of locality :
and the yard measure, in the same way, varies from the
standard yard to a fractional degree more or less whenever
it is in a temperature different from that agreed upon for the
standard yard; for all bodies contract and expand under the
influence of temperature, and temperature itself is equally
defective in its certainty and equally dependent on an
arranged and conventional standard, such as the various
thermometers—Fahrenheit's, Centigrade, Wedgwood's, &c.
The same thing is equally true of all the other obvious
qualities of bodies, as a little reflection will make
abundantly plain. Diversity of colour, for example, is
found to be relative and subjective to the effect of those
complementary colours on each other which when combined make white light ;. for a faint white light appears
green near an intense red light, and blue near an intense
yellow light, &c., so that all the qualities of bodies are
relative ; form, as we have said, being alone excepted. A
square is a square, a triangle a triangle, and a circle a
circle, &c., whatever be their size ; for form is not
dependent upon size, but on proportion of parts; and this
is the only peculiarity or characteristic of bodies which
the eye or the touch in their normal health can make us
absolutely certain of without calling in the aid of comparison.

Bishop Berkeley, in his Work on the Eye, tells us that
the situation of an object is determined only with respect
to the objects of the same sense; in other words, the
touch perceives the position of an object with reference
only to other objects touched, and the eye perceives the
position of an object seen only with reference to the
position of other objects seen ; and this is strictly correct
when applied to the question of erect vision, and within

the limits in which the Bishop employs the remark. But when it is used as an argument against the possibility of any comparison between the impressions of vision and the impressions of touch, &c., it instantly ceases to be true, for Berkeley has wholly overlooked the fact that it is not the physical faculty, but the Consciousness, that perceives the impressions of touch and vision, and that the Consciousness is capable of comparing all its impressions and of testing and verifying them by all the processes of reasoning and all the aids of science; so that it comes at last, as the result of perfectly correct mental investigation, to perceive that images are inverted in the eye, and yet not inverted to the touch, and that a thing may thus be logically and consistently true in all its particulars which is not apparent to the physical perception or immediate experience. The Consciousness can also test and convince us of the fact, that an object which the hand touches is the same object which the eye sees, and that the points of correspondence between them are not merely few and limited, like a set of coincidences, but are universal in all particulars, and without a single exception. This species of correspondence the Consciousness rightly perceives can amount to nothing short of identity, for nothing but identity is capable of it.

The Bishop also holds that the perception of distance is an acquired, and not an immediate perception of the eye. But in this particular he has also overlooked the fact that the Consciousness is the real perceptive power. If he had only considered the fact that a common mirror in reflecting objects shows distance and perspective correctly, and that the retina is just such a mirror, and possesses the same reflecting qualities and powers, which are fixed and uniform in their action under unalterable optical laws, and that the retina's impressions therefore do not and cannot improve or alter by the effect of education or experience—that it acquires no new or improved mode of mirroring by use—he could not have fallen into this error. He might have been correct had it been true that the objects presented by a mirror are seen on the flat surface of the mirror, for then a mirrored image would have been a flat picture; but we do not see reflected images *on the surface* of the mirror by which they are reflected; for the eye, or the Consciousness as our perceptive power, has no physical contact whatever with that surface. We perceive them only by the incident rays which are reflected or thrown off from the flat surface of the mirror after being intercepted by it. We perceive them, in fact, just as if there had been no mirror whatever, but merely as if the direction of the original rays proceeding from the objects themselves had been changed; for a mirror does not serve the purpose of flattening and localising a picture of the objects it is said to represent; it merely alters the direction of the rays from the objects themselves. And the question comes to be one of the very greatest difficulty whether we perceive the images on the retina in any other way—whether the Consciousness is in actual contact with the concave surface of the retina, or whether the rays of light are reflected from that concave surface to the Consciousness seated to receive them elsewhere. To solve such a question, it must be admitted, is no ordinary labour of thought. We shall endeavour to approach it by divesting it of its inessentialities—of those associated circumstances which are not elements of the question. The first of these is the point whether the Consciousness is seated in the retina or seated elsewhere. Now it matters not whether it is or is not seated elsewhere, for there can be no doubt, wherever it is situated, that the imaging rays are the means by which it perceives the appearances of objects. It is not the retina which Consciousness perceives, but the imaging light, for

these, and not the retina, convey the images. All that the
retina can do as a mirror is merely to intercept and change
the direction of these rays, and it matters nothing, therefore, whether the Consciousness receives these rays at the
surface of the retina or intercepts them elsewhere—*these
rays are what it receives.* Berkeley has said that we
do not see by geometrical lines, and that our idea of
distance cannot be derived from the angularity of these
lines, and he has been pleased to treat this proposition
with some little ridicule. But that we do not see by
geometrical lines is a statement easier to make than to
establish. If, as has been just shown, the Consciousness
perceives all objects by means of rays proceeding from
them, and impinged upon it at the surface of the retina
or elsewhere, it is perfectly certain that those rays proceed from the objects in geometrical lines, and that the
angularity of these lines and the consequent presentation
of the images is affected both by the fact of relative size
and the fact of relative distance. It may be a question
whether the Consciousness in contact with these rays is
extended as a mere surface to receive them at their point
of impact, or has depth as well as surface through which
the rays angularly penetrate and so aid it in perceiving
geometrically : but this question is beyond investigation.
What is much more relevant and certain is that the educated eye does perceive geometrical relation in the position of objects, and that it does so not because the eye,
as the effect of education, has acquired any new or improved
mode of receiving images or radiation, but merely because
the Consciousness has become more capable of appreciating
the images received. It must be borne in mind that
vision is accomplished from first to last in human beings
only in one way, namely, by radiation impinging on our
Consciousness with the velocity of light, and therefore in
a continuous stream of luminous motion affecting our Con-

sciousness, and not by the contemplation of a fixed picture in a state of rest. The only fixed appearance involved in the exercise of vision is the real object itself from which the radiation continuously proceeds, and that we do not see, but only its radiated image ; so that to human optics *the source of sight is not even the object seen, but the original influence of light*, which, falling upon objects, and picking up their images by the way, carries those images as an *incidence* to our Consciousness ; for the *incident rays* of optical science, after all, are not those rays which, reflected from an imaging surface, form what we would otherwise call reflected rays, but those rays of light which, falling on such objects in their course, make the limits and peculiarities of these objects their first mirror or imaging surface, and from mirrors purely so called *pick up nothing*, but merely suffer additional or further and renewed deflection, and bear with them thence, and still un-impaired, the first image they have acquired in their progress from originally pure light. This is probably not the mode in which a disengaged Consciousness, freed from the eye and its optical arrangements, and in actual contact with objects, would perceive them—not the way in which a spirit, or in which God perceives objects. It is, in fact, a limited mode of perception—perfectly accurate in all likelihood within its limits, but only showing us how objects appear under applied and special light, not how they appear in their own reality independent of light, or to the vision of Him to whom the light and the darkness are both alike. How absolutely imperative therefore does it become for us in presence of such a fact to subordinate our rash judgments to the wisdom of Him who is perfect in knowledge, and who judgeth not after the seeing of the Eye, but judgeth righteous judgment !

CHAPTER IV.

The limited range of our positive or absolute knowledge of external matter—How much our knowledge is merely comparative—How necessary, therefore, that we should test everything where we can— Difference in the mode in which truth and falsehood demand our credence—Spiritualism and its séances—Its profanation of the dead—Table-turning—Faraday's exposure of it—Simple application of his indicator for the detection of unconscious lateral pressure and of confederacy—Mesmerism—Its more preposterous pretensions abated—Our tendency to neglect the true knowledge of what is familiar—Our ignorance of why or how our hands instantly obey our will—Consciousness can control and direct the operations of matter—Is it the force by which motion is accomplished?—Probability that it is not—The vital forces and the forces of motion distinguished—The blood the life, a mystery— Electricity as a motive force in animals—Probability of its being the only motive force—Structure of the muscles and electric action on them—Ampère's theory of electric currents—Telegraphic and electro-mechanical nature of animal motion.

FROM what has been explained in the preceding chapters, it will now be apparent that there are but two absolute qualities of matter, that is, of bodies external to us, which are positive and capable of instantaneous verification by the senses, viz., the reality of the matter itself, when within the reach of touch, and the form of matter presented to the eye or the touch. How small a number of bodies this would make realizable to the blind man, how limited an amount of the qualities of those bodies it would present, even to the man who sees, must be very evident. How narrow therefore would be our knowledge if we depended on these self-evidencing qualities of bodies only; for of how few of them would touch and form give a complete or satisfactory description. Yet this is the absolute boundary of man's positive knowledge as to matter. All the other qualities he knows of it are relative, the result of comparison and the perception of difference and distinctiveness. Had we but one body only to handle or look at, of its form and reality we could at once convince ourselves; but its colour, if it have any, depends on the light under which it is seen or the colours by which it is surrounded, and the fact whether it is qualified to reflect the primary, or only the complementary of the colour or light under which it is seen. Its weight, its size, its temperature, &c., are all equally relative, and only capable of being negatively ascertained. It is not so heavy, so large, or so warm as this, or not so light, so small, or so cold as that object of comparison, is the whole amount of our knowledge in regard to these qualities; but what its absolute weight, size, or temperature is, we cannot tell, for we do not know the absolute weight, size, or temperature of anything; we merely know that such qualities do exist in things.

It must hence be obvious that our knowledge of the relative qualities of bodies is much more comprehensive than our knowledge of their positive qualities, and that wherever we are deprived of the opportunity of applying those standards of comparison to objects by which alone their relative qualities can be determined we are helplessly thrown on mere trust and assumption for our knowledge, and completely within the power of Natural Magic—or appearances instead of realities—and at the mercy of misconception or delusion instead of accuracy. Indeed, so much of our knowledge lies within this region, guarded only by our power of reasoning from analogy, which is a mere intellectual extension of our means of comparison and

relative examination, that we are in no instance justified
in neglecting or dispensing with all the practical verification in our power. We are entitled to assume nothing
where we have the power to test or verify, and neglect to
do so. And as corroboration forms the great convincing
power of the senses, when more than one of them are
brought to bear upon a subject, if the subject be what it
appears—and the want of corroboration is instantly manifested where it appears to be what it is not—no charlatan
or pretender has a right to demand our credence till he
has fully satisfied *every right and requisite of true evidence,
and every means of possible corroboration,* which the demand
upon us, if justifiable, ought to allow. No teacher of real or
important truth will ever ask our credence on less fair and
fully satisfactory terms; ' for teachers of truth are not
anxious that it should stand on a weak, precarious, or
inadequate basis; their desire, above all things, is that it
should be clear and convincing in itself, and as immaculate in appearance as it is in reality. We may make
perfectly certain therefore that whatever claims secrecy or
the dark, or partial obscurity for any point or detail of its
manifestation, is stamped with deception or imposture. Of
this class, Spiritualism or Spirit-rapping, together with all
the Séances and their accessories, in which it darkly or
dimly delights, is deeply and indelibly tainted by the
very obscurity in which it is self-arrayed. Its stain is
inherent in its associations. It dare not come forward
and challenge full investigation in the open light; and no
pretended or even real disinterestedness in the operator
can rescue it from the brand of imposture. Truth does
not so proclaim itself : it disdains the aid of the charlatan
or the aspect of mystery. Its most glorious attribute is
that it is self-assertive, self-demonstrative, and that it
claims in the modesty of its noble and immaculate integrity
to be nothing but what it is. · But when a rap professes to

be a spirit, we are only led to the conclusion that the operators in connection with this imposture are possessed with the ignorant idea that the souls of the departed have more sound than sense, are little improved by their advent into eternity, and have become only fit to be outrageously insulted before audiences as ignorant as the insulter, and not less profane. *Nil nisi bonus mortis* seems to be no part of the Spiritualist's motto. In his hands men of sense and virtue are only liable to lose their characters after they have joined the array of the just made perfect, and have no voice of wisdom and propriety left among their unworthy relatives on earth to screen their memories from being made an element of ridicule, misrepresentation, and swindling. The kind of evidence which is required to justify our belief in such a case, is not that a spirit should reveal itself, but that those who assert it has to any extent done so should afford us every means, so far as they are concerned, of making certain that there is no collusion.

But there are other pretensions which have not claimed concealment or darkness as essential to their success. Of these, Table-turning and Mesmerism are examples. The former has gone down before the light it has invoked, and the latter has greatly receded from its first assertions. Michael Faraday showed that while continued muscular pressure might, from the strain and weariness of the effort, become unconscious of lateral tendency, even while actually exerting it in a very strong degree, a simple index could make us conscious of the fact, and also enable us to detect confederacy ; and thenceforward gyraceous and peripatetic tables ceased to move. Table-turning is at an end, and its history only affords one of those useful illustrations of misconceived phenomena which, when fairly placed under the light of general intelligence, science never fails to explain. A simple application of the principle involved

in Faraday's index may be made by any one, with two slips
of paper; one of them narrow, and a few inches long, being
wafered down to the table at right angles to the edge, or
to a tangent to that point of the edge F G H at G if the
table be round, and the other slip not wafered, but laid
down transversely on the first piece. This second paper
being about six or eight inches long, and an inch or two
broad, so that the fingers of a hand may rest upon it, when
pressing the table, thus :

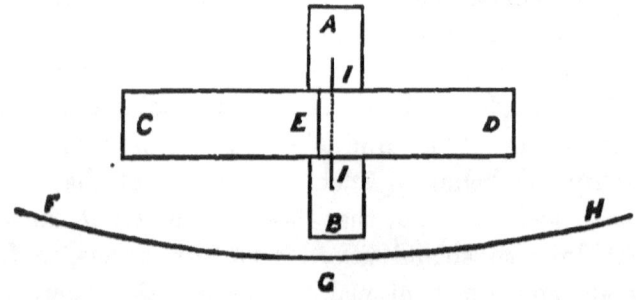

This simple arrangement is quite enough for ordinary
purposes where the table is a polished one, as the first
slip of paper A B, wafered to the table at A and B, with
the index line I I upon it, will remain fixed, while the
paper C D, on which the fingers are to rest in pressing
the table, but not on that part of it which is over the
other slip A B, will move from right to left if there be
lateral pressure in the fingers, and the line E drawn
across its centre and connecting the line I I, and occupying the position of the dotted line when the papers
are first adjusted, will move to one side or other of the
index line I in the direction of the lateral pressure, and
so at once prove its existence.

But Mesmerism, while it has much abated in interest
and modified its pretensions, has not been so satisfactorily
met by scientific intelligence. A good deal of confederacy
and imposture associated with many of its manifestations

have been detected and exposed, but the more consistent
adherents of Mesmerism have complained, and perhaps not
unjustly, that quacks and impostors, for the sake of money-
making by sensational exhibitions, have perverted the
scientific truths which they maintain, and thereby brought
discredit on phenomena which are beyond dispute. It is not
the purpose here to investigate whether Mesmerism bo true
or false. The present writer is too little acquainted with
its phenomena to pronounce a judgment one way or other.
He has seen some few attempts at Mesmerising, but they
must have been exceedingly bungled and blundering
attempts indeed if Mesmerism be anything but a stupid
hoax. The object of the following remarks is not to
investigate Mesmerism, but to consider whether we have
not within the limits of human knowledge, and admittedly
familiar experience, a set of natural facts far surpassing
in their reality all the phenomena which Mesmerism now
professes to have successfully manifested, and with some of
the peculiarities of which Mesmerists may after all be
only floundering in the dark.

It is one of the disadvantages of the student of nature
that life-long familiarity with certain phenomena too often
leads him rather to assume them as matter of course than
to study them as matter of fact—to regard them as too
commonplace for investigation, because it is accepted as a
conclusion too trite for further iteration that they are
exhaustively seen under their familiar aspects, and that
man must know and understand fully and to the uttermost
that which he is encountering every day. Were man's in-
tellectuality equal to his opportunities there would be much
probability in this conclusion. And it is only when we
are privileged through the eyes and understanding of
some rarely endowed intelligence, whose mind has opened
up a new page of nature where we had thought all was
already known, that we discover the fallacy of our assump-

tion, and find we have hitherto been looking at the half calf and gilt edges of the volume only, and that the Book in the running Brook, and the Sermon in the Stone, do not preach or expose their letter-press to every one, but, like sensitive and highly-gifted ministers, pause till the audience is sufficiently reverential and attentive. Much of the very best elements of philosophic truth and wisdom is hid under the aspect of commonplace, and familiarity with facts is not necessarily knowledge. The man who has used his hands from youth to age until they have acquired such a property of easiness in custom that for them to go right has become intuitive, and to use them wrong would involve the necessity of special direction, does not from all this experience of his powers know one bit the more how or why it is that the hand so instantly obeys the Will, or by what sprite-quick and Ariel agency the sympathy between the master and the servant is so full that, ere the pulse beats twice, or even once, the hand has acted the thought or seized what the volition has resolved on, and holds it prisoner to our further purpose. Why or how is it that our motions obey our will? Has all our life-long familiarity with this fact led us a step nearer to the solution of its *modus operandi?* Or has our experience only intensified our stupidity, and schooled us into arrogant indifference and self-satisfied ignorance?

All we have said of the great perceptive power of our being—Consciousness, we see no reason to qualify here, but neither do we feel it possible to expand the range of what we have said, or propound an extension of its energies, save in only one direction. Consciousness is not physical, nor possessed of physical powers or agencies. It is an intelligence, not material, nor incapable of separate existence from matter. But its connection with matter, in addition to its contact with and powers of perceiving it which have been already dealt with, appears to consist of a further *power to control and direct the operations of matter*. But this, after all, tells us nothing more than we already know, though perhaps under a different aspect, when we say that we will, and our members obey our will. We ask for further satisfaction than this, and the prominent question occurs : Is Consciousness the force by which the will is carried out and reduced to physical action? Mankind have hitherto lived and died, under the passive assumption that *it is;* but a little consideration will render this assumption very doubtful at least, if it do not conclusively show that *it is not.*

It is true that the Consciousness can direct the physical actions of our body, but it is not true that the body is incapable of physical action after the Consciousness is withdrawn. The living body moves its limbs as our Consciousness directs, but the dead body may be also made to move its limbs; and all that is deficient in their motions as compared with those of the living body is that the Consciousness and its directing power are not there. Electricity will make the dead move, but it cannot replace the Consciousness or its directing power. Hence the physical force or agency which carried the will into effect may be replaced, but the Will itself cannot. The physical force, therefore, is not the Will or Consciousness; neither, reciprocally, is the Consciousness or Will the physical force. The Will cannot move a paralyzed limb, but electricity properly applied can. The inference from these facts is inevitable : The physical motions of our bodies are accomplished by the agency of electricity, under the direction of our will, so far as they are voluntary, but independently of our will so far as they are involuntary. Now, without reference to the electric action of dead bodies, there are voluntary and involuntary actions in the bodies of the living, and they form two large and comprehensive divisions of our physical system. The heart, the stomach, the lungs, the liver, and numerous other departments of our physical system move and operate by involuntary action over which the Will has no direct influence or control. So that Consciousness or Will are not the forces by which these physical operations are performed, and have no presiding power over them. We know but of four departments of human existence— the Life, the Mind, the Feeling, and the Material body; but these operating forces of our physical system are obviously not fruits of either the mind or the feeling. Are they, then, part of the Life? We have no means of discovering that they are, but we have some reasons for concluding that they are not. The dead stomach has been made to digest under the action of electricity, therefore electricity can to some extent supply the necessary force involved in its action without life. Besides, its action is a physical action, and Life is not physical, nor inherent in, nor an attribute of, physical matter. No doubt life exists in a tree, and controls its vital actions, which are its only actions; but the force of those actions even in a tree is a physical force, and it is impossible to perceive how Life, which is not a physical element, can be a physical force. Yet it is here that the difficulty presents itself in its profoundest form, and here, if at all, that we are bound, as far as possible, to reason it out. Life is not inherent in vegetation, but if life be withdrawn from any member of the Vegetable World its whole forces are suspended, and their whole motions suppressed. It is not physical, and hence not a physical force; yet when it is present there is physical force—when it is absent there is none. Must our reason here recede before the great mystery of Life, and confess itself power-less? Electricity will kill a tree, but it will not enable it to perform any of the operations of its vitality. It will not make the roots of a plant digest and absorb pabulum, and send up suitable elements for bud and blossom and fruit, though it may be, and no doubt is, a subordinate agency in these operations. We must, however, meekly confess we cannot penetrate the mystery of Life. But does this stop the line of inquiry we have pursued so far in all other respects? We think not. All the actions of a plant are vital actions, and we can neither understand Life, nor that kind of action to which Life is essential. But it is not so of man and other animals. All the actions of a man are not vital actions. His muscular actions may be produced without the presence of Life. They form an extension of action beyond the range of trees and plants, and beyond the limited range therefore of essentially vital actions. Perhaps we shall be able to discover that they are as much mechanical actions as those of the steam-engine and other machinery, and as much accomplished by physical forces and agencies. The motions of a tree or plant are only those hydraulic energies by which its sap is absorbed, analyzed, distributed, and applied in the development of the plant; and in this respect they are allied to those motions of the blood in animals by which the vital energies are kept in operation, and seem to be restricted exclusively to the processes of growth or development, renovation, and reproduction. In this respect, whether it be disputed that the Scriptures teach science or not, there can be no doubt whatever that they put the finger of revelation on a remarkable scientific fact, not hitherto considered so fully as it ought to have been, when they say of animal nature that the blood is the Life thereof. If the sap of a tree be not the life of the tree, its operations are so intimately united and identified with the vital forces and actions of the tree as to be utterly indistinguishable from it by any power of human discrimination; and in like manner the operation of the blood in animal nature is utterly indistinguishable from the vital

F

energies of animal life.   Electricity, as we have said, may make the dead body move, and the dead stomach digest ; but it cannot make the blood circulate, or the dead pulse throb.   Instead of re-energizing the blood it destroys it. A shock of electricity passed through the blood after death, so far from vivifying, separates that fluid into its three component and subordinate elements—the red globular colouring matter, the gummy serum, and the watery serum, and renders it altogether unfit for the purposes of vital circulation.   But not so with regard to those motions with which animals are endowed, as distinguished from and in addition to the vital energies they possess in common with vegetable life.   These motions may be produced after life has departed from the members, and they are thence, we may warrantably conclude, separate and distinct from what we have considered as the vital actions. If electricity may produce every kind of physical motion but vital action, as we find it can in the dead, are we warranted in concluding that anything in addition to electric agency is required or employed to produce such physical motion in the living?   Unless we can charge nature in some department of her operations with superfluity, we are not entitled to assume superfluity here ·by the only light of reasoning we have to aid us in our determination of this question—the light of analogy. Nature is nowhere chargeable with superfluity that we positively know of, and we are excluded by that fact from gratuitously assuming that she may be chargeable with superfluity here.   In the living, as in the dead, physical motion may be produced by electricity, and we are warranted by all analogy of nature in concluding that it is produced by that agency alone—the Life and the Consciousness having merely a presiding and directing power over it.   But a little study of the anatomical structure of animal bodies will lead very much to the strengthening of this conclusion, for while electricity may act on inorganic bodies and cause motion, independent of organic structure in them, here it does not so act, but operates in harmony with the organic structure only, and in conformity to the aim of predetermined motive arrangements. Applied to a dead muscle it will make that muscle act, not as if it were inorganic matter and had no special structure, but as a muscle should act, and in harmony and strict subordination to its organic structure and purpose ; and this it can only do because the structure of the muscle is such as to allow the operation by it of some electric law of motion, which, if it be not specially and exclusively designed to facilitate, it at all events fully and perfectly coincides with. On this point we feel fully entitled to say that if such perfect adaptation of muscular organization to electric laws be not the result of predetermined purpose in the arrangement of nature, it is a solecism unparalleled by all mere blind coincidence. But let us now see whether we can detect the electric law from the organization and motion of the muscle ; for its anatomy has been fully ascertained. The electric law, we have said, operates in strict conformity with the muscular structure ; *ergo*, as matter of induction, the *muscular action* under electricity *is the electric action*, or identical with it, and must therefore involve the operation of the electric law. Now a muscle consists of a large number of very fine fibres arranged together, terminating at each end in a tendon, and these two terminal tendons respectively form the tendinous origin and tendinous insertion of the muscle ; and muscles are so constructed that they contract or shorten, and extend or lengthen, as may be required when under action. In contracting, the belly of the muscle, or that part of it between the two terminal tendons, swells out. In extending, the belly of the muscle collapses. This is the mode or form of mus-

cular motion ; and having satisfied ourselves of this much
it is now our duty to investigate what known law of
electricity such a motion coincides with. This, in the
advanced state of electric science, is fortunately not difficult to find. M. Ampère's theory of electric currents
supplies us with the fact that two parallel, or nearly
parallel, currents of electricity, when proceeding in the
same direction, attract each other, and when proceeding
in opposite directions, or counter to each other, they repel
each other. We have only therefore to suppose that when
the electricity passes along the fibres of the muscle in the
same direction they attract each other, and the belly of
the muscle collapses, the muscle being extended ; and
that when the currents of electricity proceed in opposite
directions, that is, so many of them along one set of the
muscular fibres from one end of the muscle—the tendinous
origin, for example—and so many more of them proceed
from the opposite end of the muscle, or the tendinous
insertion, these currents passing each other through the
belly of the muscle repel each other and swell the belly,
thereby causing the muscle to contract. The immense
number of fibres in a powerful muscle, and the number of
electric currents thus passing along them, will readily
account for the great strength and literally electric
rapidity of muscular action ; and we know of no other
explanation which furnishes the faintest indication of an
adequate cause for this familiar, but not the less remarkable phenomenon. If there be any other force which can
produce this action, mankind, as yet, know nothing of it.
We do know that electricity can, and does cause it, and we
also know that the above is the only law of electricity
man has been able to discover by which it can be done in
harmony with muscular organization, and that it is a law
adequate to the result. We also know that it is by passing through the muscle that electricity causes muscular

action, and that the muscular fibres are conductors; so that our conclusion amounts, we may almost say, to as complete demonstration as the subtle nature of electricity allows. In fact, our nerves and muscles seem to be a series of telegraphic wires and electric mechanism combined, by which our volition has accomplished its purposes in our physical nature ever since the creation of animal life, and that, great and marvellous as modern electric and telegraphic discoveries are, they are after all only a lucky stumble upon an old law, and an unconscious imitation of an old application of it, as commonplace as humanity and as hoary as antiquity itself.

We also know from Ampère's theory that currents of electricity influence each other, so that of two transverse currents the stronger controls the weaker, and are therefore prepared to find that where the distance between them is not sufficiently great, or the insulation not perfect, singular and marked effects might be produced from their proximity. And all this suggests to us that the normal and strictly legitimate electric action of animal bodies is far more extensive, and far more wonderful and powerful in the most familiar and ordinary results of animal motion, than anything Mesmerism and Animal Magnetism have been able to establish. Indeed, we are led to conclude that, if there be any grain of truth in the pretensions which Mesmerism has made, it is only a dimly and feebly perceived fragment of this great and common law of animal life on which it has alighted, and which it cannot fully explain. And if so, it is well to observe that its experiments, unless conducted under the light of science, may in many instances be injurious and exhausting to the parties operated on, in consequence of their not being conducted in strict deference to the normal laws of animal action; and that they ought to be discouraged in all but adequately enlightened and prudent hands; for everything done in the way of experiment on man ought

to be in a direction tending to promote and invigorate
healthy and natural action only.

We are now in a condition to contemplate with some
degree of wonder that most astonishing of all the phenomena of natural magic—that fearfully and wonderfully
made compound of immortality and evanescence—that
" paragon of animals," Man ! To contemplate, too, after
more than four thousand years of recorded fact and philosophy, how much and how very little we know of ourselves.
Familiar in daily life with those who are continually setting
up their arrogant and hasty opinions as the finality of
knowledge, though they have never exhibited intellectual
energy enough to penetrate or discover a fraction of what
such a work as this has recorded, or to know how much
and how long philosophy has laboured for so little, the
conclusion of the Preacher seems to hover like an abiding
epitaph over the achievements of man's boasted wisdom
in the sighing and disappointed trisyllable—Vanity !

How small a portion of the great eternal whole is
man's present existence, and yet of how many varied and
wonderful combinations is it made up ! A physical
system which possesses powers of assimilating food and
matter, both by analysis and synthesis, which no laboratory can equal, no skill in science compare with—a
system whose arrangements eclipse telegraphy by the
rapidity and completeness with which they communicate
from Will to Act, from sense to sense, intelligence and
mandate — whose electro-mechanical motive power no
machinery of human invention has yet been able to
approach—a system of pneumatic, hydrostatic, optic,
and acoustic combination, each finer in its parts and more
perfect in its action than ingenuity can even hope ever
fully to understand—and added to all these, Life, and
Mind, and Feeling forming a metaphysical co-operation, of
which we can only say IT IS, and then sink our vaunted
knowledge into lip-sealed and humbled ignorance.

CHAPTER V.

*Animal motion—Spontaneous, involuntary and diseased motions—
Capable of being artificially produced—Defects in Mesmerism—
Want of uniformity in its results—Electro-biology and Phrenology
—The brain—Propensities—Cerebral development no proof of
propensity—Alleged propensity not consistently shown in experience—Propensity not material but metaphysical, and cannot be
indicated by size and quantity of matter—Exercise causes development—Small mental power capable of great achievements—
Accountability of human life—Right and wrong divide the universe—Danger of error—Tendencies of the age—Opinion—Difference between Opinion and Conviction—Not necessary to form
opinion as a basis of action—Opinion not truth—An impediment
to correct action—An illustration of this—Case of an African
traveller — Confusion as to opinion—Our means of protection
against error.*

HAVING so far considered in the preceding chapter the
laws and forces engaged in the production of animal
motion, and which appear to result in showing that
physical action in animals is accomplished by what may
be called strictly electro-mechanical appliances, let us
now devote some attention to those animal motions in
connection with the Will and the Consciousness, and also
to a few of the phenomena of spontaneous, involuntary,
diseased and artificially-produced motions.

It appears then, from many well-established experiences,
that the Consciousness may be to a large extent separated
from physical motions which ordinarily never take place
save under its immediate direction and control, and also
that a large number of diseased motions are possible over

which the Will and the Consciousness never have any control. Thus the motions of the somnambulist are to a large extent performed without the Consciousness, though they are of a nature over which the Will, in ordinary circumstances, would preside and exercise direction. On the other hand, cramp, lock-jaw, and other diseased actions of the muscles, are of a nature over which the will unfortunately never has any control, and they prove to us conclusively that, though Consciousness may be associated with, and part of the vital force, it is not the motive force, nor necessarily associated with it—that, in fact, the motive force is not a vital, but merely a mechanical force.

But all mechanical forces are capable of mechanical regulation and control, and it is therefore quite possible and within the limits of legitimate logic to conceive that what can be produced naturally or by disease in the mechanical motions of the human body may be produced by the application of artificial control over the body. For if motion in a dead body may be produced by the application of electricity, why may not involuntary motion be also produced in a living body by the application of it? If muscular action be produced by electric currents obeying the volition, why may not more powerful currents, as M. Ampère has shown, be so applied as to control these currents in opposition to the individual will? If somnambulism and dreaming, and lock-jaw and cramp, may be produced by natural causes, why may they not be produced also by artificial means, if we know how to use these means? And yet some of these phenomena go far beyond anything that Mesmerists have been able to prove, and show an involuntary mechanical and electric action in our physical nature beyond the Mesmerist's absolute power, whatever may be said of his pretensions. It may be said that these facts go to prove the phenomena of Mesmerism. We have no objection to prove them if they be true. But we rather think they go directly to disprove Mesmerism, and establish a set of facts which show that if Mesmerism were true—if it had really discovered the key to producing by artificial means that which Nature produces by eccentric action and disease—then it ought to have no failures in the application of its key, and ought to meet with no impracticable and no unimpressible subjects. Mesmerists confess that there are individuals who cannot be mesmerised; but the facts we have been dealing with are facts to which all men are subject. And if Mesmerists cannot produce these uniformly in all, and with perfect certainty, their failure gives a strong probability to the suspicion that they have not the true key to produce them in any one, and that their experiments, so far as they have any truthfulness in them, are wholly empirical, of uncertain issue, and unworthy of yet being recognized as having established anything within the legitimate precincts of science. Our aim is neither to support Mesmerism and its pretensions, nor to be severe against anything on account of which its adherents honestly think it can really lay claim to consideration. The aim here is to direct inquiry and attention to what is known to be truth, and stimulate . investigation in the right direction. It is quite plain that nature does accomplish in a natural way phenomena and effects fully as wonderful as anything mesmerism has asserted; and if mesmerists think it of importance to produce similar effects, let them turn to the means by which Nature itself operates, and they may have some prospect of making discoveries more worthy of consideration than the pretensions of quacks, and more uniform in their results than the accident of *unaccountable susceptibilities.*

With regard to Electro-Biology and Phrenology, which are closely connected with this subject, it is perhaps right that we should also say something, because here too a great deal of falsehood appears to have got mixed up with a very small amount of physical truth.   No anatomist asserts in these days, if indeed anatomists ever made the assertion, that the brain is an inorganic mass of medullary Chaos, or that its various parts have not distinct functions and purposes, whatever these may be; but it is the pretension made by the phrenologist to forecast human character by reading the "Organs," and predicate even criminal and other life by talking of "propensities" founded on organic development and the relative dimensions of so-called faculties, that produces scientific repugnance and the well-founded disgust of sensible men.   Assuming, for the sake of argument, that phrenologists have been successful in localising the various organs of the brain which they have named in their charts and busts, how do they prove, let us ask, that the size of an organ, or the relative size of a set of organs, proves a propensity, or justifies the predication of a character therefrom?   Does the size of a man's hand, or the physical formation and power of his arm, prove, because he possesses great strength, that he is fond of hard labour, or has a propensity for laborious pursuits?   We have seen little and delicate men who have taken to manual industry and become strong-armed by practice from the extremest degree of primary weakness; and physical giants, on the other hand, who have never taken to greater toil than that of the brain, nor wielded a much heavier weapon than a goose quill.   Nay, though a certain amount of cerebral capacity is indicated by the form and dimensions of the skull, there is nothing to indicate that the brain, like the feeble arm, may not develop by exercise, or collapse and diminish from the want of it; nor to show that portions of the brain may not be largely developed and exercised at one period of life, and wholly unexercised

at another; just as much as that a man who may have
toiled fifty years, and suddenly succeeds to fortune, or
slowly matures it during that period, all at once abandons
his hard physical labour, and becomes a mere overseer or
master, employing and directing the labour of others,
or retires altogether into the leisure of life. If size of
cerebral organization meant propensity instead of merely
power or capacity, the propensity would be persistently
and continuously manifested from the beginning to the
end of existence ; but many men's lives are only a per-
sistent contradiction to their cerebral development, as
much as the lives of others are a contradiction to their
energies and physical strength. No one can look on the
fine head of Shakespeare without being struck with the
impress of pre-eminent intellect which it bears; but a
question with regard to it still arises—whether Nature
gave this evidence precedently, and stamped the physical
formation with that calm and concentrated aspect of
mental energy and seated power, or whether the trium-
phant progress of achievement did not enlarge the
expression and open the windows of the soul, and thereby
mould the physical material to its exposition, just as
practice indues the right hand with its cunning, and modifies
the nervous and muscular development of the exercised arm
into harmony with its use. If there be such evidence for
propensity as phrenologists have contended, where is the
evidence for energetic achievement, and of culpable and
degrading neglect ? But it is utterly fatal to all this
argument upon assumption that *Propensity is not Material,
nor an attribute of Matter*. It is no more Material than we
have already shown Feeling to be. There is no other propensity known as an attribute of matter than the propensities of gravitation, attraction, repulsion, and chemical
affinity, which are not living, but dead ; not inherent, but
factitious powers purely physical, and variable under

varying physical circumstances. Moral propensity is a
vital and a living power wholly metaphysical, and
incapable therefore of being evidenced by the dimensions
of a physical organ, or the relative preponderance of
physical arrangements. The biologist who does not
know this is little better than a mere materialist, like
Epicurus, and must be profoundly ignorant of metaphysics,
without which such conclusions as he draws cannot
legitimately be even approached. Matter is but a fourth
part of the elements which go to the constitution of a
human being, as we have shown at the outset of these
chapters; and the phrenologist who proceeds to assert the
existence of propensity on the bare evidence of physical
or material development omits consideration of three-
fourths of the elements necessary to the determination of
the subject, and is no wiser than he who, looking at a .
set of palsied and paralytic limbs, would assert, on the
bare ground of their apparent size and formation, that
the possessor of them must be able to walk and leap.
Physical development can at best give partial evidence
of *Capacity only*, not of *Propensity*, and only partial evidence
we insist, for men are not uniformly strong in proportion
to their appearance of strength, nor uniformly active-
minded in proportion to their appearance or capacity,
or even *possession* of intellect. The intensity, the vigour,
and the quantity of the vital power, purely immaterial
and beyond the range of scientific investigation, have
much to do with character, as well as all the circumstances
which attend its development, and, as external influences,
test and call it into operation. And the quality and
texture of the material elements, when matter itself is
at last condescended on, has more to do with its sustained
activity and enduring power than that crude, primary,
and dominant assumption of the phrenologist — the
superficial appearance of mere brute weight or quantity.

No sane man would trust the strength of a rope merely because it is thick, any more than he would endeavour to make a rope of sand because sand will bear his weight when he stands upon it ; yet the phrenologist's predications of human character are just as illogically based and inferred as such conclusions and misdirected efforts would be, and the honest mind, to which truth is everything, cannot be too earnestly warned against them. A good deal of what mental and moral power may be in achievement is evidenced by the small piecemeal and inglorious labours of that being, too much despised among mankind—the poor Plodder; for just as the Bees send forth a thousand workers to gather wax and honey for the hive, which at the end of the flower season contains a plentitude of treasure and fortune, so the Plodder, intent on achieving some worthy aim beyond the instantaneous energy of his powers, calculates the value of little by little, and adds under the sanction of forbearing time his thousandth time repeated contribution to his work, until it at last swells by slow but steady increase into the full development of his purpose, and he is enabled to leave a monument of his industry behind him not less respectable, sanctified as it is by the fortitude of patience and the heroism of perseverance, and often as beneficial to mankind as the triumphs and masterpieces of genius itself. Who will say that small things are contemptible only, or that the Ant is not the greater a giant from the very disproportion between its pigmy personality and its mighty hill—the exponent of a grander and more heroic will than genius oft can claim as its associate? And so of these small mental organs in men, on the ground of which phrenologists would predicate failure in the intellectual achievements of life. It is the exercised limb of the little man that contains the developed strength, not the idle arm of the giant. And the intellect, **too,**

improves by action. It is a mistake to suppose that the
skull is a hard incasement of bone which allows no
enlargement of its prisoner : it is an arch strong as a
groined vault of masonry to resist pressure from without,
but it is the very reversal of an arch, with all its powers
of resistance inverted and turned against itself, when
opposed to pressure from within. Let us then, by every
attribute of our manhood, resist and defy these miserable
doctrines that would foredoom our noblest powers, and
write the scaring word " impossibility " across our paths—
the arrogant fiat of charlatans and quacks. No cranium,
no physical form of our organization, exhibits at the
outset of this life the full development of which it is
capable. Adequate exercise only can give it that. The
metaphysical part of our being is the dominant part—
the animating, energising, and controlling power—and
the physical is merely subjective to it, just as external
matter also is to the forces which operate upon it. It is
quite as baseless and arrogant an assumption to say
that the physical development is the cause of propensity,
as that it is the cause of feeling and of life. The very
reverse is the case; for life, and feeling, and propensity,
on the contrary, are the causes of the physical development, which never would grow an inch from childhood to
age but for them. It is impossible to reason further
therefore with those who, assuming the position of
philosophers, mistake the effect for the cause, and the
cause for the effect, and invert the whole principles of
logic and sequences of truth to arrive at their ridiculous
conclusions ; for to them truth must appear only to be
error, and error only to be truth—an idiosyncracy as
compared with which even lunacy has some lucid intervals
in its favour.

But the result of all these various considerations of the
being and faculties of man, his internal Consciousness

in spite of all his mental resistance, to appear and to be just what it is and what he perceives it to be; and such a perception is a Conviction. It is self-evidenced and independent of our will; for a Conviction is a perception either of the mind or the senses which is unalterable by the exercise of will or choice. But suppose that two persons looking at a tree go into a discussion as to the age of the tree—which is not cut, and the age of which cannot be accurately ascertained till it is cut and the transverse section of the stem with its rings revealed—and that, without knowing anything of the number of those rings the two persons dispute and argue, one, that the tree is only eighty years old, the other, that it *is upwards of a hundred years*—these are Opinions. The one holds by the one view, and the other holds by the other, on the maxim that every one is entitled to his opinion, and that one man's opinion is as good as another. Yes, but what of the truth involved? Will the tree become only eighty years old to please the one person, or a hundred years old to please the other? Are the opinions worth anything as a matter of fact where the absolute truth, and it alone, is requisite? And when is it not requisite, if anything be requisite about the matter at all? Can either opinion be relied on and accepted as truth if a question of the slightest importance depended upon it? They may be called approximations to the truth. But are approximations *the truth*? And is anything that is not the truth other than untruth? In every instance in which the actual truth is required an opinion is worth absolutely nothing. Conviction is a perception of the truth itself; Opinion is only a guess at it. No man is entitled to hold it as the truth, or act upon it as such, *for it is plain that he can at will change his opinions, but the truth will not change.*

But we are told that men must form opinions and act upon them in the business of life. Perhaps many men

G

do so; but let us show the fallacy of their so doing by an
illustration. Very lately a celebrated African traveller
was said to have been murdered by savage natives while
pursuing his magnanimous journey in the interior of that
country. When the news reached England, they were
fully credited by some and wholly discredited by
others. Neither of these parties by believing or dis-
believing could fix the actual fact; their views of the
matter were mere opinions. But what we have to do with
here is, whether these opinions, either or both of them,
were, or could be, of any use as the basis of any action
that required to be taken in the circumstances. If the
parties who believed the illustrious traveller to be dead
were to take any action, what could their action be on the
basis of their opinion? Could it be anything more than
merely to send out at their leisure and ascertain the
reality of the fact, which they held to be true already—
hurry in the matter being unnecessary and out of the
question, because the traveller they were satisfied was
really dead? On the other hand, what action could those
who did not believe the news of the traveller's murder
take on the basis of their opinion? Was it necessary
for them to do anything at all, seeing they were satisfied
that all was right? It would be to discredit the wisdom
of their own opinion were they to do anything. Where,
then, is the value of opinion as a basis of action in such a
case? and where is there any case to which it better
applies? Any action taken by those who considered it
necessary to act in the case of the eminent traveller we
have mentioned was not taken on the basis of these
opinions, but by steering clear altogether of them. It did
occur in a sensible way, and as matter of fact, that certain
of the companions of the traveller's journey had returned—
that was matter of fact. Part of the contemplated strength
of the enterprise was not with it, whatever its condition

might be. It was therefore obvious as matter of *fact* and of *duty* that we were bound to send out aid to replace the ascertained deficiency, so that, if in time, it might not be required in vain. These were truths and obligations—not opinions arrogantly expressed, but duty clearly ascertained, without absolutely fixing anything but the wisdom of distrusting opinions altogether. True, we are told that men take and act on legal opinions day by day. But this is really a confusion of ideas arising from misapplication of language. A lawyer has the facts of a case laid before him, and a sound lawyer states what the law *is* in reference to these facts, not what in his opinion it is; not what he thinks, but what he knows it to be; and just in proportion as he states what he competently *knows* is he a prudent adviser, and as he states what he merely *thinks* is he utterly unsafe.

A mere opinion, even from a lawyer, is of very little value, and the word is really a misnomer for the purpose to which it is so applied in law. Clients wish to be informed of the law which is certainly applicable to their case, not of that uncertain thing opinion, the accuracy of which has no present certainty, but has wholly to be ascertained by a future result. Opinionative people are great self-deceivers, and besides being very dogmatic members of society, they are the most easy of all to be misled. They are continually encountering those who cannot be made, and are under no obligation, to think as they do, but who could, if they chose to flatter, easily encourage error rather than oppose it, with the most obvious disadvantage to the opinionist. Surely such people should take warning for their own sakes, as well as for the comfort of others, to refrain from making dogmatists of themselves; for after all their labour and persistency their opinions are really worth nothing. It is a very small unction to lay to their souls to say their opinions are as good as the opinions of others; for all opinions are utterly worthless, and there is but one set of fools greater than those who pertinaciously insist on having their opinions respected, namely, those who respect them. If there be noisy discussion and intemperate language it is sure to be over an opinion indiscreetly maintained, and not over a truth that it is held, for opinionative people spend many words and much labour to prove *Nothing*. They may as well rest assured at once that Truth is everything, and that, besides Truth, there is only Error. But if they will not discipline their own minds to appreciate this fact, how can they expect to be armed by accurate logical habit to correct the' errors fallen into, or, worse and more dangerous still, the impostures practised by others? *It ought ever to be remembered that opinions are conclusions in the dark, and before the truth is ascertained, about which all minds may justifiably differ.*

Assertion of Opinion, therefore, provokes only certain and inevitable defeat, for in such encounters the person who merely disputes the Opinion is not and never can be in the wrong. It is the person who asserts the Opinion who is in error, for the simple reason that Opinion is not truth, and that in the absence of the truth the Opinion cannot justifiably be insisted on. After the truth is apparent, and can no longer be resisted, the region of *Opinion* disappears, and anything but *Conviction* is impossible.

So much, then, for the proposition *that every one is entitled to have his own Opinion,* which is only the most arrogant assertion that can possibly be propounded by those who are determined at all hazards to stick to and justify their errors, and inflict on others their own imperious, petulant, and blundering wilfulness. Truth, and that manifestation of it which justifies Conviction, will very rarely be disputed or mistaken, but Opinion can never justifiably claim to be acquiesced in. It may be modestly stated, but never as more than an Opinion, and it would be better even then that it should wait till it is asked for.

We have endeavoured, and the task is by no means an easy one, nor one on the results of which we can very greatly congratulate ourselves, to popularise within a reasonable limit one of the most abstruse and important departments of philosophy, strictly in unison with, though antecedent to the subject of Natural Magic, and which deserves from mankind a much more respectful attention than it obtains as a means of self-knowledge, demonstration, and mental direction. Many of our readers will probably have tired of the subject before reaching the present page, even though our matter has been necessarily limited to our space, and to the aim of dealing lucidly and fully with a few, rather than ponderously and exhaustively with many things; for our facts have been selected and explained at considerable length for the purpose of showing that there are elements essential to accuracy of judgment which are greatly neglected in the age in which we live : an age in which correct and competent judgment is pre-eminently required to guard against deceptions ever increasing, and becoming more subtle and intricate in their character from the advancing discovery of new scientific facts and appliances. If these chapters are the means of showing without undue tediousness to those who do care for such subjects the powers of accurate perception and conviction at our command, and the absence of any necessity for forming fixed and positive opinions on matters of which we are not thoroughly certain—that no mere opinion is worth forming after all—*that the judgment may in all cases be safely and wisely suspended*

without any practical inconvenience till the truth itself appears
—let us hope they will sufficiently arm the prudent and
those who have a due respect for wisdom. Those who
prefer to learn in the school of experience must be left
to the lessons that instructor applies.

LETTERS ON NATURAL MAGIC.

LETTERS ON NATURAL MAGIC,

ADDRESSED TO

SIR WALTER SCOTT, BART.

LETTER I.

*Extent and interest of the subject—Science employed by ancient govern-
ments to deceive and enslave their subjects—Influence of the supernatural upon ignorant minds—Means employed by the ancient
magicians to establish their authority—Derived from a knowledge
of the phenomena of Nature—From the influence of narcotic
drugs upon the victims of their delusion—From every branch of
science—Acoustics—Hydrostatics—Mechanics—Optics—M. Salverte's work on the occult sciences—Object of the following Letters.*

MY DEAR SIR WALTER,

As it was at your suggestion that I undertook to
draw up a popular account of those prodigies of the
material world which have received the appellation of
Natural Magic, I have availed myself of the privilege of
introducing it under the shelter of your name. Although
I cannot hope to produce a volume at all approaching
in interest to that which you have contributed to the
Family Library, yet the popular character of some of
the topics which belong to this branch of Demonology
may atone for the defects of the following Letters ; and I
shall deem it no slight honour if they shall be considered
as forming an appropriate supplement to your valuable
work.

H

The subject of Natural Magic is one of great extent as well as of deep interest. In its widest range, it embraces the history of the governments and the superstitions of ancient times,—of the means by which they maintained their influence over the human mind,—of the assistance which they derived from the arts and the sciences, and from a knowledge of the powers and phenomena of nature. When the tyrants of antiquity were unable or unwilling to found their sovereignty on the affections and interests of their people, they sought to entrench themselves in the strongholds of supernatural influence, and to rule with the delegated authority of heaven. The prince, the priest, and the sage, were leagued in a dark conspiracy to deceive and enslave their species; and man who refused his submission to a being like himself, became the obedient slave of a spiritual despotism, and willingly bound himself in chains when they seemed to have been forged by the gods.

This system of imposture was greatly favoured by the ignorance of these early ages. The human mind is at all times fond of the marvellous, and the credulity of the individual may be often measured by his own attachment to the truth. When knowledge was the property of only one caste, it was by no means difficult to employ it in the subjugation of the great mass of society. An acquaintance with the motions of the heavenly bodies, and the variations in the state of the atmosphere, enabled its possessor to predict astronomical and meteorological phenomena with a frequency and an accuracy which could not fail to invest him with a divine character. The power of bringing down fire from the heavens, even at times when the electric influence was itself in a state of repose, could be regarded only as a gift from heaven. The power of rendering the human body insensible to fire was an irresistible instrument of imposture; and in the combinations of chemistry, and the influence of drugs and soporific embrocations on the human frame, the ancient magicians found their most available resources.

The secret use which was thus made of scientific discoveries and of remarkable inventions, has no doubt prevented many of them from reaching the present times; but though we are very ill informed respecting the progress of the ancients in various departments of the physical sciences, yet we have sufficient evidence that almost every branch of knowledge had contributed its wonders to the magician's budget, and we may even obtain some insight into the scientific acquirements of former ages, by a diligent study of their fables and their miracles.

The science of *Acoustics* furnished the ancient sorcerers with some of their best deceptions. The imitation of thunder in their subterranean temples could not fail to indicate the presence of a supernatural agent. The golden virgins whose ravishing voices resounded through the temple of Delphos;—the stone from the river Pactolus, whose trumpet notes scared the robber from the treasure which it guarded;—the speaking head which uttered its oracular responses at Lesbos;—and the vocal statue of Memnon, which began at the break of day to accost the rising sun,—were all deceptions derived from science, and from a diligent observation of the phenomena of nature.

The principles of *Hydrostatics* were equally available in the work of deception. The marvellous fountain which Pliny describes in the Island of Andros as discharging wine for seven days, and water during the rest of the year,—the spring of oil which broke out in Rome to welcome the return of Augustus from the Sicilian war, —the three empty urns which filled themselves with wine at the annual feast of Bacchus in the city of Elis,—the glass tomb of Belus which was full of oil, and which, when once emptied by Xerxes, could not again be filled,—the weeping statues, and the perpetual lamps of the ancients,—were all the obvious effects of the equilibrium and pressure of fluids.

Although we have no direct evidence that the philosophers of antiquity were skilled in *Mechanics*, yet there are indications of their knowledge, by no means equivocal, in the erection of the Egyptian obelisks, and in the transportation of huge masses of stone, and their subsequent elevation to great heights in their temples. The powers which they employed, and the mechanism by which they operated, have been studiously concealed, but their existence may be inferred from results otherwise inexplicable, and the inference derives additional confirmation from the mechanical arrangements which seem to have formed a part of their religious impostures. When in some of the infamous mysteries of ancient Rome, the unfortunate victims were carried off by the gods, there is reason to believe that they were hurried away by the power of machinery; and when Apollonius, conducted by the Indian sages to the temple of their god, felt the earth rising and falling beneath his feet like the agitated sea, he was no doubt placed upon a moving floor capable of imitating the heavings of the waves. The rapid descent of those who consulted the oracle in the cave of Trophonius,—the moving tripods which Apollonius saw in the Indian temples,—the walking statues at Antium, and in the Temple of Hierapolis,—and the wooden pigeon of Archytas, are specimens of the mechanical resources of the ancient magic.

But of all the sciences *Optics* is the most fertile in marvellous expedients. The power of bringing the remotest objects within the very grasp of the observer, and of swelling into gigantic magnitude the almost invisible bodies of the material world, never fails to inspire with astonishment even those who understand the means by which these prodigies are accomplished. The ancients, indeed, were not acquainted with those combinations of lenses and mirrors which constitute the telescope and the microscope, but they must have been familiar with the property of lenses and mirrors to form erect and inverted images of objects. There is reason to think that they employed them to effect the apparition of their gods; and in some of the descriptions of the optical displays which hallowed their ancient temples, we recognize all the transformations of the modern phantasmagoria.

It would be an interesting pursuit to embody the information which history supplies respecting the fables and incantations of the ancient superstitions, and to show how far they can be explained by the scientific knowledge which then prevailed. This task has, to a certain extent, been performed by M. Eusebe Salverte, in a work on the occult sciences, which has recently appeared; but notwithstanding the ingenuity and learning which it displays, the individual facts are too scanty to support the speculations of the author, and the descriptions are too meagre to satisfy the curiosity of the reader.*

In the following letters I propose to take a wider range, and to enter into more minute and popular details. The principal phenomena of nature, and the leading combinations of art, which bear the impress of a supernatural character, will pass under our review, and our attention will be particularly called to those singular illusions of sense, by which the most perfect organs either cease to

* We must caution the young reader against some of the views given in M. Salverte's work. In his anxiety to account for every thing miraculous by natural causes, he has ascribed to the same origin some of those events in sacred history which Christians cannot but regard as the result of divine agency.

perform their functions, or perform them faithlessly; and
where the efforts and the creations of the mind pre-
dominate over the direct perceptions of external nature.

In executing this plan, the task of selection is rendered
extremely difficult, by the superabundance of materials,
as well as from the variety of judgments for which these
materials must be prepared. Modern science may be
regarded as one vast miracle, whether we view it in
relation to the Almighty Being, by whom its objects and
its laws were formed, or to the feeble intellect of man, by
which its depths have been sounded, and its mysteries
explored:—And if the philosopher who is familiarized
with its wonders, and who has studied them as necessary
results of general laws, never ceases to admire and adore
their Author, how great should be their effect upon less
gifted minds, who must ever view them in the light of
inexplicable prodigies.—Man has in all ages sought for a
sign from heaven, and yet he has been habitually blind to
the millions of wonders with which he is surrounded. If
the following pages should contribute to abate this de-
plorable indifference to all that is grand and sublime in
the universe, and if they should inspire the reader with a
portion of that enthusiasm of love and gratitude which
can alone prepare the mind for its final triumph, the
labours of the author will not have been wholly fruitless.

LETTER II.

*The Eye the most important of our organs—Popular description of it—
The eye is the most fertile source of mental illusions—Disappearance of objects when their images fall upon the base of the optic
nerve—Disappearance of objects when seen obliquely—Deceptions
arising from viewing objects in a faint light—Luminous figures
created by pressure on the eye either from external causes or from
the fulness of the blood-vessels—Ocular spectra or accidental
colours—Remarkable effects produced by intense light—Influence
of the imagination in viewing these spectra—Remarkable illusion
produced by this affection of the eye—Duration of impressions of
light on the eye—Thaumatrope—Improvements upon it suggested—
Disappearance of halves of objects or of one of two persons—Insensibility of the eye to particular colours—Remarkable optical
illusion described.*

OF all the organs by which we acquire a knowledge of
external nature the eye is the most remarkable and the
most important.   By our other senses the information we
obtain is comparatively limited.   The touch and the taste
extend no further than the surface of our own bodies.
The sense of smell is exercised within a very narrow
sphere, and that of recognizing sounds is limited to the
distance at which we hear the bursting of a meteor and
the crash of a thunderbolt.   But the eye enjoys a bound-
less range of observation.   It takes cognizance not only
of other worlds belonging to the solar system, but of other
systems of worlds infinitely removed into the immensity
of space ; and when aided by the telescope, the invention
of human wisdom, it is able to discover the forms, the
phenomena, and the movements of bodies whose distance

is as inexpressible in language as it is inconceivable in thought.

While the human eye has been admired by ordinary observers for the beauty of its form, the power of its movements, and the variety of its expression, it has excited the wonder of philosophers by the exquisite mechanism of its interior, and its singular adaptation to the variety of purposes which it has to serve. The eyeball is nearly globular, and is about an inch in diameter. It is formed externally by a tough opaque membrane called the *sclerotic* coat, which forms the white of the eye, with the exception of a small circular portion in front called the *cornea*. This portion is perfectly transparent, and so tough in its nature as to afford a powerful resistance to external injury. Immediately within the cornea, and in contact with it, is the *aqueous* humour, a clear fluid, which occupies only a small part of the front of the eye. Within this humour is the *iris*, a circular membrane with a hole in its centre called the pupil. The colour of the eye resides in this membrane, which has the curious property of contracting and expanding so as to diminish or enlarge the pupil,—an effect which human ingenuity has not been able even to imitate. Behind the iris is suspended the *crystalline* lens in a fine transparent capsule or bag of the same form with itself. It is then succeeded by the *vitreous humour*, which resembles the transparent white of an egg, and fills up the rest of the eye. Behind the vitreous humour, there is spread out on the inside of the eyeball a fine delicate membrane, called the *retina*, which is an expansion of the *optic nerve*, entering the back of the eye, and communicating with the brain.

A perspective view and horizontal section of the left eye, shown in the annexed figure, will convey a popular idea of its structure. It is, as it were, a small camera obscura, by means of which the pictures of external objects are painted on the retina, and in a way of which we are ignorant, it conveys the impression of them to the brain.

Fig. 1.

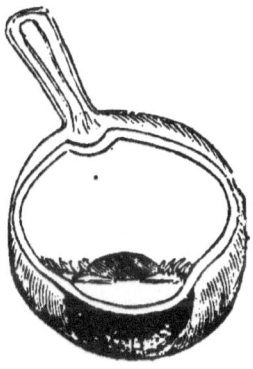

This wonderful organ may be considered as the sentinel which guards the pass between the worlds of matter and of spirit, and through which all their communications are interchanged. The optic nerve is the channel by which the mind peruses the handwriting of Nature on the retina, and through which it transfers to that material tablet its decisions and its creations. The eye is consequently the principal seat of the supernatural. When the indications of the marvellous are addressed to us through the ear, the mind may be startled without being deceived, and reason may succeed in suggesting some probable source of the illusion by which we have been alarmed : but when the eye in solitude sees before it the forms of life, fresh in their colours and vivid in their outline; when distant or departed friends are suddenly presented to its view; when visible bodies disappear and reappear without any intelligible cause ; and when it beholds objects, whether real or imaginary, for whose presence no cause can be assigned, the conviction of supernatural agency becomes under ordinary circumstances unavoidable.

Hence it is not only an amusing but an useful occupation to acquire a knowledge of those causes which are capable of producing so strange a belief, whether it arises from the delusions which the mind practises upon itself, or from the dexterity and science of others. I shall therefore proceed to explain those illusions which have their origin in the eye, whether they are general, or only occasionally exhibited in particular persons, and under particular circumstances.

There are few persons aware that when they look with one eye there is some particular object before them to which they are absolutely blind. If we look with the right eye this point is always about 15° to the right of the object which we are viewing, or to the right of the axis of the eye or the point of most distinct vision. If we look with the left eye the point is as far to the left. In order to be convinced of this curious fact, which was discovered by M. Mariotte, place two coloured wafers upon a sheet of white paper at the distance of three inches, and look at the left-hand wafer with the right eye at the distance of about 11 or 12 inches, taking care to keep the eye straight above the wafer, and the line which joins the eyes parallel to the line which joins the wafers. When this is done, and the left eye closed, the right-hand wafer will no longer be visible. The same effect will be produced if we close the right eye and, look with the left eye at the right-hand wafer. When we examine the retina to discover to what part of it this insensibility. to light belongs, we find that the image of the invisible wafer has fallen on the base of the optic nerve, or the place where this nerve enters the eye and expands itself to form the retina. This point is shown in the preceding figure by a convexity at the place where the nerve enters the eye.

But though light of ordinary intensity makes no impression upon this part of the eye, a very strong light does, and even when we use candles or highly luminous bodies in place of wafers the body does not wholly disappear, but leaves behind a faint cloudy light, without, however, giving anything like an image of the object from which the light proceeds.

When the objects are *white* wafers upon a *black* ground, the white wafer absolutely disappears, and the space which it covers appears to be completely black ; and as the light which illuminates a landscape is not much different from that of a white wafer, we should expect, whether we use one or both eyes,[*] to see a black or a dark spot upon every landscape, within 15° of the point which most particularly attracts our notice. The Divine Artificer, however, has not left his work thus imperfect. Though the base of the optic nerve is insensible to light that falls directly upon it, yet it has been made susceptible of receiving luminous impressions from the parts which surround it, and the consequence of this is, that when the wafer disappears, the spot which it occupied, in place of being black, has always the same colour as the ground upon which the wafer is laid, being white when the wafer is placed upon a white ground, and red when it is placed upon a red ground. This curious effect may be rudely illustrated by comparing the retina to a sheet of blotting-paper, and the base of the optic nerve to a circular portion of it covered with a piece of sponge. If a shower falls upon the paper, the protected part will not be wetted by the rain which falls upon the sponge that covers it, but in a few seconds it will be as effectually wetted by the moisture which it absorbs from the wet paper with which

---

[*] When both eyes are open, the object whose image falls upon the insensible spot of the one eye is seen by the other, so that though it is not invisible, yet it will only be half as luminous, and therefore two dark spots ought to be seen.

it is surrounded. In like manner the insensible spot on the retina is stimulated by a borrowed light, and the apparent defect is so completely removed that its existence can be determined only by the experiment already described.

Of the same character, but far more general in its effects, and important in its consequences, is another illusion of the eye which presented itself to me several years ago. When the eye is steadily occupied in viewing any particular object, or when it takes a fixed direction while the mind is occupied with any engrossing topic of speculation or of grief, it suddenly loses sight of, or becomes blind to, objects seen indirectly, or upon which it is not fully directed.* This takes place whether we use one or both eyes, and the object which disappears will reappear without any change in the position of the eye, while other objects will vanish and revive in succession without any apparent cause. If a sportsman, for example, is watching with intense interest the motions of one of his dogs, his companion, though seen with perfect clearness by indirect vision, will vanish, and the light of the heath or of the sky will close in upon the spot which he occupied.

In order to witness this illusion, put a little bit of white paper on a green cloth, and within three or four inches of it, place a narrow strip of white paper. At the distance of twelve or eighteen inches, fix one eye steadily upon the little bit of white paper, and in a short time a part or even the whole of the strip of paper will vanish as if it had been removed from the green cloth. It will again reappear, and again vanish, the effect depending greatly on the steadiness with which the eye is kept fixed. This illusion takes place when both the eyes are open, though it is easier to observe it when one of them is closed. The same thing happens when the object is luminous. When a candle is thus seen by indirect vision, it never wholly disappears, but it spreads itself out into a cloudy mass, the centre of which is blue, encircled with a bright ring of yellow light.

This inability of the eye to preserve a sustained vision of objects seen obliquely, is curiously compensated by the greater sensibility of those parts of the eye that have this defect. The eye has the power of seeing objects with perfect distinctness, only when it is directed straight upon them; that is, all objects seen indirectly are seen indistinctly; but it is a curious circumstance, that when we wish to obtain a sight of a very faint star, such as one of the satellites of Saturn, we can see it most distinctly *by looking away from it*, and when the eye is turned full upon it, it immediately disappears.

Effects still more remarkable are produced in the eye when it views objects that are difficult to be seen from the small degree of light with which they happen to be illuminated. The imperfect view which we obtain of such objects forces us to fix the eye more steadily upon them; but the more exertion we make to ascertain what they are, the greater difficulties do we encounter to accomplish our object. The eye is actually thrown into a state of the most painful agitation, the object will swell and contract, and partly disappear, and it will again become visible when the eye has recovered from the delirium into which it has been thrown. This phenomenon may be most distinctly seen when the objects in a room are illuminated with the feeble gleam of a fire almost extinguished; but it may be observed in daylight by the sportsman when he endeavours to mark upon the monotonous heath the particular spot where moor-game has alighted. Availing himself of the slightest difference of tint in the adjacent heath, he keeps his eye steadily fixed on it as he advances, but whenever the contrast of illumination is feeble, he will invariably lose sight of his mark and if the retina is capable of taking it up, it is only to lose it a second time.

This illusion is likely to be most efficacious in the dark, when there is just sufficient light to render white objects faintly visible, and to persons who are either timid or credulous must prove a frequent source of alarm. Its influence too is greatly aided by another condition of the eye, into which it is thrown during partial darkness. The pupil expands nearly to the whole width of the iris in order to collect the feeble light which prevails; but it is demonstrable that in this state the eye cannot accommodate itself to see near objects distinctly, so that the forms of persons and things actually become more shadowy and confused when they come within the very distance at which we count upon obtaining the best view of them. These affections of the eye are, we are persuaded, very frequent causes of a particular class of apparitions which are seen at night by the young and the ignorant. The spectres which are conjured up are always *white*, because no other colour can be seen, and they are either formed out of inanimate objects which reflect more light than others around them, or of animals or human beings whose colour or change of place renders them more visible in the dark. When the eye dimly descries an inanimate object whose different parts reflect different degrees of light, its brighter parts may enable the spectator to keep up a continued view of it; but the disappearance and reappearance of its fainter parts, and the change of shape which ensues, will necessarily give it the semblance of a living form, and if it occupies a position which is unapproachable, and where animate objects cannot find their way, the mind will soon transfer to it a supernatural existence. In like manner a human figure shadowed forth in a feeble twilight may undergo similar changes, and after being distinctly seen while it is in a situation favourable for receiving and reflecting light, it may suddenly disappear in a position fully before, and within the reach of, the observer's eye; and if this evanescence takes place in a path or road where there was no side-way by which the figure could escape, it is not easy for an ordinary mind to efface the impression which it cannot fail to receive. Under such circumstances, we never think of distrusting an organ which we have never found to deceive us ; and the truth of the maxim that "seeing is believing," is too universally admitted, and too deeply rooted in our nature to admit on any occasion of a single exception.

In these observations we have supposed that the spectator bears along with him no fears or prejudices, and is a faithful interpreter of the phenomena presented to his senses; but if he is himself a believer in apparitions, and unwilling to receive an ocular demonstration of their reality, it is not difficult to conceive the picture which will be drawn when external objects are distorted and caricatured by the imperfect indications of his senses, and coloured with all the vivid hues of the imagination.

Another class of ocular deceptions have their origin in a property of the eye which has been very imperfectly examined. The fine nervous fabric which constitutes the retina, and which extends to the brain, has the singular property of being *phosphorescent by pressure*. When we press the eyeball outwards by applying the point of the finger between it and the nose, a circle of light will be seen, which Sir Isaac Newton describes as "a circle of colours like those in the feather of a peacock's tail." He adds, that "if the eye and the finger remain quiet, these colours vanish in a second of time, but if the finger be moved with a quavering motion they appear again." In the numerous observations which I have made on these luminous circles, I have never been able to observe any colour but white, with the exception of a general red tinge which is seen when the eyelids are closed, and which is produced by the light which passes through them. The luminous circles too always continue while the pressure is applied, and they may be produced as readily after the eye has been long in darkness as when it has been recently exposed to light. When the pressure is very gently applied, so as to compress the fine pulpy substance of the retina, light is immediately created when the eye is in total darkness; and when in this state light is allowed to fall upon it, the part compressed is more sensible to light than any other part, and consequently appears more luminous. If we increase the pressure, the eyeball, being filled with incompressible fluids, will protrude all round the point of pressure, and consequently the retina at the protruded part will be *compressed* by the outward pressure of the contained fluid, while the retina on each side, namely, under the point of pressure and beyond the protruded part, will be drawn towards the protruded part or *dilated*. Hence the part under the finger which was originally compressed is now *dilated*, the adjacent parts *compressed*, and the more remote parts immediately without this *dilated* also. Now we have observed, that when the eye is, under these circumstances, exposed to light, there is a bright luminous circle shading off externally and internally into total darkness. We are led therefore to the important conclusions, that when the retina is compressed in total darkness it gives out light; that when it is compressed when exposed to light, its sensibility to light is increased; and that when it is *dilated under exposure to light, it becomes absolutely blind, or insensible to all luminous impressions.*

When the body is in a state of perfect health, this phosphorescence of the eye shows itself on many occasions. When the eye or the head receives a sudden blow, a bright flash of light shoots from the eyeball. In the act of sneezing, gleams of light are emitted from each eye, both during the inhalation of the air, and during its subsequent protrusion, and in blowing air violently through the nostrils, two patches of light appear above the axis of the eye and in front of it, while other two luminous spots unite into one, and appear as it were about the point of the nose when the eyes are directed to it. When we turn the eyeball by the action of its own muscles, the retina is affected at the place where the muscles are inserted, and there may be seen opposite each eye and towards the nose, two semicircles of light, and other two extremely faint towards the temples. At particular times, when the retina is more phosphorescent than at others, these semicircles are expanded into complete circles of light.

In a state of indisposition, the phosphorescence of the retina appears in new and more alarming forms. When the stomach is under a temporary derangement accompanied with headache, the pressure of the blood-vessels upon the retina shows itself, in total darkness, by a faint blue light floating before the eye, varying in its shape, and passing away at one side. This blue light increases in intensity, becomes *green* and then *yellow*, and sometimes rises to *red*, all these colours being frequently seen at once, or the mass of light shades off into darkness. When we consider the variety of distinct forms which in a state of perfect health the imagination can conjure up when looking into a burning fire, or upon an irregularly shaded surface,* it is easy to conceive how the masses of coloured

* A very curious example of the influence of the imagination in creating distinct forms out of an irregularly shaded surface, is mentioned in the life of Peter Heaman, a Swede, who was executed for piracy and murder at Leith in 1822. We give it in his own words :   [" One

light which float before the eye may be moulded by the
same power into those fantastic and natural shapes which
so often haunt the couch of the invalid, even when the
mind retains its energy, and is conscious of the illusion
under which it labours.   In other cases, temporary
blindness is produced by pressure upon the optic nerve,
or upon the retina, and under the excitation of fever or
delirium, when the physical cause which produces spectral
forms is at its height, there is superadded a powerful
influence of the mind, which imparts a new character to
the phantasms of the senses.

In order to complete the history of the illusions which
originate in the eye, it will be necessary to give some
account of the phenomena called *ocular spectra*, or *accidental colours*.   If we cut a figure out of red paper, and
placing it on a sheet of white paper, view it steadily for
some seconds with one or both eyes fixed on a particular
part of it, we shall observe the red colour to become less
brilliant.   If we then turn the eye from the red figure
upon the white paper, we shall see a distinct *green* figure,
which is the *spectrum*, or accidental colour of the *red*
figure.   With differently coloured figures we shall ob-

"One remarkable thing was, one day as we mended a sail, it
being a very thin one, after laying it upon deck in folds, I took the
tar-brush and tarred it over in the places which I thought needed
to be strengthened.   But when we hoisted it up, I was astonished
to see that the tar I had put upon it represented a gallows and a
man under it without a head.   The head was lying beside him.   He
was complete, body, thighs, legs, arms, and in every shape like a
man.   Now, I oftentimes made remarks upon it, and repeated them
to the others.   I always said to them all, you may depend upon it
that something will happen.   I afterwards took down the sail
on a calm day, and sewed a piece of canvas over the figure to cover
it, for I could not bear to have it always before my eyes."

serve differently coloured spectra, as in the following table :

Colour of the Original figures.	Colour of the Spectral figures.
Red,	Bluish-green.
Orange,	Blue.
Yellow,	Indigo.
Green,	Reddish-violet.
Blue,	Orange-red.
Indigo,	Orange-yellow.
Violet,	Yellow.
White,	Black.
Black,	White.

The two last of these experiments, viz., white and black figures, may be satisfactorily made by using a white medallion on a dark ground, and a black profile figure. The spectrum of the former will be found to be black, and that of the latter white.

These ocular spectra often show themselves without any effort on our part, and even without our knowledge. In a highly-painted room illuminated by the sun, those parts of the furniture on which the sun does not directly fall have always the opposite or accidental colour. If the sun shines through a chink in a *red* window-curtain, its light will appear *green*, varying, as in the above table, with the colour of the curtain; and if we look at the image of a candle reflected from the water in a *blue* finger glass, it will appear *yellow*. Whenever, in short, the eye is affected with one prevailing colour, it sees at the same time the spectral or accidental colour, just as when a musical string is vibrating, the ear hears at the same time its fundamental and its harmonic sounds.

If the prevailing light is *white* and *very strong*, the spectra which it produces are no longer black, but of various colours in succession. If we look at the sun, for example, when near the horizon, or when reflected from

glass or water, so as to moderate its brilliancy, and keep
the eye upon it steadily for a few seconds, we shall see
even for hours afterwards, and whether the eye is open
or shut, a spectre of the sun varying in its colours. At
first, with the eye open, it is *brownish-red* with a *sky-blue*
border, and when the eye is shut, it is *green* with a *red*
border. The *red* becomes more brilliant, and the *blue*
more vivid, till the impression is gradually worn off; but
even when they become very faint, they may be revived
by a gentle pressure on the eyeball.

Some eyes are more susceptible than others of these
spectral impressions, and Mr. Boyle mentions an individual who continued for years to see the spectre of the
sun when he looked upon bright objects. This fact
appeared to Locke so interesting and inexplicable, that he
consulted Sir Isaac Newton respecting its cause, and
drew from him the following interesting account of a
similar effect upon himself: " The observation you mention
in Mr. Boyle's book of colours, I once made upon myself
with the hazard of my eyes. The manner was this : I
looked a very little while upon the sun in the looking-
glass with my right eye, and then turned my eyes into a
dark corner of my chamber, and winked, to observe the
impression made, and the circles of colours which encom-
passed it, and how they decayed by degrees, and at last
vanished. This I repeated a second and a third time.
At the third time, when the phantasm of light and
colours about it were almost vanished, intending my
fancy upon them to see their last appearance, I found, to
my amazement, that they began to return, and by little
and little to become as lively and vivid as when I had
newly looked upon the sun. But when I ceased to intend
my fancy upon them they vanished again. After this, I
found that, as often as I went into the dark, and intended
my mind upon them, as when a man looks earnestly to

see anything which is difficult to be seen, I could make the phantasm return without looking any more upon the sun; and the oftener I made it return, the more easily I could make it return again. And at length, by repeating this without looking any more upon the sun, I made such an impression on my eye, that, if I looked upon the clouds, or a book, or any bright object, I saw upon it a round bright spot of light like the sun, and, which is still stranger, though I looked upon the sun with my right eye only, and not with my left, yet my fancy began to make an impression upon my left eye as well as upon my right. For if I shut my right eye, and looked upon a book or the clouds with my left eye, I could see the spectrum of the sun almost as plain as with my right eye, if I did but intend my fancy a little while upon it; for at first, if I shut my right eye, and looked with my left, the spectrum of the sun did not appear till I intended my fancy upon it; but by repeating, this appeared every time more easily. And now in a few hours' time I had brought my eyes to such a pass, that I could look upon no bright object with either eye but I saw the sun before me, so that I durst neither write nor read; but to recover the use of my eyes, shut myself up in my chamber made dark, for three days together, and used all means in my power to direct my imagination from the sun. For if I thought upon him, I presently saw his picture, though I was in the dark. But by keeping in the dark, and employing my mind about other things, I began in three or four days to have more use of my eyes again; and by forbearing to look upon bright objects, recovered them pretty well; though not so well but that, for some months after, the spectrums of the sun began to return as often as I began to meditate upon the phenomena, even though I lay in bed at midnight with my curtains drawn. But now I have been very well for many years, though I am apt to think, if I durst venture my eyes, I could still make the phantasm return by the power of my fancy. This story I tell you, to let you understand, that in the observation related by Mr. Boyle, the man's fancy probably concurred with the impression made by the sun's light to produce that phantasm of the sun which he constantly saw in bright objects."*

I am not aware of any effects that had the character of supernatural having been actually produced by the causes above described; but it is obvious, that, if a living figure had been projected against the strong light which imprinted these durable spectra of the sun, which might really happen when the solar rays are reflected from water, and diffused by its ruffled surface, this figure would have necessarily accompanied all the luminous spectres which the fancy created. Even in ordinary lights strange appearances may be produced by even transient impressions, and if I am not greatly mistaken, the case which I am about to mention is not only one which may occur, but which actually happened. A figure dressed in *black* and mounted upon a *white* horse was riding along exposed to the bright rays of the sun, which, through a small opening in the clouds, was throwing its light only upon that part of the landscape. The *black* figure was projected against a white cloud, and the white horse shone with particular brilliancy by its contrast with the dark soil against which it was seen. A person interested in the arrival of such a stranger had been for some time following his movements with intense anxiety, but upon his disappearance behind a wood, was surprised to observe the spectre of the mounted stranger in the form of a *white* rider upon a *black* steed, and this spectre was seen for some time in the sky, or upon any pale ground to which the eye was directed. Such an occurrence, especially if

* See the *Edinburgh Encyclopædia*, Art. ACCIDENTAL COLOURS.

accompanied with a suitable combination of events, might, even in modern times, have formed a chapter in the history of the marvellous.

It is a curious circumstance, that when the image of an object is impressed upon the retina only for a few moments, the picture which is left is exactly of the same colour with the object. If we look, for example, at a window at some distance from the eye, and then transfer the eye quickly to the wall, we shall see it distinctly but momentarily with *light* panes and *dark* bars; but in a space of time incalculably short, this picture is succeeded by the spectral impression of the window, which will consist of *black* panes and *white* bars. The similar spectrum, or that of the same colour as the object, is finely seen in the experiment of forming luminous circles by whirling round a burning stick, in which case the circles are always red.

In virtue of this property of the eye an object may be seen in many places at once ; and we may even exhibit at the same instant the two opposite sides of the same object, or two pictures painted on the opposite sides of a piece of card. It was found by a French philosopher, M. D'Arcet, that the impression of light continued on the retina about the eighth part of a second after the luminous body was withdrawn, and upon this principle Dr. Paris has constructed the pretty little instrument, called the *Thaumatrope*, or the *Wonder-turner*. It consists of a number of circular pieces of card about two or three inches broad, which may be twirled round with great velocity by the application of the forefinger and thumb of each hand to pieces of silk string attached to opposite points of their circumference. On each side of the circular piece of card is painted part of a picture, or a part of a figure, in such a manner that the two parts would form a group or a whole figure if we could see both sides at once. Harlequin, for example, is painted on one side, and

Columbine on the other, so that by twirling round the card the two are seen at the same time in their usual mode of combination. The body of a Turk is drawn on one side, and his head on the reverse, and by the rotation of the card the head is replaced upon his shoulders. The principle of this illusion may be extended to many other contrivances. Part of a sentence may be written on one side of a card and the rest on the reverse. Particular letters may be given on one side, and others upon the other, or even halves or parts of each letter may be put upon each side, or all these contrivances may be combined, so that the sentiment which they express can be understood only when all the scattered parts are united by the revolution of the card.

As the revolving card is virtually transparent, so that bodies beyond it can be seen through it, the power of the illusion might be greatly extended by introducing into the picture other figures, either animate or inanimate. The setting sun, for example, might be introduced into a landscape : part of the flame of a fire might be seen to issue from the crater of a volcano, and cattle grazing in a field might make part of the revolutionary landscape. For such purposes, however, the form of the instrument would require to be completely changed, and the rotation should be effected round a standing axis by wheels and pinions, and a screen placed in front of the revolving plane with open compartments or apertures, through which the principal figures would appear. Had the principle of this instrument been known to the ancients, it would doubtless have formed a powerful engine of delusion in their temples, and might have been more effective than the optical means which they seem to have employed for producing the apparitions of their gods.

In certain diseased conditions of the eye effects of a very remarkable kind are produced. The faculty of seeing objects double is too common to be noticed as remarkable; and though it may take place with only one eye, yet, as it generally arises from a transient inability to direct the axes of both eyes to the same point, it excites little notice. That state of the eye, however, in which we lose sight of half of every object at which we look, is more alarming and more likely to be ascribed to the disappearance of part of the object than to a defect of sight. Dr. Wollaston, who experienced this defect twice, informs us that, after taking violent exercise, he " suddenly found that he could see but half of a man whom he met, and that, on attempting to read the name of JOHNSON over a door, he saw only   SON, the commencement of the name being wholly obliterated from his view." In this instance, the part of the object which disappeared was towards his left, but on a second occurrence of the same affection, the part which disappeared was towards his right. There are many occasions on which this defect of the eye might alarm the person who witnessed it for the first time. At certain distances from the eye one of two persons would necessarily disappear ; and by a slight change of position either in the observer or the person observed, the person that vanished would reappear, while the other would disappear in his turn. The circumstances under which these evanescences would take place could not be supposed to occur to an ordinary observer, even if he should be aware that the cause had its origin in himself. When a phenomenon so strange is seen by a person in perfect health, as it generally is, and who has never had occasion to distrust the testimony of his senses, he can scarcely refer it to any other cause than a supernatural one.

Among the affections of the eye which not only deceive the person who is subject to them, but those also who witness their operation, may be enumerated the insensibility of the eye to particular colours. This defect is not accompanied with any imperfection of vision, or connected with any disease either of a local or a general nature, and it has hitherto been observed in persons who possess a strong and a sharp sight. Mr. Huddart has described the case of one Harris, a shoemaker, at Maryport, in Cumberland, who was subject to this defect in a very remarkable degree. He seems to have been insensible to every colour, and to have been capable of recognizing only the two opposite tints of *black* and *white*. " His first suspicion of this defect arose when he was about four years old. Having by accident found in the street a child's stocking, he carried it to a neighbouring house to inquire for the owner : he observed the people call it a *red stocking*, though he did not understand why they gave it that denomination, as he himself thought it completely described by being called a stocking. The circumstance, however, remained in his memory, and, with other subsequent observations, led him to the knowledge of his defect. He observed also that, when young, other children could discern cherries on a tree by some pretended difference of colour, though he could only distinguish them from the leaves by their difference of size and shape. He observed also that, by means of this difference of colour, they could see the cherries at a greater distance than he could, though he could see other objects at as great a distance as they, that is, where the sight was not assisted by the colour." Harris had two brothers whose perception of colours was nearly as defective as his own. One of these, whom Mr. Huddart examined, constantly mistook *light green* for *yellow*, and *orange* for *grass green*.

Mr. Scott has described in the Philosophical Transactions his own defect in perceiving colours. He states that he does not know any *green* in the world ; that a *pink* colour and a *pale blue* are perfectly alike; that he has often thought a *full red* and a *full green* a good match ;

that he is sometimes baffled in distinguishing a *full purple* from a *deep blue*, but that he knows light, dark, and middle *yellows*, and all degrees of *blue* except *sky-blue*. " I married my daughter to a genteel, worthy man, a few years ago : the day before the marriage he came to my house dressed in a new suit of fine cloth clothes. I was much displeased that he should come, as I supposed, in *black ;* and said that he should go back to change his colour. But my daughter said, No—No ; the colour is very genteel ; that it was my eyes that deceived me. He was a gentleman of the law, in a fine rich claret-coloured dress, which is as much a black to my eyes as any black that ever was dyed." Mr. Scott's father, his maternal uncle, one of his sisters, and her two sons, had all the same imperfection. Dr. Nichol has recorded a case where a naval officer purchased a *blue* uniform coat and waistcoat with *red* breeches to match the blue, and Mr. Harvey describes the case of a tailor at Plymouth, who, on one occasion, repaired an article of dress with *crimson* in place of *black* silk, and on another, patched the elbow of a *blue* coat with a piece of *crimson* cloth. It deserves to be remarked that our celebrated countrymen the late Mr. Dugald Stewart, Mr. Dalton, and Mr. Troughton, have a similar difficulty in distinguishing colours. Mr. Stewart discovered this defect when one of his family was admiring the beauty of the Siberian crab-apple, which he could not distinguish from the leaves but by its form and size. Mr. Dalton cannot distinguish *blue* from pink, and the solar spectrum consists only of two colours, *yellow* and *blue*. Mr. Troughton regards *red*, *ruddy pinks*, and brilliant *oranges*, as *yellows*, and *greens* as *blues*, so that he is capable only of appreciating *blue* and *yellow* colours.

In all those cases which have been carefully studied, at least in three of them in which I have had the advantage of making personal observations, namely, those of

Mr. Troughton, Mr. Dalton, and Mr. Liston, the eye is capable of seeing the whole of the prismatic spectrum, the red space appearing to be yellow. If the red space consisted of homogeneous or simple red rays, we should be led to infer that the eyes in question were not insensible to red light, but were merely incapable of discriminating between the impressions of red and yellow light. I have lately shown, however, that the prismatic spectrum consists of three equal and coincident spectra of *red*, *yellow*, and *blue* light, and consequently, that much yellow and a small portion of blue light exist in the red space; —and hence it follows that those eyes which see only two colours, viz., *yellow* and *blue*, in the spectrum, are really insensible to the red light of the spectrum, and see only the yellow with the small portion of blue with which the red is mixed. The faintness of the yellow light which is thus seen in the red space, confirms the opinion that the retina has not appreciated the influence of the simple red rays.

If one of the two travellers who, in the fable of the chameleon, are made to quarrel about the colour of that singular animal, had happened to possess this defect of sight, they would have encountered at every step of their journey new grounds of dissension without the chance of finding an umpire who could pronounce a satisfactory decision. Under certain circumstances, indeed, the arbiter might set aside the opinions of both the disputants, and render it necessary to appeal to some higher authority

—— to beg he'd tell 'em if he knew
Whether the thing was *red* or *blue*.

In the course of writing the preceding observations, an ocular illusion occurred to myself of so extraordinary a nature, that I am convinced it never was seen before, and I think it far from probable that it will ever be seen again. Upon directing my eyes to the candles that were standing before me, I was surprised to observe, apparently among my hair, and nearly straight above my head, and far without the range of vision, a distinct image of one of the candles inclined about 45° to the horizon, as shown at A in Fig. 2. The image was as distinct and perfect

Fig. 2.

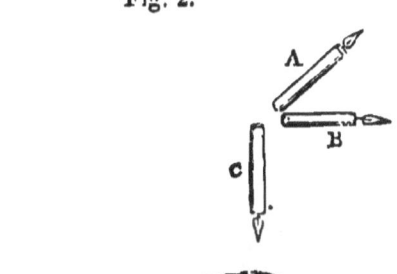

as if it had been formed by reflexion from a piece of mirror glass, though of course much less brilliant, and the position of the image proved that it must be formed by reflexion from a perfectly flat and highly-polished surface. But where such a surface could be placed, and how, even if it were fixed, it could reflect the image of the candle up through my head, were difficulties not a little perplexing. Thinking that it might be something lodged in the eyebrow, I covered it up from the light, but the image still retained its place. I then examined the eyelashes with as little success, and was driven to the extreme supposition that a crystallization was taking place in some part of the aqueous humour of the eye, and that the image was formed by the reflexion of the light of the candle from one of the crystalline faces. In this state of uncertainty, and, I may add, of anxiety, for this last supposition was by no means an agreeable one, I set myself down to examine the phenomenon experimentally. I found that the image varied its place by the motion of the head and of the eyeball, which proved that it was either attached to the eyeball or occupied a place where it was affected by that motion. Upon inclining the candle at different angles the image suffered corresponding variations of position. In order to determine the exact place of the reflecting substance, I now took an opaque circular body and held it between the eye and the candle till it eclipsed the mysterious image. By bringing the body nearer and nearer the eyeball till its shadow became sufficiently distinct to be seen, it was easy to determine the locality of the reflector, because the shadow of the opaque body must fall upon it whenever the image of the candle was eclipsed. In this way I ascertained that the reflecting body was in the upper eyelash, and I found that, in consequence of being disturbed, it had twice changed its inclination, so as to represent a vertical candle in the horizontal position B, and afterwards in the inverted position C. Still, however, I sought for it in vain, and even with the aid of a magnifier I could not discover it. At last, however, Mrs. B., who possesses the perfect vision of short-sighted persons, discovered, after repeated examinations, between two eyelashes, a minute speck, which, upon being removed with great difficulty, turned out to be a chip of red wax not above the hundredth part of an inch in diameter, and having its surface so perfectly flat and so highly polished that I could see in it the same image of the candle, by placing it extremely near the eye. This chip of wax had no doubt received its flatness and its polish from the surface of a seal, and had started into my eye when breaking the seal of a letter.

That this reflecting substance was the cause of the

image of the candle cannot admit of a doubt; but the wonder still remains how the images which it formed occupied so mysterious a place as to be seen without the range of vision, and apparently through the head. In order to explain this, let *m n*, Fig. 2, be a lateral view of the eye. The chip of wax was placed at *m* at the root of the eyelashes, and being nearly in contact with the outer surface of the cornea, the light of the candle which it reflected passed very obliquely through the pupil and fell upon the retina somewhere to the left of *n*, very near where the retina terminates; but a ray thus falling obliquely on the retina is seen, in virtue of the law of visible direction already explained, in a line *n* C perpendicular to the retina at the point near *n*, where the ray fell. Hence the candle was necessarily seen through the head as it were of the observer, and without the range of ordinary vision. The comparative brightness of the reflected image still surprises me; but even this, if the image really was brighter, may be explained by the fact, that it was formed on a part of the retina upon which light had never before fallen, and which may therefore be supposed to be more sensible, than the parts of the membrane in constant use, to luminous impressions.

Independent of its interest as an example of the marvellous in vision, the preceding fact may be considered as a proof that the retina retains its power to its very termination near the ciliary processes, and that the law of visible direction holds true even without the range of ordinary vision. It is therefore possible that a reflecting surface favourably placed on the outside of the eye, or that a reflecting surface in the inside of the eye, may cause a luminous image to fall nearly on the extreme margin of the retina, the consequence of which would be that it would be seen in the back of the head half way between a vertical and a horizontal line.

LETTER III.

*Subject of spectral illusions—Recent and interesting case of Mrs. A.—
Her first illusion affecting the ear—Spectral apparition of her
husband—Spectral . apparition of a cat—Apparition of a near
and living relation in grave-clothes seen in a looking-glass—Other
illusions affecting the ear—Spectre of a deceased friend sitting in
an easy-chair—Spectre of a coach and four filled with skeletons—
Accuracy and value of the preceding cases—State of health under
which they arose—Spectral apparitions are pictures on the retina
—The ideas of memory and imagination are also pictures on the
retina—General views of the subject—Approximate explanation of
spectral apparitions.*

THE preceding account of the different sources of illusion
to which the eye is subject, is not only useful as indicating
the probable cause of any individual deception, but it has
a special importance in preparing the mind for understanding those more vivid and permanent spectral illusions to
which some individuals have been either occasionally or
habitually subject.

In these lesser phenomena we find the retina so powerfully influenced by external impressions as to retain the
view of visible objects long after they are withdrawn ; we
observe it to be so excited by local pressures of which we
sometimes know neither the nature nor the origin, as to
see in total darkness moving and shapeless masses of
coloured light; and we find, as in the case of Sir Isaac
Newton and others, that the imagination has the power
of reviving the impressions of highly-luminous objects,
months and even years after they were first made. From
such phenomena, the mind feels it to be no violent transi-

tion to pass to those spectral illusions which, in particular states of health, have haunted the most intelligent individuals, not only in the broad light of day, but in the very heart of the social circle.

This curious subject has been so ably and fully treated in your Letters on Demonology, that it would be presumptuous in me to resume any part of it on which you have even touched; but as it forms a necessary branch of a Treatise on Natural Magic, and as one of the most remarkable cases on record has come within my own knowledge, I shall make no apology for giving a full account of the different spectral appearances which it embraces, and of adding the results of a series of observations and experiments on which I have been long occupied, with the view of throwing some light on this remarkable class of phenomena.

A few years ago I had occasion to spend some days under the same roof with the lady to whose case I have above referred. At that time she had seen no spectral illusions, and was acquainted with the subject only from the interesting volume of Dr. Hibbert. In conversing with her about the cause of these apparitions, I mentioned that, if she should ever see such a thing, she might distinguish a genuine ghost existing externally, and seen as an external object, from one created by the mind, by merely pressing one eye or straining them both so as to see objects double; for in this case the external object or supposed apparition would invariably be doubled, while the impression on the retina created by the mind would remain single. This observation recurred to her mind when she unfortunately became subject to the same illusions; but she was too well acquainted with their nature to require any such evidence of their mental origin; and the state of agitation which generally accompanies them seems to have prevented her from making the experiment as a matter of curiosity.

K

1. The first illusion to which Mrs. A. was subject was one which affected only the ear. On the 26th of December, 1830, about half-past four in the afternoon, she was standing near the fire in the hall, and on the point of going up stairs to dress, when she heard, as she supposed, her husband's voice calling her by name, " —— Come here! come to me!" She imagined that he was calling at the door to have it opened, but upon going there and opening the door she was surprised to find no person there. Upon returning to the fire, she again heard the same voice calling out very distinctly and loudly, " —— Come, come here!" She then opened two other doors of the same room, and upon seeing no person she returned to the fire-place. After a few moments she heard the same voice still calling, " —— Come to me, come! come away!" in a loud, plaintive, and somewhat impatient tone. She answered as loudly, "Where are you? I don't know where you are;" still imagining that he was somewhere in search of her: but receiving no answer she shortly went up stairs. On Mr. A.'s return to the house, about half an hour afterwards, she inquired why he called to her so often, and where he was; and she was of course greatly surprised to learn that he had not been near the house at the time. A similar illusion, which excited no particular notice at the time, occurred to Mrs. A. when residing at Florence about ten years before, and when she was in perfect health. When she was undressing after a ball, she heard a voice call her repeatedly by name, and she was at that time unable to account for it.

2. The next illusion which occurred to Mrs. A. was of a more alarming character. On the 30th of December, about four o'clock in the afternoon, Mrs. A. came down stairs into the drawing-room, which she had quitted only a few minutes before, and on entering the room she saw her husband, as she supposed, standing with his back to

the fire. As he had gone out to take a walk about half an hour before, she was surprised to see him there, and asked him why he had returned so soon. The figure looked fixedly at her with a serious and thoughtful expression of countenance, but did not speak. Supposing that his mind was absorbed in thought, she sat down in an arm-chair near the fire, and within two feet at most of the figure, which she still saw standing before her. As its eyes, however, still continued to be fixed upon her, she said after the lapse of a few minutes, " Why don't you speak —— ?" The figure immediately moved off towards the window at the farther end of the room, with its eyes still gazing on her, and it passed so very close to her in doing so that she was struck by the circumstance of hearing no step nor sound, nor feeling her clothes brushed against, nor even any agitation in the air. Although she was now convinced that the figure was not her husband, yet she never for a moment supposed that it was anything supernatural, and was soon convinced that it was a spectral illusion. As soon as this conviction had established itself in her mind, she recollected the experiment which I had suggested, of trying to double the object; but before she was able distinctly to do this, the figure had retreated to the window, where it disappeared. Mrs. A. immediately followed it, shook the curtains and examined the window, the impression having been so distinct and forcible that she was unwilling to believe that it was not a reality. Finding, however, that the figure had no natural means of escape, she was convinced that she had seen a spectral apparition like those recorded in Dr. Hibbert's work, and she consequently felt no alarm or agitation. The appearance was seen in bright daylight, and lasted four or five minutes. When the figure stood close to her it concealed the real objects behind it, and the apparition was fully as vivid as the reality.

3. On these two occasions Mrs. A. was alone, but when the next phantasm appeared her husband was present. This took place on the 4th of January, 1830. About ten o'clock at night, when Mr. and Mrs. A. were sitting in the drawing-room, Mr. A. took up the poker to stir the fire, and when he was in the act of doing this, Mrs. A. exclaimed, "Why there's the cat in the room!"—"Where?" asked Mr. A. "There, close to you," she replied.— "Where?" he repeated. "Why on the rug to be sure, between yourself and the coal-scuttle." Mr. A., who had still the poker in his hand, pushed it in the direction mentioned. "Take care," cried Mrs. A., "take care, you are hitting her with the poker." Mr. A. again asked her to point out exactly where she saw the cat. She replied, "Why sitting up there close to your feet on the rug: she is looking at me. It is Kitty—come here, Kitty!"— There were two cats in the house, one of which went by this name, and they were rarely if ever in the drawing-room. At this time Mrs. A. had no idea that the sight of the cat was an illusion. When she was asked to touch it, she got up for the purpose, and seemed as if she were pursuing something which moved away. She followed a few steps, and then said, "It has gone under the chair." Mr. A. assured her it was an illusion, but she would not believe it. He then lifted up the chair, and Mrs. A. saw nothing more of it. The room was then searched all over, and nothing found in it. There was a dog lying on the hearth, who would have betrayed great uneasiness if a cat had been in the room, but he lay perfectly quiet. In order to be quite certain, Mr. A. rung the bell, and sent for the two cats, both of which were found in the house-keeper's room.

4. About a month after this occurrence, Mrs. A., who had taken a somewhat fatiguing drive during the day, was preparing to go to bed about eleven o'clock at night, and,

sitting before the dressing-glass, was occupied in arrang-
ing her hair. She was in a listless and drowsy state of
mind, but fully awake. When her fingers were in active
motion among the papillotes, she was suddenly startled
by seeing in the mirror the figure of a near relation, who
was then in Scotland, and in perfect health. The apparition appeared over her left shoulder, and its eyes met
hers in the glass. It was enveloped in grave-clothes,
closely pinned, as is usual with corpses, round the head
and under the chin, and though the eyes were open, the
features were solemn and rigid. The dress was evidently
a shroud, as Mrs. A. remarked even the punctured pattern
usually worked in a peculiar manner round the edges of
that garment. Mrs. A. described herself as at the time
sensible of a feeling like what we conceive of fascination,
compelling her for a time to gaze on this melancholy
apparition, which was as distinct and vivid as any reflected reality could be, the light of the candles upon the
dressing-table appearing to shine fully upon its face.
After a few minutes, she turned round to look for the
reality of the form over her shoulder; but it was not
visible, and it had also disappeared from the glass when
she looked again in that direction.

5. In the beginning of March, when Mr. A. had been
about a fortnight from home, Mrs. A. frequently heard
him moving near her. Nearly every night, as she lay
awake, she distinctly heard sounds like his breathing
hard on the pillow by her side, and other sounds such as
he might make while turning in bed.

6. On another occasion, during Mr. A.'s absence, while
riding with a neighbour, Mr. ——, she heard his voice
frequently as if he were riding by his side. She heard
also the tramp of his horse's feet, and was almost puzzled
by hearing him address her at the same time with the
person really in company. His voice made remarks on

the scenery, improvements, &c., such as he probably would have done had he been present. On this occasion, however, there was no visible apparition.

7. On the 17th March, Mrs. A. was preparing for bed. She had dismissed her maid, and was sitting with her feet in hot water. Having an excellent memory, she had been thinking upon and repeating to herself a striking passage in the Edinburgh Review, when, on raising her eyes, she saw seated in a large easy-chair before her the figure of a deceased friend, the sister of Mr. A. The figure was dressed, as had been usual with her, with great neatness, but in a gown of a peculiar kind, such as Mrs. A. had never seen her wear, but exactly such as had been described to her by a common friend as having been worn by Mr. A.'s sister during her last visit to England. Mrs. A. paid particular attention to the dress, air, and appearance of the figure, which sat in an easy attitude in the chair, holding a handkerchief in one hand. Mrs. A. tried to speak to it, but experienced a difficulty in doing so, and in about three minutes the figure disappeared. About a minute afterwards, Mr. A. came into the room, and found Mrs. A. slightly nervous, but fully aware of the delusive nature of the apparition. She described it as having all the vivid colouring and apparent reality of life; and for some hours preceding this and other visions, she experienced a peculiar sensation in her eyes, which seemed to be relieved when the vision had ceased.

8. On the 5th October, between one and two o'clock in the morning, Mr. A. was awoke by Mrs. A., who told him that she had just seen the figure of his deceased mother draw aside the bed-curtains and appear between them. The dress and the look of the apparition were precisely those in which Mr. A.'s mother had been last seen by Mrs. A. at Paris in 1824.

9. On the 11th October, when sitting in the drawing-

room, on one side of the fire-place, she saw the figure of another deceased friend moving towards her from the window at the farther end of the room. It approached the fire-place, and sat down in the chair opposite. As there were several persons in the room at the time, she describes the idea uppermost in her mind to have been a fear lest they should be alarmed at her staring, in the way she was conscious of doing, at vacancy, and should fancy her intellect disordered. Under the influence of this fear, and recollecting a story of a similar effect in your work on Demonology, which she had lately read, she summoned up the requisite resolution to enable her to cross the space before the fire-place, and seat herself in the same chair with the figure. The apparition remained perfectly distinct till she sat down, as it were, in its lap, when it vanished.

10. On the 26th of the same month, about two P.M., Mrs. A. was sitting in a chair by the window in the same room with her husband. He heard her exclaim "What have I seen?" And on looking at her, he observed a strange expression in her eyes and countenance. A carriage and four had appeared to her to be driving up the entrance road to the house. As it approached, she felt inclined to go up stairs to prepare to receive company, but, as if spell-bound, she was unable to move or speak. The carriage approached, and as it arrived within a few yards of the window, she saw the figures of the postilions and the persons inside take the ghastly appearance of skeletons and other hideous figures. The whole then vanished entirely, when she uttered the above-mentioned exclamation.

11. On the morning of the 30th October, when Mrs. A. was sitting in her own room with a favourite dog in her lap, she distinctly saw the same dog moving about the room during the space of about a minute, or rather more.

12. On the 3rd December, about 9 P.M., when Mr. and

Mrs. A. were sitting near each other in the drawing-room occupied in reading, Mr. A. felt a pressure on his foot. On looking up, he observed Mrs. A.'s eyes fixed with a strong and unnatural stare on a chair about nine or ten feet distant. Upon asking her what she saw, the expression of her countenance changed, and upon recovering herself, she told Mr. A. that she had seen his brother, who was alive and well at the moment in London, seated in the opposite chair, but dressed in grave-clothes, and with a ghastly countenance, as if scarcely alive.

Such is a brief account of the various spectral illusions observed by Mrs. A.—In describing them I have used the very words employed by her husband in his communications to me on the subject; * and the reader may be assured that the descriptions are neither heightened by fancy nor amplified by invention. The high character and intelligence of the lady, and the station of her husband in society, and as a man of learning and science, would authenticate the most marvellous narrative, and satisfy the most scrupulous mind, that the case has been philosophically as well as faithfully described. In narrating events which we regard as of supernatural character, the mind has a strong tendency to give more prominence to what appears to itself the most wonderful; but from the very same cause, when we describe extraordinary and inexplicable phenomena which we believe to be the result of natural causes, the mind is prone to strip them of their most marvellous points, and bring them down to the level of ordinary events. From the very commencement of the spectral illusions seen by Mrs. A. both she and her husband were well aware of their nature and origin, and both of them paid the most minute attention to the circumstances which accompanied them, not only

* *Edinburgh Journal of Science*, New Series, No. iv. p. 218, 219; No. vi. p. 244; and No. viii. p. 261.

with the view of throwing light upon so curious a subject, but for the purpose of ascertaining their connection with the state of health under which they appeared.

As the spectres seen by Nicolai and others had their origin in bodily indisposition, it becomes interesting to learn the state of Mrs. A.'s health when she was under the influence of these illusions. During the six weeks within which the three first illusions took place, she had been considerably reduced and weakened by a troublesome cough, and the weakness which this occasioned was increased by her being prevented from taking a daily tonic. Her general health had not been strong, and long experience has put it beyond a doubt, that her indisposition arises from a disordered state of the digestive organs. Mrs. A. has naturally a morbidly sensitive imagination, which so painfully affects her corporeal impressions, that the account of any person having suffered severe pain by accident or otherwise occasionally produces acute twinges of pain in the corresponding parts of her person. The account, for example, of the amputation of an arm will produce an instantaneous and severe sense of pain in her own arm. She is subject to talk in her sleep with great fluency, to repeat long passages of poetry, particularly when she is unwell, and even to cap verses for half an hour together, never failing to quote lines beginning with the final letter of the preceding one till her memory is exhausted.

Although it is not probable that we shall ever be able to understand the actual manner in which a person of sound mind beholds spectral apparitions in the broad light of day, yet we may arrive at such a degree of knowledge on the subject as to satisfy rational curiosity, and to strip the phenomena of every attribute of the marvellous. Even the vision of natural objects presents to us insurmountable difficulties, if we seek to understand the pre-

cise part which the mind performs in perceiving them;
but the philosopher considers that he has given a satisfactory explanation of vision when he demonstrates that
distinct pictures of external objects are painted on the
retina, and that this membrane communicates with the
brain by means of nerves of the same substance as itself,
and of which it is merely an expansion. Here we reach
the gulf which human intelligence cannot pass; and if
the presumptuous mind of man shall dare to extend its
speculations farther, it will do it only to evince its inca-
pacity and mortify its pride.

In his admirable work on this subject, Dr. Hibbert has
shown that spectral apparitions are nothing more than
ideas or the recollected images of the mind, which in
certain states of bodily indisposition have been rendered
more vivid than actual impressions, or, to use other words,
that the pictures in the "mind's eye" are more vivid
than the pictures in the body's eye. This principle has
been placed by Dr. Hibbert beyond the reach of doubt;
but I propose to go much farther, and to show that the
"mind's eye" is actually the body's eye, and that the
retina is the common tablet on which both classes of impressions are painted, and by means of which they receive
their visual existence according to the same optical laws.
Nor is this true merely in the case of spectral illusions.
It holds good of all ideas recalled by the memory or
created by the imagination, and may be regarded as a
fundamental law in the science of pneumatology.

It would be out of place in a work like this to adduce
the experimental evidence on which it rests, or even to
explain the manner in which the experiments themselves
must be conducted; but I may state in general, that the
spectres conjured up by the memory or the fancy have
always a "local habitation," and that they appear in front
of the eye, and partake in its movements exactly like the

impressions of luminous objects after the objects themselves are withdrawn.

In the healthy state of the mind and body, the relative intensity of these two classes of impressions on the retina are nicely adjusted. The mental pictures are transient and comparatively feeble, and in ordinary temperaments are never capable of disturbing or effacing the direct images of visible objects. The affairs of life could not be carried on if the memory were to intrude bright representations of the past into the domestic scene, or scatter them over the external landscape. The two opposite impressions, indeed, could not coexist: the same nervous fibre which is carrying from the brain to the retina the figures of memory, could not at the same instant be carrying back the impressions of external objects from the retina to the brain. The mind cannot perform two different functions at the same instant, and the direction of its attention to one of the two classes of impressions necessarily produce the extinction of the other: but so rapid is the exercise of mental power, that the alternate appearance and disappearance of the two contending impressions is no more recognized than the successive observations of external objects during the twinkling of the eyelids. If we look, for example, at the façade of St. Paul's, and, without changing our position, call to mind the celebrated view of Mont Blanc from Lyons, the picture of the cathedral, though actually impressed upon the retina, is momentarily lost sight of by the mind, exactly like an object seen by indirect vision; and during the instant the recollected image of the mountain, towering over the subjacent range, is distinctly seen, but in a tone of subdued colouring, and indistinct outline. When the purpose of its recall is answered, it quickly disappears, and the picture of the cathedral again resumes the ascendency.

In darkness and solitude, when external objects no longer interfere with the pictures of the mind, they become more vivid and distinct; and in the state between waking and sleeping, the intensity of the impressions approaches to that of visible objects. With persons of studious habits, who are much occupied with the operations of their own minds, the mental pictures are much more distinct than in ordinary persons; and in the midst of abstract thought, external objects even cease to make any impression on the retina. A philosopher absorbed in his contemplations experiences a temporary privation of the use of his senses. His children or his servants will enter the room directly before his eyes without being seen. They will speak to him without being heard; and they will even try to rouse him from his reverie without being felt; although his eyes, his ears, and his nerves, actually receive the impressions of light, sound, and touch. In such cases, however, the philosopher is voluntarily pursuing a train of thought on which his mind is deeply interested; but even ordinary men, not much addicted to speculations of any kind, often perceive in their mind's eye the pictures of deceased or absent friends, or even ludicrous creations of fancy, which have no connection whatever with the train of their thoughts. Like spectral apparitions, they are entirely involuntary, and though they may have sprung from a regular series of associations, yet it is frequently impossible to discover a single link in the chain.

If it be true, then, that the pictures of the mind and spectral illusions are equally impressions upon the retina, the latter will differ in no respect from the former, but in the degree of vividness with which they are seen; and those frightful apparitions become nothing more than our ordinary ideas, rendered more brilliant by some accidental and temporary derangement of the vital functions. Their very vividness too, which is their only characteristic, is capable of explanation. I have already shown that the retina is rendered more sensible to light by voluntary local pressure, as well as by the involuntary pressure of the blood-vessels behind it; and if, by looking at the sun, we impress upon the retina a coloured image of that luminary, which is seen even when the eye is shut, we may by pressure alter the colour of that image, in consequence of having increased the sensibility of that part of the retina on which it is impressed. Hence we may readily understand how the vividness of the mental pictures must be increased by analogous causes.

In the case both of Nicolai and Mrs. A. the immediate cause of the spectres was a deranged action of the stomach. When such a derangement is induced by poison, or by substances which act as poisons, the retina is peculiarly affected, and the phenomena of vision singularly changed. Dr. Patouillet has described the case of a family of *nine* persons who were all driven mad by eating the root of the *Hyoscyamus niger*, or black Henbane. One of them leapt into a pond. Another exclaimed that his neighbour would lose a cow in a month, and a third vociferated that the crown piece of sixty pence would in a short time rise to five livres. On the following day they had all recovered their senses, but recollected nothing of what had happened. On the same day they all saw objects double, and, what is still more remarkable, on the third day *every object appeared to them as red as scarlet.* Now this red light was probably nothing more than the red phosphorescence produced by the pressure of the blood-vessels on the retina, and analogous to the masses of *blue, green, yellow,* and *red* light, which have been already mentioned as produced by a similar pressure in headaches, arising from a disordered state of the digestive organs.

Were we to analyse the various phenomena of **spectral**

illusions, we should discover many circumstances favourable to these views. In those seen by Nicolai the individual figures were always somewhat paler than natural objects. They sometimes grew more and more indistinct, and became perfectly white; and, to use his own words, " he could always distinguish, with the greatest precision, phantasms from phenomena." Nicolai sometimes saw the spectres when his eyes were shut, and sometimes they were thus made to disappear,—effects perfectly identical with those which arise from the impressions of very luminous objects. Sometimes the figures vanished entirely, and at other times only pieces of them disappeared, exactly conformable to what takes place with objects seen by indirect vision, which most of those figures must necessarily have been.

Among the peculiarities of spectral illusions there is one which merits particular attention, namely, that they seem to cover or conceal objects immediately beyond them. It is this circumstance more than any other which gives them the character of reality, and at first sight it seems difficult of explanation. The distinctness of any impression on the retina is entirely independent of the accommodation of the eye to the distinct vision of external objects. When the eye is at rest, and is not accommodated to objects at any particular distance, it is in a state for seeing distant objects most perfectly. When a distinct spectral impression, therefore, is before it, all other objects in its vicinity will be seen indistinctly, for while the eye is engrossed with the vision, it is not likely to accommodate itself to any other object in the same direction. It is quite common, too, for the eye to see only one of two objects actually presented to it. A sportsman who has been in the practice of shooting with both his eyes open actually sees a double image of the muzzle of his fowling-piece, though it is only with one of these images that he covers his game, having no perception whatever of the other. But there is still another principle upon which only one of two objects may be seen at a time. If we look very steadily·and continuously at a double pattern, such as those on a carpet composed of two single patterns of different colours, suppose *red* and *yellow;* and if we direct the mind particularly to the contemplation of the red one, the green pattern will sometimes vanish entirely, leaving the red one alone visible, and by the same process the *red* one may be made to disappear. In this case, however, the two patterns, like the two images, may be seen together; but if the very same. portion of the retina is excited by the direct rays of an external object, when it is excited by a mental impression, it can no more see them both at the same time than a vibrating string can give out two different fundamental sounds. It is quite possible, however, that the brightest parts of a spectral figure may be distinctly seen along with the brightest parts of an object immediately behind it, but then the bright parts of each object will fall upon different parts of the retina.

These views are illustrated by a case mentioned by Dr. Abercrombie. A gentleman, who was a patient of his, of an irritable habit, and liable to a variety of uneasy sensations in his head, was sitting alone in his dining-room in the twilight, when the door of the room was a little open. He saw distinctly a female figure enter, wrapped in a mantle, with the face concealed by a large black bonnet. She seemed to advance a few steps towards him, and then stop. He had a full conviction that the figure was an illusion of vision, and he amused himself for some time by watching it; at the same time observing that he could see through the figure so as to perceive the lock of the door, and other objects behind it.*

* Inquiries concerning the Intellectual Powers, and the Investigation of Truth.

If these views be correct the phenomena of spectral apparitions are stripped of all their terror, whether we view them in their supernatural character or as indications of bodily indisposition. Nicolai, even, in whose case they were accompanied with alarming symptoms, derived pleasure from the contemplation of them, and he not only recovered from the complaint in which they originated, but survived them for many years.—Mrs. A., too, who sees them only at distant intervals, and with whom they have but a fleeting existence, will, we trust, soon lose her exclusive privilege, when the slight indisposition which gives them birth has subsided.

LETTER IV.

*Science used as an instrument of imposture—Deceptions with plane
and concave mirrors practised by the ancients—The magician's
mirror—Effects of concave mirrors—Aërial Images—Images on
smoke—Combination of mirrors for producing pictures from
living objects—The mysterious dagger—Ancient miracles with
concave mirrors—Modern necromancy with them, as seen by
Cellini—Description and effects of the magic lantern—Improvements upon it—Phantasmagoric exhibitions of Philipstal and
others—Dr. Young's arrangement of Lenses, &c., for the Phantasmagoria—Improvements suggested—Catadioptrical phantasmagoria for producing the pictures from living objects—Method
of cutting off parts of the figures—Kircher's mysterious handwriting on the wall—His hollow cylindrical mirror for aërial
images—Cylindrical mirror for reforming distorted pictures—
Mirrors of variable curvature for producing caricatures.*

IN the preceding observations man appears as the victim
of his own delusions—as the magician unable to exorcise
the spirits which he has himself called into being. We
shall now see him the dupe of preconcerted imposture—
the slave of his own ignorance—the prostrate vassal of
power and superstition. I have already stated that the
monarchs and priests of ancient times carried on a sys-
tematic plan of imposing upon their subjects—a mode of
government which was in perfect accordance with their
religious belief: but it will scarcely be believed that the
same delusions were practised after the establishment of
Christianity, and that even the Catholic sanctuary was
often the seat of these unhallowed machinations. Nor
was it merely the low and cunning priest who thus sought
to extort money and respect from the most ignorant of his

L

flock: bishops and pontiffs themselves wielded the magician's wand over the diadems of kings and emperors, and,
by the pretended exhibition of supernatural power, made
the mightiest potentates of Europe tremble upon their
thrones. It was the light of science alone which dispelled
this moral and intellectual darkness, and it is entirely in
consequence of its wide diffusion that we live in times
when sovereigns seek to reign only through the affections
of their people, and when the minister of religion asks no
other reverence but that which is inspired by the sanctity
of his office and the purity of his character.

It was fortunate for the human race that the scanty
knowledge of former ages afforded so few elements of
deception. What a tremendous engine would have been
worked against our species by the varied and powerful
machinery of modern science! Man would still have
worn the shackles which it forged, and his noble spirit
would still have groaned beneath its fatal pressure.

There can be little doubt that the most common, as
well as the most successful, impositions of the ancients
were of an optical nature, and were practised by means of
plane and concave mirrors. It has been clearly shown by
various writers that the ancients made use of mirrors of
steel, silver, and a composition of copper and tin, like
those now used for reflecting specula. It is also very
probable from a passage in Pliny, that glass mirrors were
made at Sidon ; but it is evident that, unless the object
presented to them was illuminated in a very high degree,
the images which they formed must have been very faint
and unsatisfactory. The silver mirrors, therefore, which
were universally used, and which are superior to those
made of any other metal, are likely to have been most
generally employed by the ancient magicians. They
were made to give multiplied and inverted images of
objects, that is, they were plane, polygonal or many-

sided, and concave. There is one property, however, mentioned by Aulus Gellius, which has given unnecessary perplexity to commentators. He states that there were specula which, when put in a particular place, gave no images of objects, but, when carried to another place, recovered their property of reflection.* M. Salverte is of opinion that, in quoting Varro, Aulus Gellius was not sufficiently acquainted with the subject, and erred in supposing that the phenomenon depended on the *place* instead of the position of the mirror; but this criticism is obviously made with the view of supporting an opinion of his own, that the property in question · may be analogous to the phenomenon of polarised light, which at a certain angle refuses to suffer reflection from particular bodies. If this idea has any foundation, the mirror must have been of glass or some other body not metallic, or, to speak more correctly, there must have been *two* such mirrors, so nicely adjusted not only to one another, but to the light incident upon each, that the effect could not possibly be produced but by a philosopher thoroughly acquainted with the modern discovery of the polarisation of light by reflection. Without seeking for so profound an explanation of the phenomenon, we may readily understand how a silver mirror may instantly lose its reflecting power, in a damp atmosphere, in consequence of the precipitation of moisture upon its surface, and may immediately recover it when transported into drier air.

One of the simplest instruments of optical deception is the plane mirror, and when two are combined for this purpose it has been called the magician's mirror. An observer in front of a plane mirror sees a distinct image of himself; but if two persons take up a mirror, and if the one person is as much to one side of a line perpen-

* *Ut speculum in loco certo positum nihil imaginet ; aliorsum translatum faciat imagines.* Aul. Gel. Noct. Attic. lib. xvi. cap. 18.

dicular to the middle of it as the other is to the other side, they will see each other but not themselves. If we now suppose M C, C D, N C, C D to be the partitions of two adjacent apartments, let square openings be made in the partitions at A and B, about five feet above the floor, and let them be filled with plate glass, and surrounded with a picture frame, so as to have the appearance of two mirrors. Place two mirrors E, F, one behind each opening at A and B, inclined 45° to the partition M N, and so large that a person looking into the plates of glass at A and B will not see their edges. When this is done it is obvious

Fig. 3.

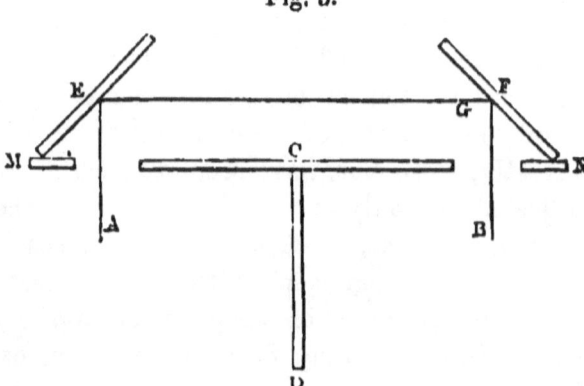

that a person looking into the mirror A will not see himself but will see any person or figure placed at B. If he believes that he is looking into a common mirror at A, his astonishment will be great at seeing himself transformed into another person, or into any living animal that may be placed at B. The success of this deception would be greatly increased if a plane mirror suspended by a pulley could be brought immediately behind the plane glass at A, and drawn up from it at pleasure. The spectator at A having previously seen himself in this moveable mirror, would be still more astonished when he afterwards perceived in the same place a face different from his own. By drawing the moveable mirror half up, the spectator at A might see half of his own face joined to half of the face placed at B ; but in the present day the most ignorant persons are so familiar with the properties of a looking-glass that it would be very difficult to employ this kind of deception with the same success which must have attended it in a more illiterate age. The optical reader will easily see that the mirror F and the apartment N C D are not absolutely necessary for carrying on this deception ; for the very same effects will be produced if the person at B is stationed at G, and looks towards the mirror F in the direction G F. As the mirror F, however, must be placed as near to A as possible, the person at G would be too near the partition C N, unless the mirror F was extremely large.

The effect of this and every similar deception is greatly increased when the persons are illuminated with a strong light, and the rest of the apartment as dark as possible ; but whatever precautions are taken, and however skilfully plane mirrors are combined, it is not easy to produce with them any very successful illusions.

The concave mirror is the staple instrument of the magician's cabinet, and must always perform a principal part in all optical combinations. In order to be quite perfect, every concave mirror should have its surface elliptical, so that if any object is placed in one focus of the ellipse, an inverted image of it will be formed in the other focus. This image, to a spectator rightly placed, appears suspended in the air, so that if the mirror and the object are hid from his view, the effect must appear to him almost supernatural.

The method of exhibiting the effect of concave mirrors most advantageously is shown in Fig. 3, where C D is the partition of a room having in it a square opening E F, the centre of which is about five feet above the floor. This opening might be surrounded with a picture-frame, and a painting which exactly filled it might be so connected with a pulley that it could be either slipped aside, or raised so as to leave the frame empty. A large concave mirror M N is then placed in another apartment, so that when any object is placed at A, a distinct image of it may be formed in the centre of the opening E F. Let us suppose this object to be a plaster cast of any object made as white as possible, and placed in an *inverted* position at A. A strong light should then be thrown upon it by a

Fig. 4.

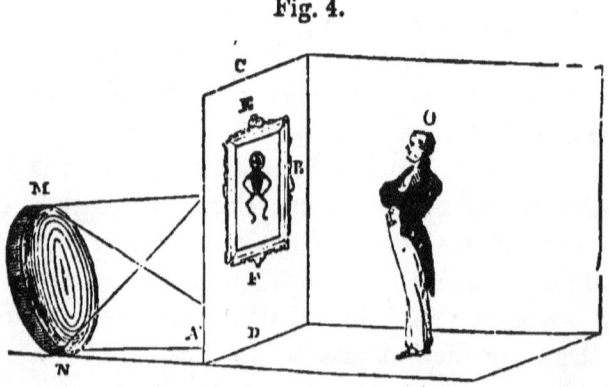

powerful lamp, the rays of which are prevented from reaching the opening E F. When this is done, a spectator placed at O will see an erect image of the statue at B the centre of the opening—standing in the air, and differing from the real statue only in being a little larger, while the apparition will be wholly invisible to other spectators placed at a little distance on each side of him.

If the opening E F is filled with smoke rising either from a chafing dish, in which incense is burnt, or made to issue in clouds from some opening below, the image will appear in the middle of the smoke depicted upon it as upon a ground, and capable of being seen by those spectators who could not see the image in the air. The rays of light, in place of proceeding without obstruction to an eye at O, are reflected as it were from those minute particles of which the smoke is composed, in the same manner as a beam of light is rendered more visible by passing through an apartment filled with dust or smoke.

It has long been a favourite experiment to place at A, a white and strongly-illuminated human skull, and to exhibit an image of it amid the smoke of a chafing dish at B; but a more terrific effect would be produced if a small skeleton, suspended by invisible wires, were placed as an object at A. Its image suspended in the air at B, or painted upon smoke, could not fail to astonish the spectator.

The difficulty of placing a living person in an inverted position, as an object at A, has no doubt prevented the optical conjurer from availing himself of so admirable a resource; but this difficulty may be removed by employing a second concave mirror. This second mirror must be so placed as to reflect towards M N, the rays proceeding from an erect living object, and to form an inverted image of this object at A. An erect image of this inverted image will then be formed at B, either suspended in the air or depicted upon a wreath of smoke. This aërial image will exhibit the precise form and colours and movements of the living object, and it will maintain its character as an apparition if any attempt is made by the spectator to grasp its unsubstantial fabric.

A deception of an alarming kind, called the *Mysterious dagger*, has been long a favourite exhibition. If a person with a drawn and highly-polished dagger, illuminated by a strong light, stands a little farther from a concave mirror than its principal focus, he will perceive in the air, between himself and the mirror, an inverted and diminished image of his own person with the dagger similarly brandished: if he aims the dagger at the centre

of the mirror's concavity, the two daggers will meet point
to point, and, by pushing it still farther from him towards
the mirror, the imaginary dagger will strike at his heart.
In this case it is necessary that the direction of the real
dagger coincides with a diameter of the sphere of which
the mirror is a part; but if its direction is on one side of
that diameter, the direction of the imaginary dagger will
be as far on the other side of the diameter, and the latter
will aim a blow at any person who is placed in the proper
position for receiving it. If the person who bears the
real dagger is therefore placed behind a screen, or otherwise concealed from the view of the spectator who is
made to approach to the place of the image, the thrust of
the polished steel at his breast will not fail to produce a
powerful impression. The effect of this experiment would
no doubt be increased by covering with black cloth the
person who holds the dagger, so that the image of his
hand only should be seen, as the inverted picture of him
would take away from the reality of the appearance. By
using two mirrors, indeed, this defect might be remedied,
and the spectator would witness an exact image of the
assassin aiming the dagger at his life.

The common way of making this experiment is to place
a basket of fruit above the dagger, so that a distinct aërial
image of the fruit is formed in the focus of the mirror.
The spectator having been desired to take some fruit from
the basket, approaches for that purpose, while a person
properly concealed withdraws the real basket of fruit
with one hand, and with the other advances the dagger,
the image of which, being no longer covered by the fruit,
strikes at the body of the astonished spectator.

The powers of the concave mirror have been likewise
displayed in exhibiting the apparition of an absent or
deceased friend. For this purpose a strongly-illuminated
bust or picture of the person is placed before the concave

mirror, and a distinct image of the picture will be seen either in the air or among smoke in the manner already described. If the background of the picture is temporarily covered with lamp-black, so that there is no light about the picture but what falls upon the figure, the effect will be more complete.

As in all experiments with concave mirrors the size of the aërial image is to that of the real object as their distances from the mirror, we may, by varying the distance of the object, increase or diminish the size of the image. In doing this, however, the distance of the image from the mirror is at the same time changed, so that it would quit the place most suitable for its exhibition. This defect may be removed by simultaneously changing the place both of the mirror and the object, so that the image may remain stationary, expanding itself from a luminous spot to a gigantic size, and again passing through all intermediate magnitudes, till it vanishes in a cloud of light.

Those who have studied the effects of concave mirrors of a small size, and without the precautions necessary to insure deception, cannot form any idea of the magical effect produced by this class of optical apparitions. When the instruments of illusion are themselves concealed—when all extraneous lights but those which illuminate the real object are excluded—when the mirrors are large and well polished and truly formed—the effect of the representation on ignorant minds is altogether overpowering, while even those who know the deception, and perfectly understand its principles, are not a little surprised at its effects. The inferiority in the effects of a common concave mirror to that of a well-arranged exhibition, is greater even than that of a perspective picture hanging in an apartment to the same picture exhibited under all the imposing accompaniments of a dioramic representation.

It can scarcely be doubted, that a concave mirror was the principal instrument by which the heathen gods were made to appear in the ancient temples. In the imperfect accounts which have reached us of these apparitions, we can trace all the elements of an optical illusion. In the ancient temple of Hercules at Tyre, Pliny mentions that there was a seat made of a consecrated stone, "from which the gods easily rose." Esculapius often exhibited himself to his worshippers in his temple at Tarsus; and the temple of Enguinum in Sicily was celebrated as the place where the goddesses exhibited themselves to mortals. Jamblichus actually informs us that the ancient magicians caused the gods to appear among the vapours disengaged from fire; and when the conjurer Maximus terrified his audience by making the statue of Hecate laugh, while in the middle of the smoke of burning incense, he was obviously dealing with the image of a living object dressed in the costume of the sorceress.

The character of these exhibitions in the ancient temples is so admirably depicted in the following passage of Damascius quoted by M. Salverte, that we recognize all the optical effects which have been already described. "In a manifestation," says he, "which ought not to be revealed . . . . there appeared on the wall of the temple a mass of light which at first seemed to be very remote; it transformed itself in coming nearer, into a face evidently divine and supernatural, of a severe aspect, but mixed with gentleness, and extremely beautiful. According to the institutions of a mysterious religion the Alexandrians honoured it as Osiris and Adonis."

Among more modern examples of this illusion, we may mention the case of the Emperor Basil of Macedonia. Inconsolable at the loss of his son, this sovereign had recourse to the prayers of the Pontiff Theodore Santabaren, who was celebrated for his power of working miracles. The ecclesiastical conjurer exhibited to him the image of his beloved son magnificently dressed and mounted upon a superb charger: the youth rushed towards his father, threw himself into his arms, and disappeared. M. Salverte judiciously observes, that this deception could not have been performed by a real person who imitated the figure of the young prince. The existence of this person, betrayed by so remarkable a resemblance, and by the trick of the exhibition, could not fail to have been discovered and denounced, even if we could explain how the son could be so instantaneously disentangled from his father's embrace. The emperor, in short, saw the aërial image of a picture of his son on horseback, and as the picture was brought nearer the mirror, the image advanced into his arms, when it of course eluded his affectionate grasp.

These and other allusions to the operations of the ancient magic, though sufficiently indicative of the methods which were employed, are too meagre to convey any idea of the splendid and imposing exhibitions which must have been displayed. A national system of deception, intended as an instrument of government, must have brought into requisition not merely the scientific skill of the age, but a variety of subsidiary contrivances, calculated to astonish the beholder, to confound his judgment, to dazzle his senses, and to give a predominant influence to the peculiar imposture which it was thought desirable to establish. The grandeur of the means may be inferred from their efficacy, and from the extent of their influence.

This defect, however, is to a certain degree supplied by an account of a modern necromancy, which has been left us by the celebrated Benvenuto Cellini, and in which he himself performed an active part.

"It happened," says he, "through a variety of odd

accidents, that I made acquaintance with a Sicilian priest, who was a man of genius, and well versed in the Latin and Greek authors. Happening one day to have some conversation with him when the subject turned upon the art of necromancy, I, who had a great desire to know something of the matter, told him that I had all my life felt a curiosity to be acquainted with the mysteries of this art.

" The priest made answer, ' That the man must be of a resolute and steady temper who enters upon that study.' I replied, ' That I had fortitude and resolution enough, if I could but find an opportunity.' The priest subjoined, ' If you think you have the heart to venture, I will give you all the satisfaction you can desire.' Thus we agreed to enter upon a plan of necromancy. The priest one evening prepared to satisfy me, and desired me to look out for a companion or two. I invited one Vincenzio Romoli, who was my intimate acquaintance: he brought with him a native of Pistoia, who cultivated the black art himself. We repaired to the Colosseo, and the priest, according to the custom of necromancers, began to draw circles upon the ground, with the most impressive cere- monies imaginable: he likewise brought hither assa- fœtida, several precious perfumes, and fire, with some compositions also, which diffused noisome odours. As soon as he was in readiness, he made an opening to the circle, and having taken us by the hand, ordered the other necromancer, his partner, to throw the perfumes into the fire at a proper time, intrusting the care of the fire and perfumes to the rest; and thus he began his incantations. This ceremony lasted above an hour and a half, when there appeared several legions of devils, insomuch that the amphitheatre was quite filled with them. I was busy about the perfumes, when the priest, perceiv- ing there was a considerable number of infernal spirits, turned to me and said, 'Benvenuto, ask them something?' I answered, 'Let them bring me into the company of my Sicilian mistress Angelica.' That night he obtained no answer of any sort; but I had received great satisfaction in having my curiosity so far indulged. The necromancer told me it was requisite we should go a second time, assuring me that I should be satisfied in whatever I asked; but that I must bring with me a pure immaculate boy.

"I took with me a youth who was in my service, of about twelve years of age, together with the same Vincenzio Romoli, who had been my companion the first time, and one Agnolino Gaddi, an intimate acquaintance, whom I likewise prevailed on to assist at the ceremony. When we came to the place appointed, the priest having made his preparations as before, with the same and even more striking ceremonies, placed us within the circle, which he had likewise drawn with a more wonderful art, and in a more solemn manner, than at our former meeting. Thus, having committed the care of the perfumes and the fire to my friend Vincenzio, who was assisted by Agnolino Gaddi, he put into my hand a pintaculo or magical chart, and bid me turn it towards the places that he should direct me; and under the pintaculo I held the boy. The necromancer, having begun to make his tremendous invocations, called by their names a multitude of demons who were the leaders of the several legions, and questioned them, by the power of the eternal uncreated God, who lives for ever, in the Hebrew language, as likewise in Latin and Greek; insomuch that the amphitheatre was almost in an instant filled with demons more numerous than at the former conjuration. Vincenzio Romoli was busied in making a fire, with the assistance of Agnolino, and burning a great quantity of precious perfumes. I, by the directions of the necromancer, again desired to be in the company of my Angelica. The former thereupon turning to me, said, 'Know, they have declared that in the space of a month you shall be in her company.'

"He thus requested me to stand resolutely by him, because the legions were now above a thousand more in number than he had designed; and besides, these were the most dangerous; so that, after they had answered my question, it behoved him to be civil to them and dismiss them quietly. At the same time the boy under the pintaculo was in a terrible fright, saying that there were in that place a million of fierce men, who threatened to destroy us; and that, moreover, four armed giants of enormous stature were endeavouring to break into our circle. During this time, whilst the necromancer, trembling with fear, endeavoured by mild and gentle methods to dismiss them in the best way he could, Vincenzio Romoli, who quivered like an aspen leaf, took care of the perfumes. Though I was as much terrified as any of them, I did my utmost to conceal the terror I felt; so that I greatly contributed to inspire the rest with resolution; but the truth is, I gave myself over for a dead man, seeing the horrid fright the necromancer was in. The boy placed his head between his knees and said, 'In this posture will I die; for we shall all surely perish.' I told him that all these demons were under us, and what he saw was smoke and shadow; so bid him hold up his head and take courage. No sooner did he look up than he cried out, 'The whole amphitheatre is burning, and the fire is just falling upon us.' So covering his eyes with his hands, he again exclaimed, 'That destruction was inevitable, and desired to see no more.' The necromancer entreated me to have a good heart, and take care to burn proper perfumes; upon which I turned to Romoli, and bid him burn all the most precious perfumes he had. At the same time I cast my eye upon Agnolino Gaddi, who was terrified to such a degree that he could scarce distinguish objects, and seemed to be half-dead. Seeing him in this condition, I said, 'Agnolino, upon these occasions a man should not yield to fear, but should stir about and give his assistance, so come directly and put on some more of these.' The effects of poor Agnolino's fear were overpowering. The boy hearing a crepitation ventured once more to raise his head, when, seeing me laugh, he began to take courage, and said 'That the devils were flying away with a vengeance.'

"In this condition we stayed till the bell rung for morning prayers. The boy again told us, that there remained but few devils, and these were at a great distance. When the magician had performed the rest of his ceremonies, he stripped off his gown, and took up a wallet full of books which he had brought with him.

"We all went out of the circle together, keeping as close to each other as we possibly could, especially the boy, who had placed himself in the middle, holding the necromancer by the coat, and me by the cloak. As we were going to our houses in the quarter of Banchi, the boy told us that two of the demons whom we had seen at the amphitheatre went on before us leaping and skipping, sometimes running upon the roofs of the houses, and sometimes upon the ground. The priest declared, that though he had often entered magic circles, nothing so extraordinary had ever happened to him. As we went along, he would fain persuade me to assist with him at consecrating a brook from which, he said, we should derive immense riches : we should then ask the demons to discover to us the various treasures with which the earth abounds, which would raise us to opulence and power ; but that these love-affairs were mere follies, from whence no good could be expected. I answered, 'That I would readily have accepted his proposal, if I under-

stood Latin.' He redoubled his persuasions, assuring me
that the knowledge of the Latin language was by no
means material. He added, that he could have Latin
scholars enough, if he had thought it worth while to look
out for them, but that he could never have met with a
partner of resolution and intrepidity equal to mine, and
that I should by all means follow his advice. Whilst we
were engaged in this conversation, we arrived at our respective houses, and all that night dreamt of nothing but
devils."

It is impossible to peruse the preceding description
without being satisfied that the legions of devils were not
produced by any influence upon the imaginations of the
spectators, but were actual optical phantasms, or the
images of pictures or objects produced by one or more
concave mirrors or lenses. A fire is lighted, and perfumes
and incense are burnt, in order to create a ground for the
images, and the beholders are rigidly confined within the
pale of the magic circle. The concave mirror and the
objects presented to it having been so placed that the
persons within the circle could not see the aërial image
of the objects by the rays directly reflected from the
mirror, the work of deception was ready to begin. The
attendance of the magician upon his mirror was by no
means necessary. He took his place along with the spectators within the magic circle. The images of the devils
were all distinctly formed in the air immediately above
the fire, but none of them could be seen by those within
the circle. The moment, however, that perfumes were
thrown into the fire to produce smoke, the first wreath of
smoke that rose through the place of one or more of the
images would reflect them to the eyes of the spectator,
and they could again disappear if the wreath was not
followed by another. More and more images would be
rendered visible as new wreaths of smoke arose, and the

whole group would appear at once when the smoke was uniformly diffused over the place occupied by the images.

The "compositions which diffused noisome odours" were intended to intoxicate or stupify the spectators, so as to increase their liability to deception, or to add to the real phantasms which were before their eyes others which were the offspring only of their own imaginations. It is not easy to gather from the description what parts of the exhibition were actually presented to the eyes of the spectators, and what parts of it were imagined by themselves. It is quite evident that the boy, as well as Agnolino Gaddi, were so overpowered with terror that they fancied many things which they did not see; but when the boy declares that four armed giants of an enormous stature were threatening to break into their circle, he gives an accurate description of the effect that would be produced by pushing the figures nearer the mirror, and then magnifying their images, and causing them to advance towards the circle. Although Cellini declares that he was trembling with fear, yet it is quite evident that he was not entirely ignorant of the machinery which was at work, for in order to encourage the boy, who was almost dead with fear, he assured them that the devils were under their power, and that "what he saw was smoke and shadow."

Mr. Roscoe, from whose Life of Cellini the preceding description is taken, draws a similar conclusion from the consolatory words addressed to the boy, and states that they "confirm him in the belief, that the whole of these appearances, like a phantasmagoria, were merely the effects of a magic lantern produced on volumes of smoke from various kinds of burning wood." In drawing this conclusion, Mr. Roscoe has not adverted to the fact, that this exhibition took place about the middle of the sixteenth century, while the magic lantern was not invented by

M

Kircher till towards the middle of the seventeenth century, Cellini having died in 1570, and Kircher having been born in 1601. There is no doubt that the effects described could be produced by this instrument, but we are not entitled to have recourse to any other means of explanation but those which were known to exist at the time of Cellini. If we suppose, however, that the necromancer either had a regular magic lantern, or that he had fitted up his concave mirror in a box containing the figures of his devils, and that this box with its lights was carried home with the party, we can easily account for the declaration of the boy, " that, as they were going home to their houses in the quarter of Banchi, *two of the demons whom we had seen at the amphitheatre, went on before us leaping and skipping, sometimes running upon the roofs of the houses, and sometimes upon the ground.*"

The introduction of the magic lantern as an optical instrument, supplied the magicians of the seventeenth century with one of their most valuable tools. The use of the concave mirror, which does not appear to have been even put up into the form of an instrument, required a separate apartment, or at least that degree of concealment which it was difficult on ordinary occasions to command; but the magic lantern, containing in a small compass its lamp, its lenses, and its sliding figures, was peculiarly fitted for the itinerant conjurer, who had neither the means of providing a less portable and more expensive apparatus, nor the power of transporting and erecting it.

The magic lantern shown in the annexed figure consists of a dark lantern A B, containing a lamp G, and a concave metallic mirror M N; and it is so constructed that when the lamp is lighted, not a ray of light is able to escape from it. Into the side of the lantern is fitted a double tube C D, the outer half of which D, is capable of moving within the other half. A large plano-convex lens C, is fixed at the inner end of the double tube, and a small convex lens D, at the outer end; and to the fixed tube C E, there is joined a groove E F, in which the sliders containing the painted objects are placed, and through which they can be moved. Each slider contains a series of figures or pictures painted on glass with highly-

Fig. 5.

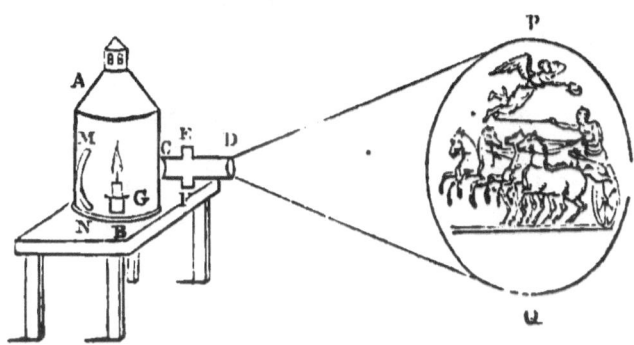

transparent colours. The direct light of the lamp G, and the light reflected from the mirror M N, falling upon the illuminating lens C, is concentrated by it so as to throw a brilliant light upon the painting on the slider, and as this painting is in the conjugate focus of the convex lens D, a magnified image of it will be formed on a white wall or white cloth placed at P Q. If the lens D is brought nearer to E F, or to the picture, the distinct image will be more magnified, and will be formed at a greater distance from D, so that if there is any particular distance of the image which is more convenient than another, or any particular size of the object which we wish, it can be obtained by varying the distance of the lens D from E F.

When the image is received on an opaque ground, as is commonly the case, the spectators are placed in the same room with the lantern; but for the purposes of deception, it would be necessary to place the lantern in another apartment like the mirror in Fig. 4, and to throw the magnified pictures on a large plate of ground glass, or a transparent gauze screen, stretched across an opening E F, Fig. 4, made in the partition which separates the spectators from the exhibitor. The images might, like those of the concave mirror, be received upon wreaths of smoke. These images are of course always inverted in reference to the position of the painted objects; but in order to render them really erect, we have only to invert the sliders. The representations of the magic lantern never fail to excite a high degree of interest, even when exhibited with the ordinary apparatus; but by using double sliders, and varying their movements, very striking effects may be produced. A smith, for example, is made to hammer upon his anvil,—a figure is thrown into the attitude of terror by the introduction of a spectral appa- rition,—and a tempest at sea is imitated, by having the sea on one slider, and the ships on other sliders, to which an undulatory motion is communicated.

The magic lantern is susceptible of great improvement in the painting of the figures, and in the mechanism and combination of the sliders. A painted figure which ap- pears well executed to the unassisted eye, becomes a mere daub when magnified 50 or 100 times; and when we consider what kind of artists are employed in their execu- tion, we need not wonder that this optical instrument has degenerated into a mere toy for the amusement of the young. Unless for public exhibition, the expense of exceedingly minute and spirited drawings could not be afforded; but I have no doubt that if such drawings were executed, a great part of the expense might be saved by engraving them on wood, and transferring their outline to the glass sliders.

A series of curious representations might be effected,

by inserting glass plates containing suitable figures in a trough having two of its sides parallel, and made of plate glass. The trough must be introduced at E F, so that the figure on the glass is at the proper distance from the object lens D. When the trough is filled with water or with any transparent fluid, the picture at P Q will be seen with the same distinctness as if the figure had been introduced by itself into the groove E F; but if any transparent fluid of a different density from water is mixed with it, so as to combine with it quickly or slowly, the appearance of the figure displayed at P Q will undergo singular changes. If spirits of wine, or any ardent spirit, are mixed with the water, so as to produce throughout its mass partial variations of density, the figure at P Q will be as it were broken down into a thousand parts, and will recover its continuity and distinctness when the two fluids have combined. If a fluid of less density than water is laid gently upon the water, so as to mix with it gradually, and produce a regular diminution of density downwards; or if saline substances soluble in water are laid at the bottom of the trough, the density will diminish upwards, and the figure will undergo the most curious elongations and contractions. Analogous effects may be produced by the application of heat to the surface or sides of the trough, so that we may effect at the same time both an increase and a diminution in the density of the water, in consequence of which the magnified images will undergo the most remarkable transformations. It is not necessary to place the glass plate which contains the figure within the trough. It may be placed in front of it, and by thus creating as it were an atmosphere with local variations of density we may exhibit the phenomena of the mirage and of looming, in which the inverted images of ships and other objects are seen in the air, as described in another letter.

The power of the magic lantern has been greatly extended by placing it on one side of the transparent screen of taffetas which receives the images while the spectators are placed on the other side, and by making every part of the glass sliders opaque, excepting the part which forms the figures. Hence all the figures appear luminous on a black ground, and produce a much greater effect with the same degree of illumination. An exhibition depending on these principles was brought out by M. Philipstal in 1802 under the name of the *Phantasmagoria*, and when it was shown in London and Edinburgh it produced the most impressive effects upon the spectators. The small theatre of exhibition was lighted only by one hanging lamp, the flame of which was drawn up into an opaque chimney or shade when the performance began. In this "darkness visible" the curtain rose, and displayed a cave with skeletons and other terrific figures in relief upon its walls. The flickering light was then drawn up beneath its shroud, and the spectators, in total darkness, found themselves in the middle of thunder and lightning. A thin transparent screen had, unknown to the spectators, been let down after the disappearance of the light, and upon it the flashes of lightning and all the subsequent appearances were represented. This screen being half-way between the spectators and the cave which was first shown, and being itself invisible, prevented the observers from having any idea of the real distance of the figures, and gave them the entire character of aërial pictures. The thunder and lightning were followed by the figures of ghosts, skeletons, and known individuals, whose eyes and mouth were made to move by the shifting of combined sliders. After the first figure had been exhibited for a short time, it began to grow less and less, as if removed to a great distance, and at last vanished in a small cloud of light. Out of this same cloud the germ of another figure began to appear, and gradually grow larger and larger, and approached the spectators till it attained its perfect development. In this manner, the head of Dr. Franklin was transformed into a skull; figures which retired with the freshness of life came back in the form of skeletons, and the retiring skeletons returned in the drapery of flesh and blood.

The exhibition of these transmutations was followed by spectres, skeletons, and terrific figures, which, instead of receding and vanishing as before, suddenly advanced upon the spectators, becoming larger as they approached them, and finally vanished by appearing to sink into the ground. The effect of this part of the exhibition was naturally the most impressive. The spectators were not only surprised but agitated, and many of them were of opinion that they could have touched the figures. M. Robertson, at Paris, introduced along with his pictures the direct shadows of living objects, which imitated coarsely the appearance of those objects in a dark night or in moonlight.

All these phenomena were produced by varying the distance of the magic lantern A B, Fig. 5, from the screen P Q, which remained fixed, and at the same time keeping the image upon the screen distinct, by increasing the distance of the lens D from the sliders in E F. When the lantern approached to P Q, the circle of light P Q, or the section of the cone of rays P D Q, gradually diminished, and resembled a small bright cloud, when D was close to the screen. At this time a new figure was put in, so that when the lantern receded from the screen, the old figure seemed to have been transformed into the new one. Although the figure was always at the same distance from the spectators, yet, owing to its gradual diminution in size, it necessarily appeared to be retiring to a distance. When the magic lantern was withdrawn from P Q, and the lens D at the same time brought nearer to E F, the image in P Q gradually increased in size, and therefore seemed in the same proportion to be approaching the spectators.

Superior as this exhibition was to any representation that had been previously made by the magic lantern, it still laboured under several imperfections. The figures were poorly drawn, and in other respects not well executed, and no attempt whatever was made to remove the optical incongruity of the figures becoming more luminous when they retired from the observer, and more obscure when they approached to him. The variation of the distance of the lens D from the sliders in E F was not exactly adapted to the motion of the lantern to and from the screen, so that the outline of the figures was not equally distinct during their variations of magnitude.

Dr. Thomas Young suggested the arrangement shown in Fig. 6 for exhibiting the phantasmagoria. The magic

Fig. 6.

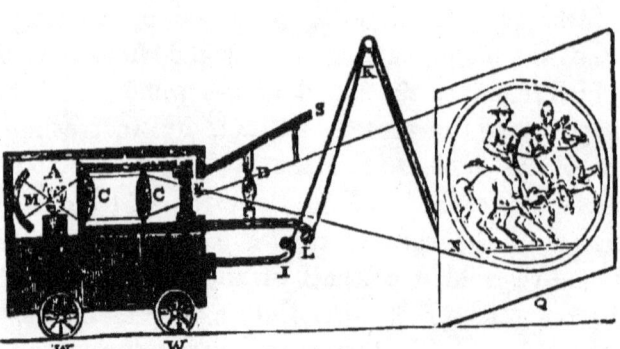

lantern is mounted on a small car II, which runs on wheels W W. The direct light of the lamp G, and that reflected from the mirror M, is condensed by the illuminating lenses C C, upon the transparent figures in the opaque sliders at E, and the image of these figures is formed at

P Q, by the object lens D. When the car H is drawn back on its wheels, the rod I K brings down the point K, and, by means of the rod K L, pushes the lens D nearer to the sliders in E F, and when the car advances to P Q, the point K is raised, and the rod K L draws out the lens D from the slider, so that the image is always in the conjugate focus of D, and therefore distinctly painted on the screen. The rod K N must be equal in length to I K, and the point I must be twice the focal length of the lens D before the object, L being immediately under the focus of the lens. In order to diminish the brightness of the image when it grows small and appears remote, Dr. Young contrived that the support of the lens D should suffer a screen S to fall and intercept a part of the light. This method, however, has many disadvantages; and we are satisfied that the only way of producing a variation in the light corresponding to the variation in the size of the image, is to use a single illuminating lens C, and to cause it to approach E F, and throw less light upon the figures when D is removed from E F, and to make C recede from E F when D approaches to it. The lens C should therefore be placed in a mean position corresponding to a mean distance of the screen and to the ordinary size of the figures, and should have the power of being removed from the slider E F, when a greater intensity of light is required for the images when they are rendered gigantic, and of being brought close to E F when the images are made small. The size of the lens C ought of course to be such that the section of its cone of rays at E F is equal to the size of the figure on the slider when C is at its greatest distance from the slider.

The method recommended by Dr. Young for pulling out and pushing in the object lens D, according as the lantern approaches to or recedes from the screen, is very ingenious and effective. It is, however, clumsy in itself, and the connexion of the levers with the screen, and their interposition between it and the lantern, must interfere with the operations of the exhibitor. It is, besides, suited only to short distances between the screen and the lantern; for when that distance is considerable, as it must sometimes require to be, the levers K L, K I, K T would bend by the least strain, and become unfitted for their purpose. For these reasons, the mechanism which adjusts the lens D should be moved by the axle of the front wheels, the tube which contains the lens should be kept at its greatest distance from E F by a slender spring, and should be pressed to its proper distance by the action of a spiral cam suited to the optical relation between the two conjugate focal distances of the lens.

Superior as the representations of the phantasmagoria are to those of the magic lantern, they are still liable to the defect which we have mentioned, namely, the necessary imperfection of the minute transparent figures when magnified. This defect cannot be remedied by employing the most skilful artists. Even Michael Angelo would have failed in executing a figure an inch long with transparent varnishes, when all its imperfections were to be magnified. In order, therefore, to perfect the art of representing phantasms, the objects must be living ones, and in place of chalky ill-drawn figures mimicking humanity by the most absurd gesticulations, we shall have phantasms of the most perfect delineation, clothed in real drapery, and displaying all the movements of life. The apparatus by which such objects may be used may be called the *catadioptrical phantasmagoria,* as it operates both by reflection and refraction.

The combination of mirrors and lenses which seems best adapted for this purpose is shown in Fig. 7, where A B is a living figure placed before a large concave mirror M N, by means of which a diminished and inverted image of it is formed at *a b*. If P Q is the transparent screen upon which the image is to be shown to the spectators on the right hand of it, a large lens L L must be so placed before the image *a b* as to form a distinct and erect picture of it at A' B' upon the screen. When the image A' B' is required to be the exact size of A B, the lens L L must magnify the small image *a b* as much as the mirror M N diminishes the figure A B. The living object A B, the mirror M N, and the lens L L, must all be placed in a moveable car for the purpose of producing the variations in the size of the phantasms, and the transformations of one figure into another. The contrivance for adjusting the lens L L to give a distinct picture at different

Fig. 7.

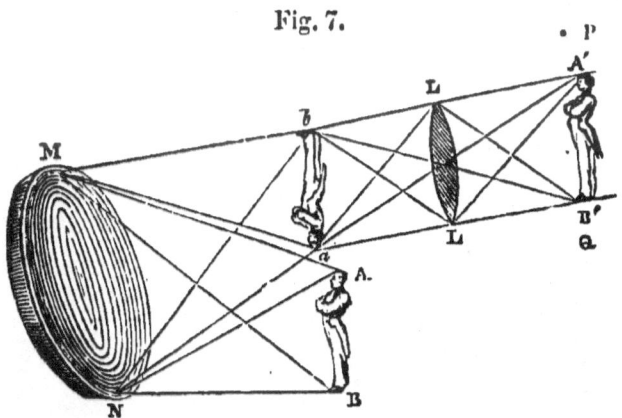

distances of the screen will of course be required in the present apparatus. In order to give full effect to the phantasms, the living objects at A B will require to be illuminated in the strongest manner, and should always be dressed either in white or in very luminous colours, and in order to give them relief a black cloth should be stretched at some distance behind them. Many interesting effects might also be produced by introducing at A B fine paintings and busts.

It would lead us into too wide a field were we to detail
the immense variety of resources which the science of optics
furnishes for such exhibitions.   One of these, however, is
too useful to be passed without notice.   If we interpose a
prism with a small refracting angle between the image *a b*,
Fig. 7, and the lens L L, the part of the figure immediately
opposite to the prism will be as it were detached from the
figure, and will be exhibited separately on the screen P Q.
Let us suppose that this part is the head of the figure.
It may be detached vertically, or lifted from the body as
if it were cut off, or it may be detached downwards and
placed on the breast as if the figure were deformed.   In
detaching the head vertically or laterally, an opaque screen
must be applied to prevent any part of the head from
being seen by rays which do not pass through the prism ;
but this and other practical details will soon occur to those
who put the method to an experimental trial.   The application of the prism is shown in Fig. 8, where *a b* is the

Fig. 8.

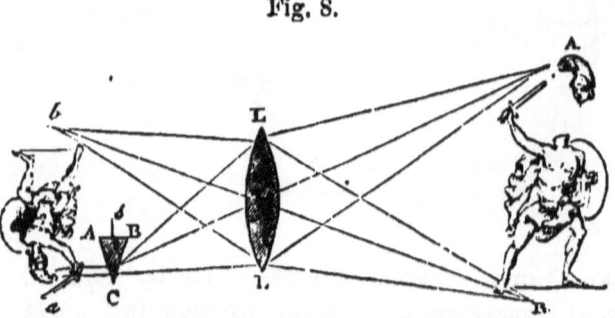

inverted image formed by a concave mirror, A B C a
prism with a small refracting angle B C A, placed between
a b and the lens L L, *s a* small opaque screen, and A B
the figure with its head detached.   A hand may be made
to grasp the hair of the head, and the aspect of death may
be given to it, as if it had been newly cut off.   Such a
representation could be easily made, and the effect upon

the spectators would be quite overpowering. The lifeless head might then be made to recover its vitality, and be safely replaced upon the figure. If the head A of the living object A B, Fig. 7, is covered with black cloth, the head of a person or of an animal placed above A might be set upon the shoulders of the figure A B by the refraction of a prism.

When the figure *a b*, Fig. 8, is of very small dimensions, as in the magic lantern, a small prism of glass would answer the purpose required of it; but in public exhibitions, where the image *a b* must be of a considerable size, if formed by a concave mirror, a very large prism would be necessary. This, however, though impracticable with solid glass, may be easily obtained by means of two large pieces of plate glass made into a prismatic vessel and filled with water. Two of the glasses of a carriage window would make a prism capable of doubling the whole of the bust of a living person placed as an object at A B, Fig. 7, so that two perfectly similar phantasms might be exhibited. In those cases where the images before the lens L L are small, they may be doubled and even tripled by interposing a well-prepared plate of calcareous spar, that is, crossed by a thin film. These images would possess the singular character of being oppositely coloured, and of changing their distances and their colours by slight variations in the positions of the plate,*

In order to render the images which are formed by the glass and water prisms as perfect as possible, it would be easy to make them achromatic, and the figures might be multiplied to any extent by using several prisms, having their refracting edges parallel, for the purpose of giving a similarity of position to all the images.

Among the instruments of natural magic which were in use at the revival of science, there was one invented by

* See *Edin. Encyclopædia*, Art. OPTICS, vol. xv. p. 611.

Kircher for exhibiting the mysterious handwriting on the wall of an apartment from which the magician and his apparatus were excluded. The annexed figure represents this apparatus, as given by Schottus. The apartment in which the spectators are placed is between L L and G H, and there is an open window in the side next L L, G H being the inside of the wall opposite to the window. Upon the face of the plane speculum E F are written the words to be introduced, and when a lens L L is placed at such a distance from the speculum, and of such a focal length that the letters and the place of their representation are in its conjugate foci, a distinct image of the

Fig. 9.

writing will be exhibited on the wall at G H. The letters on the speculum are of course inverted, as seen at E F, and when they are illuminated by the sun's rays S, as shown in the figure, a distinct image, as Schottus assures us, may be formed at the distance of 500 feet. In this experiment the speculum is by no means necessary. If the letters are cut out of an opaque card, and illuminated by the light of the sky in the day, or by a lamp during night, their delineation on the wall would be equally distinct. In the daytime it would be necessary to place the letters at one end of a tube or oblong box, and the lens at the other end. As this deception is performed when the spectators are unprepared for any such exhibition, the warning written in luminous letters on the wall, or any word associated with the fate of the individual observer, could not fail to produce a singular effect upon his mind. The words might be magnified, diminished, multiplied, coloured, and obliterated, in a cloud of light, from which they might again reappear by the methods already described, as applicable to the magic lantern.

The art of forming aërial representations was a great desideratum among the opticians of the seventeenth century. Vitellio and others had made many unsuccessful attempts to produce such images, and the speculations of Lord Bacon on the subject are too curious to be withheld from the reader.

"It would be well bolted out," says he, " whether great refractions may not be made upon reflections, as well as upon direct beams. For example, take an empty basin, put an angel or what you will into it ; then go so far from the basin till you cannot see the angel, because it is not in a right line ; then fill the basin with water, and you shall see it out of its place, because of the refraction. To proceed, therefore, put a looking-glass into a basin of water. I suppose you shall not see the image in a right line or at equal angles, but wide. I know not whether this experiment may not be extended, so as you might see the image and not the glass, which, for beauty and strangeness, were a fine proof, for then you should see the image like a spirit in the air. As, for example, if there be a cistern or pool of water, you shall place over against it the picture of the devil, or what you will, so as that you do not see the water. Then put a looking-glass in the water ; now if you can see the devil's picture aside, not seeing the water, it would look like the devil indeed. They have an old tale in Oxford, that Friar Bacon walked between two steeples, which was thought to be done by glasses, when he walked upon the ground."

Kircher also devoted himself to the production of such images, and he has given in the annexed figure his method of producing them. At the bottom of a polished cylindrical vessel A B he placed a figure C D, which we presume must have been highly illuminated from below, and to the spectators who looked into the vessel in an oblique direction there was exhibited an image placed vertically in the air as if it were ascending at the mouth of the vessel. Kircher assures us that he once exhibited in this manner a representation of the Ascension of our Saviour, and that

Fig. 10.

the images were so perfect that the spectators could not be persuaded, till they had attempted to handle them, that they were not real substances. Although Kircher does not mention it, yet it is manifest that the original figure A B must have been a deformed or anamorphous drawing, in order to give a reflected image of just proportions. We doubt, indeed, if the representation or the figure was ever exhibited. It is entirely incompatible with the laws of reflection.

Among the ingenious and beautiful deceptions of the seventeenth century, we must enumerate that of the reformation of distorted pictures by reflection from cylindrical and conical mirrors. In these representations the original image from which a perfect picture is produced is often so completely distorted, that the eye cannot trace in it the resemblance to any regular figure, and the greatest degree of wonder is of course excited, whether the original

Fig. 11.

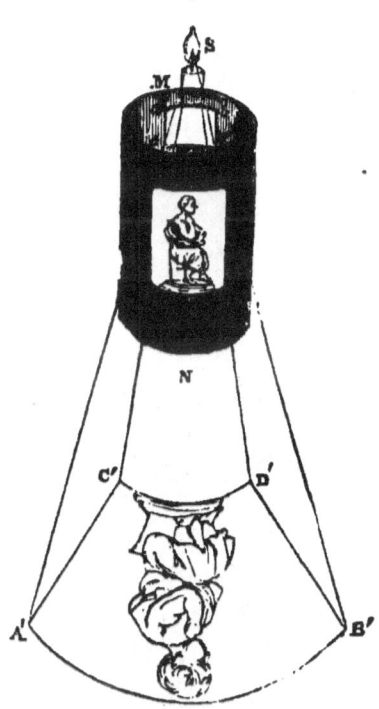

image is concealed or exposed to view. These distorted pictures may be drawn by strict geometrical rules; but I have shown in Fig. 11 a simple and practical method of executing them. Let M N be an accurate cylinder made of tin-plate or of thick pasteboard. Out of the farther side of it cut a small aperture $a\,b\,c\,d$; and out of the nearer side cut a larger one A B C D, the size of the picture to be distorted. Having perforated the outline of

N

the picture with small holes, place it on the opening A B C D so that its surface may be cylindrical. Let a candle or a bright luminous object, the smaller the better, be placed at S, as far behind the picture A B C D as the eye is afterwards to be placed before it, and the light passing through the small holes will represent on a horizontal plane a distorted image of the picture A' B' C' D', which when sketched in outline with a pencil, and shaded or coloured, will be ready for use. If we now substitute a polished cylindrical mirror of the same size in place of

Fig. 12.

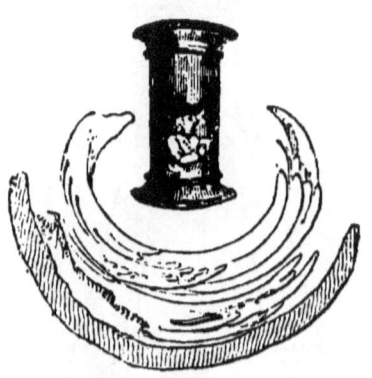

M N, then the distorted picture when laid horizontally at A' B' C' D' will be restored to its original state when seen by reflection at A B C D in the polished mirror. It would be an improvement on this method to place at A B C D a thin and flexible plate of transparent mica, having drawn upon it with a sharp point or painted upon it the figure required. The projected image of this figure at A' B' C' D' may then be accurately copied.

The effect of a cylindrical mirror is shown in Fig. 12, which is copied from an old one which we have seen in use.

The method above described is equally applicable to concave cylindrical mirrors, and to those of a conical form, and it may also be applied to mirrors of variable curvature, which produce different kinds of distortions from different parts of their surfaces.

By employing a mirror whose surface has a variable curvature like A B C, Fig. 13, we obtain an instrument for producing an endless variety of caricatures, all of which are characterized by their resemblance to the original. If a figure M N is placed before such a mirror,

Fig. 13.

it will of course appear distorted and caricatured ; but even if the figure takes different distances and positions, the variations which the image undergoes are neither sufficiently numerous or remarkable to afford much amusement. But if the figure M N is very near the mirror, so that new distortions are produced by the different distances of its different parts from the mirror, the most singular caricatures may be exhibited. If the figure, for example, bends forward his head and the upper part of his body, they will swell in size, leaving his lower extremities short and slender. If it draws back the upper part of the body, and advances the limbs, the opposite effect will take place. In like manner different sides of the head, the right or the left side of it, the brow or the chin, may be swelled and contracted at pleasure. By stretching out the arms before the body they become like those of an orang-outang, and by drawing them back they dwindle into half their regular size. All these effects, which depend greatly on the agility and skill of the performer, may be very much increased by suitable distortions in his own features and figure. The family likeness, which is of course never lost in all the variety of figures which are thus produced, adds greatly to the interest of the exhibition; and we have seen individuals so annoyed at recognizing their own likeness in the hideous forms of humanity which were thus delineated, that they could not be brought to contemplate them a second time. If the figure is inanimate, like the small cast of a statue, the effect is very curious, as the swelling and contracting of the parts and the sudden change of expression give a sort of appearance of vitality to the image. The inflexibility of such a figure, however, is unfavourable to its transformation into caricatures.

Interesting as these metamorphoses are, they lose in the simplicity of the experiment much of the wonder which they could not fail to excite if exhibited on a great scale, where the performer is invisible, and where it is practicable to give an aërial representation of the caricatured figures. This may be done by means of the apparatus shown in Fig. 7,* where we may suppose A B to be the reduced image seen in the reflecting surface A B C, Fig. 13.† By bringing this image nearer the mirror M N, Fig. 7, a magnified and inverted image of it may be formed at $a\ b$, of such a magnitude as to give the last image in P Q the same size as life. Owing to the loss of light by the two reflections, a very powerful illumination would be requisite for the original figure. If such an exhibition were well got up the effect of it would be very striking.

* Page 163.   † Page 171.

LETTER V.

Miscellaneous optical illusions—Conversions of cameos into intaglios or elevations into depressions, and the reverse—Explanation of this class of deceptions—Singular effects of illumination with light of one simple colour—Lamps for producing homogeneous yellow light—Methods of increasing the effect of this exhibition—Method of reading the inscription of coins in the dark—Art of deciphering the effaced inscription of coins—Explanation of these singular effects—Apparent motion of the eyes in portraits—Remarkable examples of this—Apparent motion of the features of a portrait, when the eyes are made to move—Remarkable experiment of breathing light and darkness.

In the preceding letter I have given an account of the most important instruments of Natural Magic which depend on optical principles; but there still remain several miscellaneous phenomena on which the stamp of the marvellous is deeply impressed, and the study of which is pregnant with instruction and amusement.

One of the most curious of these is that false perception in vision by which we conceive depressions to be elevations and elevations depressions, or by which intaglios are converted into cameos, and cameos into intaglios. This curious fact seems to have been first observed at one of the early meetings of the Royal Society of London, when one of the members, in looking at a guinea through a compound microscope of new construction, was surprised to see the head upon the coin depressed, while other members could only see it embossed as it really was.

While using telescopes and compound microscopes, Dr. Gmelin of Wurtemburg observed the same fact. The protuberant parts of objects appeared to him depressed, and the depressed parts protuberant; but what perplexed him extremely, this illusion took place at some times and not at others, in some experiments and not in others, and appeared to some eyes and not to others.

After making a great number of experiments, Dr. Gmelin is said to have constantly observed the following effects: Whenever he viewed any object rising upon a plane of any colour whatever, provided it was neither white nor shining, and provided the eye and the optical tube were directly opposite to it, the elevated parts appeared depressed, and the depressed parts elevated. This happened when he was viewing a seal, and as often as he held the tube of the telescope perpendicularly, and applied it in such a manner that its whole surface almost covered the last glass of the tube. The same effect was produced when a compound microscope was used. When the object hung perpendicularly from a plane, and the tube was supported horizontally and directly opposite to it, the illusion also took place, and the appearance was not altered when the object hung obliquely and even horizontally. Dr. Gmelin is said to have at last discovered a method of preventing this illusion, which was, by looking not towards the centre of the convexity, but at first to the edges of it only, and then gradually taking in the whole. "But why these things should so happen, he did not pretend to determine."

The best method of observing this deception is to view the engraved seal of a watch with the eye-piece of an achromatic telescope, or with a compound microscope, or any combination of lenses which inverts the objects that are viewed through it.* The depression in the seal will

---

* A single convex lens will answer the purpose, provided we hold the eye six or eight inches behind the image of the seal formed in is conjugate focus.

immediately appear an elevation, like the wax impression which is taken from it; and though we know it to be hollow, and feel its concavity with the point of our finger, the illusion is so strong that it continues to appear a protuberance. The cause of this will be understood from Fig. 14, where S is the window of the apartment,

Fig. 14.

or the light which illuminates the *hollow* seal L R, whose shaded side is of course on the same side L with the light. If we now invert the seal with one or more lenses, so that it may look in the opposite direction, it will appear to the eye as in Fig. 15, with the shaded side L

Fig. 15.

farthest from the window. But as we know that the window is still on our left land, and that the light falls in the direction R L, and as every body with its shaded side farthest from the light must necessarily be convex or protuberant, we immediately believe that the hollow seal is now a cameo or bas-relief. The proof which the eye thus receives of the seal being raised, overcomes the evidence of its being hollow derived from our actual knowledge, and from the sense of touch. In this experiment the deception takes place from our knowing the real direction of the light which falls upon the seal; for if the place of the window, with respect to the seal, had been inverted as well as the seal itself, the illusion could not have taken place.

In order to explain this better, let us suppose the seal L R, Fig. 14, to be illuminated with a candle S, the place of which we can change at pleasure. If we invert L R it will rise into a cameo, as in Fig. 15; and if we then place another candle D on the other side of it, as in Fig. 16, the hollow seal will be equally illuminated on all sides, and it will sink down into a cavity or intaglio. If the two candles do not illuminate the seal equally, or

Fig. 16.

if any accidental circumstance produces a belief that the light is wholly or principally on one side, the mind will entertain a corresponding opinion respecting the state of the seal, regarding it as a hollow if it believes the light to come wholly or principally from the right hand, and as a cameo if it believes the light to come from the left hand.

If we use a small telescope to invert the seal, and if we cover up all the candle but its flame, and arrange the experiment so that the candle may be inverted along with the image, the seal will still retain its concavity, because the shadow is still on the same side with the illuminating body.

If we make the same experiments with the raised impression of the seal taken upon wax, we shall observe the very same phenomena, the seal being depressed when it alone is inverted, and retaining its convexity when the light is inverted along with it.

The illusion, therefore, under our consideration is the result of an operation of our own minds, whereby we judge of the forms of bodies by the knowledge we have acquired of light and shadow. Hence the illusion depends on the accuracy and extent of our knowledge on this subject; and while some persons are under its influence, others are entirely insensible to it. When the seat or hollow cavity is not polished, but ground, and the surface round it of uniform colour and smoothness, almost every person, whether young or old, learned or ignorant, will be subject to the illusion; because the youngest and the most careless observers cannot but know that the shadow

Fig. 17.

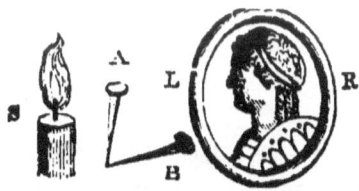

of a hollow is always on the side next the light, and the shadow of a protuberance on the side opposite to the light; but if the object is the raised impression of a seal upon wax, I have found that when inverted it still seemed raised to the three youngest of six persons, while the three eldest were subject to the deception.

This illusion may be dissipated by a process of reasoning arising from the introduction of a new circumstance in the experiment. Thus, let R L, Fig. 18, be the inverted seal, which consequently appears raised, and let an opaque and unpolished pin A be placed on one side of the seal. Its shadow will be of course opposite the candle as at B. In this case the seal which had become

a cameo by its inversion, will now sink down into a
cavity by the introduction of the pin and its shadow; for as
the pin and its shadow are inverted, as shown in Fig.
18, while the candle retains its place, the shadow of the pin
falling in the direction A B is a stronger proof to the
eye that the light is coming from the right hand, than
the actual knowledge of the candle being on the left
hand, and therefore the cameo necessarily sinks into a
cavity, or the shadow is now on the same side as the light.
This experiment will explain to us why on some occasions
an acute observer will elude the deception, while every
other person is subject to it. Let us suppose that a

Fig. 18.

particle of dust, or a little bit of wax, capable of giving
a shadow, is adhering to the surface of the seal, an
ordinary observer will take no notice of this, or if he
does, he will probably not make it a subject of consideration, and will therefore see the head on the seal raised
into a cameo; but the attentive observer noticing the
little protuberance, and observing that its shadow lies
to the left of it, will instantly infer that the light comes
in that direction, and will still see the seal hollow.

I have already mentioned that in some cases even the
sense of touch does not correct the erroneous perception.
We of course feel that the part of the hollow on which
the finger is placed is actually hollow; but if we look at
the other part of the hollow it will still appear raised.

By using two candles yielding different degrees of light,

and thus giving an uncertainty to the direction of the light, we may weaken the illusion in any degree we choose, so as to overpower it by touch or by a process of reasoning.

I have had occasion to observe a series of analogous phenomena arising from the same cause, but produced without any instrument for inverting the object. If A B, for example, is a plate of mother-of-pearl, and L R a circular or any other cavity (Fig. 19) ground or turned in it, then if this cavity is illuminated by a candle or a

Fig. 19.

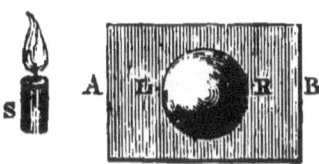

window at S, in place of there being a shadow of the margin L of the hollow next the light, as there would have been had the body been opaque, a quantity of bright refracted light will appear where there would have been a shadow, and the rest of the cavity will be comparatively obscure, as if it were in shade. The necessary consequence of this is, that the cavity will appear as an elevation when seen only by the naked eye, as it is only an elevated surface that could have its most luminous side at L.

Similar illusions take place in certain pieces of polished wood, calcedony, and mother-of-pearl, where the surface is perfectly smooth. This arises from there being at that place a knot or growth, or nodule of different transparency from the surrounding mass, and the cause of it will be understood from Fig. 20. Let m o be the surface of a mahogany table, A m o B a section of the table, and m n o a section of a knot more transparent than the rest of the mass. Owing to the transparency of the thin edge at *o*, opposite to the candle S, the side *o* is illuminated, while the rest of the knot is comparatively dark, so that on the principles already explained the spot *m n o* appears to be a hollow in the table. From this cause arises the appearance of dimples in certain plates of calcedony called hammered calcedony, owing to its having the look of being dimpled with a hammer. The surface on which these cavities are seen is a section of small spherical aggregations of siliceous matter, which exhibit the same

Fig. 20.

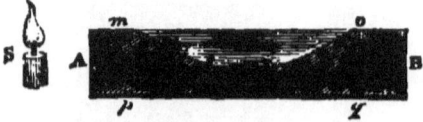

phenomena as the cavities in wood. Mother-of-pearl presents the very same phenomena, and it is indeed so common in this substance that it is nearly impossible to find a mother-of-pearl button or counter which seems to have its surface flat, although they are perfectly so when examined by the touch. Owing to the different refraction of the incident light by the different growths of the shell cut in different directions by the artificial surface, like the annual growth of wood in a dressed plank, the surface has necessarily an unequal and undulating appearance.

Among the wonders of science there are perhaps none more surprising than the effects produced upon coloured objects by illuminating them with homogeneous light, or light of one.colour. The light which emanates from the sun, and by which all the objects of the material world are exhibited to us, is composed of three different colours, *red, yellow,* and *blue,* by the mixture of which in different

proportions all the various hues of nature may be produced. These three colours, when mixed in the proportion in which they occur in the sun's rays, compose a
purely white light; but if any body on which this white
light falls shall absorb, or stop, or detain within its substance any part of any one or more of these simple colours,
it will appear to the eye of that colour which arises from
the mixture of all the rays which it does not absorb, or of
that colour which white light would have if deprived of
the colours which are absorbed. Scarlet cloth, for example,
absorbs most of the blue rays and many of the yellow, and
hence appears *red*. Yellow cloth absorbs most of the blue
and many of the red rays, and therefore appears yellow,
and blue cloth absorbs most of the yellow and red rays.
If we were to illuminate the *scarlet* cloth with pure and
unmixed *yellow* light, it would appear *yellow*, because the
scarlet cloth does not absorb all the yellow rays, but
reflects some of them ; and if we illuminate *blue* cloth
with yellow light, it will appear nearly *black*, because it
absorbs all the yellow light, and reflects almost none of it.
But whatever be the nature and colour of the bodies on
which the yellow light falls, the light which it reflects
must be yellow, for no other light falls upon them, and
those which are not capable of reflecting yellow light must
appear absolutely black, however brilliant be their colour
in the light of day.

As the methods now discovered of producing yellow
light in abundance were not known to the ancient conjurers, nor even to those of later times, they have never
availed themselves of this valuable resource. It has been
long known that salt thrown into the wick of a flame produces yellow light, but this light is mixed with blue and
green rays, and is, besides, so small in quantity that it
illuminates objects only that are in the immediate vicinity
of the flame. A method which I have found capable of

producing it in abundance is shown in Fig. 21, where A B is a lamp containing at A a large quantity of alcohol and water or ardent spirits, which gradually descends into a platina or metallic cup D. This cup is strongly heated by a spirit-lamp L, inclosed in a dark lantern; and when the diluted alcohol in D is inflamed, it will burn with a fierce and powerful yellow flame: if the flame should not be perfectly yellow, owing to an excess of alcohol, a

Fig. 21.

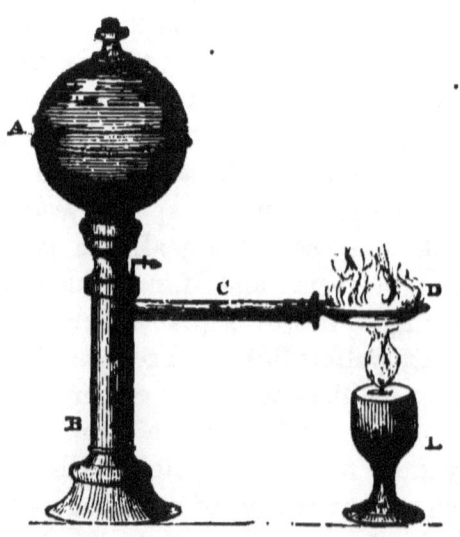

proportion of salt thrown into the cup will answer the same purpose as a further dilution of the alcohol.*

A monochromatic lamp for producing yellow light may be constructed most effectually by employing a portable gas lamp containing compressed oil gas. If we allow the gas to escape in a copious stream, and set it on fire, it will form an explosive mixture with the atmospheric air, and will no longer burn with a white flame, but will emit a bluish and reddish light. The force of the issuing gas,

* See *Edinburgh Transactions*, vol. ix. p. 435.

or any accidental current of air, is capable of blowing out
this flame, so that it is necessary to have a contrivance
for sustaining it.   The method which I used for this purpose is shown in Fig. 22.   A small gas tube *a b c*, arising
from the main burner M N of the gas lamp P Q, terminates above the burner, and has a short tube *d e*, moveable
up and down within it, so as to be gas-tight.   This tube
d e, closed at *e*, communicates with the hollow ring *f g*, in
the inside of which four apertures are perforated in such

Fig. 22.

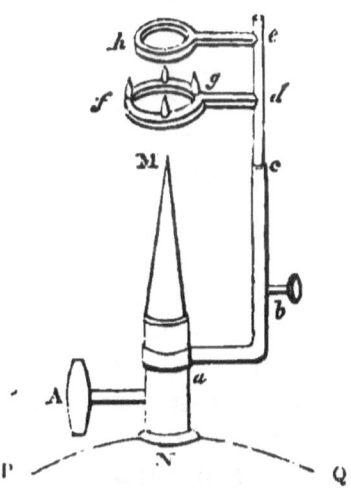

a manner as to throw their jets of gas to the apex of a
cone, of which *f g* is the base.   When we cause the gas to
flow from the burner M, by opening the main cock A, it
will rush into the tube *a b c d*, and issue in small flames
at the four holes in the ring *f g*.   The size of these flames
is regulated by the cock *b*.   The inflammation, therefore,
of the ignited gas will be sustained by these four subsidiary
flames through which it passes, independent of any agitation of the air, or of the force with which it issues from
the burner.   On a projecting arm *e h*, carrying a ring *h*,

I fixed a broad collar, made of coarse cotton wick, which had been previously soaked in a saturated solution of common salt. When the gas is allowed to escape at M, with such force as to produce a long and broad column of an explosive mixture of gas and atmospheric air, the bluish flame occasioned by the explosion passes through the salted collar, and is converted by it into a mass of homogeneous yellow light. This collar will last a long time without any fresh supply of salt, so that the gas lamp will yield a permanent monochromatic yellow flame, which will last as long as there is gas in the reservoir. In place of a collar of cotton wick, a hollow cylinder of sponge, with numerous projecting tufts, may be used, or a collar may be similarly constructed with asbestos cloth, and, if thought necessary, it might be supplied with a saline solution from a capillary fountain.

Having thus obtained the means of illuminating any apartment with yellow light, let the exhibition be made in a room with furniture of various bright colours, with oil or water coloured paintings on the wall. The party which is to witness the experiment should be dressed in a diversity of the gayest colours ; and the brightest coloured flowers and highly-coloured drawings should be placed on the tables. The room being at first lighted with ordinary lights, the bright and gay colours of everything that it contains will be finely displayed. If the white lights are now suddenly extinguished, and the yellow lamps lighted, the most appalling metamorphosis will be exhibited. The astonished individuals will no longer be able to recognise each other. All the furniture in the room and all the objects which it contains will exhibit only one colour. The flowers will lose their hues. The paintings and drawings will appear as if they were executed in China ink, and the gayest dresses, the brightest scarlets, the purest lilacs, the richest blues, and the most vivid greens will all be converted into one monotonous yellow. The complexions of the parties too will suffer a corresponding change. One pallid death-like yellow,

————like the unnatural hue
Which autumn plants upon the perished leaf,

will envelop the young and the old, and the sallow faces will alone escape from the metamorphosis. Each individual derives merriment from the cadaverous appearance of his neighbour, without being sensible that he is himself one of the ghostly assemblage.

If, in the midst of the astonishment which is thus created, the white lights are restored at one end of the room, while the yellow lights are taken to the other end, one side of the dress of every person, namely, that next the white light, will be restored to its original colours, while the other side will retain its yellow hue. One cheek will appear in a state of health and colour, while the other retains the paleness of death, and, as the individuals change their position, they will exhibit the most extraordinary transformations of colour.

If, when all the lights are yellow, beams of white light are transmitted through a number of holes like those in a sieve, each luminous spot will restore the colour of the dress or furniture upon which it falls, and the nankeen family will appear all mottled over with every variety of tint. If a magic lantern is employed to throw upon the walls or upon the dresses of the company luminous figures of flowers or animals, the dresses will be painted with these figures in the real colour of the dress itself. Those alone who appeared in yellow, and with yellow complexions, will to a great degree escape all these singular changes.

I red and blue light could be produced with the same facility and in the same abundance as yellow light, the

o

illumination of the apartment with these lights in succession would add to the variety and wonder of the exhibition. The red light might perhaps be procured in sufficient quantity from the nitrate and other salts of strontian; but it would be difficult to obtain a blue flame of sufficient intensity for the suitable illumination of a large room. Brilliant white lights, however, might be used, having for screens glass troughs containing a mass one or two inches thick of a solution of the ammoniacal carbonate of copper. This solution absorbs all the rays of the spectrum but the blue, and the intensity of the blue light thus produced would increase in the same proportion as the white light employed.

Among the numerous experiments with which science astonishes and sometimes even strikes terror into the ignorant, there is none more calculated to produce this effect than that of displaying to the eye in absolute darkness the legend or inscription upon a coin. To do this, take a silver coin (I have always used an old one), and after polishing the surface as much as possible, make the parts of it which are raised rough by the action of an acid, the parts not raised, or those which are to be rendered darkest, retaining their polish. If the coin thus prepared is placed upon a mass of red-hot iron, and removed into a dark room, the inscription upon it will become less luminous than the rest, so that it may be distinctly read by the spectator. The mass of red-hot iron should be concealed from the observer's eye, both for the purpose of rendering the eye fitter for observing the effect, and of removing all doubt that the inscription is really read in the dark, that is, without receiving any light, direct or reflected, from any other body. If, in place of polishing the depressed parts, and roughening its raised parts, we make the raised parts polished, and roughen the depressed parts, the inscription will now be less luminous than the depressed parts, and we shall still be able to read it, from its being as it were written in black letters on a white ground. The first time I made this experiment, without being aware of what would be the result, I used a French shilling of Louis XV., and I was not a little surprised to observe upon its surface in black letters the inscription BENEDICTUM SIT NOMEN DEI.

The most surprising form of this experiment is when we use a coin from which the inscription has been either wholly obliterated, or obliterated in such a degree as to be illegible. When such a coin is laid upon the red-hot iron, the letters and figures become oxidated, and the film of oxide radiating more powerfully than the rest of the coin will be more luminous than the rest of the coin, and the illegible inscription may be now distinctly read, to the great surprise of the observer, who had examined the blank surface of the coin previous to its being placed upon the hot iron. The different appearances of the same coin, according as the raised parts are polished or roughened, are shown in Figs. 23 and 24.

In order to explain the cause of these remarkable effects, we must notice a method which has been long known, though never explained, of deciphering the inscriptions on worn-out coins. This is done by merely placing the coin upon a hot iron. An oxidation takes place over the whole surface of the coin, the film of oxide changing its tint with the intensity or continuance of the heat. The parts, however, where the letters of the inscription had existed oxidate at a different rate from the surrounding parts, so that these letters exhibit their shape, and become legible, in consequence of the film of oxide which covers them having a different thickness, and therefore reflecting a different tint from that of the adjacent parts. The tints thus developed sometimes pass through many orders of brilliant colours, particularly *pink* and *green*, and settle in a bronze, and sometimes a black tint, resting upon the inscription alone. In some cases the tint left on the trace of the letters is so very faint that it can just be seen, and may be entirely removed by a slight rub of the finger.

When the experiment is often repeated with the same coin, and the oxidations successively removed after each experiment, the film of oxide continues to diminish, and at last ceases to make its appearance. It recovers the property, however, in the course of time. When the coin is put upon the hot iron, and consequently when the oxidation is the greatest, a considerable smoke arises from

Fig. 23.   Fig. 24.

the coin, and this diminishes, like the film of oxide, by frequent repetition. A coin which had ceased to emit this smoke, smoked slightly after having been exposed twelve hours to the air. I have found from numerous trials that it is always the raised parts of the coin, and in modern coins the elevated ledge round the inscription, that becomes first oxidated. In an English shilling of 1816 this ledge exhibited a brilliant yellow tint before it appeared on any other part of the coin.

If we use an uniform and homogeneous disc of silver that has never been hammered or compressed, its surface will oxidate equally, provided all its parts are equally heated. In the process of converting this disc into a coin, the *sunk* parts have obviously been *most compressed* by the prominent parts of the die, and the *elevated* parts *least compressed*, the metal being in the latter left as it were in its natural state. The raised letters and figures on a coin have therefore less density than the other parts, and these parts oxidate sooner, or at a lower temperature. When the letters of the legend are worn off by friction, the parts immediately below them have also less density than the surrounding metal, and the site as it were of the letters therefore receives from heat a degree of oxidation, and a colour different from that of the surrounding surface. Hence we obtain an explanation of the revival of the invisible letters by oxidation.

The same influence of difference of density may be observed in the beautiful oxidations which are produced on the surface of highly-polished steel, heated in contact with air, at temperatures between 430° and 630° of Fahrenheit.* When the steel has hard portions called *pins* by the workmen, the uniform tint of the film of oxide stops near these hard portions, which always exhibit colours different from those of the rest of the mass. These parts, on account of their increased density, absorb the oxygen of atmospheric air less copiously than the surrounding portions. Hence we see the cause why steel expanded by heat absorbs oxygen, which, when united with the metal, forms the coloured superficial film. As the heat increases, a greater quantity of oxygen is absorbed, and the film increases in thickness.

These observations enable us to explain the legibility of inscriptions in the dark, whether the coin is in a perfect state, or the letters of it worn off. All *black* or *rough* surfaces radiate light more copiously than *polished* or *smooth* surfaces, and hence the inscription is *luminous* when it is *rough*, and *obscure* when it is polished, and the letters

* See *Edinburgh Encyclopædia*, Art. Steel, vol xviii. p. 387.

covered with black oxide are more luminous than the
adjacent parts, on account of the superior radiation of
light by the black oxide which covers them.

By the means now described invisible writing might be
conveyed by impressing it upon a metallic surface, and
afterwards erasing it by grinding and polishing that
surface perfectly smooth.   When exposed to a proper
degree of heat, the secret would display itself. written in
oxidated letters. Many amusing experiments might be
made upon the same principle.

A series of curious and sometimes alarming deceptions,
arises from the representation of objects in perspective
upon a plane surface. One of the most interesting of
these depends on the principles which regulate the
apparent direction of the eyes in a portrait.   Dr. Wollaston
has thought this subject of sufficient importance to be
treated at some length in the Philosophical Transactions.
When we look at any person we direct to them both our
face and our eyes, and in this position the circular iris
will be in the middle of the white of the eyeball, or, what
is the same thing, there will be the same quantity of white
on each side of the iris.   If the eyes are now moved to
either side, while the head remains fixed, we shall readily
judge of the change of their direction by the greater or
less quantity of white on each side of the iris.   This test,
however, accurate as it is, enables us only to estimate the
extent to which the eyes deviate in direction from the
direction of the face to which they belong.   But their
direction in reference to the person who views them is
entirely a different matter;   and Dr. Wollaston is of
opinion, that we are not guided by the eyes alone, but are
unconsciously aided by the concurrent position of the
entire face.

If a skilful painter draws a pair of eyes with great
correctness directed to the spectator, and deviating from

the general position of the face as much as is usual in good portraits, it is very difficult to determine their direction, and they will appear to have different directions to different persons.   But what is very curious, Dr. Wollaston has shown that the same pair of eyes may be made to direct themselves either to or from the spectator by the addition of other features in which the position of the face is changed.   Thus in Fig. 25, the pair of eyes are

Fig. 25.

looking intently at the spectator, and the face has a corresponding direction; but when we cover up the face in Fig. 25 with the face in Fig. 26, which looks to the right, the eyes change their direction, and look to the right also. In like manner, eyes drawn originally to look a little to the right or the left of the spectator may be made to look directly at him by adding suitable features.

The nose is obviously the principal feature which produces this change of direction, as it is more subject to change of perspective than any of the other features; but Dr. Wollaston has shown, by a very accurate experiment, that even a small portion of the nose introduced with the features will carry the eyes along with it.   He obtained four exact copies of the same pair of eyes looking at the spectator, by transferring them upon copper from a steel plate, and having added to each of two pair of them, a nose in one case directed to the right, and in the other, to the left, and to each of the other two pairs a very small portion of the upper part of the nose, all the four pair of eyes lost their front direction, and looked to the right or to the left, according to the direction of the nose, or of the portion of it which was added.

But the effect thus produced is not limited, as Dr. Wollaston remarks, to the mere change in the direction of the eyes, "for a total difference of character may be given to the same eyes by a due representation of the other features. A lost look of devout abstraction in an uplifted countenance may be exchanged for an appearance of inquisitive archness in the leer of a younger face turned downwards and obliquely towards the opposite side," as in Fig. 27, 28. This, however, is perhaps not an exact expression of the fact. The new character which is said to be given to the eyes is given only to the eyes in combination with the new features, or, what is probably more correct, the inquisitive archness is in the other features, and the eye does not belie it.

Dr. Wollaston has not noticed the converse of these illusions, in which a change of direction is given to fixed features by a change in the direction of the eyes. This effect is finely seen in some magic lantern sliders, where a pair of eyes is made to move in the head of a figure which invariably follows the motion of the eyeballs.

Having thus determined the influence which the general perspective of the face has upon the apparent direction of the eyes in a portrait, Dr. Wollaston applies it to the explanation of the well-known fact, that when the eyes of a portrait look at a spectator in front of it they will follow him, and appear to look at him in every other direction. This curious fact, which has received less consideration than it merits, has been often skilfully employed by the novelist, in alarming the fears or exciting the courage of his hero. On returning to the hall of his ancestors, his attention is powerfully fixed on the grim portraits which surround him. The parts which they have respectively performed in the family history rise to his mind: his own actions, whether good or evil, are called up in contrast, and as the preserver or the destroyer of his line, he stands as it were in judgment before them.

Fig. 27.

His imagination, thus excited by conflicting feelings, transfers a sort of vitality to the canvas, and if the personages do not "start from their frames," they will at least bend upon him their frowns or their approbation. It is in vain that he tries to evade their scrutiny. Wherever he goes their eyes eagerly pursue him;—they will seem even to look at him over their shoulders, and he will find it impossible to shun their gaze but by quitting the apartment.

As the spectator in this case changes his position in a horizontal plane, the effect which we have described is accompanied by an apparent diminution in the breadth of the human face, from only seven or eight inches till it disappears at a great obliquity. In moving, therefore, from a front view to the most oblique view of the face, the change in its apparent breadth is so slow that the apparent motion of the head of the figure is scarcely recognized as it follows the spectator. But if the perspective figure has a great breadth in a horizontal plane, such as a soldier firing his musket, an artilleryman his piece of ordnance, a bowman drawing his bow, or a lancer pushing his spear, the apparent breadth of the figure will vary from five to six feet or upwards till it disappears, and therefore the change of apparent magnitude is sufficiently rapid to give the figure the dreaded appearance of turning round, and following the spectator. One of the best examples of this must have been often observed in the foreshortened figure of a dead body lying horizontally, which has the appearance of following the observer with great rapidity, and turning round upon the head as the centre of motion.

The cause of this phenomenon is easily explained. Let us suppose a portrait with its face and its eyes directed straight in front, so as to look at the spectator. Let a straight line be drawn through the tip of the nose and half way between the eyes, which we shall call the middle line. On each side of this middle line there will be the same breadth of head, of cheek, of chin, and of neck, and each iris will be in the middle of the whole of the eye. If we now go to one side, the apparent horizontal breadth of every part of the head and face will be diminished, but the parts on each side of the middle line will be diminished equally, and at any position, however oblique, there will be the same breadth of face on each side of the middle line, and the iris will be in the centre of the whole of the eyeball, so that the portrait preserves all the characters of a figure looking at the spectator, and must necessarily do so wherever he stands.

This explanation might be illustrated by a picture which represents three artillerymen, each firing a piece of ordnance in parallel directions. Let the gun of the middle one be pointed accurately to the eye of the spectator, so that he sees neither its right side nor its left, nor its upper nor its under side, but directly down its muzzle, so that if there was an opening in the breech he would see through it. In like manner the spectator will see the left side of the gun on his left hand, and the right side of the gun on his right hand. If the spectator now changes his place, and takes ever such an oblique position, either laterally or vertically, he must still see the same thing, because nothing else is presented to his view. The gun of the middle soldier must always point to his eye, and the other guns to the right and left of him. They must therefore all three seem to move as he moves, and follow his eye in all its changes of place. The same observations are of course applicable to buildings and streets seen in perspective.

In common portraits the apparent motion of the head is generally rendered indistinct by the canvas being imperfectly stretched, as the slightest concavity or convexity entirely deforms the face when the obliquity is considerable. The deception is therefore best seen when the painting is executed on a very flat board, and in colours sufficiently vivid to represent every line in the face with tolerable distinctness at great obliquities. This distinctness of outline is indeed necessary to a satisfactory exhibition of this optical illusion. The most perfect

exhibition, indeed, that I ever saw of it was in the case
of a painting of a ship upon a sign-board executed in
strongly gilt lines. It contained a view of the stern, and
side of a ship in the stocks, and, owing to the flatness
of the board and the brightness of the lines, the gradual
development of the figure from the most violent fore-
shortening at great obliquities till it attained its perfect
form, was an effect which surprised every person that saw
it.

The only other optical illusion which our limits will
permit us to explain, is the very remarkable experiment
of what may be truly called *breathing light or darkness*.
Let S be a candle where light falls at an angle of 56° 45'
upon two glass plates A, B, placed close to each other,
and let the reflected rays A C, B D, fall at the same
angle upon two similar plates C, D, but so placed that
the plane of reflection from the latter is at right angles
to the plane of reflection from the former. An eye placed

Fig. 29.

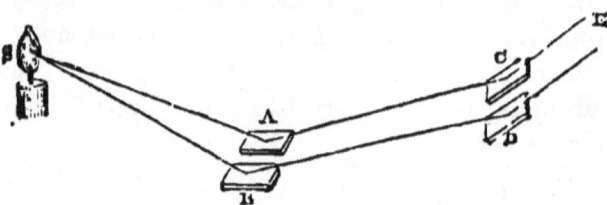

at E, and looking at the same time into the two plates
C and D, will see very faint images of the candle S, which
by a slight adjustment of the place may be made to disappear almost wholly. Allowing the plate C to remain
as it is, change the position of D, till its inclination to
the ray B D is diminished about 3¼°, or made nearly
53° 11'. When this is done, the image that had disappeared on looking into D will be restored, so that the

spectator at E, upon looking into the two mirrors C, D, will see no light in C, because the candle has nearly disappeared, while the candle is distinctly seen in D. If, while the spectator is looking into these two mirrors, either he or another person breathes upon them gently and quickly, the breath will revive the extinguished image in C, and will extinguish the visible image in D. The following is the cause of this singular result. The light A C, B D, is polarized by reflection from the plates A, B, because it is incident at the polarizing angle of 56° 45' for glass. When we breathe upon the plates C, D, we form upon their surface a thin film of water, whose polarizing angle is 53° 11', so that if the polarized rays A C, B D, fell upon the plates C, D, at an angle of 53° 11', the candle from which they proceeded would not be visible, or they would not suffer reflection from the plates C D. At all other angles the light would be reflected and the candles visible. Now the plate D is placed at an angle of 53° 11', and C at an angle of 56° 45', so that when a film of water is breathed upon them the light will be reflected from the latter, and none from the former: that is, the act of breathing upon the plates will restore the invisible, and extinguish the visible image.

LETTER VI.

Natural phenomena marked with the marvellous—Spectre of the Brocken described—Analogous phenomena—Aërial spectres seen in Cumberland—Fata Morgana in the Straits of Messina—Objects below the horizon raised and magnified by refraction—Singular example seen at Hastings—Dover Castle seen through the hill on which it stands—Erect and inverted images of distant ships seen in the air—Similar phenomena seen in the Arctic regions—Enchanted coast—Mr. Scoresby recognizes his father's ship by its aërial image—Images of cows seen in the air—Inverted images of horses seen in South America—Lateral images produced by refraction—Aërial spectres by reflection—Explanation of the preceding phenomena.

Among the wonders of the natural world which are every day presented to us, without either exciting our surprise or attracting our notice, some are occasionally displayed which possess all the characters of supernatural phenomena. In the names by which they are familiarly known, we recognize the terror which they inspired, and even now, when science has reduced them to the level of natural phenomena, and developed the causes from which they arise, they still retain their primitive importance, and are watched by the philosopher with as intense an interest as when they were deemed the immediate effects of Divine power. Among these phenomena we may enumerate the *Spectre of the Brocken*, the *Fata Morgana* of the Straits of Messina, the *Spectre Ships* which appear in the air, and the other extraordinary effects of the *Mirage.**

* In the Sanscrit, says Baron Humboldt, the phenomenon of the Mirage is called *Mriga Trichna*, " thirst or desire of the antelope," no

The Brocken is the name of the loftiest of the Hartz Mountains, a picturesque range which lies in the kingdom of Hanover. It is elevated 3300 feet above the sea, and commands the view of a plain seventy leagues in extent, occupying nearly the two-hundredth part of the whole of Europe, and animated with a population of above five millions of inhabitants. From the earliest periods of authentic history, the Brocken has been the seat of the marvellous. On its summits are still seen huge blocks of granite, called the Sorcerer's Chair and the Altar. A spring of pure water is known by the name of the Magic Fountain, and the anemone of the Brocken is distinguished by the title of the Sorcerer's Flower. These names are supposed to have originated in the rites of the great Idol Cortho, whom the Saxons worshipped in secret on the summit of the Brocken, when Christianity was extending her benignant sway over the subjacent plains.

As the locality of these idolatrous rites, the Brocken must have been much frequented, and we can scarcely doubt that the spectre which now so often haunts it at sunrise must have been observed from the earliest times; but it is nowhere mentioned that this phenomenon was in any way associated with the objects of their idolatrous worship. One of the best accounts of the spectre of the Brocken is that which is given by M. Hauc, who saw it on the 23rd of May, 1797. After having been on the summit of the mountain no less than thirty times, he had at last the good fortune of witnessing the object of his curiosity. The sun rose about four o'clock in the morning through a serene atmosphere. In the south-west, towards Achter-

doubt because this animal, *Mriga*, compelled by thirst, *Trichna*, approaches those barren plains where, from the effect of unequal refraction, he thinks he perceives the undulating surface of the waters.—*Personal Narrative*, vol. iii. p. 554.

mannshohe, a brisk west wind carried before it the transparent vapours, which had not yet been condensed into thick heavy clouds. About a quarter past four he went towards the inn, and looked round to see whether the atmosphere would afford him a free prospect towards the south-west, when he observed at a very great distance, towards Achtermannshohe, a human figure of a monstrous size. His hat, having been almost carried away by a violent gust of wind, he suddenly raised his hand to his head, to protect his hat, and the colossal figure did the same. He immediately made another movement by

Fig. 30.

bending his body,—an action which was repeated by the spectral figure. M. Haue was desirous of making further experiments, but the figure disappeared. He remained, however, in the same position, expecting its return, and in a few minutes it again made its appearance on the Achtermannshohe, when it mimicked his gestures as before. He then called the landlord of the inn, and having both taken the same position which he had before, they looked towards the Achtermannshohe but saw nothing. In a very short space of time, however, two colossal figures were formed over the above eminence, and after bending their bodies and imitating the gestures of the two spectators, they disappeared. Retaining their position, and keeping their eyes still fixed upon the same spot, the two gigantic spectres again stood before them, *and were joined by a third.* Every movement that they made was imitated by the three figures, but the effect varied in its intensity, being sometimes weak and faint, and at other times strong and well defined.

In the year 1798 M. Jordan saw the same phenomenon at sunrise, and under similar circumstances, but with less distinctness and without any duplication of the figures.*

Phenomena perfectly analogous to the preceding, though seen under less imposing circumstances, have been often witnessed. When the spectator sees his own shadow opposite to the sun upon a mass of thin fleecy vapour passing near him, it not only imitates all his movements, but its head is distinctly encircled with a halo of light. The aërial figure is often not larger than life, its size and its apparent distance depending, as we shall afterwards see, upon particular causes. I have often seen a similar shadow when bathing in a bright summer's day in au extensive pool of deep water. When the fine mud deposited at the bottom of the pool is disturbed by the feet of the bather, so as to be disseminated through the mass of water in the direction of his shadow, his shadow is no longer a shapeless mass formed upon the bottom, but is a regular figure formed upon the floating particles of mud, and having the head surrounded with a halo, not only luminous, but consisting of distinct radiations.

One of the most interesting accounts of aërial spectres with which we are acquainted has been given by Mr. James Clarke, in his Survey of the Lakes of Cumberland, and the accuracy of this account was confirmed by the

* See J. F. Gmelin's *Gottingischen Journal der Wissenchaften,* vol. i. part iii. 1798.

attestations of two of the persons by whom the phenomena were first seen. On a summer's evening in the
year 1743, when Daniel Stricket, servant to John Wren
of Wilton Hall, was sitting at the door along with his
master, they saw the figure of a man with a dog pursuing
some horses along Souterfell side, a place so extremely
steep that a horse could scarcely travel upon it at all.
The figures appeared to run at an amazing pace, till they
got out of sight at the lower end of the Fell. On the
following morning Stricket and his master ascended the
steep side of the mountain, in the full expectation of
finding the man dead, and of picking up some of the shoes
of the horses, which they thought must have been cast
while galloping at such a furious rate. Their expectations, however, were disappointed. No traces either of
man or horse could be found, and they could not even
discover upon the turf the single mark of a horse's hoof.
These strange appearances, seen at the same time by two
different persons in perfect health, could not fail to make
a deep impression on their minds. They at first concealed what they had seen, but they at length disclosed it,
and were laughed at for their credulity.

In the following year, on the 23rd June, 1744, Daniel
Stricket, who was then servant to Mr. Lancaster of Blakehills (a place near Wilton Hall, and both of which places
are only about half a mile from Souterfell), was walking,
about seven o'clock in the evening, a little above the
house, when he saw a troop of horsemen riding on
Souterfell side in pretty close ranks, and at a brisk pace.
Recollecting the ridicule that had been cast upon him the
preceding year, he continued to observe the figures for
some time in silence; but being at last convinced that
there could be no deception in the matter, he went to the
house and informed his master that he had something
curious to show him. They accordingly went out to·

gether; but before Stricket had pointed out the place
Mr. Lancaster's son had discovered the aërial figures.
The family was then summoned to the spot, and the
phenomena were seen alike by them all. The equestrian
figures seemed to come from the lowest parts of Souterfell
and became visible at a place called Knott. They then
advanced in regular troops along the side of the Fell, till
they came opposite to Blakehills, when they went over
the mountain, after describing a kind of curvilineal path.
The pace at which the figures moved was a regular swift
walk, and they continued to be seen for upwards of two
hours, the approach of darkness alone preventing them
from being visible. Many troops were seen in succession; and frequently the last but one in a troop quitted
his position, galloped to the front, and took up the same
pace with the rest. The changes in the figures were seen
equally by all the spectators, and the view of them was
not confined to the farm of Blakehills only, but they were
seen by every person at every cottage within the distance
of a mile, the number of persons who saw them amounting
to about twenty-six. The attestation of these facts, signed
by Lancaster and Stricket, bears the date of the 21st
July, 1744.

These extraordinary sights were received not only with
distrust but with absolute incredulity. They were not
even honoured with a place in the records of natural
phenomena, and the philosophers of the day were neither
in possession of analogous facts, nor were they acquainted
with those principles of atmospherical refraction upon
which they depend. The strange phenomena, indeed, of
the *Fata Morgana*, or the *Castles of the Fairy Morgana*,
had been long before observed, and had been described by
Kircher in the seventeenth century, but they presented
nothing so mysterious as the aërial troopers of Souterfell;
and the general characters of the two phenomena were so

unlike, that even a philosopher might have been excused for ascribing them to different causes.

This singular exhibition has been frequently seen in the Straits of Messina between Sicily and the coast of Italy, and whenever it takes place, the people, in a state of exultation, as if it were not only a pleasing but a lucky phenomenon, hurry down to the sea, exclaiming *Morgana, Morgana.* When the rays of the rising sun form an angle of 45° on the sea of Reggio, and when the surface of the water is perfectly unruffled either by the wind or the current, a spectator placed upon an eminence in the city, and having his back to the sun and his face to the sea, observes upon the surface of the water superb palaces with their balconies and windows, lofty towers, herds and flocks grazing in wooded valleys and fertile plains, armies of men on horseback and on foot, with multiplied fragments of buildings, such as columns, pilasters, and arches. These objects pass rapidly in succession along the surface of the sea during the brief period of their appearance. The various objects thus enumerated are pictures of palaces and buildings actually existing on shore, and the living objects are of course only seen when they happen to form a part of the general landscape.

If at the time that these phenomena are visible the atmosphere is charged with vapour or dense exhalations, the same objects which are depicted upon the sea will be seen also in the air occupying a space which extends from the surface to the height of twenty-five feet. These images, however, are less distinctly delineated than the former.

If the air is in such a state as to deposit dew, and is capable of forming the rainbow, the objects will be seen only on the surface of the sea, but they all appear fringed with red, yellow, and blue light as if they were seen through a prism.

In our own country, and in our own times, facts still more extraordinary have been witnessed. From Hastings, on the coast of Sussex, the cliffs on the French coast are fifty miles distant, and they are actually hid by the convexity of the earth; that is, a straight line drawn from Hastings to the French coast would pass through the sea. On Wednesday, the 26th July, 1798, about five o'clock in the afternoon, Mr. Latham, a Fellow of the Royal Society, then residing at Hastings, was surprised to see a crowd of people running to the seaside. Upon inquiry into the cause of this, he learned that the coast of France could be seen by the naked eye, and he immediately went down to witness so singular a sight. He distinctly saw the cliffs extending for some leagues along the French coast, and they appeared as if they were only a few miles off. They gradually appeared more and more elevated, and seemed to approach nearer to the eye. The sailors with whom Mr. Latham walked along the water's edge were at first unwilling to believe in the reality of the appearance, but they soon became so thoroughly convinced of it, that they pointed out and named to him the different places which they had been accustomed to visit, and which they conceived to be as near as if they were sailing at a small distance into the harbour. These appearances continued for nearly an hour, the cliffs sometimes appearing brighter and nearer, and at other times fainter and more remote. Mr. Latham then went upon the eastern cliff or hill, which is of considerable height, when, as he remarks, a most beautiful scene presented itself to his view. He beheld at once Dungeness, Dover Cliffs, and the French coast all along from Calais, Boulogne, &c., to St. Vallery, and, as some of the fishermen affirmed, as far west as Dieppe. With the help of a telescope, the French fishing-boats were plainly seen at anchor, and the different colours of the land upon the heights, together with the buildings, were perfectly discernible. Mr. Latham likewise states that the cape of land called Dungeness, which extends nearly two miles into the sea, and is about sixteen miles in a straight line from Hastings, appeared as if quite close to it, and the vessels and fishing-boats which were sailing between the two places appeared equally near, and were magnified to a high degree. These curious phenomena continued "in the highest splendour" till past eight o'clock, although a black cloud had for some time totally obscured the face of the sun.

A phenomenon no less marvellous was seen by Professor Vince of Cambridge and another gentleman on the

Fig. 31.

6th August, 1806, at Ramsgate. The summits *v w x y* of the four turrets of Dover Castle are usually seen over the hill A B, upon which it stands, lying between Ramsgate and Dover; but on the day above mentioned, at seven o'clock in the evening, when the air was very still and a little hazy, not only were the tops *v w x y* of the four towers of Dover Castle seen over the adjacent hill A B, *but the whole of the castle, m n r s, appeared as if it were situated on the side of the hill next Ramsgate*, and rising above the hill as much as usual. This phenomenon was so very singular and unexpected, that at first sight Dr. Vince thought it an illusion; but upon continuing his observations, he became satisfied that it was a real image of the castle. Upon this he gave a telescope to a person present, who, upon attentive examination, saw also a very clear image of the castle, as the Doctor had described it. He continued to observe it for about twenty minutes, during which time the appearance remained precisely the same, but rain coming on, they were prevented from making any further observations. Between the observers and the land from which the hill rises, there was about six miles of sea, and from thence to the top of the hill there was about the same distance. Their own height above the surface of the water was about seventy feet.

This illusion derived great force from the remarkable circumstance, that the hill itself did not appear through the image, as it might have been expected to do. The image of the castle was very strong and well defined, and though the rays from the hill behind it must undoubtedly have come to the eye, yet the strength of the image of the castle so far obscured the background, that it made no sensible impression on the observers. Their attention was, of course, principally directed to the image of the castle; but if the hill behind had been at all visible, Dr. Vince conceives that it could not have escaped their observation, as they continued to look at it for a considerable time with a good telescope.

Hitherto our aërial visions have been seen only in their erect and natural positions, either projected against the ground or elevated in the air; but cases have occurred in which both erect and inverted images of objects have been seen in the air, sometimes singly, sometimes combined, sometimes when the real object was invisible, and sometimes when a part of it had begun to show itself to the spectator.

In the year 1793, Mr. Huddart, when residing at Allonby, in Cumberland, perceived the inverted image of a ship beneath the image, as shown in Fig. 32; but

Dr. Vince, who afterwards observed this phenomenon under a greater variety of forms, found that the ship

Fig. 32.

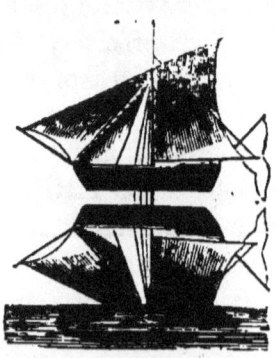

which was here considered the real one, was only an erect image of the real ship, which was at the time beneath the horizon, and wholly invisible.

In August, 1798, Dr. Vince observed a great variety of these aërial images of vessels approaching the horizon.

Fig. 33.

Sometimes there was seen only one inverted image above the real ship, and this was generally the case when the real ship was full in view. But when the real ship was just beginning to show its topmast above the horizon, as at A, Fig. 33, two aërial images of it were seen, one at B inverted, and the other in its natural position at C. In this case the sea was distinctly visible between the erect and inverted images, but in other cases the hull of the one image was immediately in contact with the hull of the other.

Analogous phenomena were seen by Captain Scoresby when navigating with the ship *Baffin* in the icy sea in the immediate neighbourhood of West Greenland. On the 28th of June, 1820, he observed about eighteen sail of ships at the distance of ten or fifteen miles. The sun had shone during the day without the interposition of a cloud, and his rays were peculiarly powerful. The intensity of its light occasioned a painful sensation in the eyes, while its heat softened the tar in the rigging of the ship, and melted the snow on the surrounding ice with such rapidity, that pools of fresh water were formed on almost every place, and thousands of rills carried the excess into the sea. There was scarcely a breath of wind: the sea was as smooth as a mirror. The surrounding ice was crowded together, and exhibited every variety, from the smallest lumps to the most magnificent sheets. Bears traversed the fields and floes in unusual numbers, and many whales sported in the recesses and openings among the drift ice. About six in the evening, a light breeze at N.W. having sprung up, a thin stratus or "fog bank," at first considerably illuminated by the sun, appeared in the same quarter, and gradually rose to the altitude of about a quarter of a degree. At this time most of the ships navigating at the distance of ten or fifteen miles began to change their form and magnitude, and when examined by a telescope from the masthead exhibited some extra-ordinary appearances, which differed at almost every point of the compass. One ship had a perfect image, as dark and distinct as the original, united to its masthead in a reverse position. Two others presented two distinct inverted images in the air, one of them a perfect figure of the original, and the other wanting the hull. Two or three more were strangely distorted, their masts appearing of at least twice their proper height, the top-gallant mast forming one-half of the total elevation, and other vessels exhibited an appearance totally different from all the preceding, being as it were compressed in place of elongated. Their masts seemed to be scarcely one-half of their proper altitude, in consequence of which one would have supposed that they were greatly heeled to one side, or in the position called careening. Along with all the images of the ships a reflection of the ice, sometimes in two strata, also appeared in the air, and these reflections suggested the idea of cliffs composed of vertical columns of alabaster.

On the 15th, 16th, and 17th of the same month, Mr. Scoresby observed similar phenomena, sometimes extending continuously through half the circumference of the horizon, and at other times appearing only in detached spots in various quarters. The inverted images of distant vessels were often seen in the air, *while the ships themselves were far beyond the reach of vision.* Some ships were elevated to twice their proper height, while others were compressed almost to a line. Hummocks of ice were surprisingly enlarged, and every prominent object in a proper position was either magnified or distorted.

But of all the phenomena witnessed by Mr. Scoresby, that of the *Enchanted Coast*, as it may be called, must have been the most remarkable. This singular effect was seen on the 18th July, when the sky was clear, and a tremulous and perfectly transparent vapour was particularly sensible and profuse. At nine o'clock in the morning, when the phenomenon was first seen, the thermometer stood at 42° Fahr., but in the preceding evening it must have been greatly lower, as the sea was in many places covered with a considerable pellicle of new ice,—a circumstance which in the very warmest time of the year must be considered as quite extraordinary, especially when it is known that 10° farther to the north no freezing of the sea at this season had ever before been observed. Having approached on this occasion so near the unexplored shore of Greenland that the land appeared distinct and bold, Mr. Scoresby was anxious to obtain a drawing of it, but on making the attempt he found that the outline was constantly changing, and he was induced to examine the coast with a telescope, and to sketch the various appearances which presented themselves. These are shown, without any regard to their proper order, in Fig. 34, which we shall describe in Mr. Scoresby's own words: "The general telescopic appearance of the coast was that of an extensive ancient city abounding with the ruins of castles, obelisks, churches and monuments, with other large and conspicuous buildings. Some of the hills seemed to be surmounted by turrets, battlements, spires, and pinnacles; while others, subjected to one or two reflections, exhibited large masses of rock, apparently suspended in the air, at a considerable elevation above the actual termination of the mountains to which they referred. The whole exhibition was a grand phantasmagoria. Scarcely was any particular portion sketched before it changed its appearance, and assumed the form of an object totally different. It was perhaps alternately a castle, a cathedral, or an obelisk; then expanding horizontally, and coalescing with the adjoining hills, united the intermediate valleys, though some miles in width, by a bridge of a single arch, of the most magnificent appearance and extent.   Notwithstanding these repeated changes, the various figures represented in the drawing had all the distinctness of reality ; and not only the different strata, but also the veins of the rocks, with the wreaths of snow occupying ravines and fissures, formed sharp and distinct lines, and exhibited every appearance of the most perfect solidity."

Fig. 34.

One of the most remarkable facts respecting aërial images presented itself to Mr. Scoresby in a later voyage which he performed to the coast of Greenland in 1822. Having seen an inverted image of a ship in the air he directed to it his telescope ; he was able to discover it to be his father's ship, which was at the time below the horizon. "It was," says he, "so well defined, that I could distinguish by a telescope every sail, the general rig of the ship, and its particular character; insomuch, that I confidently pronounced it to be my father's ship, the *Fame*, which it afterwards proved to be; though, on comparing notes with my father, I found that our relative position, at the time, gave a distance from one another of very nearly thirty miles, being about seventeen miles beyond the horizon, and some leagues beyond the limit of direct vision. I was so struck with the peculiarity of the circumstance, that I mentioned it to the officer of the watch, stating my full conviction that the *Fame* was then cruising in the neighbouring inlet."

Several curious effects of the mirage were observed by Baron Humboldt during his travels in South America. When he was residing at Cumana, he frequently saw the islands of Picuita and Boracha suspended in the air, and sometimes with an inverted image. On one occasion he observed small fishing-boats swimming in the air, during more than three or four minutes, above the well-defined horizon of the sea, and when they were viewed through a telescope, one of the boats had an inverted image accompanying it in its movements. This distinguished traveller observed similar phenomena in the barren steppes of the Caraccas, and on the borders of the Orinoco, where the river is surrounded by sandy plains. Little hills and chains of hills appeared suspended in the air, when seen from the steppes, at three or four leagues distance. Palm trees standing single in the Llanos appeared to be cut off at bottom, as if a stratum of air separated them from the ground; and, as in the African desert, plains destitute of vegetation appeared to be rivers or lakes. At the Mesa de Pavona M. Humboldt and M. Bonpland *saw cows suspended in the air* at the distance of 1000 toises, and having their feet elevated 3' 20" above the soil. In this case the images were erect, but the travellers learned from good authority that *inverted images of horses had been seen suspended in the air* near Calabozo.

In all these cases of aërial spectres the images were directly above the real object; but a curious case was observed by MM. Jurine and Soret on the 17th September, 1818, where the image of the vessel was on one side of the real one.   About 10_h P.M. a bark at the distance of about 4000 toises from Bellerive, on the lake of Geneva, was seen approaching to Geneva, by the *left* bank of the lake, and at the same time an image of the sails was observed above the water, which, instead of following the direction of the bark, separated from it, and appeared to approach Geneva by the right bank of the lake, the *image* moving from *east* to *west*, while the *bark* moved from *north* to *south*.   When the image first separated from the bark they had both the same magnitude, but the image diminished as it receded from it, and was reduced to one-half when the phenomenon disappeared.

A very unusual example of aërial spectres occurred to Dr. A. P. Buchan while walking on the cliff about a mile to the east of Brighton on the morning of the 28th November, 1804.   "While watching the rising of the sun," says he, "I turned my eyes directly towards the sea, just as the solar disc emerged from the surface of the water, and saw the face of the cliff on which I was standing represented precisely opposite to me at some distance on the ocean.   Calling the attention of my companion to this appearance, we discerned our own figures standing on the summit of the apparent opposite cliff, as well as the representation of the windmill near at hand.

"The reflected images were most distinct precisely opposite to where we stood, and the false cliff seemed to fade away, and to draw near to the real one, in proportion as it receded towards the west.   This phenomenon lasted about ten minutes, or till the sun had risen nearly his own diameter above the surface of the ocean.   The whole then seemed to be elevated into the air, and successively disappeared, giving an impression very similar to that which is produced by the drawing up of a drop scene in the theatre. The horizon was cloudy, or perhaps it might with more propriety be said that the surface of the sea was covered with a dense fog of many yards in height, and which gradually receded before the rays of the sun."

An illusion of a different kind, though not less interesting, is described by the Reverend Mr. Hughes in his Travels in Greece, as seen from the summit of Mount Ætna. "I must not forget to mention," says he, "one extraordinary phenomenon which we observed, and for which I have searched in vain for a satisfactory solution. At the extremity of the vast shadow which Ætna projects across the island, appeared a perfect and distinct image of the mountain itself elevated above the horizon, and diminished as if viewed in a concave mirror. Where or what the reflector could be which exhibited this image I cannot conceive; we could not be mistaken in its appearance, for all our party observed it, and we had been prepared for it beforehand by our Catanian friends. It remained visible about *ten* minutes, and disappeared as the shadow decreased. Mr. Jones observed the same phenomenon, as well as some other friends with whom I conversed upon the subject in England."

It is impossible to study the preceding phenomena without being impressed with the conviction that nature is full of the marvellous, and that the progress of science and the diffusion of knowledge are alone capable of dispelling the fears which her wonders must necessarily excite even in enlightened minds. When a spectre haunts the couch of the sick, or follows the susceptible vision of the invalid, a consciousness of indisposition divests the apparition of much of its terror, while its invisibility to surrounding friends soon stamps it with the impress of a false perception. The spectres of the conjurer too, however skilfully they may be raised, quickly lose their supernatural character, and even the most ignorant beholder regards the modern magician as but an ordinary man, who borrows from the sciences the best working implements of his art. But when, in the midst of solitude, and in situations where the mind is undisturbed by sublunary cares, we see our own image delineated in the air, and mimicking in gigantic perspective the tiny movements of humanity :—when we see troops in military array performing their evolutions on the very face of an almost inaccessible precipice;—when in the eye of day a mountain seems to become transparent, and exhibits on one side of it a castle which we know to exist only on the other;—when distant objects, concealed by the roundness of the earth, and beyond the cognizance of the telescope, are actually transferred over the intervening convexity and presented in distinct and magnified outline to our accurate examination;—when such varied and striking phantasms are seen also by all around us, and therefore appear in the character of real phenomena of nature, our impressions of supernatural agency can only be removed by a distinct and satisfactory knowledge of the causes which gave them birth.

It is only within the last forty years that science has brought these atmospherical spectres within the circle of her dominion; and not only are all their phenomena susceptible of distinct explanation, but we can even reproduce them on a small scale with the simplest elements of our optical apparatus.

In order to convey a general idea of the causes of these phenomena, let A B C D, Fig. 35, be a glass trough filled with water, and let a small ship be placed at S. An eye situated about E, will see the topmast of the ship S directly through the plate of glass B D. Fix a convex lens a of short focus upon the plate of glass B D, and a little above a straight line S E joining the ship and the eye; and immediately above the convex lens a place a concave one *b*. The eye will now see through the convex lens *a* an *inverted* image of the ship at S', and through the concave lens *b*, an erect image of the ship at S", representing in a

Fig. 35.

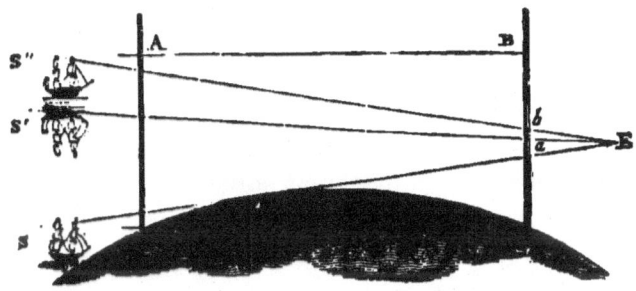

general way the phenomena shown in Fig. 33. But it will be asked, where are the lenses in nature to produce these effects? This question is easily answered. If we take a tin tube with glass plates at each end, and fill it with water, and if we cool it on the outside with ice, it will act like a *concave* lens when the cooling effect has reached the axis; and, on the other hand, if we heat the same tube filled with water, on the outside, it will act as a *convex* glass. In the first case the density of the water diminishes towards the centre, and in the second it increases towards the centre. The very same effects are produced in the air, only a greater tract of air is necessary for showing the effect produced, by heating and cooling it unequally. If we now remove the lenses *a*, *b*, and hold a heated iron horizontally above the water in the trough A B C, the heat will gradually descend, expanding or rendering rarer the upper portions of the fluid. If, when the heat has reached within a little of the bottom, we look through the trough at the ship S in the direction E S', we shall see an inverted image at S', and an erect one at S", and if we hide from the eye at E all

Q

the ship S excepting the topmast, we shall have an exact representation of the phenomenon in Fig. 33. The experiment will succeed better with oil in place of water; and the same result may be obtained without heat, by pouring clear syrup into the glass trough till it is nearly one-third full, and then filling it up with water. The water will gradually incorporate with the syrup, and produce, as Dr. Wollaston has shown, a regular gradation of density, diminishing from that of the pure syrup to that of the pure water. Similar effects may be obtained by using masses of transparent solids, such as glass, rock salt, &c.

Now it is easy to conceive how the changes of density which we can thus produce artificially may be produced in nature. If in serene weather the surface of the sea is much colder than the air of the atmosphere, as it frequently is, and as it was to a very great degree during the phenomena described by Mr. Scoresby, the air next the sea will gradually become colder and colder, by giving out its heat to the water; and the air immediately above will give out its heat to the cooler air immediately below it, so that the air from the surface of the sea, to a considerable height upwards, will gradually diminish in density, and therefore must produce the very phenomena we have described.

The phenomenon of Dover Castle, seen on the Ramsgate side of the hill, was produced by the air being more dense near the ground, and above the sea, than at greater heights, and hence the rays proceeding from the castle reached the eye in curved lines, and the cause of its occupying its natural position on the hill, and not being seen in the air, was that the top of the hill itself, in consequence of being so near the castle, suffered the same change from the varying density of the air, and therefore the castle and the hill were equally elevated and retained their relative positions. The reason why the image of the castle and the hill appeared erect was that the rays from the top and bottom of the castle had not crossed before they reached Ramsgate; but as they met at Ramsgate, an eye at a greater distance from the castle, and in the path of the rays, would have seen the image inverted. This will be better understood from the annexed diagram, which represents the actual progress of the rays, from a ship S P, concealed from the observer at E by the convexity of the

Fig. 36.

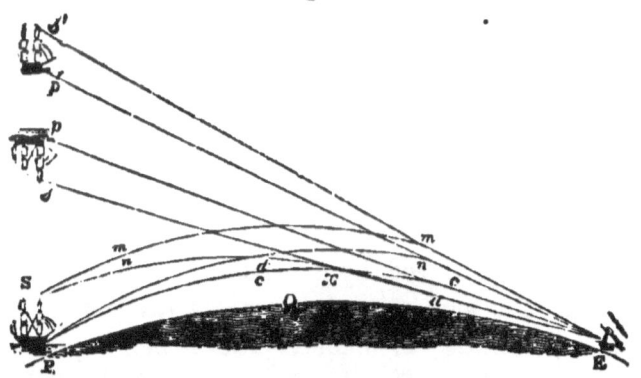

earth P Q E. A ray proceeding from the keel of the ship P is refracted into the curve line P c x c E, and a ray proceeding from the topmast S is refracted in the direction S d x d E, the two rays crossing at x, and proceeding to the eye E with the ray from the keel P uppermost; hence the ship must appear inverted as at s p. Now if the eye E of the observer had been placed nearer the ship as at x, before the rays crossed, as was the case at Ramsgate, it would have seen an erect image of the ship raised a little above the real ship S P. Rays S m, S n, proceeding higher up in the air, are refracted in the directions S m m E, S n n E, but do not cross before they reach the eye, and therefore they afford the erect image of the ship shown at s' p'.

The aërial troopers seen at Souterfell were produced by the very same process as the spectre of Dover Castle, having been brought by unequal refraction from one side of the hill to the other. It is not our business to discover how a troop of soldiers came to be performing their evolutions on the other side of Souterfell; but if there was then no road along which they could be marching, it is highly probable that they were troops exercising among the hills in secret previous to the breaking out of the Rebellion in 1745.

The image of the Genevese bark which was seen sailing at a distance from the real one, arose from the same cause as the images of ships in the air, with this difference only, that in this case the strata of equal density were vertical or perpendicular to the water, whereas in the former cases they were horizontal or parallel to the water. The state of the air which produced the lateral image may be produced by a headland or island, or even rocks, near the surface, and covered with water. These headlands, islands, or sunken rocks being powerfully heated by the sun in the daytime, will heat the air immediately above them, while the adjacent air over the sea will retain its former coolness and density. Hence there will necessarily arise a gradation of density varying in the same horizontal direction, or where the lines of equal density are vertical. If we suppose the very same state of the air to exist in a horizontal plane which exists in a vertical plane, in Fig. 36, then the same images would be seen in a horizontal line, viz., an inverted one at $s\,p$, and an erect one at $s'\,p'$. In the case of the Genevese bark the rays had not crossed before they reached the eye, and therefore the image was an erect one. Had the real Genevese bark been concealed by some promontory or other cause from the observation of MM. Jurine and Soret, they might have attached a supernatural character to the spectral image, especially if they had seen it gradually decay, and finally disappear on the still and unbroken surface of the lake. No similar fact had been previously observed, and there were no circumstances in the case to have excited the suspicion that it was the spectre of a real vessel produced by unequal refraction.

The spectre of the Brocken and other phenomena of the same kind have essentially a different origin from those which arise from unequal refraction. They are merely shadows of the observer projected on dense vapour or thin fleecy clouds, which have the power of reflecting much light. They are seen most frequently at sunrise, because it is at that time that the vapours and clouds necessary for their production are most likely to be generated; and they can be seen only when the sun is throwing his rays horizontally, because the shadow of the observer would otherwise be thrown either up in the air, or down upon the ground. If there are two persons looking at the phenomenon, as when M. Haue and the landlord saw it together, each observer will see his own image most distinctly, and the head will be more distinct than the rest of the figure, because the rays of the sun will be more copiously reflected at a perpendicular incidence; and as from this cause the light reflected from the vapour or cloud becomes fainter farther from the shadow, the appearance of a halo round the head of the observer is frequently visible. M. Haue mentions the extraordinary circumstance of the two spectres of him and the landlord being joined by a *third figure*, but he unfortunately does not inform us which of the two figures was doubled, for it is impossible that a person could have joined their party unobserved. It is very probable that the new spectre forms a natural addition to the group, as we have represented it in Fig. 30, and if this was the case, it could only have been produced by a duplication of one of the figures produced by unequal refraction.

The reflected spectre of Dr. Buchan standing upon the cliff at Brighton arose from a cause to which we have not yet adverted. It was obviously no shadow, for it is certain, from the locality, that the rays of the sun fell upon the face of the cliff and upon his person at an angle of about 73° from the perpendicular, so as to illuminate them strongly. Now there are two ways in which such an image may have been reflected, namely, either from strata of air of variable density, or from a vertical stratum of vapour, consisting of exceedingly minute globules of water. Whenever light suffers refraction, either in passing at once from one medium into another, or from one part of the same medium into another of different density, a portion of it suffers reflection. If an object, therefore, were strongly illuminated, a sufficiently distinct image, or rather shadow of it, might be seen by reflection from strata of air of different density. As the temperature at which moisture is deposited in the atmosphere varies with the density of the air, then at the same temperature moisture might be depositing in a stratum of one density, while no deposition is taking place in the adjacent stratum of a different density. Hence there would exist as it were in the air a vertical wall or stratum of minute globules of water, from the surface of which a sufficiently distinct image of a highly-illuminated object might be reflected. That this is possible may be proved by breathing upon glass. If the particles deposited upon the glass are large, then no distinct reflection will take place; but if the particles be very small, we shall see a distinct image formed by the surface of the aqueous film.

The phenomena of the Fata Morgana have been too imperfectly described to enable us to offer a satisfactory explanation of them. The aërial images are obviously those formed by unequal refraction. The pictures seen on the sea may be either the aërial images reflected from its surface, or from a stratum of dense vapour, or they may be the direct reflections from the objects themselves. The coloured images, as described by Minasi, have never been seen in any analogous phenomena, and require to be better described before they can be submitted to scientific examination.

The representation of ships in the air by unequal refraction has no doubt given rise in early times to those superstitions which have prevailed in different countries respecting " phantom ships," as Mr. Washington Irving calls them, which always sail in the eye of the wind, and plough their way through the smooth sea, where there is not a breath of wind upon its surface. In his beautiful story of the storm ship, which makes its way up the Hudson against wind and tide, this elegant writer has finely embodied one of the most interesting superstitions of the early American colonists. The Flying Dutchman had in all probability a similar origin, and the wizard beacon-keeper of the Isle of France, who saw in the air the vessels bound to the island long before they appeared in the offing, must have derived his power from a diligent observation of the phenomena of nature.

LETTER VII.

Illusions depending on the ear—Practised by the ancients—Speaking and singing heads of the ancients—Exhibition of the invisible girl described and explained—Illusions arising from the difficulty of determining the direction of sounds—Singular example of this illusion—Nature of ventriloquism—Exhibitions of some of the most celebrated ventriloquists—M. St. Gille—Louis Brabant—M. Alexandre—Captain Lyon's account of Esquimaux ventriloquists.

NEXT to the eye the ear is the most fertile source of our illusions, and the ancient magicians seem to have been very successful in turning to their purposes the doctrines of sound. In the labyrinth of Egypt, which contained twelve palaces and 1500 subterraneous apartments, the gods were made to speak in a voice of thunder; and Pliny, in whose time this singular structure existed, informs us that some of the palaces were so constructed that their doors could not be opened without permitting the peals of thunder from being heard in the interior. When Darius Hystaspes ascended the throne, and allowed his subjects to prostrate themselves before him as a god, the divinity of his character was impressed upon his worshippers by the bursts of thunder and flashes of lightning which accompanied their devotion. History has of course not informed us how these effects were produced; but it is probable that, in the subterraneous and vaulted apartments of the Egyptian labyrinth, the reverberated sounds arising from the mere opening and shutting of the doors themselves afforded a sufficient imitation of ordinary thunder. In the palace of the Persian king, however, a more artificial imitation is likely to have been employed, and it is not improbable that the method used in our modern theatres was known to the ancients. A thin sheet of iron, three or four feet long, such as that used for German stoves, is held by one corner between the finger and the thumb, and allowed to hang freely by its own weight. The hand is then moved or shaken horizontally, so as to agitate the corner in a direction at right angles to the surface of the sheet. By this simple process a great variety of sounds will be produced, varying from the deep growl of distant thunder to those loud and explosive bursts which rattle in quick succession from clouds immediately over our heads. The operator soon acquires great power over this instrument, so as to be able to produce from it any intensity and character of sound that may be required. The same effect may be produced by sheets of tin plate, and by thin plates of mica; but on account of their small size, the sound is shorter and more acute. In modern exhibitions an admirable imitation of lightning is produced by throwing the powder of rosin, or the dust of lycopodium, through a flame, and the rattling showers of rain which accompany these meteors are well imitated by a well-regulated shower of peas.

. The principal pieces of acoustic mechanism used by the ancients were *speaking* or *singing heads*, which were constructed for the purpose of representing the gods, or of uttering oracular responses. Among these, the speaking head of Orpheus, which uttered its responses at Lesbos, is one of the most famous. It was celebrated not only throughout Greece, but even in Persia, and it had the credit of predicting, in the equivocal language of the heathen oracles, the bloody death which terminated the expedition of Cyrus the Great into Scythia. Odin, the mighty magician of the north, who imported into Scandinavia the magical arts of the east, possessed a speaking head, said to be that of the sage Minos, which he had enchased in gold, and which uttered responses that had all the authority of a divine revelation. The celebrated mechanic Gerbert, who filled the Papal chair A.D. 1000, under the name of Sylvester II., constructed a speaking head of brass. Albertus Magnus is said to have executed a head in the thirteenth century, which not only moved but spoke. It was made of earthenware, and Thomas Aquinas is said to have been so terrified when he saw it, that he broke it in pieces, upon which the mechanist exclaimed, " There goes the labour of thirty years."

It has been supposed by some authors, that in the ancient speaking-machines the deception was effected by means of ventriloquism, the voice issuing from the juggler himself; but it is more probable that the sound was conveyed by pipes from a person in another apartment to the mouth of the figure. Lucian, indeed, expressly informs us that the impostor Alexander made his figure of Æsculapius speak, by transmitting his voice through the gullet of a crane to the mouth of the statue; and that this method was general, appears from a passage in Theodoretus, who assures us that in the fourth century, when Bishop Theophilus broke to pieces the statues at Alexandria, he found some which were hollow, and which were so placed against a wall, that the priest could conceal himself behind them, and address the ignorant spectators through their mouths.

Even in modern times, speaking-machines have been constructed on this principle. The figure is frequently a mere head placed upon a hollow pedestal, which, in order to promote the deception, contains a pair of bellows, a sounding-board, a cylinder and pipes supposed to represent the organs of speech. In other cases these are dispensed with, and a simple wooden head utters its sounds through a speaking-trumpet. At the court of Charles II. this deception was exhibited with great effect by one Thomas Irson, an Englishman, and when the astonishment had become very general, a popish priest was discovered by one of the pages in an adjoining apartment. The questions had been proposed to the wooden figure by whispering into its ear, and this learned personage had answered them all with great ability, by speaking through a pipe in the same language in which the questions were proposed. Professor Beckmann informs us that children and women were generally concealed either in the juggler's box, or in the adjacent apartment, and that the juggler gave them every assistance by means of signs previously agreed upon. When one of these exhibitions was shown at Gottingen, the Professor was allowed, on the promise of secrecy, to witness the process of deception. He saw the assistant in another room, standing before the pipe with a card in his hand, upon which the signs agreed upon had been marked, and he had been introduced so privately into the house that even the landlady was ignorant of his being there.

An exhibition of the very same kind has been brought forward in our own day, under the name of the *Invisible Girl;* and as the mechanism employed was extremely ingenious, and is well fitted to convey an idea of this class of deceptions, we shall give a detailed description of it.

The machinery, as contructed by M. Charles, is shown in Fig. 37 in perspective, and a plan of it in Fig. 38. The four upright posts A, A, A, A, are united at top by a cross rail B, B, and by two similar rails at bottom. Four bent wires a, a, a, a, proceeded from the top of these posts, and terminated at c. A hollow copper ball M, about a foot in diameter, was suspended from these wires by four slender ribands b, b, b, b, and into the copper ball were fixed the extremities of four trumpets T, T, T, T, with their mouths outwards.

Fig. 37.

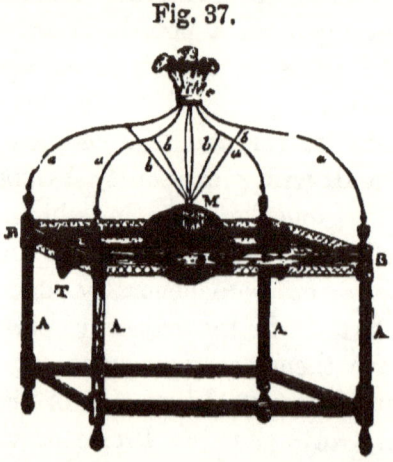

The apparatus now described was all that was visible to the spectator; and though fixed in one spot, yet it had the appearance of a piece of separate machinery, which might have occupied any other part of the room.

Fig. 38.

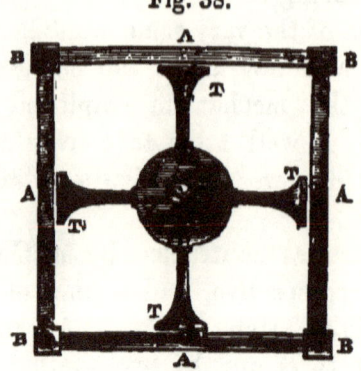

When one of the spectators was requested by the exhibitor to propose some question, he did it by speaking into one of the trumpets at T. An appropriate answer was then returned from all the trumpets, and the sound issued with sufficient intensity to be heard by an ear applied to any of them, and yet it was so weak that it appeared to come from a person of very diminutive size. Hence the sound was supposed to come from an invisible girl, though the real speaker was a full-grown woman. The invisible lady conversed in different languages, sang beautifully, and made the most lively and appropriate remarks on the persons in the room.

This exhibition was obviously far more wonderful than the speaking heads which we have described, as the latter invariably communicated with a wall, or with a pedestal through which pipes could be carried into the next apartment. But the ball M and its trumpets communicated with nothing through which sound could be conveyed. The spectator satisfied himself by examination that the ribands b, b, were real ribands, which concealed nothing, and which could convey no sound, and as he never conceived that the ordinary piece of frame-work A B, could be of any other use than its apparent one of supporting the sphere M, and defending it from the spectators, he was left in utter amazement respecting the origin of the sound, and his surprise was increased by the difference between the sounds which were uttered and those of ordinary speech.

Though the spectators were thus deceived by their own reasoning, yet the process of deception was a very simple one. In two of the horizontal railings A, A, Fig. 38, opposite the trumpet mouths T, there was an aperture communicating with a pipe or tube which went to the vertical post B, and descending it, as shown at T A A, Fig. 39, went beneath the floor $f f$ in the direction $p, p,$ and entered the apartment N, where the invisible lady sat. On the side of the partition about h, there was a small hole, through which the lady saw what was going on in the exhibition room, and communications were no doubt made to her by signals from the person who attended the machine. When one of the spectators asked a question by speaking into one of the trumpets T, the sound was reflected from the mouth of the trumpet back to the aperture at A, in the horizontal rail, Fig. 38.

Fig. 39.

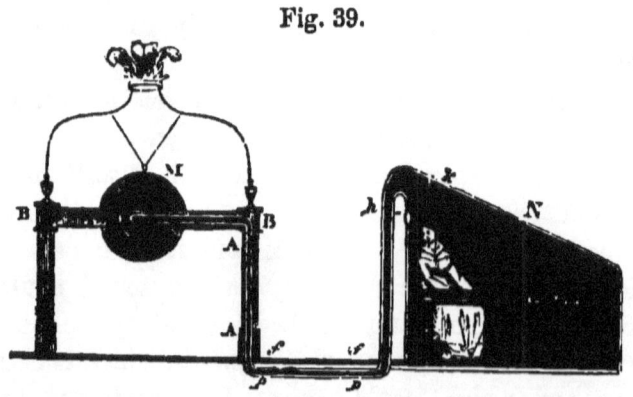

and was distinctly conveyed along the closed tube into the apartment N. In like manner the answer issued from the aperture A, and being reflected back to the ear of the spectator by the trumpet, he heard the sounds with that change of character which they receive when transmitted through a tube and then reflected to the ear.

The surprise of the auditors was greatly increased by the circumstance, that an answer was returned to questions put in a whisper, and also by the conviction that nobody but a person in the middle of the audience could observe the circumstances to which the invisible figure frequently adverted.

Although the performances of speaking heads were generally effected by the methods now described. yet there is reason to think that the ventriloquist sometimes presided at the exhibition, and deceived the audience by his extraordinary powers of illusion. There is no species of deception more irresistible in its effects than that which arises from the uncertainty with which we judge of the direction and distance of sounds. · Every person must have noticed how a sound in their own ears is often mistaken for some loud noise moderated by the distance from which it is supposed to come; and the sportsman must have frequently been surprised at the existence of musical sounds humming remotely in the extended heath, when it was only the wind sounding in the barrel of his gun. The great proportion of apparitions that haunt old castles and apartments associated with death exist only in the sounds which accompany them. The imagination even of the boldest inmate of a place hallowed by superstition, will transfer some trifling sound near his own person to a direction and to a distance very different from the truth, and the sound which otherwise might have no peculiar complexion will derive another character from its new locality. Spurning the idea of a supernatural origin, he determines to unmask the spectre, and grapple with it in its den. All the inmates of the house are found to be asleep—even the quadrupeds are in their lair—there is not a breath of wind to ruffle the lake that reflects through the casement the reclining crescent of the night; and the massive walls in which he is inclosed forbid the idea that he has been disturbed by the warping of panelling or the bending of partitions. His search is vain ; and he remains master of his own secret, till he has another opportunity of investigation. The same sound again disturbs him, and, modified probably by his own position at the time, it may perhaps appear to come in a direction slightly different from the last. His searches are resumed, and he is again disappointed. If this incident should recur night after night with the same result ;—if the sound should appear to depend upon his own motions, or be anyhow associated with himself, with his present feelings, or with his past history, his personal courage will give way, a superstitious dread, at which he himself perhaps laughs, will seize his mind, and he will rather believe that the sounds have a supernatural origin than that they could continue to issue from a spot where he knows there is no natural cause for their production.

I have had occasion to have personal knowledge of a case much stronger than that which has now been put. A gentleman, devoid of all superstitious feelings, and living in a house free from any gloomy associations, heard night after night in his bedroom a singular noise unlike any ordinary sound to which he was accustomed. Ho had slept in the same room for years without hearing it, and he attributed it at first to some change of circumstances in the roof or in the walls of the room, but after the strictest examination no cause could be found for it. It occurred only once in the night; it was heard almost every night, with few interruptions. It was over in an instant, and it never took place till after the gentleman had gone to bed. It was always distinctly heard by his companion, to whose time of going to bed it had no relation. It depended on the gentleman alone, and it followed him into another apartment with another bed, on the opposite side of the house. Accustomed to such investigations, he made the most diligent but fruitless search into its cause. The consideration that the sound had a special reference to him alone, operated upon his imagination, and he did not scruple to acknowledge that the recurrence of the mysterious sound produced a superstitious feeling at the moment. Many months afterwards it was found that the sound arose from the partial opening of the door of a wardrobe which was within a few feet of the gentleman's head, and which had been taken into the other apartment. This wardrobe was almost always opened before he retired to bed, and the door being a little too tight, it gradually forced itself open with a sort of dull sound, resembling the note of a drum. As the door had only started half an inch out of its place, its change of place never attracted attention. The sound, indeed, seemed to come in a different direction, and from a greater distance.

When sounds so mysterious in their origin are heard by persons predisposed to a belief in the marvellous, their influence over the mind must be very powerful. An inquiry into their origin, if it is made at all, will be made more in the hope of confirming than of removing the original impression, and the unfortunate victim of his own fears will also be the willing dupe of his own judgment.

This uncertainty with respect to the direction of sound is the foundation of the art of ventriloquism. If we place ten men in a row at such a distance from us that they are included in the angle within which we cannot judge of the direction of sound, and if in a calm day each of them speaks in succession, we shall not be able with closed eyes to determine from which of the ten men any of the sounds proceeds, and we shall be incapable of perceiving that there is any difference in the direction of the sounds emitted by the two uttermost. If a man and a child are placed within the same angle, and if the man speaks with the accent of a child without any corresponding motion in his mouth or face, we shall necessarily believe that the voice comes from the child : nay, if the child is so distant from the man that the voice actually appears to us to come from the man, we will still continue in the belief that the child is the speaker ; and this con- viction would acquire additional strength if the child favoured the deception by accommodating its features and

R

gestures to the words spoken by the man. So powerful, indeed, is the influence of this deception, that if a jack-ass placed near the man were to open its mouth, and shake its head responsive to the words uttered by his neighbour, we would rather believe that the ass spoke than that the sounds proceeded from ·a person whose mouth was shut, and the muscles of whose face were in perfect repose. If our imagination were even directed to a marble statue or a lump of inanimate matter, as the source from which we were to expect the sounds to issue, we would still be deceived, and would refer the sounds even to these lifeless objects. The illusion would be greatly promoted if the voice were totally different in its tone and character from that of the man from whom it really comes; and if he occasionally speak in his own full and measured voice, the belief will be irresistible that the assumed voice proceeds from the quadruped or from the inanimate object.

When the sounds which are required to proceed from any given object are such as they are actually calculated to yield, the process of deception is extremely easy, and it may be successfully executed even if the angle between the real and the supposed directions of the sound is much greater than the angle of uncertainty. Mr. Dugald Stewart has stated some cases in which deceptions of this kind were very perfect. He mentions his having seen a person who, by counterfeiting the gesticulations of a performer on the violin, while he imitated the music by his voice, riveted the eyes of his audience on the instrument, though every sound they heard proceeded from his own mouth. The late Savile Carey, who imitated the whistling of the wind through a narrow chink, told Mr. Stewart that he had frequently practised this deception in the corner of a coffee-house, and that he seldom failed to see some of the company rise to examine the tightness of the windows, while others, more intent on their newspapers, contented themselves with putting on their hats and buttoning their coats. Mr. Stewart likewise mentions an exhibition formerly common in some of the continental theatres, where a performer on the stage displayed the dumb show of singing with his lips and eyes and gestures, while another person unseen supplied the music with his voice. The deception in this case he found to be at first so complete as to impose upon the nicest ear and the quickest eye; but in the progress of the entertainment he became distinctly sensible of the imposition, and sometimes wondered that it should have misled him for a moment. In this case there can be no doubt that the deception was at first the work of the imagination, and was not sustained by the acoustic principle. The real and the mock singer were too distant, and when the influence of the imagination subsided, the true direction of the sound was discovered. This detection of the imposture, however, may have arisen from another cause. If the mock singer happened to change the position of his head, while the real singer made no corresponding change in his voice, the attentive spectator would at once notice this incongruity, and discover the imposition.

In many of the feats of ventriloquism the performer contrives, under some pretence or other, to conceal his face, but ventriloquists of great distinction, such as M. Alexandre, practise their art without any such concealment.

Ventriloquism loses its distinctive character if its imitations are not performed with a voice from the belly. The voice, indeed, does not actually come from that region, but when the ventriloquist utters sounds from the larynx without moving the muscles of his face, he gives them strength by a powerful action of the abdominal muscles. Hence he speaks by means of his belly, although the throat is the real source from which the sounds proceed. Mr. Dugald Stewart has doubted the fact, that ventriloquists possess the power of fetching a voice from within : he cannot conceive what aid could be derived from such an extraordinary power; and he considers that the imagination, when seconded by such powers of imitation as some mimics possess, is quite sufficient to account for all the phenomena of ventriloquism which he has heard. This opinion, however, is strongly opposed by the remark made to Mr. Stewart himself by a ventriloquist, "that his art would be perfect if it were possible only to speak distinctly without any movement of the lips at all." But, independent of this admission, it is a matter of absolute certainty, that this internal power is exercised by the true ventriloquist. In the account which the Abbé Chapelle has given of the performances of M. St. Gille and Louis Brabant, he distinctly states that M. St. Gille appeared to be absolutely mute while he was exercising his art, and that no change in his countenance could be discovered.* He affirms also that the countenance of Louis Brabant exhibited no change, and that his lips were close and inactive. M. Richerand, who attentively watched the performances of M. Fitz-James, assures us that during his exhibition there was a distension in the epigastric region, and that he could not long continue the exertion without fatigue.

The influence over the human mind which the ventriloquist derives from the skilful practice of his art is greater than that which is exercised by any other species of conjurer. The ordinary magician requires his theatre, his accomplices, and the instruments of his art, and he enjoys but a local sovereignty within the precincts of his

* *Edinburgh Journal of Science,* No. xviii. p. 254.

own magic circle. The ventriloquist, on the contrary, has the supernatural always at his command. In the open fields, as well as in the crowded city, in the private apartment, as well as in the public hall, he can summon up innumerable spirits ; and though the persons of his fictitious dialogue are not visible to the eye, yet they are as unequivocally present to the imagination of his auditors as if they had been shadowed forth in the silence of a spectral form. In order to convey some idea of the influence of this illusion, I shall mention a few well-authenticated cases of successful ventriloquism.

M. St. Gille, a grocer of St. Germain-en-Laye, whose performances have been recorded by the Abbé de la Chapelle, had occasion to shelter himself from a storm in a neighbouring convent, where the monks were in deep mourning for a much-esteemed member of their community who had been recently buried. While lamenting over the tomb of their deceased brother the slight honours which had been paid to his memory, a voice was suddenly heard to issue from the roof of the choir, bewailing the condition of the deceased in purgatory, and reproving the brotherhood for their want of zeal. The tidings of this supernatural event brought the whole brotherhood to the church. The voice from above repeated its lamentations and reproaches, and the whole convent fell upon their faces, and vowed to make a reparation of their error. They accordingly chanted in full choir a *De Profundis*, during the intervals of which the spirit of the departed monk expressed his satisfaction at their pious exercises. The prior afterwards inveighed against modern scepticism on the subject of apparitions, and M. St. Gille had great difficulty in convincing the fraternity that the whole was a deception.

On another occasion, a commission of the Royal Academy of Sciences at Paris, attended by several persons of the highest rank, met at St. Germain-en-Laye to witness the performances of M. St. Gille. The real object of their meeting was purposely withheld from a lady of the party, who was informed that an aërial spirit had lately established itself in the neighbourhood, and that the object of the assembly was to investigate the matter. When the party had sat down to dinner in the open air, the spirit addressed the lady in a voice which seemed to come from above their heads, from the surface of the ground at a great distance, or from a considerable depth under her feet. Having been thus addressed at intervals during two hours the lady was firmly convinced of the existence of the spirit, and could with difficulty be undeceived.

Another ventriloquist, Louis Brabant, who had been valet de chambre to Francis I., turned his powers to a more profitable account. Having fallen in love with a rich and beautiful heiress, he was rejected by her parents as an unsuitable match for their daughter. On the death of her father, Louis paid a visit to the widow, and he had no sooner entered the house than she heard the voice of her deceased husband addressing her from above, "Give my daughter in marriage to Louis Brabant, who is a man of large fortune and excellent character. I endure the inexpressible torments of purgatory for having refused her to him. Obey this admonition, and give everlasting repose to the soul of your poor husband." This awful command could not be resisted, and the widow announced her compliance with it.

As our conjurer, however, required money for the completion of his marriage, he resolved to work upon the fears of one Cornu, an old banker at Lyons, who had amassed immense wealth by usury and extortion. Having obtained an interview with the miser, he intro-

duced the subjects of demons and spectres and the
torments of purgatory, and, during an interval of silence,
the voice of the miser's deceased father was heard complaining of his dreadful situation in purgatory, and
calling upon his son to rescue him from his sufferings
by enabling Louis Brabant to redeem the Christians that
were enslaved by the Turks. The awe-struck miser was
also threatened with eternal damnation if he did not thus
expiate his own sins; but such was the grasp that the
banker took of his gold that the ventriloquist was
obliged to pay him another visit. On this occasion, not
only his father, but all his deceased relations appealed to
him in behalf of his own soul and theirs, and such was
the loudness of their complaints that the spirit of the
banker was subdued, and he gave the ventriloquist ten
thousand crowns to liberate the Christian captives.
When the miser was afterwards undeceived, he is said to
have been so mortified that he died of vexation.

The ventriloquists of the nineteenth century made great
additions to their art, and the performances of M. Fitz-
James and M. Alexandre, which must have been seen by
many of our countrymen, were far superior to those of
their predecessors. Besides the art of speaking by the
muscles of the throat and the abdomen, without moving
those of the face, these artists had not only studied with
great diligence and success the modifications which sounds
of all kinds undergo from distance, obstructions and other
causes, but had acquired the art of imitating them in the
highest perfection. The ventriloquist was therefore able
to carry on a dialogue in which the *dramatis voces*, as they
may be called, were numerous ; and when on the outside
of an apartment he could personate a mob with its infinite
variety of noise and vociferation. Their influence over an
audience was still further extended by a singular power
over the muscles of the body. M. Fitz-James actually

succeeded in making the opposite or corresponding muscles act differently from each other; and while one side of his face was merry and laughing, the other was full of sorrow and in tears. At one moment he was tall, thin, and melancholic, and after passing behind a screen he came out "bloated with obesity and staggering with fulness." M. Alexandre possessed the same power over his face and figure, and so striking was the contrast of two of these forms, that an excellent sculptor, Mr. Joseph, has perpetuated them in marble.

This new acquirement of the ventriloquist enabled him, in his own single person and with his own single voice, to represent upon the stage a dramatic composition which would have required the assistance of several actors. Although only one character in the piece could be seen at the same time, yet they all appeared during its performance, and the change of face and figure on the part of the ventriloquist was so perfect that his personal identity could not be recognised in the *dramatis personæ.* This deception was rendered still more complete by a particular construction of the dresses, which enabled the performer to reappear in a new character after an interval so short that the audience necessarily believed that it was another person.

It is a curious circumstance that Captain Lyon found among the Esquimaux of Igloolik ventriloquists of no mean skill. There is much rivalry amongst the professors of the art, who do not expose each other's secrets, and their exhibitions derive great importance from the rarity of their occurrence. The following account of one of them is so interesting that we shall give the whole of it in Captain Lyon's words.

"Amongst our Igloolik acquaintances were two females and a few male wizards, of whom the principal was Toolemak. This personage was cunning and intelligent, and, whether professionally, or from his skill in the chase, but perhaps from both reasons, was considered by all the tribe as a man of importance. As I invariably paid great deference to his opinion on all subjects connected with his calling, he freely communicated to me his superior knowledge, and did not scruple to allow of my being present at his interviews with Tornga, or his patron spirit. In consequence of this, I took an early opportunity of requesting my friend to exhibit his skill in my cabin. His old wife was with him, and by much flattery and an accidental display of a glittering knife and some beads, she assisted me in obtaining my request. All light excluded, our sorcerer began chanting to his wife with great vehemence, and she in return answered by singing the Amna-aya, which was not discontinued during the whole ceremony. As far as I could hear, he afterwards began turning himself rapidly round, and in a loud powerful voice vociferated for Tornga with great impatience, at the same time blowing and snorting like a walrus. His noise, impatience, and agitation increased every moment, and he at length seated himself on the deck, varying his tones, and making a rustling with his clothes. Suddenly the voice seemed smothered, and was so managed as to sound as if retreating beneath the deck, each moment becoming more distant, and ultimately giving the idea of being many feet below the cabin, when it ceased entirely. His wife now, in answer to my queries, informed me very seriously that he had dived, and that he would send up Tornga. Accordingly, in about half a minute, a distant blowing was heard very slowly approaching, and a voice, which differed from that at first heard, was at times mingled with the blowing, until at length both sounds became distinct, and the old woman informed me that Tornga was come to answer my questions. I accordingly asked several questions of the sagacious spirit, to each of which inquiries I received an answer by two loud claps on the deck, which I was given to understand were favourable.

"A very hollow, yet powerful voice, certainly much different from the tones of Toolemak, now chanted for some time, and a strange jumble of hisses, groans, shouts, and gabblings like a turkey succeeded in rapid order. The old woman sang with increased energy, and as I took it for granted that this was all intended to astonish the Kabloona, I cried repeatedly that I was very much afraid. This, as I expected, added fuel to the fire, until the poor immortal, exhausted by its own might, asked leave to retire.

"The voice gradually sunk from our hearing as at first, and a very indistinct hissing succeeded; in its advance it sounded like the tone produced by the wind on the bass chord of an Æolian harp. This was soon changed to a rapid hiss like that of a rocket, and Toolemak with a yell announced his return. I had held my breath at the first distant hissing, and twice exhausted myself, yet our conjurer did not once respire, and even his returning and powerful yell was uttered without a previous stop or inspiration of air.

"Light being admitted, our wizard, as might be expected, was in a profuse perspiration, and certainly much exhausted by his exertions, which had continued for at least half an hour. We now observed a couple of bunches, each consisting of two stripes of white deer-skin and a long piece of sinew, attached to the back of his coat. These we had not seen before, and were informed that they had been sewn on by Tornga while he was below."*

Captain Lyon had the good fortune to witness another of Toolemak's exhibitions, and he was much struck with

* *Private Journal of Captain G. F. Lyon*, pp. 358, 361.

the wonderful steadiness of the wizard throughout the whole performance, which lasted an hour and a half. He did not once appear to move, for he was so close to the skin behind which Captain Lyon sat, that if he had done so he must have perceived it. Captain Lyon did not hear the least rustling of his clothes, or even distinguish his breathing, although his outcries were made with great exertion.*

* *Private Journal of Captain G. F. Lyon,* p. 363.

LETTER VIII.

*Musical and harmonic sounds explained—Power of breaking glasses
with the voice—Musical sounds from the vibration of a column of
air—And of solid bodies—Kaleidophone—Singular acoustic
figures produced on sand laid on vibrating plates of glass, and
on stretched membranes— Vibration of flat rulers, and cylinders
of glass—Production of silence from two sounds—Production of
darkness from two lights—Explanation of these singular effects—
Acoustic automaton—Droz's bleating sheep—Maillardet's singing
bird—Vaucanson's flute-player—His pipe and tabor player—
Baron Kempelen's talking engine — Kratzenstein's speaking
machine—Mr. Willis's researches.*

AMONG the discoveries of modern science there are few
more remarkable than those which relate to the production of harmonic sounds. We are all familiar with the
effects of musical instruments, from the deep-toned voice
of the organ to the wiry shrill of the Jew's harp. We sit
entranced under their magical influence, whether the ear
is charmed with the melody of their sounds, or the heart
agitated by the sympathies which they rouse. But
though we may admire their external form, and the skill
of the artist who constructed them, we never think of
inquiring into the cause of such extraordinary combinations.

Sounds of all kinds are conveyed to the organ of hearing
through the air ; and if this element were to be destroyed
all nature would be buried in the deepest silence. Noises
of every variety, whether they are musical or discordant,
high or low, move through the air of our atmosphere at
the surface of the earth with a velocity of 1090 feet in a

second, or 765 miles per hour ; but in sulphurous acid gas sound moves only through 751 feet in a second, while in hydrogen gas it moves with the great velocity of 3000 feet. Along fluid and solid bodies its progress is still more rapid. Through water it moves at the rate of 4708 feet in a second, through tin at the rate of 8175 feet, and through iron, glass, and some kinds of wood, at the rate of 18,530 feet.

When a number of single and separate sounds follow each other in rapid succession, they produce a continued sound, in the same manner as a continuous circle of light is produced by whirling round a burning stick before the eye. In order that the sound may appear a single one to the ear, nearly sixteen separate sounds must follow one another every second. When these sounds are exactly similar, and recur at equal intervals, they form a musical sound. In order to produce such sounds from the air, it must receive at least sixteen equally distant impulses or strokes in a second. The most common way of producing this effect is by a string or wire A B, Fig. 40, stretched between the fixed points A, B. If this string is taken by the middle and pulled aside, or if it is suddenly struck, it will vibrate between its two fixed points, as shown in the figure, passing alternately on each side of its axis A B, the vibrations gradually diminishing by the resistance of the air till the string is brought to rest. Its vibrations, however, may be kept up by drawing a rosined fiddle-bow across it, and while it is vibrating it will give out a sound corresponding to the rapidity of its vibrations, and arising from the successive blows or impulses given to the air by the string. This sound is called the fundamental sound of the string, and its acuteness or sharpness increases with the number of vibrations which the string performs in a second.

If we now touch the vibrating string A' B' lightly with

the finger, or with a feather at the middle point C, Fig.
40, it will give out a more acute but fainter sound than
before, and while the extent of its vibrations is diminished,
their frequency is doubled.   In like manner, if we touch
the string A" B", Fig. 40, at a point C, so that A" C is
one-third of A" B", the note will be still more acute, and
correspond to thrice the number of vibrations.   All this
might have been expected, but the wonderful part of the
experiment is, that the vibrating string A' B' divides
itself at C into two parts A' C, C B', the part A' C
vibrating round A' and C as fixed points, and the part
C B' round C and B', but always so that the part A' C is

Fig. 40.

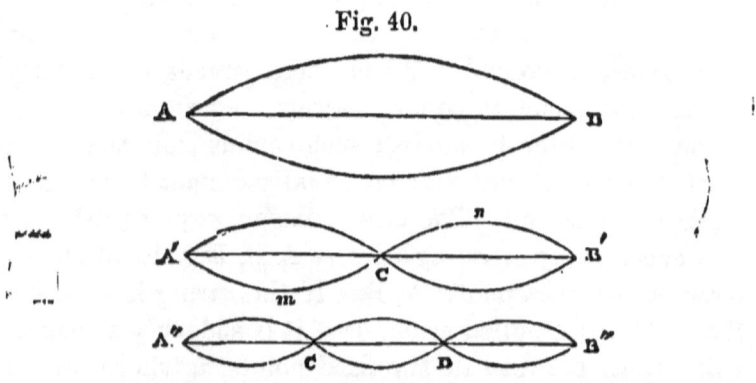

at the same distance on the one side of the axis A' B' as
at A m C, while the part C B is on the other side, as at
C n B.   Hence the point C, being always pulled by equal
and opposite forces, remains at rest as if it were absolutely
fixed.   This stationary point is called a *node*, and the
vibrating portions A' m C, C n B' loops.   The very same
is true of the string A" B", the points C and D being
stationary points; and upon the same principle a string
may be divided into any number of vibrating portions.
In order to prove that the string is actually vibrating in
these equal subdivisions, we have only to place a piece of
light paper with a notch in it on different parts of the

string. At the nodes C and D it will remain perfectly at rest, while at *m* or *n* in the middle of the loops it will be thrown off or violently agitated.

The acute sounds given out by each of the vibrating portions are called *harmonic sounds*, and they accompany the fundamental sound of the string in the very same manner, as we have already seen, that the eye sees the accidental or harmonic colours while it is affected with the fundamental colour.

The subdivision of the string, and consequently the production of harmonic sounds, may be effected without touching the string at all, and by means of a sympathetic action conveyed by the air. If a string A B, for example, Fig. 40, is at rest, and if a shorter string A" C, one-third of its length, fixed at the two points A" and C is set a-vibrating in the same room, the string A B will be set a-vibrating in three loops like A" B", giving out the same harmonic sounds as the small string A" C.

It is owing to this property of sounding bodies that singers with great power of voice are able to break into pieces a large tumbler glass, by singing close to it its proper fundamental note; and it is from the same sympathetic communication of vibrations that two pendulum clocks fixed to the same wall, or two watches lying upon the same table, will take the same rate of going, though they would not agree with one another if placed in separate apartments. Mr. Ellicott even observed that the pendulum of the one clock will stop that of the other, and that the stopped pendulum will after a certain time resume its vibrations, and in its turn stop the vibrations of the other pendulum.

The production of musical sounds by the vibrations of a column of air in a pipe is familiar to every person, but the extraordinary mechanism by which it is effected is known principally to philosophers. A column of air in a

pipe may be set a-vibrating by blowing over the open end
of it, as is done in Pan's pipes, or by blowing over a hole
in its side as in the flute, or by blowing through an aperture called a reed, with a flexible tongue, as in the
clarionet.   In order to understand the nature of this
vibration, let A B, Fig. 41, be a pipe or tube, and let us
place in it a spiral spring A B, in which the coil or spire
are at equal distances, each end of the spiral being fixed to
the end of the tube. This elastic spring may be supposed
to represent the air in the pipe, which is of equal density
throughout. If we take hold of the spring at m, and push

Fig. 41.

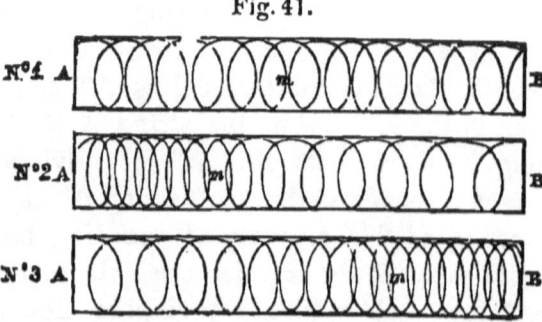

the point m towards A and towards B in succession, it
will give us a good idea of the vibration of an elastic
column of air.   When m is pushed towards A, the spiral
spring will be compressed or condensed, as shown at m A,
No. 2, while at the other end it will be dilated or rarefied,
as shown at m B, and in the middle of the tube it will
have the same degree of compression as in No. 1.   When
the string is drawn to the other end of the tube B, the
spring will be, as in No. 3, condensed at the end B, and
dilated at the end A.   Now when a column of air vibrates
in a pipe A B, the whole of it rushes alternately from B
to A, as in No. 2, and from A to B, as in No. 3, being
condensed at the end A, No. 2, and dilated or rarefied at
the end B, while in No. 3 it is rarefied at A and con-

densed at B, preserving its natural density at the middle point between A and B. In the case of the spring the ends A B are alternately pushed outwards and pulled inwards by the spring, the end A being pushed outwards in No. 2, and B pulled inwards, while in No. 3 A is pulled inwards and B pushed outwards.

That the air vibrating in a pipe is actually in the state now described may be shown by boring small holes in the pipe, and putting over them pieces of a fine membrane. The membrane opposite to the middle part between A and B, where the particles of the air have the greatest motion, will be violently agitated, while at points nearer the ends A and B it will be less and less affected.

Let us now suppose two pipes A B, B C, to be joined together as in Fig. 42, and to be separated by a fixed

Fig. 42.

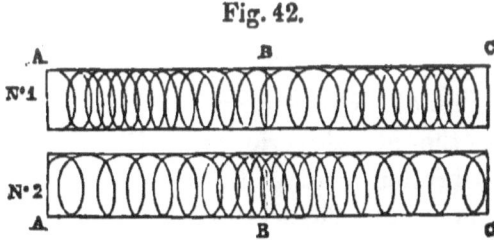

partition at B; and let a spiral spring be fixed in each. Let the spring A B be now pushed to the end A, while the spring B C is pushed to C, as in No. 1, and back again, as in No. 2, but always in opposite directions; then it is obvious that the partition B is in No. 1 drawn in opposite directions towards A and towards C, and always with forces equal to each other, that is, when B is drawn slightly towards A, which it is at the beginning of the motion, it is also drawn slightly towards C, and when it is drawn forcibly towards A, as it is at the end of the. motion of the spring, it is also drawn forcibly towards C. If the partition B, therefore, is moveable, it will still remain fixed during the opposite excursions of the spiral springs: nay, if we remove the partition, and hook the end of one spiral spring to the end of the other, the node or point of junction will remain stationary during the movements of the springs, because at every instant that point is drawn by equal and opposite forces. If *three*, *four*, or *five* spiral springs are joined in a similar manner, we may conceive them all vibrating between their nodes in the same manner.

Upon the very same principles we may conceive a long column of air without partitions dividing itself into two, three, or four smaller columns, each of which will vibrate between its nodes in the same manner as the spiral spring. At the middle point of each small vibrating column the air will be of its natural density like that of the atmosphere, while at the nodes B, &c., it will be in a state of condensation and rarefaction alternately.

If, when the air is vibrating in one column in the pipe A B, as in Fig. 41, Nos. 2, 3, we conceive a hole made in the middle, the atmospheric air will not rush in to disturb the vibration, because the air within the pipe and without it has exactly the same density. Nay, if, instead of a single hole, we were to cut a ring out of the pipe at the middle point, the column would vibrate as before. But if we bore a hole between the middle and one of the ends, where the vibrating column must be either in a state of condensation or rarefaction, the air must either rush out or rush in, in order to establish the equilibrium. The air opposite the hole will then be brought to the state of the external air like that in the middle of the pipe, it will become the middle of a vibrating column, and the whole column of air, instead of vibrating as one, will vibrate as two columns, each column vibrating with twice the velocity, and yielding harmonic sounds along with the fundamental sound of the whole columns, in the same manner as we have already explained with regard to vibrating strings. By opening other holes we may sub-divide a vibrating column into any number of smaller vibrating columns. The holes in flutes, clarionets, &c., are made for this purpose. When they are all closed up the air vibrates in one column, and by opening and shutting the different holes in succession, the number of vibrating columns is increased or diminished at pleasure, and consequently the harmonic sounds will vary in a similar manner.

Curious as these phenomena are, they are still surpassed by those which are exhibited during the vibration of solid bodies. A rod or bar of metal or glass may be made to vibrate either longitudinally or laterally.

An iron rod will vibrate longitudinally like a column of air if we strike it at one end in the direction of its length, or rub it in the same direction with a wetted finger, and it will emit the same fundamental note as a column of air *ten* or *eleven* times as long, because sound moves as much faster in iron than in air. When the iron rod is thus vibrating along its length, the very same changes which we have shown in Fig. 41, as produced in a spiral spring or in a column of air, take place in the solid metal. All its particles move alternately towards A and towards B, the metal being in the one case condensed at the end to which the particles move, and expanded at the end from which they move, and retaining its natural density in the middle of the rod. If we now hold this rod in the middle, by the finger and thumb lightly applied, and rub it in the middle either of A B or B C with a piece of cloth sprinkled with powdered rosin, or with a well-rosined fiddle-bow drawn across the rod, it will divide itself into two vibrating portions A B, B C, each of which will vibrate, as shown in Fig. 42, like the two adjacent columns of air, the section of the rod, or the

particles which compose that section at B, being at perfect
rest.   By holding the rod at any intermediate point between A and B, so that the distance from A to the finger
and thumb is one-third, one-fourth, one-fifth, &c., of the
whole length A C, and rubbing one of the divisions in
the middle, the rod will divide itself into 3, 4, 5, &c.,
vibrating portions, and give out corresponding harmonic
sounds.

A rod of iron may be made to vibrate laterally or
transversely by fixing one end of it firmly as in a vice,
and leaving the other free, or by having both ends free or
both fixed.   When a rod, fixed at one end and free at the
other, is made to vibrate, its mode of vibrating may be
rendered evident to the eye; and for the purpose of doing
this Mr. Wheatstone has contrived a curious instrument
called the *Kaleidophone*, which is shown in Fig. 43.   It

Fig. 43.

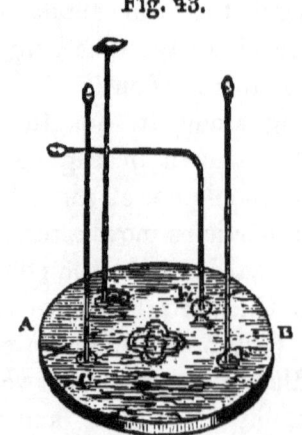

consists of a circular base of wood A B, about *nine* inches
in diameter and one inch thick, and having four brass
sockets firmly fixed into it at C, D, E, and F.   Into these
sockets are screwed four vertical steel rods, C, D, E, and
F, about 13 or 14 inches long, one being a square rod,
another a bent cylindrical one, and the other two cylin-

drical ones of different diameters. On the extremities of these rods are fixed small quicksilvered glass beads, either singly or in groups, so that when the instrument is placed in the light of the sun or in that of a lamp, bright images of the sun or candle are seen reflected on each bead. If any of these rods is set a-vibrating, these luminous images will form continuous and returning curve lines in a state of constant variation, each different rod giving curves of different characters.

The melodion, an instrument of great power, embracing five octaves, operates by means of the vibrations of metallic rods of unequal lengths, fixed at one end and free at the other.* A narrow and thin plate of copper is screwed to the free extremity of each. rod, and at right angles to its length ; and its surface is covered with a small piece of felt impregnated with rosin. This narrow band is placed near the circumference of a revolving cylinder, and by touching the key it is made to descend till it touches the revolving cylinder, and gives out its sound. The sweetness and power of this instrument are unrivalled, and such is the character of its tones, that persons of a nervous temperament are often entirely overpowered by its effects.

The vibrations of plates of metal or glass of various forms exhibit a series of the most extraordinary phenomena which are capable of being shown by very simple means. These phenomena are displayed in an infinite variety of regular figures assumed by sand, or fine lycopodium powder, strewed over the surface of the glass plate. In order to produce these figures, we must pinch or damp the plate at one or more places, and when the sand is. strewed upon its surface it is thrown into vibrations by drawing a fiddle-bow over different parts of its circum-

* See *Edinburgh Encyclopædia*, Art. SCIENCE, CURIOSITIES IN, vol. xvii. p. 563.

ference.   The method of damping or pinching plates is
shown in Fig. 44.   In No. 1 a square plate of glass A B,
ground smooth at its edges, is pinched by the finger and
thumb.   In No. 2 a circular plate is held by the thumb
against the top *c* of a perpendicular rod, and damped by
the fingers at two different points of its circumference.
In No. 3 it is damped at three points of its circumference,
c and *d*, by the thumb and finger, and at *e* by pressing it
against a fixed obstacle *a b*.   By means of a clamp like
that at No. 4, it may be damped at a greater number of
points.

Fig. 44.

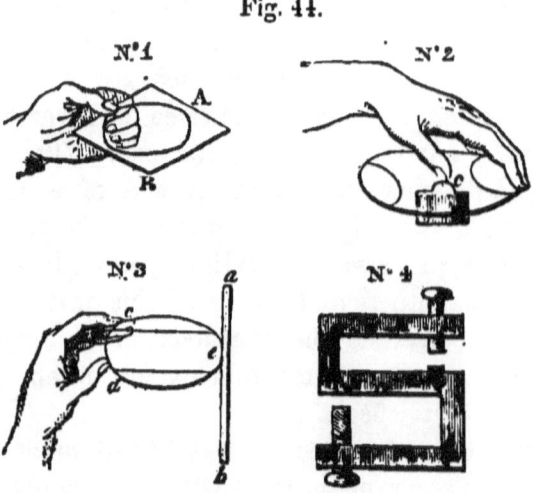

If we take a *square* plate of glass, such as that shown in
Fig. 45, No. 1, and pinching it at its centre, draw the
fiddle-bow near one of its angles, the sand will accumulate
in the form of a cross, as shown in the figure, being
thrown off the parts of the plate that are in a state of
vibration, and settling in the nodes or parts which are at
rest.   If the bow is drawn across the middle of one of the
edges, the sand will accumulate as in No. 2.   If the plate
is pinched at N, No. 3, and the bow applied at F, and
perpendicular to A B, the sand will arrange itself in three

parallel lines, perpendicular to a fourth passing through F and N. But if the point N, where it is pinched, is a little farther from the edge than in No. 3, the parallel lines will change into curves as in No. 4.

If the plate of glass is circular and pinched at its centre, and also at a point of its circumference, and if the bow is applied at a point 45° from the last point, the figure of the sand will be as in Fig. 46, No. 1. If with

Fig 45.

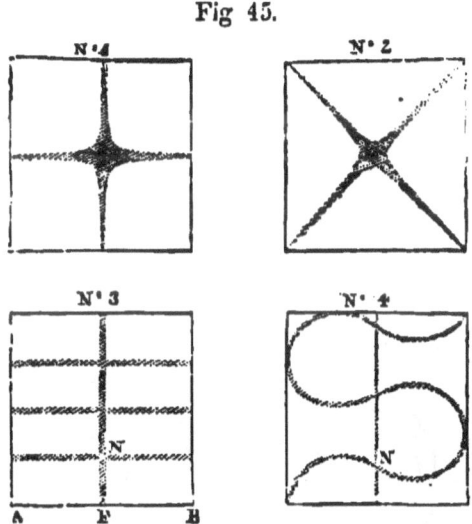

the same plate, similarly pinched, the bow is drawn over a part 30° from the pinched point of the circumference, the sand will form six radii as in No. 2. When the centre of the plate is left free, a different set of figures is produced, as shown in No. 3 and No. 4. When the plate is pinched near its edge, and the bow applied 45° from the point pinched, a circle of sand will pass through that point, and two diameters of sand at right angles to each other will be formed, as in No. 3. When a point of the circumference is pressed against a fixed obstacle, and the bow applied 30° from that point, the figure in No. 4 is produced,

If, in place of a solid plate, we strew the sand over a
stretched membrane, the sand will form itself into figures,
even when the vibrations are communicated to the
membrane through the air. In order to make these
experiments, we must stretch a thin sheet of wet paper,
such as vegetable paper, over the mouth of a tumbler
glass with a footstalk, and fix it to the edges with glue.
When the paper is dry, a thin layer of dry sand is strewed
upon its surface. If we place this membrane upon a

Fig. 46.

No. 1.   No. 2.

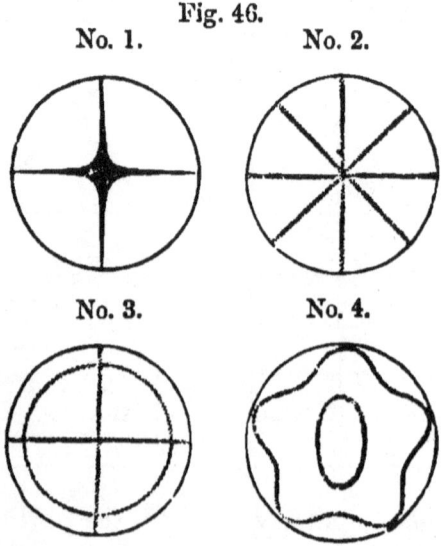

No. 3.   No. 4.

table, and hold immediately above it, and parallel to the
membrane, a plate of glass vibrating so as to give any of
the figures shown in Fig. 46, the sand upon the membrane
will imitate exactly the figure upon the glass. If the
glass plate, in place of vibrating horizontally, is made to
vibrate in an inclined position, the figures on the membrane will change with the inclination, and the sand will
assume the most curious arrangements. The figures thus
produced vary with the size of the membrane, with its
material, its tension, and its shape. When the same

figure occurs several times in succession, a breath upon the paper will change its degree of tension and produce an entirely new figure, which, as the temporary moisture evaporates, will return to the original figure, through a number of intermediate ones. The pipe of an organ at the distance of a few feet, or the notes of a flute at the distance of half a foot, will arrange the sand on the membrane into figures which perpetually change with the sound that is produced.

The manner in which flat rulers and cylinders of glass perform their vibrations is very remarkable. If a glass plate about twenty-seven inches long, six-tenths of an inch broad, and six-hundredths of an inch thick, is held by the edges between the finger and thumb, and has its lower surface, near either end, rubbed with a piece of wet cloth, sand laid upon its upper surface will arrange itself in parallel lines at right angles to the length of the plate. If the place of these lines is marked with a dot of ink, and the other side of the glass ruler is turned upwards, and the ruler made to vibrate as before, the sand will now accumulate in lines intermediate between the former lines, so that the motions of one-half the thickness of the glass ruler are precisely the reverse of those of the corresponding parts of the other half.

As these singular phenomena have not yet been made available by the scientific conjurer, we must be satisfied with this brief notice of them; but there is still one property of sound, which has its analogy also in light, too remarkable to be passed without notice. This property has more of the marvellous in it than any result within the wide range of the sciences. *Two loud sounds may be made to produce silence, and two strong lights may be made to produce darkness!*

If two equal and similar strings, or the columns of air in two equal and similar pipes, perform exactly 100 vibrations in a second, they will produce each equal waves of sound, and these waves will conspire in generating an uninterrupted sound, double of either of the sounds heard separately. If the two strings or the two columns of air are not in unison, but nearly so, as in the case where the one vibrates 100, and the other 101 times in a second, then at the first vibration the two sounds will form one of double the strength of either; but the one will gradually gain upon the other, till at the fiftieth vibration it has gained half a vibration on the other. At this instant the two sounds will *destroy one another*, and an interval of perfect silence will take place. The sound will instantly commence, and gradually increase till it becomes loudest at the hundredth vibration, where the two vibrations conspire in producing a sound double of either. An interval of silence will again occur at the 150th, 250th, 350th vibration, or every second, while a sound of double the strength of either will be heard at the 200dth, 300dth, and 400dth vibration. When the unison is very defective, or when there is a great difference between the number of vibrations which the two strings or columns of air perform in a second, the successive sounds and intervals of silence resemble a rattle. With a powerful organ the effect of this experiment is very fine, the repetition of the sounds *wow—wow—wow*—representing the doubled sound and the interval the silence arising from the total extinction of the two separate sounds.

The phenomena corresponding to this in the case of light are perhaps still more surprising. If a beam of *red* light issues from a luminous point, and falls upon the retina, we shall see distinctly the luminous object from which it proceeds; but if another pencil of red light issues from another luminous point anyhow situated, provided the difference between its distance and that of the other luminous point from the point of the retina, on

which the first beam fell, is the 258th thousandth part
of an inch, or exactly *twice, thrice, four* times, &c., that
distance; and if this second beam falls upon the same
point of the retina, the one light will increase the intensity of the other, and the eye will see *twice* as much light
as when it received only one of the beams separately.
All this is nothing more than what might be expected
from our ordinary experience. But if the difference in
the distances of the two luminous points is only *one-half*
of the 258th thousandth part of an inch, or $1\frac{1}{2}$, $2\frac{1}{2}$, $3\frac{1}{2}$, $4\frac{1}{2}$
times that distance, *the one light will extinguish the other,
and produce absolute darkness.* If the two luminous points
are so situated, that the difference of their distances from
the point of the retina is intermediate between 1 and $1\frac{1}{2}$,
or 2 and $2\frac{1}{2}$, above the 258th thousandth part of an inch,
the intensity of the effect which they produce will vary
from absolute darkness to double the intensity of either
light. At $1\frac{1}{4}$, $2\frac{1}{4}$, $3\frac{1}{4}$ times, &c., the 258th thousandth of
an inch, the intensity of the two combined lights will be
equal only to one of them acting singly. If the lights,
in place of falling upon the retina, fall upon a sheet of
white paper, the very same effect will be produced; a
black spot being produced in the one case, and a bright
white one in the other, and intermediate degrees of brightness in intermediate cases. If the two lights are *violet*,
the difference of distances at which the preceding phenomena will be produced will be the 157th thousandth
part of an inch, and it will be intermediate between the
258th and the 157th thousandth part of an inch, for the
intermediate colours. This curious phenomenon may be
easily shown to the eye, by admitting the sun's light into
a dark room through a small hole about the 40th or 50th
part of an inch in diameter, and receiving the light on a
sheet of paper. If we hold a needle or piece of slender
wire in this light, and examine its shadow, we shall find

that the shadow consists of bright and dark stripes suc·
ceeding each other alternately, the stripe in the very
middle or axis of the shadow being a bright one. The
rays of light which are bent into the shadow, and which
meet in the very middle of the shadow, have exactly the
same length of path, so that they form a bright fringe of
double the intensity of either ; but the rays which fall
upon a point of the shadow at a certain distance from the
middle have a difference in the length of their paths,
corresponding to the difference at which the lights destroy
each other, so that a *black* stripe is produced on each side
of the middle bright one.   At a greater distance from the
middle, the difference becomes such as to produce a bright
stripe, and so on, a bright and a dark stripe succeeding
each other to the margin of the shadow.

The explanation which philosophers have given of these
strange phenomena is very satisfactory, and may be easily
understood.   When a wave is made on the surface of a
still pool of water, by plunging a stone into it, the wave
advances along the surface, while the water itself is never
carried forward, but merely rises into a height and falls
into a hollow, each portion of the surface experiencing an
elevation and a depression in its turn.   If we suppose two
waves equal and similar to be produced by two separate stones, and if they reach the same spot at the same
time, that is, if the two elevations should exactly coincide,
they would unite their effects and produce a wave twice
the size of either ; but if the one wave should be just so
far before the other that the hollow of the one coincided
with the elevation of the other, and the elevation of the
one with the hollow of the other, the two waves would
obliterate or destroy one another, the elevation as it were
of the one filling up half the hollow of the other, and the
hollow of the one taking away half the elevation of the
other, so as to reduce the surface to a level.   These

effects will be actually exhibited by throwing two equal stones into a pool of water, and it will be seen that there are certain lines of a hyperbolic form where the water is quite smooth, in conseqence of the equal waves obliterating one another, while in other adjacent parts the water is raised to a height corresponding to both the waves united.

In the tides of the ocean, we have a fine example of the same principle. The two immense waves arising from the action of the sun and moon upon the ocean produce our spring-tides by their combination, or when the elevations of each coincide, and our neap-tides, when the elevation of the one wave coincides with the depression of the other. If the sun and moon had exerted exactly the same force upon the ocean, or produced tide waves of the same size, then our neap-tides would have disappeared altogether, and the spring-tide would have been a wave double of the wave produced by the sun and moon separately. An example of the effect of the equality of the two waves occurs in the port of Batsha, where the two waves arrive by channels of different lengths, and actually obliterate each other.

Now, as sound is produced by undulations or waves in the air, and as light is supposed to be produced by waves or undulations in an ethereal medium, filling all nature, and occupying the pores of transparent bodies, the successive production of sound and silence, by two loud sounds, or of light and darkness by two bright lights, may be explained in the very same manner as we have explained the increase and the obliteration of waves formed on the surface of water. If this theory of light be correct, then the breadth of a wave of *red* light will be the 258th thousandth part of an inch, the breadth of a wave of green light the 207th thousandth part of an inch, and the breadth of a wave of violet light the 157th thousandth part of an inch.

Among the wonders of modern skill, we must enumerate those beautiful automata by which the motions and actions of man and other animals have been successfully imitated. I shall therefore describe at present some of the most remarkable acoustic automata, in which the production of musical and vocal sounds has been the principal object of the artist.

Many very ingenious pieces of acoustic mechanism have been from time to time exhibited in Europe. The celebrated Swiss mechanist, M. le Droz, constructed for the King of Spain the figure of a sheep, which imitated in the most perfect manner the bleating of that animal, and likewise the figure of a dog watching a basket of fruit, which, when any of the fruit was taken away, never ceased barking till it was replaced.

The singing-bird of M. Maillardet, which he exhibited in Edinburgh many years ago, is still more wonderful.* An oval box, about three inches long, was set upon the table, and in an instant the lid flew up, and a bird of the size of the humming-bird, and of the most beautiful plumage, started from its nest. After fluttering its wings, it opened its bill and performed four different kinds of the most beautiful warbling. It then darted down into its nest, and the lid closed upon it. The moving power in this piece of mechanism is said to have been springs which continued their action only four minutes. As there was no room, within so small a figure, for accommodating pipes to produce the great variety of notes which were warbled, the artist used only one tube, and produced all the variety of sounds by shortening and lengthening it with a moveable piston.

Ingenious as these pieces of mechanism are, they sink into insignificance when compared with the machinery of M. Vaucanson, which had previously astonished all

* A similar piece of mechanism had been previously made by M. le Droz.

Europe. His two principal automata were the flute-player, and the pipe and tabor player. The flute-player was completed in 1736, and wherever it was exhibited it produced the greatest sensation. When it came to Paris it was received with great suspicion. The French savans recollected the story of M. Raisin, the organist of Troyes, who exhibited an automaton player upon the harpsichord, which astonished the French court by the variety of its powers. The curiosity of the King could not be restrained, and in consequence of his insisting upon examining the mechanism, there was found in the figure a pretty little musician five years of age. It was natural, therefore, that a similar piece of mechanism should be received with some distrust; but this feeling was soon removed by M. Vaucanson, who exhibited and explained to a committee of the Academy of Sciences the whole of the mechanism. This learned body was astonished at the ingenuity which it displayed; and they did not hesitate to state, that the machinery employed for producing the sounds of the flute performed in the most exact manner the very operations of the most expert flute-player, and that the artist had imitated the effects produced, and the means employed by nature, with an accuracy which had exceeded all expectation. In 1738, M. Vaucanson published a memoir, approved of by the Academy, in which he gave a full description of the machinery employed, and of the principles of its construction. Following this memoir, I shall therefore attempt to give as popular a description of the automaton as can be done without lengthened details and numerous figures.

The body of the flute-player was about 5½ feet high, and was placed upon a piece of rock, surrounding a square pedestal 4½ feet high by three and a half wide. When the panel which formed the front of the pedestal was opened, there was seen on the right a clock movement, which, by the aid of several wheels, gave a rotatory motion to a steel axis about 2½ feet long, having cranks at six equidistant points of its length, but lying in different directions. To each crank was attached a cord, which descended and was fixed by its other end to the upper board of a pair of bellows, 2½ feet long and six inches wide. Six pair of bellows arranged along the bottom of the pedestal were then wrought, or made to blow in succession, by turning the steel axis.

At the upper face of the pedestal, and upon each pair of bellows, is a double pulley, one of whose rims is 3 inches in diameter, and the other 1½. The cord which proceeds from the crank coils round the smallest of these pulleys, and that which is fixed to the upper board of the bellows goes round the larger pulley. By this means the upper board of the bellows is made to rise higher than if the cords went directly from them to the cranks.

Round the larger rims of three of these pulleys, viz., those on the right hand, there are coiled three cords, which, by means of several smaller pulleys, terminate in the upper boards of other three pairs of bellows placed on the top of the box.

The tension of each cord when it begins to raise the board of the bellows to which it is attached, gives motion to a lever placed above it between the axis and the double pulley in the middle and lower region of the box. The other end of this lever keeps open the valve in the lower board of the bellows, and allows the air to enter freely, while the upper board is rising to increase the capacity of the bellows. By this means there is not only power gained, in so far as the air gains easier admission through the valve, but the fluttering noise produced by the action of the air upon the valves is entirely avoided, and the nine pair of bellows are wrought with great ease, and without any concussion or noise.

These nine bellows discharge their wind into three different and separate tubes. Each tube receives the wind of three bellows, the upper boards of one of the three pair being loaded with a weight of four pounds, those of the second three pair with a weight of two pounds, and those of the other three pair with no weight at all. These three tubes ascended through the body of the figure, and terminated in three small reservoirs placed in its trunk. These reservoirs were thus united into one, which, ascending into the throat, formed by its enlargement the cavity of the mouth terminated by two small lips, which rested upon the hole of the flute. These lips had . the power of opening more or less, and by a particular mechanism they could advance or recede from the hole in the flute. Within the cavity of the mouth there is a small moveable tongue for opening and shutting the passage for the wind through the lips of the figure.

The motions of the fingers, lips, and tongue, of the figure were produced by means of a revolving cylinder thirty inches long, and twenty-one in diameter. By means of pegs and brass staples fixed in fifteen different divisions in its circumference, fifteen different levers, similar to those in a barrel-organ, were raised and depressed. Seven of these regulated the motions of the seven fingers for stopping the holes of the flute, which they did by means of steel chains rising through the body and directed by pulleys to the shoulder, elbow, and fingers. Other three of the levers, communicating with the valves of the three reservoirs, regulated the ingress of the air, so as to produce a stronger or a weaker tone. Another lever opened the lips so as to give a free passage to the air, and another contracted them for the opposite purpose. A third lever drew them backwards from the orifice of the flute, and a fourth pushed them forward. The remaining lever enabled the tongue to stop up the orifice of the flute.

T

Such is a very brief view of the general mechanism by which the requisite motions of the flute-player were produced. The airs which it played were probably equal to those executed by a living performer, and its construction, as well as its performances, continued for many years to delight and astonish the philosophers and musicians of Europe.

Encouraged by the success of this machine M. Vaucanson exhibited in 1741 other automata, which were equally, if not more, admired. One of these was the automaton duck, which performed all the motions of that animal, and not only ate its food, but digested it;* and the other was his pipe and tabor-player, a piece of mechanism which required all the resources of his fertile genius. Having begun this machine before he was aware of its peculiar difficulties, he was often about to abandon it in despair, but his patience and his ingenuity combined enabled him not only to surmount every difficulty, but to construct an automaton which performed complete airs, and greatly excelled the most esteemed performers on the pipe and tabor.

The figure stands on a pedestal, and is dressed like a dancing shepherd. He holds in one hand a flageolet, and in the other the stick with which he beats the tambourin as an accompaniment to the airs of the flageolet, about twenty of which it is capable of performing. The flageolet has only three holes, and the variety of its tones depends principally on a proper variation of the force of the wind, and on the different degrees with which the orifices are covered. These variations in the force of the wind required to be given with a rapidity which the ear can scarcely follow, and the articulation of the tongue was required for the quickest notes, otherwise the effect was far from agreeable. As the human tongue is not capable of giving the requisite articulations to a rapid succession

* See Letter XI.

of notes, and generally slurs over one-half of them, the automaton was thus able to excel the best performers, as it played complete airs with articulations of the tongue at every note.

In constructing this machine M. Vaucanson observed that the flageolet must be a most fatiguing instrument for the human lungs, as the muscles of the chest must make an effort equal to 56 pounds in order to produce the highest notes. A single ounce was sufficient for the lowest notes, so that we may, from this circumstance, form an idea of the variety of intermediate effects required to be produced.

While M. Vaucanson was engaged in the construction of these wonderful machines, his mind was filled with the strange idea of constructing an automaton containing the whole mechanism of the circulation of the blood. From some birds which he made he was satisfied of its practicability ; but as the whole vascular system required to be made of elastic gum or caoutchouc, it was supposed that it could only be executed in the country where the caoutchouc-tree was indigenous. Louis XVI. took a deep interest in the execution of this machine. It was agreed that a skilful anatomist should proceed to Guiana to superintend the construction of the blood-vessels, and the King had not only approved of, but had given orders for, the voyage. Difficulties, however, were thrown in the way : Vaucanson became disgusted, and the scheme was abandoned.

The two automata which we have described were purchased by Professor Bayreuss of Helmstadt; but we have not been able to learn whether or not they still exist.

Towards the end of the nineteenth century a bold and almost successful attempt was made to construct a *talking automaton*. In the year 1779, the Imperial Academy of Sciences at St. Petersburgh proposed as the subject of one of their annual prizes an inquiry into the nature of the vowel sounds A, E, I, O and U, and the construction of an instrument for artificially imitating them. This prize was gained by M. Kratzenstein, who showed that all the vowels could be distinctly pronounced by blowing through a reed into the lower ends of the pipes of the annexed figures, as shown in Fig. 47, where the corresponding vowels are marked on the different pipes. The vowel I is

Fig. 47.

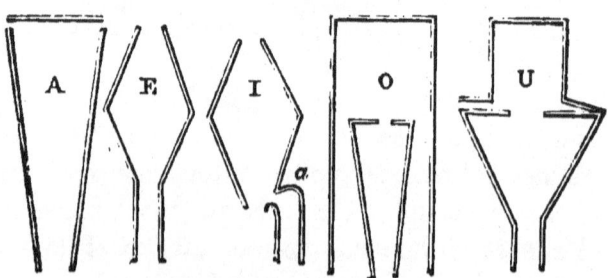

pronounced by merely blowing into the pipe $a\,b$, of the pipe marked I, without the use of a reed.

About the same time that Kratzenstein was engaged in these researches, M. Kempelen of Vienna, a celebrated mechanician, was occupied with the same subject. In his first attempt he produced the vowel sounds, by adapting a reed R, Fig. 48, to the bottom of a funnel-shaped cavity A B, and placing his hand in various positions within the funnel. This contrivance, however, was not fitted for his purpose; but after long study, and a diligent examination of the organs of speech, he contrived a hollow oval box, divided into two portions attached by a hinge so as to resemble jaws. This box received the sound which issued from the tube connected with the reed, and by opening and closing the jaws he produced the sounds A, O, O U, and an imperfect E, but no indications of an I. After two years' labour he succeeded in obtaining from different jaws the sounds of the consonants P, M, L, and by means of these vowels and consonants, he could compose syllables and words, such as *mama, papa, aula, lama, mulo*. The sounds of two adjacent letters, however, run into each other, and an aspiration followed some of the consonants, so that instead of *papa* the word sounded *phaa-ph-a;* these difficulties he contrived with much labour to surmount, and he found it necessary to imitate the human organs of speech

Fig. 48.

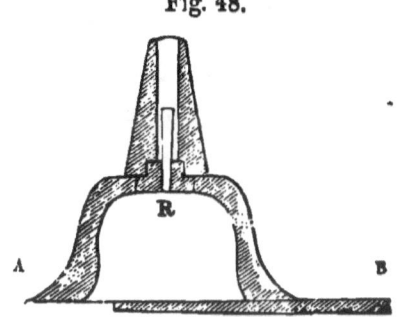

by having only one mouth and one glottis. The mouth consisted of a funnel or bell-shaped piece of elastic gum, which approximated, by its physical properties, to the softness and flexibility of the human organs.* To the mouth-piece was added a nose made of two tin tubes, which communicated with the mouth. When both these tubes were open, and the mouth-piece closed, a perfect M was produced, and when one was closed and the other open, an N was sounded. M. Kempelen could have succeeded in obtaining the four letters D, G, K, T, but by using a P instead of them, and modifying the sound in a particular manner, he contrived to deceive the ear by a tolerable resemblance of these letters.

* Had M. Kempelen known the modern discovery of giving caoutchouc any degree of softness, by mixing it with molasses or sugar, which is always absorbing moisture from the atmosphere, he might have obtained a still more perfect imitation of the human organs.

There seems to be no doubt that he at last was able to produce entire words and sentences, such as *opera, astronomy, Constantinopolis, vous êtes mon ami, je vous aime de tout mon cœur, venez avec moi à Paris, Leopoldus secundus, Romanorum imperator semper Augustus, &c.*, but he never fitted up a speaking figure, and probably, from being dissatisfied with the general result of his labours, he exhibited only to his private friends the effects of the apparatus, which was fitted up in the form of a box.

This box was rectangular, and about three feet long, and was placed upon a table and covered with a cloth. When any particular word was mentioned by the company, M. Kempelen caused the machine to pronounce it, by introducing his hands beneath the cloth, and apparently giving motion to some parts of the apparatus. Mr. Thomas Collinson, who had seen this machine in London, mentions in a letter to Dr. Hutton, that he afterwards saw it at M. Kempelen's own house in Vienna, and that he then gave it the same word to be pronounced which he gave it in London, viz., the word *Exploitation*, which, he assures us, it again distinctly pronounced with the French accent.

M. Kratzenstein seems to have been equally unsuccessful, for though he assured M. De Lalande, when he saw him in Paris in 1786, that he had made a machine which could speak pretty well, and though he showed him some of the apparatus by which it could sound the vowels, and even such syllables as *papa* and *mama*, yet there is no reason to believe that he had accomplished more than this.

The labours of Kratzenstein and Kempelen have been recently pursued with great success by our ingenious countryman Mr. Willis of Cambridge. In repeating Kempelen's experiment shown in Fig. 48, he used a shallower cavity, such as that in Fig. 49, and found that

he could entirely dispense with the introduction of the
hand, and could obtain the whole series of vowels, by
sliding a flat board C D over the mouth of the cavity.
Mr. Willis then conceived the idea of adapting to the reed
cylindrical tubes, whose length could be varied by sliding
joints. When the tube was greatly less than the length
of a stopped pipe in unison with the reed, it sounded I,
and by increasing the length of the tube it gave E, A, O
and U in succession. But what was very unexpected,

Fig. 49.

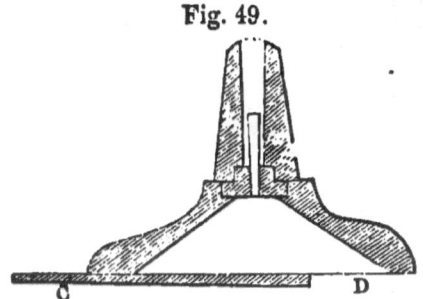

when the tube was so much lengthened as to be 1½ times
the length of a stopped pipe in unison with the reed, the
vowels began to be again sounded in an inverted order,
viz., U, O, A, E, and then again in a direct order, I, E, A,
O, U, when the length of the tube was equal to twice that
of a stopped pipe, in unison with the reed.

Some important discoveries have been recently made by
M. Savart respecting the mechanism of the human voice,*
and we have no doubt that, before another century is
completed, a *Talking* and a *Singing machine* will be
numbered among the conquests of Science.

* See *Edinburgh Journal of Science*, No. viii. p. 200.

LETTER IX.

Singular effects in nature depending on sound—Permanent character of speech—Influence of great elevations on the character of sounds, and on the powers of speech—Power of sound in throwing down buildings—Dog killed by sound—Sounds greatly changed under particular circumstances—Great audibility of sounds during the night explained—Sounds deadened in media of different densities—Illustrated in the case of a glass of champagne, and in that of new-fallen snow—Remarkable echoes—Reverberations of thunder—Subterranean noises—Remarkable one at the Solfaterra—Echo at the Menai Suspension Bridge—Temporary deafness produced in diving-bells—Inaudibility of particular sounds to particular ears—Vocal powers of the statue of Memnon—Sounds in granite rocks—Musical mountain of El-Nakous.

ALTHOUGH among the phenomena of the material world there is scarcely one which, when well considered, is not an object of wonder, yet those which we have been accustomed to witness from our infancy lose all their interest from the frequency of their occurrence, while to the natives of other countries they are unceasing objects of astonishment and delight. The inhabitant of a tropical climate is confounded at the sight of falling snow, and he almosts discredits the evidence of his senses when he sees a frozen river carrying loaded waggons on its surface. The diffusion of knowledge by books, as well as by frequent communication between the natives of different quarters of the globe, have deprived this class of local wonders of their influence, and the Indian and the Scandinavian can visit each other's lands without any violent excitement of surprise. Still, however, there are phenomena of rare occurrence, of which no description can convey the idea, and which continue to be as deeply marked with the marvellous as if they had been previously unknown. Among these we may rank the remarkable modifications which sound undergoes in particular situations and under particular circumstances.

In the ordinary intercourse of life, we recognise individuals as much by their voice as by the features of their face and the form of their body. A friend who has been long absent will often stand before us as a stranger, till his voice supplies us with the full power of recognition. The brand imprinted by time on his outer form may have effaced the youthful image which the memory had cherished, but the original character of his voice and its yet remembered tones will remain unimpaired.

An old friend with a new face is not more common in its moral than in its physical acceptation, and though the sagacity of proverbial wisdom has not supplied us with the counterpart in relation to the human voice, yet the influence of its immutability over the mind has been recorded by the poet in some of his most powerful conceptions. When Manfred was unable to recognise in the hectic phantom of Astarte the endeared lineaments of the being whom he loved, the mere utterance of his name recalled "the voice which was his music," and invested her with the desired reality :

> Say on, say on—
> I live but in the Sound—It is thy voice!

> BYRON.

The permanence of character thus impressed upon speech exists only in those regions to whose atmosphere our vocal organs are adapted. If either the speaker or the hearer is placed in air differing greatly in density from that to which they are accustomed, the voice of the one will emit different sounds, or the same sounds will pro-

duce a different impression on the ear of the other. But
if both parties are placed in this new atmosphere, their
tones of communication will suffer the most remarkable
change. The two extreme positions, where such effects
become sufficiently striking, are in the compressed air of
the diving-bell, when it is immersed to a great depth in
the sea, or in the rarefied atmosphere which prevails on
the summit of the Himalaya or the Andes.

In the region of common life, and even at the stillest
hour of night, the ear seldom rests from its toils. When
the voice of man and the bustle of his labours have ceased,
the sounds of insect life are redoubled, the night breeze
awakens among the rustling leaves, and the swell of the
distant ocean, and the sounds of the falling cataract or of
the murmuring brook, fill the air with their pure and
solemn music. The sublimity of deep silence is not to
be found even in the steppes of the Volga, or in the
forests of the Orinoco. It can be felt only in those lofty
regions
>   Where the tops of the Andes
>   Shoot soaringly forth.

As the traveller rises above the limit of life and motion,
and enters the region of habitual solitude, the death-like
silence which prevails around him is rendered still more
striking by the diminished density of the air which he
breathes. The voice of his fellow-traveller ceases to be
heard even at a moderate distance, and sounds which
would stun the ear at a lower level make but a feeble
impression. The report of a pistol on the top of Mont
Blanc is no louder than that of an Indian cracker. But
while the thinness of the air thus subdues the loudest
sounds, the voice itself undergoes a singular change : the
muscular energy by which we speak experiences a great
diminution, and our powers of utterance, as well as our
power of hearing, are thus singularly modified. Were the

magician, therefore, who is desirous to impress upon his
victim or upon his pupil the conviction of his supernatural
power, to carry him, under the injunction of silence,

———————————————— to breathe
The difficult air of the iced mountain's top,
Where the birds dare not build, nor insect's wing
Flit o'er the herbless granite,

he would experience little difficulty in asserting his power
over the elements, and still less in subsequently communicating the same influence to his companion.

But though the air at the tops of our highest mountains
is scarcely capable of transmitting sounds of ordinary
intensity, yet sounds of extraordinary power force their
way through its most attenuated strata. At elevations
where the air is three thousand times more rare than that
which we breathe, the explosion of meteors is heard like
the sound of cannon on the surface of the earth, and the
whole air is often violently agitated by the sound. This
fact alone may give us some idea of the tremendous nature
of the forces which such explosions create, and it is
fortunate for our species that they are confined to the
upper regions of the atmosphere. If the same explosions
were to take place in the dense air which rests upon the
earth, our habitations and our lives would be exposed to
the most imminent peril.

Buildings have often been thrown down by violent
concussions of the air, occasioned either by the sound of
great guns or by loud thunder, and the most serious
effects upon human and animal life have been produced
by the same cause. Most persons have experienced the
stunning pain produced in the ear when placed near a
cannon that is discharged. Deafness has frequently been
the result of such sudden concussions, and if we may
reason from analogy, death itself must often have been the
consequence. When peace was proclaimed in London in

1697, two troops of horse were dismounted and drawn up in line in order to fire their volleys. Opposite the centre of the line was the door of a butcher's shop, where there was a large mastiff dog of great courage. This dog was sleeping by the fire, but when the first volley was fired, it immediately started up, ran into another room, and hid itself under a bed. On the firing of the second volley, the dog rose, run several times about the room, trembling violently and apparently in great agony. When the third volley was fired, the dog ran about once or twice with great violence, and instantly fell down dead, throwing up blood from his mouth and nose.

Sounds of known character and intensity are often singularly changed even at the surface of the earth, according to the state of the ground and the conditions of the clouds. On the extended heath, where there are no solid objects capable of reflecting or modifying sound, the sportsman must frequently have noticed the unaccountable variety of sounds which are produced by the report of his fowling-piece. Sometimes they are flat and prolonged, at other times short and sharp, and sometimes the noise is so strange that it is referred to some mistake in the loading of the gun. These variations, however, arise entirely from the state of the air, and from the nature and proximity of the superjacent clouds. In pure air of uniform density the sound is sharp and soon over, as the undulations of the air advance without any interrupting obstacles. In a foggy atmosphere, or where the vapours produced by heat are seen dancing as it were in the air, the sound is dull and prolonged; and when these clouds are immdiately overhead, a succession of echoes from them produces a continued or a reverberating sound. When the French astronomers were determining the velocity of sound by firing great guns, they observed that the report was always single and sharp under a perfectly clear sky, but indistinct, and attended by a long-continued roll like thunder, when a cloud covered a considerable part of the horizon. It is no doubt owing to the same cause, namely, the reflection from the clouds, that the thunder rolls through the heavens, as if it were produced by a succession of electric explosions.

The great audibility of sounds during the night is a phenomenon of considerable interest, and one which had been observed even by the ancients. In crowded cities or in their vicinity, the effect was generally ascribed to the rest of animated beings, while in localities where such an explanation was inapplicable, it was supposed to arise from a favourable direction of the prevailing wind. Baron Humboldt was particularly struck with this phenomenon when he first heard the rushing of the great cataracts of the Orinoco in the plain which surrounds the mission of the Apures. These sounds he regarded as three times louder during the night than during the day. Some authors ascribed this fact to the cessation of the humming of insects, the singing of birds, and the action of the wind on the leaves of the trees, but M. Humboldt justly maintains that this cannot be the cause of it on the Orinoco, where the buzz of insects is much louder in the night than in the day, and where the breeze never rises till after sunset. Hence he was led to ascribe the phenomenon to the perfect transparency and uniform density of the air, which can exist only at night after the heat of the ground has been uniformly diffused through the atmosphere. When the rays of the sun have been beating on the ground during the day, currents of hot air of different temperatures, and consequently of different densities, are constantly ascending from the ground and mixing with the cold air above. The air thus ceases to be a homogeneous medium, and every person must have observed the effects of it upon objects seen through it which are very indistinctly visible, and have a tremulous motion, as if they were "dancing in the air." The very same effect is perceived when we look at objects through spirits and water that are not perfectly mixed, or when we view distant objects over a red-hot poker or over a flame. In all these cases the light suffers refraction in passing from a medium of one density into a medium of a different density, and the refracted rays are constantly changing their direction as the different currents rise in succession. Analogous effects are produced when sound passes through a mixed medium, whether it consists of two different mediums, or of one medium where portions of it have different densities. As sound moves with different velocities through media of different densities, the wave which produces the sound will be partly reflected in passing from one medium to the other, and the direction of the transmitted wave changed; and hence in passing through such media different portions of the wave will reach the ear at different times, and thus destroy the sharpness and distinctness of the sound. This may be proved by many striking facts. If we put a bell in a receiver containing a mixture of hydrogen gas and atmospheric air, the sound of the bell can scarcely be heard. During a shower of rain or of snow, noises are greatly deadened, and when sound is transmitted along an iron wire or an iron pipe of sufficient length, we actually hear two sounds, one transmitted more rapidly through the solid, and the other more slowly through the air. The same property is well illustrated by an elegant and easily-repeated experiment of Chladni's. When sparkling champagne is poured into a tall glass till it is half full, the glass loses its power of ringing by a stroke upon its edge, and emits only a disagreeable and puffy sound. This effect will continue while the wine is filled with bubbles of air, or as long as the effervescence lasts; but when the effervescence begins to subside, the sound becomes clearer and clearer, and the glass rings as usual when the air-bubbles have vanished. If we reproduce the effervescence by stirring the champagne with a piece of bread the glass will again cease to ring. The same experiment will succeed with other effervescing fluids.

The difference in the audibility of sounds that pass over homogeneous and over mixed media is sometimes so remarkable as to astonish those who witness it. The following fact is given on the evidence of an officer who observed it. When the British and the American forces were encamped on each side of a river, the outposts were so near that the forms of individuals could be easily distinguished. An American drummer made his appearance and began to beat his drum, but though the motion of his arms was distinctly seen, not a single sound reached the ear of the observer. A coating of snow that had newly fallen upon the ground, and the thickness of the atmosphere, had conspired to obstruct the sound. An effect the very reverse of this is produced by a coating of glazed or hardened snow, or by an extended surface of ice or water. Lieutenant Foster was able to carry on a conversation with a sailor across Port Bowen harbour, a distance of no less than a mile and a quarter, and the sound of great guns has been heard at distances varying from 120 to 200 miles. Over hard and dry ground of an uniform character, or where a thin soil rests upon a continuous stratum of rock, the sound is heard at a great distance, and hence it is the practice among many eastern tribes to ascertain the approach of an enemy by applying the ear to the ground.

Many remarkable phenomena in the natural world are produced by the reflection and concentration of sound. Every person is familiar with the ordinary *Echo* which arises from the reflection of sound from an even surface, such as the face of a wall, of a house, of a rock, of a hill, or of a cloud. As sound moves at the rate of 1090 feet in a second, and as the sound which returns to the person who emits it has travelled over a space equal to twice his distance from the reflecting surface, the distance in feet of the body which occasions the echo may be readily found by multiplying 545 by the number of seconds which elapse between the emission of the sound and its return in the form of an echo. This kind of echo, where the same person is the speaker and the hearer, never takes place unless when the observer is immediately in front of the reflecting surface, or when a line drawn from his mouth to the flat surface is nearly perpendicular to it, because in this case alone the wave of sound is reflected in the very same direction from the wall in which it reaches it. If the speaker places himself on one side of this line, then the echo will be heard most distinctly by another person as far on the other side of it, because the waves of sound are reflected like light, so that the angle of incidence or the inclination at which the sound falls upon the reflected surface is equal to the angle of reflection, or the inclination at which the sound is returned from the wall. If two persons, therefore, are placed before the reflecting wall, the one will hear the echo of the sound emitted by the other, and obstacles may intervene between these two persons so that neither of them hears the direct sound emitted by the other; in the same manner as the same persons similarly placed before a looking-glass would see each other distinctly by reflection, though objects might obstruct their direct view of each other.

Hitherto we have supposed that there is only one reflecting surface, in which case there will be only one echo; but if there are several reflecting surfaces, as is the case in an amphitheatre of mountains, or during a thunder-storm, where there are several strata or masses of clouds ; or if there are two parallel or inclined surfaces between which the sound can be repeatedly reflected, or if the surface is curved so that the sound reflected from one part falls upon another part, like the sides of a polygon inscribed in a circle—in all these cases there will be numerous echoes, which produce a very singular effect. Nothing can be more grand and sublime than the primary and secondary echoes of a piece of ordnance discharged in an amphitheatre of precipitous mountains. The direct or primary echoes from each reflecting surface reach the ear in succession, according to their different distances, and these are either blended with or succeeded by the secondary echoes which terminate in a prolonged growl ending in absolute silence. Of the same character are the reverberated claps of a thunder-bolt reflected from the surrounding clouds, and dying away in the distance. The echo which is produced by parallel walls is finely illustrated at the Marquis of Simonetta's villa near Milan, which has been described by Addison and Keysler, and which we believe is that described by Mr. Southwell in the Philosophical Transactions for 1746. Perpendicular to the main body of this villa there extend two parallel wings about fifty-eight paces distant from each other, and the surfaces of which are unbroken either with doors or windows. The sound of the human voice, or rather a word quickly pronounced, is repeated above forty times, and the report of a pistol from fifty-six to sixty times. The repetitions, however, follow in such rapid succession that it is difficult to reckon them, unless early in the morning before the equal temperature of the atmosphere is disturbed, or in a calm still evening. The echoes appear to be best heard from a window in the main building between the two projecting walls, from which the

U

pistol also is fired.   Dr. Plot mentions an echo in Wood-
stock Park which repeats seventeen syllables by day
and twenty by night.   An echo on the north side of
Shipley Church in Sussex repeats twenty-one syllables.
Sir John Herschel mentions an echo in the Manfroni
palace at Venice, where a person standing in the centre
of a square room about twenty-five feet high, with a
concave roof, hears the stamp of his foot repeated a great
many times, but as his position deviates from the centre,
the echoes become feebler, and at a short distance entirely
cease.   The same phenomenon, he remarks, occurs in the
large room of the library of the museum at Naples.
M. Genefay has described as existing near Rouen a
curious oblique echo which is not heard by the person
who emits the sound.   A person who sings hears only
his own voice, while those who listen hear only the echo,
which sometimes seems to approach, and at other times
to recede from the ear ; one person hears a single sound,
another several sounds, and one hears it on the right and
another on the left, the effect always changing as the
hearer changes his position.   Dr. Birch has described
an extraordinary echo at Roseneath in Argyleshire, which
certainly does not now exist.   When eight or ten notes
were played upon a trumpet they were correctly repeated,
but on a key a third lower.   After a short pause another
repetition of the notes was heard in a still lower tone,
and after another short interval they were repeated in a
still lower tone.

In the same manner as light is always lost by reflection,
so the waves of sound are enfeebled by reflection from
ordinary surfaces, and the echo is in such cases fainter
than the original sound.   If the reflecting surface, however, is circular, sound may be condensed and rendered
stronger in the same manner as light.   I have seen a fine
example of this in the circular turn of a garden wall

nearly a mile distant from a weir across a river. When the air is pure and homogeneous, the rushing sound of the water is reflected from the hollow surface of the wall, and concentrated in a focus, the place of which the ear can easily discover from the intensity of the sound being there a maximum. A person not acquainted with the locality conceives that the rushing noise is on the other side of the wall.

In Whispering Galleries, or places where the lowest whispers are carried to distances at which the direct sound is inaudible, the sound may be conveyed in two ways, either by repeated reflections from a curved surface in the direction of the sides of a polygon inscribed in a circle, or where the whisperer is in the focus of one reflecting surface, and the hearer in the focus of another reflecting surface, which is placed so as to receive the reflected sounds. The first of these ways is exemplified in the whispering gallery of St. Paul's, and in the octagonal gallery of Gloucester Cathedral, which conveys a whisper seventy-five feet across the nave, and the second in the baptistery of a church in Pisa, where the architect Giovanni Pisano is said to have constructed the cupola on purpose. The cupola has an elliptical form, and when one person whispers in one focus, it is distinctly heard by the person placed in the other focus, but not by those who are placed between them. The sound first reflected passes across the cupola, and enters the ears of the intermediate persons, but it is too feeble to be heard till it has been condensed by a second reflection to the other focus of ellipse. A naval officer, who travelled through Sicily in the year 1824, gives an account of a powerful whispering place in the cathedral of Girgenti, where the slightest whisper is carried with perfect distinctness through a distance of 250 feet, from the great western door to the cornice behind the high altar. By an unfortunate coincidence the focus of one of the reflecting surfaces was chosen for the place of the confessional, and when this was accidentally discovered, the lovers of secrets resorted to the other focus, and thus became acquainted with confessions of the gravest import. This divulgence of scandal continued for a considerable time, till the eager curiosity of one of the dilettanti was punished, by hearing his wife's avowal of her own infidelity. This circumstance gave publicity to the whispering peculiarity of the cathedral, and the confessional was removed to a place of greater secrecy.

An echo of a very peculiar character has been described by Sir John Herschel in his Treatise on Sound, as produced by the suspension bridge across the Menai Strait in Wales. "The sound of a blow with a hammer," says he, "on one of the main piers is returned in succession from each of the cross beams which support the road-way, and from the opposite pier at a distance of 576 feet; and in addition to this, the sound is many times repeated between the water and the road-way. The effect is a series of sounds which may be thus written : the first return is

Fig. 50.

sharp and strong from the road-way overhead; the rattling which succeeds dies away rapidly, but the single repercussion from the opposite pier is very strong, and is succeeded by a faint palpitation repeating the sound at the rate of twenty-eight times in five seconds, and which, therefore, corresponds to a distance of 184 feet, or very nearly the double interval from the road-way to the water. Thus it appears that in the repercussion between the water and road-way, that from the latter only affects the ear, the line drawn from the auditor to the water being too oblique for the sound to diverge sufficiently in that direction. Another peculiarity deserves especial notice, namely, that the echo from the opposite pier is best heard when the auditor stands precisely opposite to the middle of the breadth of the pier, and strikes just on that point. As it deviates to one or the other side, the return is proportionally fainter, and is scarcely heard by him when his station is a little beyond the extreme edge of the pier, though another person, stationed (on the same side of the water) at an equal distance from the central point, so as to have the pier between them, hears it well."

A remarkable subterranean echo is often heard when the hoofs of a horse or the wheels of a carriage pass over particular spots of ground. This sound is frequently very similar to that which is produced in passing over an arch or vault, and is commonly attributed to the existence of natural or artificial caves beneath. As such caves have often been constructed in times of war as places of security for persons and property, many unavailing attempts have been made to discover hidden treasures where their locality seemed to be indicated by subterraneous sounds. But though these sounds are sometimes produced by excavations in the ground, yet they generally arise from the nature of the materials of which the ground is composed. and from their manner of combination. If the hollow of a road has been filled up with broken rock, or with large water-worn stones, having hollows either left entirely empty, or filled up with materials of different density, then the sound will be reflected in passing from the loose to the dense materials, and there will arise a great number of echoes reaching the ear in rapid succession, and forming by their union a hollow rumbling sound. This principle has been very successfully applied by Sir John Herschel to explain the subterranean sounds with which every traveller is familiar who has visited the Solfaterra near Naples. When the ground at a particular place is struck violently by throwing a large stone against it, a peculiar hollow sound is distinctly heard. This sound has been ascribed by some geologists to the existence of a great vault communicating with the ancient seat of the volcano, by other writers to a reverberation from the surrounding hills with which it is nearly concentric, and by others to the porosity of the ground. Dr. Daubeny, who says that the hollow sound is heard when any part of the Solfaterra is struck, accounts for it by supposing that the hill is not made up of one entire rock, but of a number of detached blocks, which, hanging as it were by each other, form a sort of vault over the abyss within which the volcanic operations are going on.* Mr. Forbes, who has given the latest and most interesting description of this singular volcano,† agrees in opinion with Dr. Daubeny, while Mr. Scrope ‡ and Sir John Herschel concur in opinion that no such cavities exist. "It seems most probable," says the latter, "that the hollow reverberation is nothing more than an assemblage of partial echoes arising from the reflection of successive portions of the original sound in its progress through the soil at the innumerable half-coherent surfaces composing it : were the whole soil a mass of sand, these reflections would be so strong and frequent as to destroy the whole impulse, in too short an interval to allow of a distinguishable after-sound. It is a case analogous to that of a strong light, thrown into a milky medium or smoky atmosphere; the whole medium

* *Description of Volcanoes*, p. 170.
† *Edinburgh Journal of Science*, N. Series, No. i. p. 124.
‡ *Considerations on Volcanoes*, and *Edinburgh Journal of Science*, No. xx. p. 261, and No. xiv. p. 265.

appears to shine with a nebulous undefined light. This is to the eye what such a hollow sound is to the ear."*

It has been recently shown by M. Savart, that the human ear is so extremely sensible as to be capable of appreciating sounds which arise from about *twenty-four thousand* vibrations in a second, and consequently, that it can hear a sound which lasts only the twenty-four thousandth part of a second. Vibrations of such frequency afford only a shrill squeak or chirp; and Dr. Wollaston has shown that there are many individuals with their sense of hearing entire, who are altogether insensible to such acute sounds, though others are painfully affected by them. Nothing, as Sir John Herschel remarks, can be more surprising than to see two persons, neither of them deaf, the one complaining of the penetrating shrillness of a sound, while the other maintains there is no sound at all. Dr. Wollaston has also shown that this is true also of very grave sounds, so that the hearing or not hearing of musical notes at both extremities of the scale seems to depend wholly on the pitch or frequency of vibration constituting the note, and not upon the intensity or loudness of the noise. This affection of the ear sometimes appears in cases of common deafness, where a shrill tone of voice, such as that of women and children, is often better heard than the loud and deeper tone of men.

Dr. Wollaston remarked, that when the mouth and nose are shut, the tympanum or drum of the ear may be so exhausted by a forcible attempt to take breath by the expansion of the chest, the pressure of the external air upon the membrane gives it such a tension, that the ear becomes insensible to grave tones, without losing in any degree the perception of sharper sounds. Dr. Wollaston found, that after he had got into the habit of making the experiment, so as to be able to produce a great degree of

* Art. Sound, *Encycl. Metrop.* § 110.

exhaustion, his ears were insensible to all sounds below F, marked by the base clef. "If I strike the table before me," says he, "with the end of my finger, the whole board sounds with a deep dull note. If I strike it with my nail, there is also at the same time a sharp sound produced by quicker vibrations of parts around the point of contact. When the ear is exhausted it hears only the latter sound, without perceiving in any degree the deeper note of the whole table. In the same manner, in listening to the sound of a carriage, the deeper rumbling noise of the body is no longer heard by an exhausted ear; but the rattle of a chain or loose screw remains at least as audible as before exhaustion." Dr. Wollaston supposes that this excessive tension of the drum of the ear, when produced by the compressed air in the diving-bell, will also produce a corresponding *deafness to low tones.* This curious experiment has been since made by Dr. Colladon, when descending in the diving-bell at Howth in 1820. "We descended," says he, "so slowly that we did not notice the motion of the bell; but as soon as the bell was immersed in water, we felt about the ears and the forehead a sense of pressure, which continued increasing during some minutes. I did not, however, experience any pain in the ears; but my companion suffered so much that we were obliged to stop our descent for a short time. To remedy that inconvenience, the workmen instructed us, after having closed our nostrils and mouth, to endeavour to swallow, and to restrain our respiration for some moments, in order that, by this exertion, the internal air might act on the Eustachian tube. My companion, however, having tried it, found himself very little relieved by this remedy. After some minutes, we resumed our descent. My friend suffered considerably; he was pale; his lips were totally discoloured; his appearance was that of a man on the point of fainting; he was in involuntary low spirits,

owing, perhaps, to the violence of the pain, added to that
kind of apprehension which our situation unavoidably
inspired. This appeared to me the more remarkable, as
my case was totally the reverse. I was in a state of excitement resembling the effect of some spirituous liquor.
I suffered no pain; I experienced only a strong pressure
round my head, as if an iron circle had been bound about
it. I spoke with the workmen and had some difficulty in
hearing them. This difficulty of hearing rose to such a
height, that during three or four minutes I could not hear
them speak. I could not, indeed, hear myself speak,
though I spoke as loudly as possible; nor did even the
great noise caused by the violence of the current against
the sides of the bell reach my ears."

The effect thus described by Dr. Colladon is different
from that anticipated by Dr. Wollaston. He was not
merely deaf to low tones but to all sounds whatever; and
I have found by repeated experiment, that my own ears
become perfectly insensible even to the shrill tones of the
female voice, and of the voice of a child, when the drum
of the ear is thrown into a state of tension by yawning.

With regard to sounds of high pitch at the other
extremity of the scale, Dr. Wollaston has met with
persons, whose hearing was in other respects perfect, who
never heard the chirping of the *Gryllus campestris*, which
commonly occurs in hedges during a summer's evening,
or that of the house-cricket, or the squeak of the bat, or
the chirping of the common house-sparrow. The note of
the bat is a full octave higher than that of the sparrow;
and Dr. Wollaston believes that the note of some insects
may reach one octave more, as there are sounds decidedly
higher than that of a small pipe, one-fourth of an inch in
length, which he conceives cannot be far from six octaves
above the middle E of the pianoforte. " The suddenness
of the transition," says Dr. Wollaston, " from perfect

hearing to total want of perception occasions a degree of surprise, which renders an experiment on this subject with a series of small pipes among several persons rather amusing. It is curious to observe the change of feeling manifested by various individuals of the party, in succession, as the sounds approach and pass the limits of their hearing. Those who enjoy a temporary triumph are often compelled in their turn to acknowledge to how short a distance their little superiority extends." In concluding his interesting paper on this subject, Dr. Wollaston con-jectures that animals, like the grylli (whose powers of hearing appear to commence nearly where ours terminate), may have the power of hearing still sharper sounds which at present we do not know to exist, and that there may be other insects having nothing in common with us, but who are endowed with a power of exciting, and a sense of perceiving vibrations which make no impression upon our organs, while their organs are equally insensible to the slower vibrations to which we are accustomed.

With the view of studying the class of sounds inaudible to certain ears, we would recommend to the young naturalist to examine the sounds emitted by the insect tribe, both in relation to their effect upon the human ear, and to the mechanism by which they are produced. The Cicadæ or locusts in North America appear, from the observations of Dr. Hildreth,[*] to be furnished with a bagpipe on which they play a variety of notes. "When any one passes," says he, "they make a great noise and screaming with their air-bladder or bagpipes. These bags are placed under, and rather behind, the wings in the axilla, something in the manner of using the bagpipes with the bags under the arms,—I could compare them to nothing else; and, indeed, I suspect the first inventor of the instrument borrowed his ideas from some insect of

* Edinburgh Journal of Science, No. xvii. p. 158.

this kind. They play a variety of notes and sounds, one
of which nearly imitates the scream of the tree-toad."

Among the acoustic wonders of the natural world
may be ranked the vocal powers of the statue of Memnon,
the son of Aurora, which modern discoveries have withdrawn from among the fables of ancient Egypt. The
history of this remarkable statue is involved in much
obscurity. Although Strabo affirms that it was over-
turned by an earthquake, yet as Egypt exhibits no traces
of such a convulsion, it has been generally believed that
the statue was mutilated by Cambyses. Ph. Casselius,
in his dissertation on vocal or speaking stones, quotes
the remark of the scholiast in Juvenal, "that, when
mutilated by Cambyses, the statue which saluted both the
sun and the king, afterwards saluted only the sun."
Philostratus, in his life of Apollo, informs us, that the
statue looked to the east, and that it spoke as soon as the
rays of the rising sun fell upon its mouth. Pausanias,
who saw the statue in its dismantled state, says that it is
a statue of the sun, that the Egyptians call it Phamenophis,
and not Memnon, and *that it emits sounds every morning at
sunrise, which can be compared only to that of the breaking of
the string of a lyre.* Strabo speaks only of a single sound
which he heard; but Juvenal, who had probably heard it
often during his stay in Egypt, describes it as if it
emitted several sounds:

> Dimidio magicæ resonant ubi Memnone chordæ.
> Where broken Memnon sounds his magic strings.

The simple sounds which issued from the statue were in
the progress of time magnified into intelligible words, and
even into an oracle of seven verses, and this prodigy has
been recorded in a Greek inscription on the left leg of
the statue. But though this new faculty of the colossus
was evidently the contrivance of the Egyptian priests, yet

we are not entitled from this to call in question the
simple and perfectly credible fact that it emitted sounds.
This property, indeed, it seems to possess at the present
day; for we learn,* that an English traveller, Sir A.
Smith, accompanied with a numerous escort, examined
the statue, and that at six o'clock in the morning he
heard very distinctly the sounds which had been so celebrated in antiquity. He asserts that this sound does not
proceed from the statue but from the pedestal; and he
expresses his belief that it arises from the impulse of the
air upon the stones of the pedestal, which are arranged so
as to produce this surprising effect. This singular
description is to a certain extent confirmed by the description of Strabo, who says that he was quite certain that he
heard a sound which proceeded either *from the base*, or
from the colossus, or from some one of the assistants.
As there were no Egyptian priests in the escort of Sir
A. Smith, we may now safely reject this last, and, for
many centuries, the most probable hypothesis.

The explanation suggested by Sir A. Smith, had been
previously given in a more specific form by M. Dussaulx,
the translator of Juvenal. " The statue," says he, " being
hollow, the heat of the sun heated the air which it contained, and this air, issuing at some crevice, produced the
sounds of which the priests gave their own interpretation."

Rejecting this explanation, M. Langles, in his dissertation on the vocal statue of Memnon, and M. Salverte,
in his work on the occult sciences, have ascribed the
sounds entirely to Egyptian priestcraft, and have even
gone so far as to describe the mechanism by which the
statue not only emitted sounds, but articulated distinctly
the intonations appropriate to the seven Egyptian vowels,
and consecrated to the seven planets. M. Langles conceives that the sounds may be produced by a series of

* *Revue Encyclopédique*, 1821, Tom. ix. p. 592.

hammers, which strike either the granite itself, or sonorous stones like those which have been long used in China for musical instruments. M. Salverte improves this imperfect apparatus, by supposing that there might be adapted to these hammers a clepsydra or water-clock, or any other instrument fitted to measure time, and so constructed as to put the hammers in motion at sunrise. Not satisfied with this supposition, he conjectures that the spring of all this mechanism was to be found in the art of concentrating the rays of the sun, which was well known to the ancients. Between the lips of the statue, or in some less remarkable part of it concealed from view by its height, he conceives an aperture to be perforated, containing a lens or a mirror capable of condensing the rays of the rising sun upon one or more metallic levers which by their expansion put in motion the seven hammers in succession. Hence he explains why the sounds were emitted only at sunrise, and when the solar rays fell upon the mouth of the statue, and why they were never again heard till the sun returned to the eastern horizon. As a piece of mechanism, this contrivance is defective in not providing for the change in the sun's amplitude, which is very considerable even in Egypt, for as the statue and the lens are both fixed, and as the sounds were heard at all seasons of the year, the same lens which threw the midsummer rays of the sun upon the hammers could not possibly throw upon them his rays in winter But even if the machinery were perfect, it is obvious that it could not have survived the mutilation of the statue, and could not, short of a miracle, have performed its part in the time of Sir A. Smith.

If we abandon the idea of the whole being a trick of the priesthood, which has been generally done, and which the recent observations of Sir A. Smith authorizes us to do,

we must seek some natural cause for the phenomena
similar to that suggested by Dussaulx. It is curious to
observe how the study of nature gradually dispels the
consecrated delusions of ages, and reduces to the level of
ordinary facts what time had invested with all the
characters of the supernatural. And in the present case
it is no less remarkable that the problem of the statue of
Memnon should have been first solved by means of an
observation made by a solitary traveller wandering on the
banks of the Orinoco. "The granitic rock," says Baron
Humboldt, "on which we lay is one of those where
travellers on the Orinoco have heard from time to time,
towards sunrise, subterraneous sounds resembling those
of the organ. The missionaries call these stones *loxas de
musica*. 'It is witchcraft,' said our young Indian pilot.
We never ourselves heard these mysterious sounds either
at Carichana Vieja or in the upper Orinoco; but from
information given us by witnesses worthy of belief, the
existence of a phenomenon that seems to depend on a
certain state of the atmosphere cannot be denied. The
shelves of rock are full of very narrow and deep crevices.
They are heated during the day to about 50°. I often
found their temperature at the surface during the night
at 39°, the surrounding atmosphere being at 28°. It
may easily be conceived that the difference of temperature
between the subterraneous and the external air attains
its maximum about sunrise, or at that moment which is at
the same time farther from the period of the maximum
of the heat of the preceding day. May not these sounds
of an organ, then, which are heard when a person sleeps
upon the rock, his ear in contact with the stone, be the
effect of a current of air that issues out through the
crevices? Does not the impulse of the air against the
elastic spangles of mica that intercept the crevices contribute to modify the sounds? May we not admit that

the ancient inhabitants of Egypt, in passing incessantly up and down the Nile, had made the same observation on some rock of the Thebaid, and that the music of the rocks there led to the jugglery of the priests in the statue of Memnon ?"

This curious case of the production of sounds in granite rocks at sunrise might have been regarded as a transatlantic wonder which was not applicable to Egypt ; but by a singular coincidence of observation, MM. Jomard, Jollois, and Devilliers, who were travelling in Egypt nearly about the same time that M. Humboldt was traversing the wilds of South America, heard, *at sunrise*, *in a monument of granite*, situated near the centre of the spot on which the palace of Carnac stands, *a noise resembling that of a breaking string*, the very expression by which Pausanias characterizes the sound in the Memnonian granite. The travellers regarded these sounds as arising from the transmission of rarefied air through the crevices of a sonorous stone, and they were of the same opinion with Humboldt, that these sounds might have *suggested* to the Egyptian priests *the juggleries of the Memnonium*. Is it not strange that the Prussian and the French travellers should not have gone a step farther, and solved the problem of two thousand years, by maintaining that the sound of the statue of Memnon was itself a natural phenomenon, or a granite sound elicited at sunrise by the very same causes which operated on the Orinoco and in the Temple of Carnac, in place of regarding it as a trick in imitation of natural sounds ? If, as Humboldt supposes, the ancient inhabitants of Egypt had, in passing incessantly up and down the Nile, become familiar with the music of the granite rocks of the Thebaid, how could the imitation of such natural and familiar sounds be regarded by the priests as a means of deceiving the people ? There could be nothing marvellous in a colossal statue of granite giving out the very same sounds that were given out at the same time of the day by a granite rock; and in place of reckoning it a supernatural fact, they could regard it in no other light than as the duplicate of a well-known natural phenomenon. It is a mere conjecture, however, that such sounds were common in the Thebaid, and it is therefore probable that a granite rock, possessing the property of emitting sounds at sunrise, had been discovered by the priests, who were at the same time the philosophers of Egypt, and that the block had been employed in the formation of the Memnonian statue for the purpose of impressing upon it a supernatural character, and enabling them to maintain their influence over a credulous people.

The inquiries of recent travellers have enabled us to corroborate these views, and to add another remarkable example of the influence of subterraneous sounds over superstitious minds. About three leagues to the north of Tor, in Arabia Petræa, is a mountain, within the bosom of which the most singular sounds have been heard. The Arabs of the Desert ascribe these sounds to a convent of monks preserved miraculously under ground, and the sound is supposed to be that of the *Nakous,* a long narrow metallic ruler, suspended horizontally, which the priest strikes with a hammer for the purpose of assembling the monks to prayer. A Greek was said to have seen the mountain open, and to have descended into the subterranean convent, where he found fine gardens and delicious water; and, in order to give proof of his descent, he produced some fragments of consecrated bread, which he pretended to have brought from the subterranean convent. The inhabitants of Tor likewise declare that the camels are not only frightened but rendered furious when they hear these subterraneous sounds.

M. Seetzen, the first European traveller who visited

this extraordinary mountain, set out from Woodyel Nackel on the 17th of June at five o'clock in the morning. He was accompanied by a Greek Christian and some Bedouin Arabs, and after a quarter of an hour's walk they reached the foot of a majestic rock of hard sandstone. The mountain itself was quite bare and entirely composed of it. He found inscribed upon the rock several Greek and Arab names, and also some Koptic characters, which proved that it had been resorted to for centuries. About noon the party reached the foot of the mountains called *Nakous,* where at the foot of a ridge they beheld an insulated peaked rock. This mountain presented upon two of its sides two sandy declivities about 150 feet high, and so inclined that the white and slightly adhering sand which rests upon its surface is scarcely able to support itself; and when the scorching heat of the sun destroys its feeble cohesion, or when it is agitated by the smallest motions, it slides down the two acclivities. These declivities unite behind the insulated rock, forming an acute angle, and, like the adjacent surfaces, they are covered with steep rocks which consist chiefly of a white and friable freestone.

The first sound which greeted the ears of the travellers took place at an hour and a quarter after noon. They had climbed with great difficulty as far as the sandy declivity, a height of seventy or eighty feet, and had rested beneath the rocks where the pilgrims are accustomed to listen to the sounds.

While in the act of climbing, M. Seetzen heard the sound from beneath his knees, and hence he was led to think that the sliding of the sand was the cause of the sound, and not the effect of the vibration which it occasioned. At three o'clock the sound became louder, and continued six minutes, and after having ceased for ten minutes, it was again heard. The sound appeared to have

x

the greatest resemblance to that of the humming-top, rising and falling like that of an Eolian harp. Believing that he had discovered the true origin of the sound, M. Seetzeen was anxious to repeat the experiment, and with this view he climbed with the utmost difficulty to the highest rocks, and, sliding down as fast as he could, he endeavoured, with the help of his hands and feet, to set the sand in motion. The effect thus produced far exceeded his expectetions, and the sand in rolling beneath him made so loud a noise that the earth seemed to tremble to such a degree that he states he should certainly have been afraid if he had been ignorant of the cause.

M. Seetzen throws out some conjectures respecting the cause of these sounds. Does the rolling layer of sand, says he, act like the fiddle-bow, which on being rubbed upon a plate of glass raises and distributes into regular figures the sand with which the plate is covered? Does the adherent and fixed layer of sand perform here the part of the plate of glass, and the neighbouring rocks that of the sounding body? We cannot pretend to answer these questions, but we trust that some philosopher competent to the task will have an opportunity of examining these interesting phenomena with more attention, and describing them with greater accuracy.

The only person, so far as I can learn, who has visited El Nakous since the time of Seetzen is Mr. Gray, of University College, Oxford; but he has not added much to the information acquired by his predecessor. During the first visit which he made to the place, he heard at the end of a quarter of an hour a low continuous murmuring sound beneath his feet, which gradually changed into pulsations as it became louder, so as to resemble the striking of a clock, and at the end of five minutes it became so strong as to detach the sand. Returning to the spot next day, he heard the sound still louder than before.

He could not observe any crevices by which the external air could penetrate, and as the sky was serene and the air calm, he was satisfied that the sounds could not arise from this cause.*

* See *Edinburgh Journal of Science*, No. xi. p. 153, and No. xiii. p. 51.

LETTER X.

Mechanical inventions of the ancients few in number—Ancient and modern feats of strength—Feats of Eckeberg particularly described—General explanation of them—Real feats of strength performed by Thomas Topham — Remarkable power of lifting heavy persons when the. lungs are inflated—Belzoni's feat of sustaining pyramids of men—Deception of walking along the ceiling in an inverted position—Pneumatic apparatus in the foot of the house-fly for enabling it to walk in opposition to gravity— Description of the analogous apparatus employed by the gecko lizard for the same purpose—Apparatus used by the Echineis remora or sucking fish.

THE mechanical knowledge of the ancients was principally theoretical, and though they seem to have executed some minor pieces of mechanism which were sufficient to delude the ignorant, yet there is no reason for believing that they have executed any machinery that was capable of exciting much surprise, either by its ingenuity or its magnitude. The properties of the mechanical powers, however, seem to have been successfully employed in performing feats of strength which were beyond the reach even of strong men, and which could not fail to excite the greatest wonder when exhibited by persons of ordinary size.

Firmus, a native of Seleucia, who was executed by the Emperor Aurelian for espousing the cause of Zenobia, was celebrated for his feats of strength. In his account of the life of Firmus, who lived in the third century, Vopiscus informs us, that he could suffer iron to be forged upon an anvil placed upon his breast. In doing this he lay upon his back, and resting his feet and shoulders against some support, his whole body formed an arch as we shall afterwards more particularly explain. Until the end of the sixteenth century the exhibition of such feats does not seem to have been common. About the year 1703, a native of Kent of the name of Joyce exhibited such feats of strength in London and other parts of England, that he received the name of the second Sampson. His own personal strength was very great; but he had also discovered, without the aid of theory, various positions of his body in which men even of common strength could perform very surprising feats. He drew against horses, and raised enormous weights; but as he actually exhibited his power in ways which evinced the enormous strength of his own muscles, all his feats were ascribed to the same cause. In the course of eight or ten years, however, his methods were discovered, and many individuals of ordinary strength exhibited a number of his principal performances, though in a manner greatly inferior to Joyce.

Some time afterwards, John Charles Van Eckeberg, a native of Harzgerode in Anhalt, travelled through Europe under the appellation of Sampson, exhibiting very remarkable examples of his strength. This we believe is the same person whose feats are particularly described by Dr. Desaguliers. He was a man of the middle size, and of ordinary strength; and as Dr. Desaguliers was convinced that his feats were exhibitions of skill and not of strength, he was desirous of discovering his methods, and with this view he went to see him accompanied with the Marquis of Tullibardine, Dr. Alexander Stuart, and Dr. Pringle, and his own mechanical operator. They placed themselves round the German so as to be able to observe accurately all that he did, and their success was so great, that they were able to perform most of the feats the same evening by themselves, and almost all the rest when they had provided the proper apparatus. Dr. Desaguliers exhibited some of the experiments before the Royal Society, and has given such a distinct explanation of the principles on which they depend, that we shall endeavour to give a popular account of them.

1. The performer sat upon an inclined board A B placed upon a frame C D E, with his feet abutting against

Fig. 51.

the upright board C. Round his loins was placed a strong girdle F G, to the iron ring of which at G was fastened a rope by means of a hook. The rope passed between his legs through a hole in the board C, and several men, or two horses pulling at the other end of the rope, were unable to draw the performer out of his place. His hands at G seemed to pull against the men, but they were of no advantage to him whatever.

2. Another of the German's feats is shown in Fig. 52. Having fixed the rope above mentioned to a strong post at A, and made it pass through a fixed iron eye at B, to the ring in his girdle, he planted his feet against the post at B, and raised himself from the ground by the rope, as shown in the figure. He then suddenly stretched out his legs and broke the rope, falling back on a feather-bed at C, spread out to receive him.

3. In imitation of Firmus, he laid himself down on the ground, as shown in Fig. 53, and when an anvil A was

Fig. 52.

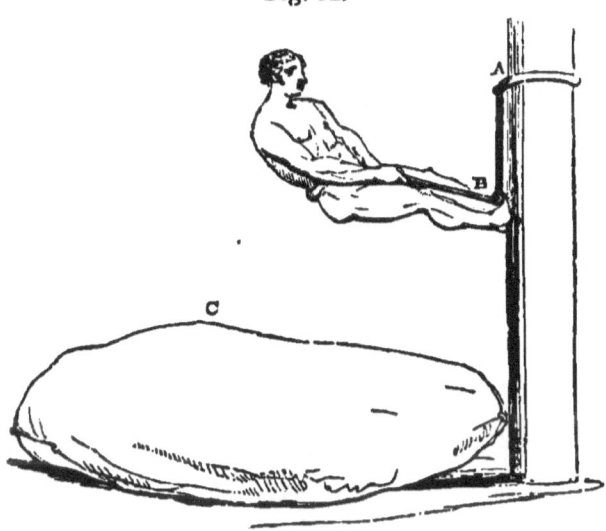

placed upon his breast, a man hammered with all his force
the piece of iron B, with a sledge-hammer, and sometimes

Fig. 53.

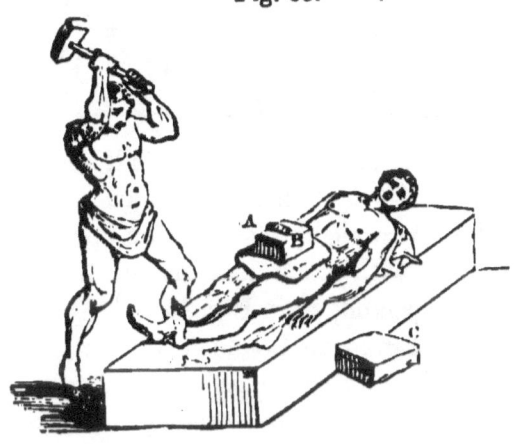

two smiths cut in two with chisels a great cold bar of iron
laid upon the anvil. At other times a stone of huge
dimensions, half of which is shown at C, was laid upon his
belly, and broken with a blow of the great hammer.

4. The performer then placed his shoulders upon one

chair, and his heels upon another, as in Fig. 54, forming
with his back-bone, thighs, and legs, an arch springing
from its abutments at A and B. One or two men then
stood upon his belly, rising up and down while the per-

Fig. 54.

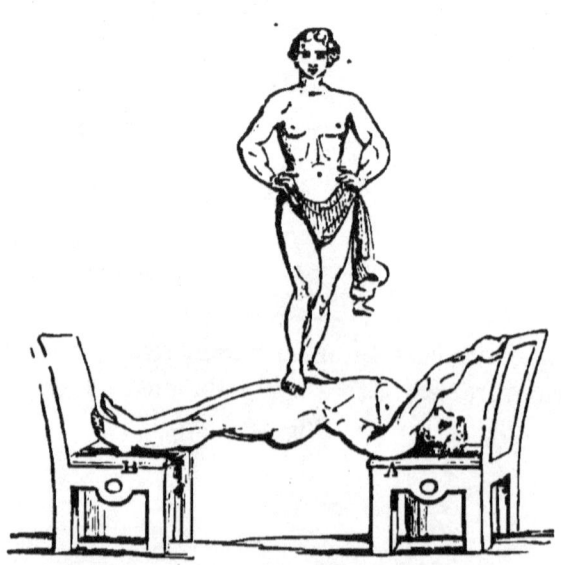

former breathed. A stone one and a half feet long, one
foot broad, and half a foot thick, was then laid upon his
belly and broken by a sledge-hammer, an operation which
may be performed with much less danger than when his
back touched the ground, as in Fig. 53.

5. His next feat was to lie down on the ground as in
Fig. 55. A man being then placed on his knees, he draws
his heels towards his body, and raising his knees, he lifts
up the man gradually, till having brought his knees
perpendicularly under him, as in Fig. 56, he raises his
own body up, and placing his arms around the man's legs,
he rises with him, and sets him down on some low table
or eminence of the same height as his knees. This feat
he sometimes performed with two men in place of one.

Fig. 55.

Fig. 56.

6. The last, and apparently the most wonderful, performance of the German is shown in Fig. 57, where he

Fig. 57.

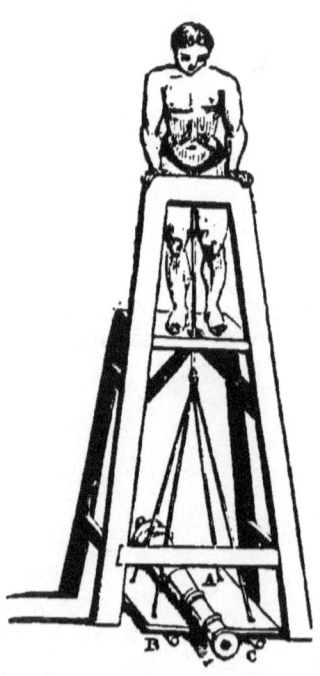

appears to raise a cannon A, placed upon a scale, the four ropes of the scale being fixed to a rope or chain attached to his girdle in the manner already described. Previous to the fixing of the ropes, the cannon and scale rest upon two rollers B C, but when all is ready, the two rollers are knocked from beneath the scale, and the cannon is sustained by the strength of his loins.

The German also exhibited his strength in twisting into a screw a flat piece of iron like A, Fig. 58. He first bent the iron into a right angle as at B, and then wrapping his handkerchief about its broad upper end, he

held that end in his left hand, and with his right applied
to the other end, twisted about the angular point, as

Fig. 58.

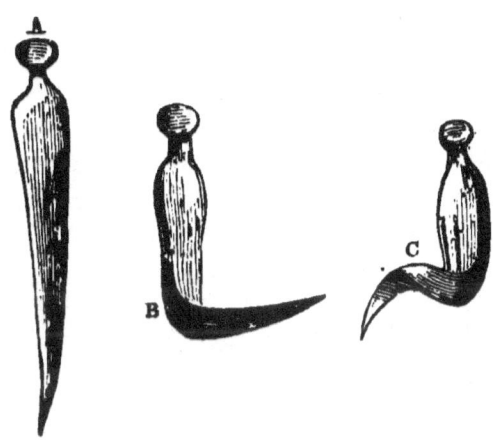

shown at C. Lord Tullibardine succeeded in doing the
same thing, and even untwisted one of the irons which
the German had twisted.

It would lead into details by no means popular, were
I to give a minute explanation of the mechanical prin
ciples upon which these feats depend. A few general
observations will perhaps be sufficient for ordinary
readers. The feats No. 1, 2, and 6, depend entirely on
the natural strength of the bones of the pelvis, which
form a double arch, which it would require an immense
force to break, by any external pressure directed to the
centre of the arch ; and as the legs and thighs are capable
of sustaining four or five thousand pounds when they
stand quite upright, the performer has no difficulty in
resisting the force of two horses, or of sustaining the
weight of a cannon weighing two or three thousand
pounds.

The feat of the anvil is certainly a very surprising one.

The difficulty, however, really consists in sustaining the anvil, for when this is done the effect of the hammering is nothing. If the anvil were a thin piece of iron, or even two or three times heavier than the hammer, the performer would be killed by a few blows; but the blows are scarcely felt when the anvil is very heavy, for the more matter the anvil has, the greater is its inertia, and it is the less liable to be struck out of its place; for when it has received by the blow the whole momentum of the hammer, its velocity will be so much less than that of the hammer, as its quantity of matter is greater. When the blow, indeed, is struck, the man feels less of the weight of the anvil than he did before, because in the reaction of the stone all the parts of it round about the hammer rise towards the blow. This property is illustrated by the well-known experiment of laying a stick with its ends upon two drinking glasses full of water, and striking the stick downwards in the middle with an iron bar. The stick will in this case be broken without breaking the glasses, or spilling the water. But if the stick is struck upwards as if to throw it up in the air, the glasses will break if the blow be strong, and if the blow is not very quick, the water will be spilt without breaking the glasses.

When the performer supports a man upon his belly as in Fig. 54, he does it by means of the strong arch formed by his backbone, and the bones of his legs and thighs. If there were room for them he could bear three or four, or, in their stead, a great stone, to be broken with one blow.

A number of feats of real and extraordinary strength were exhibited about a century ago, in London, by Thomas Topham, who was five feet ten inches high, and about 31 years of age. He was entirely ignorant of any of the methods for making his strength appear more surprising, and he often performed by his own natural powers what he learned had been done by others by artificial means. A distressing example of this occurred in his attempt to imitate the feat of the German Sampson by pulling against horses. Ignorant of the method which we have already ·described, he seated himself on the ground with his feet against two stirrups, and by the weight of his body he succeeded in pulling against a single horse ; but in attempting to pull against two horses, he was lifted out of his place and one of his knees was shattered against the stirrups, so as to deprive him of most of the strength of one of his legs. The following are the feats of real strength which Dr. Desaguliers saw him perform.

1. Having rubbed his fingers with coal ashes to keep them from slipping, he rolled up a very strong and large pewter plate.

2. Having laid seven or eight short and strong pieces of tobacco-pipe on the first and third finger, he broke them by the force of his middle finger.

3. He broke the bowl of a strong tobacco-pipe placed between his first and third finger, by pressing his fingers together sideways.

4. Having thrust such another bowl under his garter, his legs being bent, he broke it to pieces by the tendons of his hams, without altering the bending of his leg.

5. He lifted with his teeth, and held in a horizontal position for a considerable time, a table six feet long, with half a hundredweight hanging at the end of it. The feet of the table rested against his knees.

6. Holding in his right hand an iron kitchen poker three feet long and three inches round, he struck upon his bare left arm, between the elbow and the wrist, till he bent the poker nearly to a right angle.

7. Taking a similar poker, and holding the ends of it in his hands, and the middle against the back of his neck,

he brought both ends of it together before him, and he then pulled it almost straight again. This last feat was the most difficult, because the muscles which separate the arms horizontally from each other are not so strong as those which bring them together.

8. He broke a rope about two inches in circumference, which was partly wound about a cylinder four inches in diameter, having fastened the other end of it to straps that went over his shoulder.

9. Dr. Desaguliers saw him lift a rolling stone of about 800 lbs. weight with his hands only, standing in a frame above it, and taking hold of a frame fastened to it. Hence Dr. Desaguliers gives the following relative view of the strengths of individuals:

Strength of the weakest men	- -	125 lbs.
Strength of very strong men	- -	400
Strength of Topham	- - - -	800

The weight of Topham was about 200.

One of the most remarkable and inexplicable experiments relative to the strength of the human frame, which you have yourself seen and admired, is that in which a heavy man is raised with the greatest facility, when he is lifted up the instant that his own lungs and those of the persons who raise him are inflated with air. This experiment was, I believe, first shown in England a few years ago by Major H., who saw it performed in a large party at Venice under the direction of an officer of the American Navy. As Major H. performed it more than once in my presence, I shall describe as nearly as possible the method which he prescribed. The heaviest person in the party lies down upon two chairs, his legs being supported by the one and his back by the other. Four persons, one at each leg, and one at each shoulder, then try to raise him, and they find his dead weight to be very great, from the difficulty they experience in supporting him. When he is replaced in tho chair, each of tho four persons takes hold of the body as before, and the person to bo lifted gives two signals by clapping his hands. At the first signal he himself and the four lifters begin to draw a long and full breath, and when the inhalation is completed, or the lungs filled, the second signal is given, for raising the person from tho chair. To his own surprise and that of his bearers, he rises with the greatest facility, as if he were no heavier than a feather. On several occasions I have observed that when one of the bearers performs his part ill, by making tho inhalation out of time, the part of the body which he tries to raise is left as it were behind. As you have repeatedly seen this experiment, and have performed the part both of the load and of the bearer, you can testify how remarkable the effects appear to all parties, and how complete is the conviction, either that the load has been lightened, or tho bearer strengthened by the prescribed process.

At Venice the experiment was performed in a much more imposing manner. The heaviest man in the party was raised and sustained upon the points of the forefingers of six persons. Major H. declared that the experiment would not succeed if the person lifted were placed upon a board, and the strength of the individuals applied to the board. He conceived it necessary that the bearers should communicate directly with the body to be raised. I have not had an opportunity of making any experiments relative to these curious facts; but whether the general effect is an illusion, or the result of known or of new principles, the subject merits a careful investigation.

Among the remarkable exhibitions of mechanical strength and dexterity, we may enumerate that of supporting pyramids of men. This exhibition is a very ancient one. It is described, though not very clearly, by the Roman poet Claudian, and it has derived some importance

in modern times, in consequence of its having been performed in various parts of great Britain by the celebrated
traveller Belzoni, before he entered upon the more
estimable career of an explorer of Egyptian antiquities.
The simplest form of this feat consists in placing a number
of men upon each other's shoulders, so that each row consists of a man fewer till they form a pyramid terminating
in a single person, upon whose head a boy is sometimes
placed with his feet upwards.

Among the displays of mechanical dexterity, though
not grounded on any scientific principle, may be mentioned
the art of walking along the ceiling of an apartment with
the head downwards. This exhibition, which we have
witnessed in one of the London Theatres, never failed to
excite the wonder of the audience, although the movements
of the inverted performer were not such as to inspire us
with any high ideas of the mechanism by which they
were effected. The following was probably the method
by which the performer was carried along the ceiling.
Two parallel grooves or openings were made in the
ceiling at the same distance as the foot tracks of a person
walking on sand. These grooves were narrower than the
human foot, so as to permit a rope or chain or strong wire,
attached to the feet of the performer, to pass through the
ceiling, where they were held by two or more persons
above it. In this way the inverted performer might be
carried along by a sliding or shuffling motion, similar to
that which is adopted in walking in the dark, and in
which the feet are not lifted from the ground. A more
regular motion, however, might be produced by a contrivance for attaching the rope or chain to the sole of the
foot, at each step, and subsequently detaching it. In this
way, when the performer is pulled against the ceiling by
his left foot, he would lift his right foot, and having made
a step with it, and planted it against the grooves, the rope

would be attached to it, and when the rope was detached from the left foot, it would make a similar step, while the right foot was pulled against the ceiling. These effects might be facilitated and rendered more natural by attaching to the body or to the feet of the performer strong wires invisible to the audience, and by using friction wheels, if a sliding motion only is required.

A more scientific method of walking upon the ceiling is suggested by those beautiful pneumatic contrivances by which insects, fishes, and even some lizards are enabled

Fig. 59.   .

to support the weight of their bodies against the force of gravity. The house-fly is well known to have the power of walking in an inverted position upon the ceilings of rooms, as well as upon the smoothest surfaces. In this case the fly does not rest upon its legs, and must therefore adhere to the ceiling, either by some glutinous matter upon its feet, or by the aid of some apparatus given it for

that purpose. In examining the foot of the fly with a
powerful microscope, it is found to consist of two concavities, as shown in Fig. 59 and 60, the first of which is
copied from a drawing by G. Adams, published in 1746,
and the second by J. C. Keller, a painter at Nuremberg,
who drew it for a work published in 1766. The author
of this work maintains that these concavities are only
used when the fly moves horizontally, and that, when it
moves perpendicularly or on the ceiling, they are turned
up out of the way, and the progressive motion is effected
by fixing the claws shown in the figure into the irregu-
larities of the surface upon which the fly moves, whether

Fig. 60.

it is glass, porcelain, or any other subtance. Sir Everard
Home, however, supposes with great reason, that these
concave surfaces are (like the leathern suckers used by
children for lifting stones) employed to form a vacuum,
so that the foot adheres as it were by suction to the
ceiling, and enables the insect to support itself in an
inverted position.

This conclusion Sir Everard has been led to draw from an examination of the foot of the Lacerta Gecko. Sir Joseph Banks had mentioned to him in the year 1815, that this lizard, which is a native of the island of Java, comes out in the evening from the roofs of the houses, and walks down the smooth, hard, polished chunam walls in search of the flies which settle upon them, and which are its natural food. When Sir Joseph was at Batavia, he amused himself in catching this lizard. He stood close to the wall at some distance from the animal, and, by suddenly scraping the wall with a long flattened pole, he was able to bring the animal to the ground.

Having procured from Sir Joseph a very large specimen of the Gecko, which weighed 5¼ ounces avoirdupois, Sir Everard Home was enabled to ascertain the peculiar mechanism by which the feet of this animal have the power of keeping hold of a smooth, hard, perpendicular wall, and carry up so heavy a weight as that of its body.

The foot of the Gecko has five toes, and at the end of each of them, except the thumb, is a very sharp, and highly-curved claw. On the under surface of each toe are sixteen transverse slits, leading to as many cavities or pockets, the depth of which is nearly equal to the length of the slit that forms the surface. These cavities all open forwards, and the external edge of each opening is serrated like the teeth of a small toothed comb. The cavities are lined with a cuticle, which also covers the serrated edges.

This structure Sir Everard Home found to bear a considerable resemblance to that portion of the head of the *Echineis remora*, or sucking-fish, by which it attaches itself to the shark, or the bottoms of ships. It is of an oval form, and is surrounded by a broad, loose, moveable edge, capable of applying itself closely to the surface on which it is set. It consists of two rows of cartilaginous plates, connected by one edge to the surface on which they are placed, the other, or the external edge, being serrated like that in the cavities of the feet of the Gecko. The two rows are separated by a thin ligamentous partition, and the plates being raised or depressed by the voluntary mucles form so many vacua, by means of which the adhesion of the fish is effected.

These beautiful contrivances of Divine Wisdom cannot fail to arrest the attention and excite the admiration of the reader ; but though there can be little doubt that they are pneumatic suckers wrought by the voluntary muscles of the animals to which they belong, yet we would recommend the farther examination of them to the attention of those who have good microscopes at their command.

LETTER XI.

Mechanical automata of the ancients—Moving tripods—Automata of Dædalus— Wooden pigeon of Archytas — Automatic clock of Charlemagne—Automata made by Turrianus for Charles V.— Camus's automatic carriage made for Louis XIV.—Degennes's mechanical peacock—Vaucanson's duck which ate and digested its food—Du Moulin's automata—Baron Kempelen's automaton chess-player — Drawing and writing automata — Maillardet's conjurer — Benefits derived from the passion for automata— Examples of wonderful machinery for useful purposes—Duncan's tambouring machinery—Watt's statue-turning machinery—Bab. bage's calculating machinery.

WE have already seen that the ancients had attained some degree of perfection in the construction of automata or pieces of mechanism which imitated the movements of man and the lower animals. The tripods which Homer * mentions as having been constructed by Vulcan for the banqueting hall of the gods, advanced of their own accord to the table, and again returned to their place. Self-moving tripods are mentioned by Aristotle, and Philostratus informs us, in his life of Apollonius, that this philosopher saw and admired similar pieces of mechanism among the sages of India.

Dædalus enjoys also the reputation of having constructed machines that imitated the motions of the human body. Some of his statues are said to have moved about spontaneously, and Plato, Aristotle, and others have related that it was necessary to tie them, in order to prevent them

* *Iliad*, Lib. xviii. 373—378.

from running away. Aristotle speaks of a wooden Venus, which moved about in consequence of quicksilver being poured into its interior; but Callistratus, the tutor of Demosthenes, states with some probability, that the statues of Dædalus received their motion from the mechanical powers. Beckmann is of opinion that the statues of Dædalus differed only from those of the early Greeks and Egyptians in having their eyes open and their feet and hands free, and that the reclining posture of some, and the attitude of others, " as if ready to walk," gave rise to the exaggeration that they possessed the power of locomotion. This opinion, however, cannot be maintained with any show of reason; for if we apply such a principle in one case, we must apply it in all, and the mind would be left in a state of utter scepticism respecting the inventions of ancient times.

We are informed by Aulus Gellius, on the authority of Favorinus, that Archytas of Tarentum, who flourished about 400 years before Christ, constructed a wooden pigeon which was capable of flying. Favorinus relates, that when it had once alighted, it could not again resume its flight, and Aulus Gellius adds, that it was suspended by balancing, and animated by a concealed aura or spirit.

Among the earliest pieces of modern mechanism was the curious water-clock presented to Charlemagne by the Kaliph Harun al Raschid. In the dial-plate there were twelve small windows corresponding with the divisions of the hours. The hours were indicated by the opening of the windows, which let out little metallic balls, which struck the hour by falling upon a brazen bell. The doors continued open till twelve o'clock, when twelve little knights, mounted on horseback, came out at the same instant, and after parading round the dial, shut all the windows and returned to their apartments.*

* *Annales Loisiliani.* Anno 807.

The next automata of which any distinct account has been preserved are those of the celebrated John Muller or Regiomontanus, which have been mentioned by Kircher, Baptista Porta, Gassendi, Lana, and Bishop Wilkins. This philosopher is said to have constructed an artificial eagle, which flew to meet the Emperor Maximilian when he arrived at Nuremberg on the 7th June, 1470. After soaring aloft in the air, the eagle is stated to have met the Emperor at some distance from the city, and to have returned and perched upon the town gate, where it waited his approach. When the Emperor reached the gate, the eagle stretched out its wings, and saluted him by an inclination of its body. Muller is likewise reported to have constructed an iron fly, which was put in motion by wheel-work, and which flew about and leapt upon the table. At an entertainment given by this philosopher to some of his familiar friends, the fly flew from his hand, and after performing a considerable round, it returned again to the hand of its master.

The Emperor Charles V., after his abdication of the throne, amused himself in his later years with automata of various kinds. The artist whom he employed was Janellus Turrianus of Cremona. It was his custom after dinner to introduce upon the table figures of armed men and horses. Some of these beat drums, others played upon flutes, while a third set attacked each other with spears. Sometimes he let fly wooden sparrows, which flew back again to their nest. He also exhibited corn-mills so extremely small that they could be concealed in a glove, yet so powerful that they could grind in a day as much corn as would supply eight men with food for a day.

The next piece of mechanism of sufficient interest to merit our attention is that which was made by M. Camus for the amusement of Louis XIV. when a child. It consisted of a small coach, which was drawn by two horses, and which contained the figure of a lady within, with a footman and page behind. When this machine was placed at the extremity of a table of the proper size, the coachman smacked his whip, and the horses instantly set off, moving their legs in a natural manner, and drawing the coach after them. When the coach reached the opposite edge of the table, it turned sharply at a right angle, and proceeded along the adjacent edge. As soon as it arrived opposite the place where the King sat it stopped ; the page descended and opened the coach door ; the lady alighted, and with a curtsey presented a petition, which she held in her hand to the King. After waiting some time she again curtsied and re-entered the carriage. The page closed the door, and having resumed his place behind, the coachman whipped his horses and drove on. The footman who had previously alighted, ran after the carriage and jumped up behind into his former place.

Not content with imitating the movements of animals, the mechanical genius of the 17th and 18th centuries ventured to perform by wheels and pinions the functions of vitality. We are informed by M. Lobat, that General Degennes, a French officer who defended the colony of St. Christopher's against the English forces, constructed a peacock, which could walk about as if alive, pick up grains of corn from the ground, digest them as if they had been submitted to the action of the stomach, and afterwards discharge them in an altered form. Degennes is said to have invented various machines of great use in navigation and gunnery, and to have constructed clocks without weights or springs.

The automaton of Degennes probably suggested to M. Vaucanson the idea of constructing his celebrated duck, which excited so much interest throughout Europe, and which was perhaps the most wonderful piece of mechanism that was ever made. Vaucanson's duck exactly resembled the living animal in size and appearance. It executed accurately all its movements and gestures, it ate and drank with avidity, performed all the quick motions of the head and throat which are peculiar to the living animal, and like it, it muddled the water which it drank with its bill. It produced also the sound of quacking in the most natural manner. In the anatomical structure of the duck, the artist exhibited the highest skill. Every bone in the real duck had its representative in the automaton, and its wings were anatomically exact. Every cavity, apophysis, and curvature was imitated, and each bone executed its proper movements. When corn was thrown down before it, the duck stretched out its neck to pick it up, it swallowed it, digested it, and discharged it, in a digested condition. The process of digestion was effected by chemical solution, and not by trituration, and the food digested in the stomach was conveyed away by tubes to the place of its discharge.

The automata of Vaucanson were imitated by one Du Moulin, a silversmith, who travelled with them through Germany in 1752, and who died at Moscow in 1765. Beckmann informs us that he saw several of them after the machinery had been deranged; but that the artificial duck, which he regarded as the most ingenious, was still able to eat, drink, and move. Its ribs, which were made of wire, were covered with duck's feathers, and the motion was communicated through the feet of the duck by means of a cylinder and fine chains like that of a watch.

Ingenious as all these machines are, they sink into insignificance when compared with the automaton chess-player, which for a long time astonished and delighted the whole of Europe. In the year 1769, M. Kempelen, a gentleman of Presburg in Hungary, constructed an automaton chess-player, the general appearance of which is shown in the annexed figures. The chess-player is a

figure as large as life, clothed in a Turkish dress, sitting
behind a large square chest or box three feet and a half
long, two feet deep, and two and a half high.   The machine
runs on casters, and is either seen on the floor when the
doors of the apartment are thrown open, or is wheeled
into the room previous to the commencement of the exhibition.   The Turkish chess-player sits on a chair fixed to
the square chest : his right arm rests on the table, and in
the left he holds a pipe, which is removed during the
game, as it is with this hand that he makes the moves.   A
chess-board, eighteen inches square, and bearing the usual
number of pieces, is placed before the figure.   The

Fig. 61.   Fig. 62.

exhibitor then announces to the spectators his intention of
showing them the mechanism of the automaton.   For this
purpose he unlocks the door A, Fig. 61, and exposes to
view a small cupboard lined with black or dark coloured
cloth, and containing cylinders, levers, wheels, pinions,
and different pieces of machinery, which *have the appearance*
of occupying the whole space.   He next opens the door
B, Fig. 62, at the back of the same cupboard, and holding
a lighted candle at the opening, he still further displays
the enclosed machinery to the spectators, placed in front
of A, Fig. 61.   When the candle is withdrawn, the door

B is then locked ; and the exhibitor proceeds to open the drawer G, G, Fig. 61, in front of the chest. Out of this drawer he takes a small box of counters, a set of chess-men, and a cushion for the support of the automaton's arm, as if this was the sole object of the drawer. The two front doors, C, C, of the large cupboard, Fig. 61, are then opened, and at the back-door D of the same cupboard, Fig. 62, the exhibitor applies a lighted candle, as before, for the purpose of showing its interior, which is lined with dark cloth like the other, and contains only a few pieces of machinery. The chest is now wheeled round, as in Fig. 62 : the garments of the figure are lifted up, and the door E in the trunk, and another door F in the thigh, are opened, the doors B and D having been previously closed. When this exhibition of the interior of the machine is over, the chest is wheeled back into its original position on the floor. The doors A, C, C, in front, and the drawer G, G, are closed and locked, and the exhibitor, after occupying himself for some time at the back of the chest, as if he were adjusting the mechanism, removes the pipe from the hand of the figure, and winds up the machinery.

The automaton is now ready to play, and when an opponent has been found among the company, the figure takes the first move. At every move made by the automaton, the wheels of the machine are heard in action ; the figure moves its head, and seems to look over every part of the chess-board. When it gives check to its opponent, it shakes its head *thrice*, and only *twice* when it checks the queen. It likewise shakes its head when a false move is made, replaces the adversary's piece on the square from which it was taken, and takes the next move itself. In general, though not always, the automaton wins the game.

During the progress of the game, the exhibitor often

stood near the machine, and wound it up like a clock after it had made ten or twelve moves. At other times he went to a corner of the room, as if it were to consult a small square box, which stood open for this purpose.

The chess-playing machine, as thus described, was exhibited after its completion in Presburg, Vienna, and Paris, to thousands, and in 1783 and 1784 it was exhibited in London and different parts of England, without the secret of its movements having been discovered. Its ingenious inventor, who was a gentleman and a man of education, never pretended that the automaton itself really played the game. On the contrary, he distinctly stated, "that the machine was a *bagatelle*, which was not without merit in point of mechanism, but that the effects of it appeared so marvellous only from the boldness of the conception, and the fortunate choice of the methods adopted for promoting the illusion."

Upon considering the operations of this automaton, it must have been obvious that the game of chess was performed either by a person enclosed in the chest, or by the exhibitor himself. The first of these hypotheses was ingeniously excluded by the display of the interior of the machine, for as every part contained more or less machinery, the spectator invariably concluded that the smallest dwarf could not be accommodated within, and this idea was strengthened by the circumstance, that no person of this description could be discovered in the suite of the exhibitor. Hence the conclusion was drawn, that the exhibitor actuated the machine either by mechanical means conveyed through its feet, or by a magnet concealed in the body of the exhibitor. That mechanical communication was not formed between the exhibitor and the figure, was obvious from the fact, that no such communication was visible, and that it was not necessary to place the machine on any particular part of the floor. Hence the opinion became very prevalent that the agent was a magnet; but even this supposition was excluded, for the exhibitor allowed a strong and well-armed loadstone to be placed upon the machine during the progress of the game. Had the moving power been a magnet, the whole action of the machine would have been deranged by the approximation of a loadstone concealed in the pockets of any of the spectators.

As Baron Kempelen himself had admitted that there was an illusion connected with the performance of the automaton, various persons resumed the original conjecture, that it was actuated by a person concealed in its interior, who either played the game of chess himself, or performed the moves which the exhibitor indicated by signals. A Mr. J. F. Freyhere of Dresden published a book on the subject in 1789, in which he endeavoured to explain, by coloured plates, how the effect was produced; and he concluded, "that a well-taught boy, very thin and tall of his age (sufficiently so that he could be concealed in a drawer almost immediately under the chess-board), agitated the whole."

In another pamphlet which had been previously published at Paris in 1785, the author not only supposed that the machine was put in motion by a dwarf, a famous chess-player, but he goes so far as to explain the manner in which he could be accommodated within the machine. The invisibility of the dwarf when the doors were opened was explained by his legs and thighs being concealed in two hollow cylinders, while the rest of his body was out of the box, and hid by the petticoats of the automaton. When the doors were shut the clacks produced by the swivel of a ratchet-wheel permitted the dwarf to change his place and return to the box unheard; and while the machine was wheeled about the room, the dwarf had an opportunity of shutting the trap through which he passed into the machine. The interior of the figure was next shown, and the spectators were satisfied that the box contained no living agent.

Although these views were very plausible, yet they were never generally adopted; and when the automaton was exhibited in Great Britain in 1819 and 1820, by M. Maelzel, it excited as intense an interest as when it was first produced in Germany. There can be little doubt, however, that the secret has been discovered; and an anonymous writer has shown in a pamphlet, entitled "*An attempt to analyse the Automaton Chess-player* of M. Kempelen," that it is capable of accommodating an ordinary-sized man; and he has explained in the clearest manner how the inclosed player takes all the different positions, and performs all the motions which are necessary to produce the effects actually observed. The following is the substance of his observations :

The drawer G G when closed does not extend to the back of the chest, but leaves a space O behind it (see Figs. 69, 70, and 71), fourteen inches broad, eight inches high, and three feet eleven inches long. This space is never exposed to the view of spectators. The small cupboard seen at A is divided into two parts by a door or screen I, Fig. 68, which is moveable upon a hinge, and is so constructed that it closes at the same instant that B is closed. The whole of the front compartment as far as I is occupied with the machinery H. The other compartment behind I is empty, and communicates with the space O behind the drawer, the floor of this division being removed. The back of the great cupboard C C is double, and the part P Q, to which the quadrants are attached, moves on a joint Q, at the upper part, and forms when raised an opening S, between the two cupboards, by carrying with it part of the partition R, which consists of cloth tightly stretched. The false back is shown closed in Fig. 69, while Fig. 70 shows the same back raised, so as to form the opening S between the chambers.

When the spectator is allowed to look into the trunk of the figure by lifting up the dress, as in Fig. 70, it will be observed that a great part of the space is occupied by an inner trunk N, Fig. 70, 71, which passes off to the back in the form of an arch, and conceals from the spectators a portion of the interior. This inner trunk N opens and communicates with the chest by an aperture T, Fig. 72, about twelve inches broad and fifteen high. When the false back is raised, the two cupboards, the

Fig. 63.   Fig. 64.

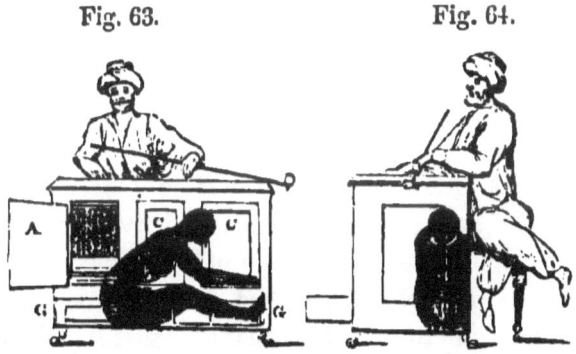

trunk N, and the space O behind the drawer, are all connected together.

The construction of the interior being thus understood, the chess-player may be introduced into the chest through the sliding panel U, Fig. 69. He will then raise the false back of the large cupboard, and assume the position represented by the shaded figure in Fig. 63 and 64. Things being in this state, the exhibitor is ready to begin his process of deception. He first opens the door A of the small cupboard, and from the crowded and very ingenious disposition of the machinery within it, the eye is unable to penetrate far beyond the opening, and the spectator concludes without any hesitation that the whole of the cupboard is filled, as it appears to be, with similar machinery. This false conclusion is greatly corroborated by observing the glimmering light which plays among the wheel-work when the door B is opened, and a candle held at the opening. This mode of exhibiting the interior of the cupboard satisfies the spectator also that no opaque body capable of holding or concealing any of the parts of a hidden agent is interposed between the light and the observer. The door B is now locked and the screen I closed, and as this is done at the time that the light is withdrawn it will wholly escape observation.

The door B is so constructed as to close by its own weight, but as the head of the chess-player will soon be placed very near it, the secret would be disclosed if, in turning round, the chest door should by any accident fly open. This accident is prevented by turning the key, and, lest this little circumstance should excite notice, it would probably be regarded as accidental, as the keys were immediately wanted for the other locks.

As soon as the door B is locked, and the screen I closed, the secret is no longer exposed to hazard, and the exhibitor proceeds to lead the minds of the spectators still farther from the real state of things. The door A is left open to confirm the opinion that no person is concealed within, and that nothing can take place in the interior without being observed.

The drawer G G is now opened, apparently for the purpose of looking at the chess-men, cushion and counters which it contains ; but the real object of it is to give time to the player to change his position, as shown in the annexed figure, and to replace the false back and partition preparatory to the opening of the great cupboard. The chess-player, as the figure shows, occupies with his body the back compartment of the small cupboard, while his legs and thighs are contained in the space O, behind the drawer G G, his body being concealed by the screen I, and his limbs by the drawer G G.

The great cupboard C C is now opened, and there is so little machinery in it that the eye instantly discovers that no person is concealed in it. To make this more certain, however, a door is opened at the back, and a lighted candle held to it, to allow the spectators to explore every corner and recess.

Fig. 65.

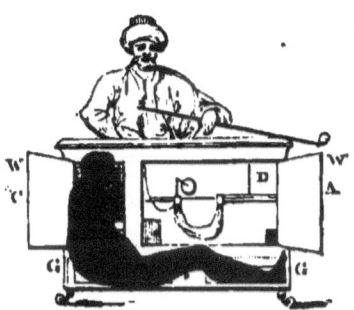

The front doors of the great and small cupboard being left opened, the chest is wheeled round to show the trunk of the figure, and the bunch of keys is allowed to remain in the door D, as the apparent carelessness of such a proceeding will help to remove any suspicion which may have been excited by the locking of the door B.

When the drapery of the figure has been raised, and the doors E and F in the trunk and thigh opened, the chest is wheeled round again into its original position, and the doors E and F closed. In the mean time the player withdraws his legs from behind the drawer, as he cannot so easily do this when the drawer G G is pushed in.

In all these operations, the spectator flatters himself that he has seen in succession every part of the chest, while in reality some parts have been wholly concealed from his view, and others but imperfectly shown, while at

z

the present time nearly half of the chest is excluded from view.

When the drawer G G is pushed in, and the doors A and C closed, the exhibitor adjusts the machinery at the back, in order to give time to the player to take the position shown in a front view in Fig. 66, and in profile in Fig. 67. In this position he will experience no difficulty in executing every movement made by the automaton. As his head is above the chess-board, he will see through

<table>
<tr><td>Fig. 66.</td><td>Fig. 67.</td></tr>
</table>

the waistcoat of the figure, as easily as through a veil, the whole of the pieces on the board, and he can easily take up and put down a chess-man without any other mechanism than that of a string communicating with the finger of the figure. His right hand being within the chest may be employed to keep in motion the wheel-work for producing the noise which is heard during the moves, and to perform the other movements of the figure, such as that of moving the head, tapping on the chest, &c.

A very ingenious contrivance is adopted to facilitate the introduction of the player's left arm into the arm of the figure. To permit this, the arm of the figure requires to be drawn backwards; and for the purpose of concealing, and at the same time explaining this strained attitude, a pipe is ingeniously placed in the automaton's hand. For this reason the pipe is not removed till all the other arrangements are completed. When everything has been thus prepared, the pipe is taken from the figure, and the exhibitor winds up as it were the inclosed machinery, for the double purpose of impressing upon the company the belief that the effect is produced by machinery, and of giving a signal to the player to put in motion the head of the automaton.

Fig. 68.   Fig. 69.

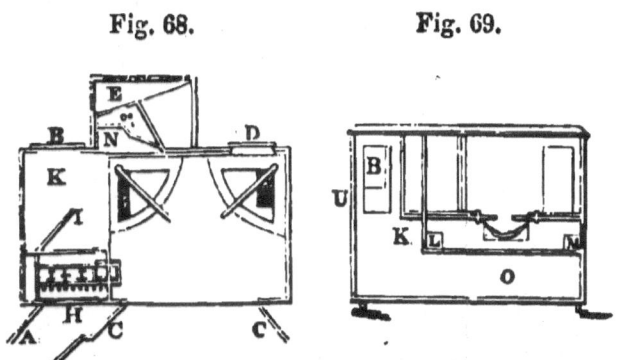

This ingenious explanation of the chess automaton is, our author states, greatly confirmed by the *regular and undeviating* mode of disclosing the interior of the chest; and he also shows that the facts which have been observed respecting the winding-up of the machine "afford positive proof that the axis turned by the key is quite free and unconnected either with a spring or weight, or any system of machinery."

In order to make the preceding description more intelligible, I shall add the following more detailed explanation of the figures.

Fig. 61 is a perspective view of the automaton seen in front with all the doors thrown open.

Fig. 62 is an elevation of the automaton, as seen from behind.

Fig. 63 is an elevation of the front of the chest, the shaded figure representing the enclosed player in his first position, or when the door A is opened.

Fig. 64 is a side elevation, the shaded figure representing the player in the same position.

Fig. 65 is a front elevation, the shaded figure showing the player in his second position, or that which he takes after the door B and screen I are closed, and the great cupboard opened.

Fig. 66 is a front elevation, the shaded figure showing the player in his third position, or that in which he plays the game.

Fig. 70.   Fig. 71.

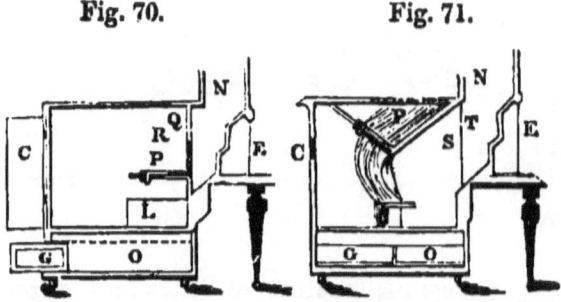

Fig. 67 is a side elevation, showing the figure in the same position.

Fig. 68 is an horizontal section of the chest through the line W W in Fig. 66.

Fig. 69 is a vertical section of the chest through the line X X in Fig. 68.

Fig. 70 is a vertical section through the line Y Y, Fig. 66 showing the false back closed.

Fig. 71 is a similar vertical section showing the false back raised.

The following letters of reference are employed in all the figures:

A. Front door of the small cupboard.

B. Back door of ditto.

C C. Front doors of large cupboard.

D. Back door of ditto.

E. Door of ditto.

F. Door of the thigh.

G G. The drawer.

H. Machinery in front of the small cupboard.

I. Screen behind the machinery.

K. Opening caused by the removal of part of the floor of the small cupboard.

L. A box which serves to conceal an opening in the floor of the large cupboard, made to facilitate the first position; and which also serves as a seat for the third position.

M. A similar box to receive the toes of the player in the first position.

N. The inner chest filling up part of the trunk.

O. The space behind the drawer.

P Q. The false back turning on a joint at Q.

R. Part of the partition formed of cloth stretched tight, which is carried up by the false back to form the opening between the chambers.

S. The opening between the chambers.

T. The opening connecting the trunk and chest, which is partly concealed by the false back.

U. Panel which is slipt aside to admit the player.

Various pieces of mechanism of wonderful ingenuity have been constructed for the purposes of drawing and writing. One of these, invented by M. Le Droz, the son of the celebrated Droz of Chaux le Fonds, has been described by Mr. Collinson. The figure was the size of life. It held in its hand a metallic style, and when a spring was touched, so as to release a detent, the figure immediately began to draw upon a card of Dutch vellum previously laid under its hand. After the drawing was executed on the first card, the figure rested. Other five cards were

then put in in succession, and upon these it delineated in
the same manner different subjects. On the first card it
drew "elegant portraits, and likenesses of the king and
queen facing each other;" and Mr. Collinson remarks,
that it was curious to observe with what precision the
figure lifted up its pencil in its transition from one point
of the drawing to another without making the slightest
mistake.

M. Maillardet has executed an automaton which both
writes and draws. The figure of a boy kneeling on one
knee holds a pencil in his hand. When the figure begins
to work, an attendant dips the pencil in ink, and adjusts
the drawing-paper upon a brass tablet. Upon touching a
spring, the figure proceeds to write, and when the line is
finished its hand returns to dot and stroke the letters
when necessary. In this manner it executes four beautiful pieces of writing in French and English, and three
landscapes, all of which occupy about one hour.

One of the most popular pieces of mechanism which we
have seen is the magician constructed by M. Maillardet
for the purpose of answering certain given questions. A
figure, dressed like a magician, appears seated at the
bottom of a wall, holding a wand in one hand and a book
in the other. A number of questions ready prepared are
inscribed on oval medallions, and the spectator takes any
of these which he chooses, and to which he wishes an
answer; and having placed it in a drawer ready to receive
it, the drawer shuts with a spring till the answer is returned.
The magician then rises from his seat, bows his head,
describes circles with his wand, and, consulting the book
as if in deep thought, he lifts it toward his face. Having
thus appeared to ponder over the proposed question, he
raises his wand, and striking with it the wall above his
head, two folding-doors fly open, and display an appropriate answer to the question. The doors again close, the

magician resumes his original position, and the drawer opens to return the medallion. There are twenty of these medallions, all containing different questions, to which the magician returns the most suitable and striking answers. The medallions are thin plates of brass of an elliptical form, exactly resembling each other. Some of the medallions have a question inscribed on each side, both of which the magician answers in succession. If the drawer is shut without a medallion being put into it, the magician rises, consults his book, shakes his head, and resumes his seat. The folding-doors remain shut, and the drawer is returned empty. If two medallions are put into the drawer together, an answer is returned only to the lower one. When the machinery is wound up, the movements continue about an hour, during which time about fifty questions may be answered. The inventor stated, that the means by which the different medallions acted upon the machinery, so as to produce the proper answers to the questions which they contained, were extremely simple.*

The same ingenious artist has constructed various other automata representing insects and other animals. One of these was a spider entirely made of steel, which exhibited all the movements of the animal. It ran on the surface of a table during three minutes, and to prevent it from running off, its course always tended towards the centre of the table. He constructed likewise a caterpillar, a lizard, a mouse, and a serpent. The serpent crawls about in every direction, opens its mouth, hisses and darts out its tongue.

Ingenious and beautiful as all these pieces of mechanism are, and surprising as their effects appear even to scientific spectators, the principal object of their inventors was to astonish and amuse the public. We should form an

* See the *Edinburgh Encyclopædia*, Art. ANDROIDES, Vol. ii. p. 66.

erroneous judgment, however, if we supposed that this was
the only result of the ingenuity which they displayed. The
passion for automatic exhibitions which characterised the
eighteenth century gave rise to the most ingenious mechanical devices, and introduced among the higher orders of
artists habits of nice and accurate execution in the formation
of the most delicate pieces of machinery. The same combination of the mechanical powers which made the spider
crawl, or which waved the tiny rod of the magician, contributed in future years to purposes of higher import.
Those wheels and pinions, which almost eluded our senses
by their minuteness, reappeared in the stupendous
mechanism of our spinning-machines and our steam-
engines. The elements of the tumbling puppet were
revived in the chronometer, which now conducts our navy
through the ocean; and the shapeless wheel which
directed the hand of the drawing automaton has served in
the present age to guide the movements of the tambouring
engine. Those mechanical wonders which in one century
enriched only the conjurer who used them, contributed in
another to augment the wealth of the nation; and those
automatic toys which once amused the vulgar, are now
employed in extending the power and promoting the
civilization of our species. In whatever way, indeed, the
power of genius may invent or combine, and to whatever
low or even ludicrous purposes that invention or combination may be originally applied, society receives a gift
which it can never lose; and though the value of the
seed may not be at once recognized, and though it may lie
long unproductive in the ungenial till of human knowledge,
it will some time or other evolve its germ, and yield to
mankind its natural and abundant harvest.

Did the limits of so popular a volume as this ought to
be permit it, I should have proceeded to give a general
description of some of these extraordinary pieces of

machinery, the construction and effects of which never fail to strike the spectator with surprise. This, however, would lead me into a field too extensive, and I shall therefore confine myself to a notice of three very remarkable pieces of mechanism which are at present very little known to the general reader, viz., the tambouring machine of Mr. Duncan, the statue-turning machine of Mr. Watt, and the calculating machinery of Mr. Babbage.

The tambouring of muslins, or the art of producing upon them ornamental flowers and figures, has been long known and practised in Britain, as well as in other countries; but it was not. long before the year 1790 that it became an object of general manufacture in the west of Scotland, where it was chiefly carried on. At first it was under the direction of foreigners; but their aid was not long necessary, and it speedily extended to such a degree as to occupy, either wholly or partially, more than 20,000 females. Many of these labourers lived in the neighbourhood of Glasgow, which was the chief seat of the manufacture; but others were scattered through every part of Scotland, and supplied by agents with work and money. In Glasgow, a tambourer of ordinary skill could not in general earn more than five or six shillings a week by constant application; but to a labouring artisan, who had several daughters, even these low wages formed a source of great wealth. At the age of five years, a child capable of handling a needle was devoted to tambouring, even though it could not earn more than a shilling or two in a week; and the consequence of this was, that female children were taken from school, and rendered totally unfit for any social or domestic duty. The tambouring population was therefore of the worst kind, and it must have been regarded as a blessing rather than as a calamity, when the work which they performed was entrusted to regular machinery.

Mr. John Duncan of Glasgow, the inventor of the tambouring machinery, was one of those unfortunate individuals who benefit their species without benefiting themselves, and who died in the meridian of life the victim of poverty and of national ingratitude. He conceived the idea of bringing into action a great number of needles at the same time, in order to shorten the process by manual labour, but he at first was perplexed about the diversification of the pattern. This difficulty, however, he soon surmounted by employing two forces at right angles to each other, which gave him a new force in the direction of the diagonal of the parallelogram, whose sides were formed by the original forces. His first machine was very imperfect; but after two years' study he formed a company, at whose expense six improved machines were put in action, and who secured the invention by a patent. At this time the idea of rendering the machine automatic had scarcely occurred to him; but he afterwards succeeded in accomplishing this great object, and the tambouring machines were placed under the surveillance of a steam-engine. Another patent was taken for these improvements. The reader who desires to have a minute account of these improvements, and of the various parts of the machinery, will be amply gratified by perusing the inventor's own account of the machinery in the article CHAINWORK in the Edinburgh Encyclopædia. At present it will be sufficient to state, that the muslin to be tamboured was suspended vertically in a frame, which was capable of being moved both in a vertical and a horizontal direction. Sixty or more needles lying horizontal occupied a frame in front of the muslin web. Each of these working-needles, as they are called, was attended by a feeding-needle, which by a circular motion round the working-needle lodged upon the stem of the latter the loop of the thread. The sixty needles then penetrated the web, and in order that they might return again without injuring the fabric, the barb or eye of the needle, which resembled the barb of a fishing hook, was shut by a slider. The muslin web then took a new position by means of the machinery that gave it its horizontal and vertical motion, so that the sixty needles penetrated it, at their next movement, at another point of the figure or flower. This operation went on till sixty flowers were completed. The web was then slightly wound up, that the needles might be opposite that part of it on which they were to work another row of flowers.

The flowers were generally at an inch distance, and the rows were placed so that the flowers formed what are called diamonds. There were seventy-two rows of flowers in a yard, so that in every square yard there were nearly 4000 flowers, and in every piece of ten yards long 40,000. The number of loops or stitches in a flower varied with the pattern, but on an average there was about thirty. Hence the number of stitches in a yard was 120,000, and the number in a piece was 1,200,000. The average work done in a week by one machine was fifteen yards, or 60,000 flowers, or 1,800,000 stitches, and by comparing this with the work done by one person with the hand, it appeared that the machine enabled one person to do the work of twenty-four persons.

One of the most curious and important applications of machinery to the arts which has been suggested in modern times was made by the late Mr. Watt, in the construction of a machine for copying or reducing statues and sculpture of all kinds. The art of multiplying busts and statues, by casts in plaster of Paris, has been the means of diffusing a knowledge of this branch of the fine arts; but from the fragile nature of the material, the copies thus produced were unfit for exposure to the weather, and therefore ill calculated for ornamenting public buildings, or for perpetuating the memory of public achievements. A machine, therefore, which is capable of multiplying the labours of the sculptor in the durable materials of marble or of brass was a desideratum of the highest value, and one which could have been expected only from a genius of the first order. During many years Mr. Watt carried on his labours in secret, and he concealed even his intention of constructing such a machine. After he had made considerable progress in its execution, and had thought of securing his invention by a patent, he learned that an ingenious individual in his own neighbourhood had been long occupied in the same pursuit; and Mr. Watt informed me, that he had every reason to believe that this gentleman was entirely ignorant of his labours. A proposal was then made that the two inventors should combine their talents, and secure the privilege by a joint patent; but Mr. Watt had experienced so frequently the fatal operation of our patent laws, that he saw many difficulties in the way of such an arrangement, and he was unwilling, at his advanced age, to embark in a project so extensive, and which seemed to require for its successful prosecution all the ardour and ambition of a youthful mind. The scheme was therefore abandoned; and such is the unfortunate operation of our patent laws, that the circumstance of two individuals having made the same invention has prevented both from bringing it to perfection, and conferring a great practical benefit upon their species. The machine which Mr. Watt had constructed had actually executed some excellent pieces of work. I have seen in his house at Heathfield copies of basso relievos, and complete statues of a small size; and some of his friends have in their possession other specimens of its performance.

Of all the machines which have been constructed in modern times, the calculating machine is doubtless the

most extraordinary. Pieces of mechanism for performing particular arithmetical operations have been long ago
constructed, but these bear no comparison either in
ingenuity or in magnitude to the grand design conceived
and nearly executed by Mr. Babbage. Great as the power
of mechanism is known to be, yet we venture to say that
many of the most intelligent of our readers will scarcely
admit it to be possible that astronomical and navigation
tables can be accurately computed by machinery; that
the machine can itself correct the errors which it may
commit; and that the results of its calculations, when
absolutely free from error, can be printed off, without the
aid of human hands, or the operation of human intelligence. All this, however, Mr. Babbage's machine can do ;
and as I have had the advantage of seeing it actually
calculate, and of studying its construction with Mr.
Babbage himself, I am able to make the above statement
on personal observation. The calculating machine now
constructing under the superintendence of the inventor
has been executed at the expense of the British Government, and is of course their property. It consists essentially of two parts, a calculating part, and a printing part,
both of which are necessary to the fulfilment of Mr.
Babbage's views, for the whole advantage would be lost
if the computations made by the machine were copied by
human hands and transferred to types by the common
process. The greater part of the calculating machinery
is already constructed, and exhibits workmanship of such
extraordinary skill and beauty that nothing approaching
to it has been witnessed. In order to execute it, particularly those parts of the apparatus which are dissimilar
to any used in ordinary mechanical constructions, tools
and machinery of great expense and complexity have been
invented and constructed ; and in many instances contrivances of singular ingenuity have been resorted to, which

cannot fail to prove extensively useful in various branches of the mechanical arts.

The drawings of this machinery, which form a large part of the work, and on which all the contrivance has been bestowed, and all the alterations made, cover upwards of 400 *square feet of surface*, and are executed with extraordinary care and precision.

In so complex a piece of mechanism, in which interrupted motions are propagated simultaneously along a great variety of trains of mechanism, it might have been supposed that obstructions would arise, or even incompatibilities occur, from the impracticability of foreseeing all the possible combinations of the parts; but this doubt has been entirely removed, by the constant employment of a system of mechanical notation invented by Mr. Babbage, which places distinctly in view, at every instant, the progress of motion through all the parts of this or any other machine, and by writing down in tables the times required for all the movements, this method renders it easy to avoid all risk of two opposite actions arriving at the same instant at any part of the engine.

In the printing part of the machine less progress has been made in the actual execution than in the calculating part. The cause of this is the greater difficulty of its contrivance, not for transferring the computations from the calculating part to the copper or other plate destined to receive it, but for giving to the plate itself that number and variety of movements which the forms adopted in printed tables may call for in practice.

The practical object of the calculating engine is to compute and print a great variety and extent of astronomical and navigation tables, which could not be done without enormous intellectual and manual labour, and which, even if executed by such labour, could not be calculated with the requisite accuracy. Mathematicians, astronomers,

and navigators do not require to be informed of the real
value of such tables; but it may be proper to state, for
the information of others, that *seventeen* large folio
volumes of logarithmic tables alone were calculated at an
enormous expense by the French Government; and that
the British Government regarded these tables to be of
such national value that they proposed to the French
Board of Longitude to print an *abridgment* of them at the
joint expense of the two nations, and offered to advance
5000*l.* for that purpose.   Besides logarithmic tables, Mr.
Babbage's machine will calculate tables of the powers and
products of numbers, and all astronomical tables for
determining the positions of the sun, moon, and planets ;
and the same mechanical principles have enabled him to
integrate innumerable equations of finite differences; that
is, when the equation of differences is given, he can, by
setting an engine, produce at the end of a given time any
distant term which may be required, or any succession of
terms commencing at a distant point.

Besides the cheapness and celerity with which this
machine will perform its work, the *absolute accuracy* of the
printed results deserves especial notice.   By peculiar
contrivances, any small error produced by accidental dust,
or by any slight inaccuracy in one of the wheels, is corrected as soon as it is transmitted to the next, and this is
done in such a manner as effectually to prevent any ac-
cumulation of small errors from producing an erroneous
figure in the result.

In order to convey some idea of this stupendous under-
taking, we may mention the effects produced by a small
trial engine constructed by the inventor, and by which he
computed the following table from the formula $x^2 + x + 41$.
The figures as they were calculated by the machine were
not exhibited to the eye as in sliding rules and similar
instruments, but were actually presented to the eye on two

opposite sides of the machine; the number 383, for example, appearing in figures before the person employed in copying.

Table calculated by a small Trial Engine.

41	131	383	797	1373
43	151	421	853	1447
47	173	461	911	1523
53	197	583	971	1601
61	223	547	1033	1681
71	251	593	1097	1763
83	281	641	1163	1847
97	313	691	1231	1933
113	347	743	1301	2021

While the machine was occupied in calculating this table, a friend of the inventor undertook to write down the numbers as they appeared. In consequence of the copyist writing quickly, he rather more than kept pace with the engine, but as soon as five figures appeared, the machine was at least equal in speed to the writer. At another trial *thirty-two* numbers of the same table were calculated in the space of *two minutes and thirty seconds*, and as these contained *eighty-two* figures, the engine produced thirty-three figures every minute, or more than one figure in every two seconds. On another occasion it produced *forty-four* figures per minute. This rate of computation could be maintained for any length of time; and it is probable that few writers are able to copy with equal speed for many hours together.

Some of that class of individuals who envy all great men, and deny all great inventions, have ignorantly stated that Mr. Babbage's invention is not new. The same persons, had it suited their purpose, would have maintained that the invention of spectacles was an anticipation of the telescope; but even this is more true than the allegation, that the arithmetical machines of Pascal and others were the types of Mr. Babbage's engine. The object of these machines was entirely different. Their highest functions were to perform the operations of common arithmetic. Mr. Babbage's engine, it is true, can perform these operations also, and can extract the roots of numbers, and approximate to the roots of equations, and even to their impossible roots. But this is not its object. Its function, in contradistinction to that of all other contrivances for calculating, is to embody in machinery the method of differences, which has never before been done ; and the effects which it is capable of producing, and the works which in the course of a few years we expect to see it execute, will place it at an infinite distance from all other efforts of mechanical genius.*

* A popular account of this engine will be found in Mr. Babbage's interesting volume *On the Economy of Manufactures.*

LETTER XII.

Wonders of chemistry—Origin, progress, and objects of alchemy—Art of breathing fire—Employed by Barchochebas, Eunus, &c.— Modern method—Art of walking upon burning coals and red-hot iron, and of plunging the hands in melted lead and boiling water— Singular property of boiling tar—Workmen plunge their hands in melted copper—Trial of ordeal by fire—Aldini's incombustible dresses—Examples of their wonderful power in resisting flame— Power of breathing and enduring air of high temperatures— Experiments made by Sir Joseph Banks, Sir Charles Blagden, and Mr. Chantry.

THE science of chemistry has from its infancy been pre-eminently the science of wonders. In her laboratory the alchemist and the magician have revelled uncontrolled, and from her treasures was forged the sceptre which was so long and so fatally wielded over human reason. The changes which take place in the bodies immediately around us are too few in number and too remote from observation to excite much of our notice ; but when the substances procured directly from nature, or formed casually by art, become objects of investigation, they exhibit in their simple or combined actions the most extraordinary effects. The phenomena which they display, and the products which they form, so little resemble those with which we are familiar, that the most phlegmatic and the least speculative observer must have anticipated from them the creation of new and valuable compounds. It can scarcely, therefore, be a matter of surprise that minds of the highest order, and spirits of the loftiest ambition, should have sought in the transmutations of chemistry for those splendid products which were conceived to be most conducive to human happiness.

The disciple of Mammon grew pale over his crucible in his ardour to convert the baser metals into gold : the philosopher pined in secret for the universal solvent which might develop the elements of the precious stones, and yield to him the means of their production ; and the philanthropist aspired after a universal medicine, which might arrest disease in its course, and prolong indefinitely the life of man. To us who live under the meridian of knowledge, such expectations must appear as presumptuous as they were delusive ; but when we consider that gold and silver were actually produced by chemical processes from the rude ores of lead and copper ;—that some of the most refractory bodies had yielded to the disintegrating and solvent powers of chemical agents ;—and that the mercurial preparations of the Arabian physicians had operated like charms in the cure of diseases that had resisted the feeble medicines of the times, we may find some apology for the extravagant expectations of the alchemists.

An object of lofty pursuit, even if it be one of impossible attainment, is not unworthy of philosophical ambition. Though we cannot scale the summit of the volcanic cone, we may yet reach its heaving flanks, and though we cannot decompose its loftiest fires, we may yet study the lava which they have melted and the products which they have sublimed. In like manner, though the philosopher's stone has not been found, chemistry has derived rich accessions from its search ;—though the general solvent has not been obtained, yet the diamond and the gems have surrendered to science their adamantine strength ;— and though the elixir of life has never been distilled, yet other medicines have soothed "the ills which flesh is heir to," and prolonged in no slight degree the average term of our existence.

Thus far the pursuits of the alchemist were honourable and useful; but when his calling was followed, as it soon was, by men prodigal of fortune and of character, science became an instrument of crime; secrets unattained were bartered for the gold of the credulous and the ignorant, and books innumerable were composed to teach these pretended secrets to the world. An intellectual reaction, however, soon took place, and those very princes who had sought to fill their exhausted treasuries at the furnace of the chemist, were the first to enact laws against the frauds which they had encouraged, and to dispel the illusions which had so long deceived their subjects.

But even when the moral atmosphere of Europe was thus disinfected, chemistry supplied the magician with his most lucrative wonders, and those who could no longer delude the public with dreams of wealth and longevity, now sought to amuse and astonish them by the exhibition of their skill. The narrow limits of this volume will not permit me to give even a general view of those extraordinary effects which this popular science can display. I must therefore select from its inexhaustible stores those topics which are most striking in their results, and most popular in their details.

One of the most ancient feats of magic was the art of breathing flame—an art which even now excites the astonishment of the vulgar. During the insurrection of the slaves in Sicily in the second century before Christ, a Syrian named Eunus acquired by his knowledge the rank of their leader. In order to establish his influence over their minds, he pretended to possess miraculous power. When he wished to inspire his followers with courage, he breathed flames or sparks among them from his mouth, at the same time that he was rousing them by his eloquence

St. Jerome informs us, that the Rabbi Barchochobas, who headed the Jews in their last revolt against Hadrian, made them believe that he was the Messiah, by vomiting flames from his mouth; and at a later period, the Emperor Constantius was thrown into a state of alarm when Valentinian informed him that he had seen one of the body guards breathing out fire and flames. We are not acquainted with the exact methods by which these effects were produced; but Florus informs us, that Eunus filled a perforated nut-shell with sulphur and fire, and having concealed it in his mouth, he breathed gently through it while he was speaking. This art is performed more simply by the modern juggler. Having rolled together some flax or hemp, so as to form a ball the size of a walnut, he sets it on fire, and allows it to burn till it is nearly consumed: he then rolls round it while burning some additional flax, and by these means the fire may be retained in it for a considerable time. At the commencement of his exhibition he introduces the ball into his mouth, and while he breathes through it the fire is revived, and a number of burning sparks are projected from his mouth. These sparks are too feeble to do any harm, provided he inhales the air through his nostrils.

The kindred art of walking on burning coals or redhot iron belongs to the same antiquity. The priestesses of Diana at Castabala in Cappadocia were accustomed, according to Strabo, to walk over burning coals; and at the annual festival, which was held in the temple of Apollo on Mount Soracte in Etruria, the Hirpi marched over burning coals, and on this account they were exempted from military service, and received other privileges from the Roman Senate. This power of resisting fire was ascribed even by Varro to the use of some liniment with which they anointed the soles of their feet.

Of the same character was the art of holding red-hot

iron in the hands or between the teeth, and of plunging the hands into boiling water or melted lead. About the close of the seventeenth century, an Englishman of the name of Richardson rendered himself famous by chewing burning coals, pouring melted lead upon his tongue, and swallowing melted glass. That these effects are produced partly by deception, and partly by a previous preparation of the parts subjected to the heat, can scarcely admit of a doubt. The fusible metal, composed of mercury, tin, and bismuth, which melts at a low temperature, might easily have been substituted in place of lead ; and fluids of easy ebullition may have been used in place of boiling water. A solution of spermaceti or sulphuric ether, tinged with alkanet root, which becomes solid at 50° of Fahrenheit, and melts and boils with the heat of the hand, is supposed to be the substance which is used at Naples when the dried blood of St. Januarius melts spontaneously, and boils over the vessel which contains it.

But even when the fluid requires a high temperature to boil, it may have other properties, which enable us to plunge our hands into it with impunity. This is the case with boiling tar, which boils at a temperature of 220°, even higher than that of water. Mr. Davenport informs us, that he saw one of the workmen in the King's Dock-yard at Chatham immerse his naked hand in tar of that temperature. He drew up his coat sleeves, dipped in his hand and wrist, bringing out fluid tar, and pouring it off from his hand as from a ladle. The tar remained in complete contact with his skin, and he wiped it off with tow. Convinced that there was no deception in this experiment, Mr. Davenport immersed the entire length of his fore-finger in the boiling cauldron, and moved it about a short time before the heat became inconvenient. Mr. Daven-port ascribes this singular effect to the slowness with which the tar communicates its heat, which he conceives to arise from the abundant volatile vapour which is evolved " carrying off rapidly the caloric in a latent state, and intervening between the tar and the skin, so as to prevent the more rapid communication of heat." He con ceives also, that when the hand is withdrawn, and the hot tar adhering to it, the rapidity with which this vapour is evolved from the surface exposed to the air cools it immediately. The workmen informed Mr. Davenport, that, if a person put his hand into the cauldron with his glove on, he would be dreadfully burnt, but this extraordinary result was not put to the test of observation.

But though the conjurers with fire may have availed themselves of these singular properties of individual bodies, yet the general secret of their art consisted in rendering the skin of the exposed parts callous and insensible to heat—an effect which may be produced by continually compressing or singeing them till the skin acquires a horny consistence. A proof of this opinion is mentioned by Beckmann, who assures us that in September, 1765, when he visited the copper-works at Awestad, one of the workmen, bribed by a little money to drink, took some of the melted copper in his hand, and after showing it to the company, threw it against a wall. He then squeezed the fingers of his horny hand close to each other, held it a few minutes under his arm-pit to make it perspire, as he said, and taking it again out, drew it over a ladle filled with melted copper, some of which he skimmed off, and moved his hand backwards and forwards very quickly by way of ostentation. During this performance M. Beckmann noticed a smell like that of singed horn or leather, though the hand of the workman was not burned. This callosity of the skin may be effected by frequently moistening it with dilute sulphuric acid. Some allege that the juices of certain plants produce the same effect, while others recommend the frequent rubbing of the skin

with oil.   The receipt given by Albertus Magnus for this
purpose was of a different nature.   It consisted of a non-
conducting calcareous paste, which was made to adhere to
the skin by the sap of the marsh-mallow, the slimy seeds
of the flea-bane, and the white of an egg.

As the ancients were acquainted with the incombus-
tibility of asbestos or amianthus, and the art of weaving
it into cloth, it is highly probable that it was employed
in the performance of some of their miracles, and it is
equally probable that it was subsequently used, along
with some of·the processes already described, in enabling
the victims of superstition to undergo without hazard the
trial of ordeal by fire.   In every country where this bar-
barous usage prevailed, whether in the sanctuary of the
Christian idolater, or in the pagan temple of the Bramin,
or under the wild orgies of the African savage, Providence
seems to have provided the means of meeting it with impunity.   In Catholic countries this exculpatory judgment
was granted chiefly to persons in weak health, who were
incapable of using arms, and particularly to monks and
ecclesiastics who could not avail themselves of the trial
by single combat.   The fire ordeal was conducted in the
church under the inspection of the clergy: mass was at
the same time celebrated, and the iron and the victims
were consecrated by the sprinkling of holy water.   The
preparatory steps were also under the direction of the
priests.   It was necessary that the accused should be
placed three days and three nights under their care, both
before and after the trial.   Under the pretence of preventing the defendant from preparing his hands by art, and
in order to ascertain the result of the ordeal, his hands
were covered up and sealed during the three days which
preceded and followed the fiery application; and it has
been plausibly conjectured by Beckmann, that during the
first three days the preventative was applied to those

whom they wished to acquit, and that the last three days were requisite to bring back the hands to their natural condition. In these and other cases, the accused could not have availed himself directly of the use of asbestos gloves, unless we could suppose them so made as to imitate the human skin at a distance; but the fibres of that mineral may have been imbedded in a paste which applied itself readily to all the elevations and depressions of the skin.

In our own times the art of defending the hands and face, and indeed the whole body, from the action of heated iron and intense fire, has been applied to the nobler purpose of saving human life, and rescuing property from the flames. The revival and the improvement of this art we owe to the benevolence and the ingenuity of the Chevalier Aldini of Milan, who has travelled through all Europe to present this valuable gift to his species. Sir H. Davy had long ago shown that a safety lamp for illuminating mines, containing inflammable air, might be constructed of wire-gauze alone, which prevented the flame within, however large or intense, from setting fire to the inflammable air without. This valuable property, which has been long in practical use, he ascribed to the conducting and radiating power of the wire-gauze, which carried off the heat of the flame, and deprived it of its power. The Chevalier Aldini conceived the idea of applying the same material in combination with other badly-conducting substances, as a protection against fire. The incombustible pieces of dress which he uses for the body, arms, and legs, are formed out of strong cloth, which has been steeped in a solution of alum, while those for the head, hands, and feet, are made of cloth of asbestos or amianthus. The head-dress is a large cap which enve-lcps the whole head down to the neck, having suitable perforations for the eyes, nose, and mouth. The stockings

and cap are single, but the gloves are made of double
amianthus cloth, to enable the fireman to take into his
hand burning or red-hot bodies. The piece of ancient
asbestos cloth preserved in the Vatican was formed, we
believe, by mixing the asbestos with other fibrous substances; but M. Aldini has executed a piece of nearly the
same size, nine feet five inches long, and five feet three
inches wide, which is much stronger than the ancient
piece, and possesses superior qualities, in consequence of
having been woven without the introduction of any
foreign substance. In this manufacture the fibres are
prevented from breaking by the action of steam, the cloth
is made loose in its fabric, and the threads are about the
fiftieth of an inch in diameter.

The metallic dress which is superadded to these means
of defence consists of five principal pieces, viz., a *casque* or
cap, with a mask large enough to leave a proper space
between it and the asbestos cap; a cuirass with its brass-
ets; a piece of armour for the trunk and thighs; a pair of
boots of double wire-gauze; and an oval shield five feet
long by 2½ wide, made by stretching the wire-gauze over
a slender frame of iron. All these pieces are made of
iron wire-gauze, having the interval between its threads
the twenty-fifth part of an inch.

In order to prove the efficacy of this apparatus, and
inspire the firemen with confidence in its protection, he
showed them that a finger first enveloped in asbestos, and
then in a double case of wire-gauze, might be held a long
time in the flame of a spirit-lamp or candle before the
heat became inconvenient. A fireman having his hand
within a double asbestos glove, and its palm protected by
a piece of asbestos cloth, seized with impunity a large
piece of red-hot iron, carried it deliberately to the distance
of 150 feet, inflamed straw with it, and brought it back
again to the furnace. On other occasions, the firemen

handled blazing wood and burning substances, and walked during five minutes upon an iron grating placed over flaming faggots.

In order to show how the head, eyes, and lungs, are protected, the fireman put on the asbestos and wire-gauze cap, and the cuirass, and held the shield before his breast. A fire of shavings was then lighted, and kept burning in a large raised chafing-dish, and the fireman plunged his head into the middle of the flames with his face to the fuel, and in that position went several times round the

Fig. 72.

chafing-dish for a period longer than a minute. In a subsequent trial at Paris, a fireman placed his head in the middle of a large brasier filled with flaming hay and wood, as in Fig. 72, and resisted the action of the fire during five or six minutes, and even ten minutes.

In the experiments which were made at Paris in the presence of a committee of the Academy of Sciences, two parallel rows of straw and brushwood, supported by iron wires, were formed at the distance of three feet from each other, and extended thirty feet in length. When this combustible mass was set on fire, it was necessary to stand at the distance of eight or ten yards to avoid the heat. The flames from both the rows seemed to fill up the whole space between them, and rose to the height of nine or ten feet. At this moment six firemen, clothed in the incombustible dresses, and marching at a slow pace behind each other, repeatedly passed through the whole length between the two rows of flame, which were constantly fed with additional combustibles. One of the firemen carried on his back a child eight years old in a wicker basket covered with metallic gauze, and the child had no other dress than a cap made of amianthine cloth.

In February, 1829, a still more striking experiment was made in the yard of the barracks of St. Gervais. Two towers were erected two stories high, and were surrounded with heaps of inflamed materials, consisting of faggots and straw. The firemen braved the danger with impunity. In opposition to the advice of M. Aldini, one of them, with the basket and child, rushed into a narrow place, where the flames were raging eight yards high. The violence of the fire was so great that he could not be seen, while a thick black smoke spread around, throwing out a heat which was unsupportable by the spectators. The fireman remained so long invisible that serious doubts were entertained of his safety. He at length, however, issued from the fiery gulf uninjured, and proud of having succeeded in braving so great a danger.

It is a remarkable result of these experiments, that the firemen are able to breathe without difficulty in the middle of the flames. This effect is owing not only to the heat being intercepted by the wire gauze as it passes to the lungs, in consequence of which its temperature becomes supportable, but also to the singular power which the body possesses of resisting great heats, and of breathing air of high temperatures.

A series of curious experiments were made on this subject by M. Tillet, in France, and by Dr. Fordyce and Sir Charles Blagden, in England. Sir Joseph Banks, Dr. Solander, and Sir Charles Blagden, entered a room in which the air had a temperature of 198° Fahr. and remained ten minutes; but as the thermometer sunk very rapidly, they resolved to enter the room singly. Dr. Solander went in alone, and found the heat 210°. and Sir Joseph entered when the heat was 211°. Though exposed to such an elevated temperature, their bodies preserved their natural degree of heat. Whenever they breathed upon a thermometer it sunk several degrees : every expiration, particularly if strongly made, gave a pleasant impression of coolness to their nostrils, and their cold breath cooled their fingers whenever it reached them. On touching his side, Sir Charles Blagden found it cold like a corpse, and yet the heat of his body under his tongue was 98°. Hence they concluded that the human body possesses the power of destroying a certain degree of heat when communicated with a certain degree of quickness. This power, however, varies greatly in different media. The same person who experienced no inconvenience from air heated to 211°, could just bear rectified spirits of wine at 130°, cooling oil at 129°, cooling water at 123°, and cooling quicksilver at 117°. A familiar instance of this occurred in the heated room. All the pieces of metal there, even their watch-chains, felt so hot, that they could scarcely bear to touch them for a moment, while the air from which the metal had derived all its heat was only unpleasant. MM. Duhamel and Tillet observed at Rochefoucault in France that the girls who were

accustomed to attend ovens in a bakehouse were capable
of enduring for ten minutes a temperature of 270°.

The same gentlemen who performed the experiments
above described ventured to expose themselves to still
higher temperatures. Sir Charles Blagden went into a
room where the heat was 1° or 2° above 260°, and remained eight minutes in this situation, frequently walking
about to all the different parts of the room, but standing
still most of the time in the coolest spot, where the heat
was above 240°. The air, though very hot, gave no pain,
and Sir Charles and all the other gentlemen were of
opinion that they could support a much greater heat.
During seven minutes, Sir C. Blagden's breathing continued perfectly good, but after that time he felt an
oppression in his lungs, with a sense of anxiety, which
induced him to leave the room. His pulse was then 144,
double its ordinary quickness. In order to prove that
there was no mistake respecting the degree of heat indicated by the thermometer, and that the air which they
breathed was capable of producing all the well-known
effects of such a heat on inanimate matter, they placed
some eggs and a beef-steak upon a tin frame near the
thermometer, but more distant from the furnace than from
the wall of the room. In the space of twenty minutes
the eggs were roasted quite hard, and in forty-seven
minutes the steak was not only dressed, but almost dry.
Another beef-steak, similarly placed, was rather overdone
in thirty-three minutes. In the evening, when the heat
was still more elevated, a third beef-steak was laid in the
same place, and as they had noticed that the effect of the
hot air was greatly increased by putting it in motion, they
blew upon the steak with a pair of bellows, and thus
hastened the dressing of it to such a degree, that the
greatest portion of it was found to be pretty well done in
thirteen minutes.

Our distinguished countryman, Mr. Chantry, has very recently exposed himself to a temperature still higher than any which we have mentioned. The furnace which he employs for drying his moulds is about 14 feet long, 12 feet high, and 12 feet broad. When it is raised to its highest temperature, with the doors closed, the thermometer stands at 350°, and the iron floor is red hot. The workmen often enter it at a temperature of 340°, walking over the iron floor with wooden clogs, which are of course charred on the surface. On one occasion Mr. Chantry, accompanied by five or six of his friends, entered the furnace, and, after remaining two minutes, they brought out a thermometer which stood at 320°. Some of the party experienced sharp pains in the tips of their ears, and in the septum of the nose, while others felt a pain in their eyes.

LETTER XIII.

Spontaneous combustion — In the absorption of air by powdered charcoal, and of hydrogen by spongy platinum — Dobereiner's lamp — Spontaneous combustion in the bowels of the earth — Burning cliffs—Burning soil—Combustion without flame—Spontaneous combustion of human beings—Countess Zangari—Grace Pett—Natural fire temples of the Guebres—Spontaneous fires in the Caspian Sea — Springs of inflammable gas near Glasgow— Natural light-house of Maracaybo—New elastic fluids in the cavities of gems—Chemical operation going on in their cavities— Explosions produced in them by heat—Remarkable changes of colour from chemical causes—Effects of the nitrous oxide or paradise gas when breathed — Remarkable cases described — Conclusion.

AMONG the wonderful phenomena which chemistry presents to us, there are few more remarkable than those of spontaneous combustion, in which bodies, both animate and inanimate, emit flames, and are sometimes entirely consumed by internal fire. One of the commonest experiments in chemistry is that of producing inflammation by mixing two fluids perfectly cold. Becker, we believe, was the first person who discovered that this singular effect was produced by mixing oil of vitrol with oil of turpentine. Borrichios showed that aquafortis produced the same effect as oil of vitrol. Tournefort proved that spirit of nitre and oil of sassafras took fire when mixed; and Homberg discovered that the same property was possessed by many volatile oils when mixed with spirit of nitre.

Every person is familiar with the phenomena of heat and combustion produced by fermentation. Ricks of hay and stacks of corn have been frequently consumed by the heat generated during the fermentation produced from moisture; and gunpowder magazines, barns, and paper-mills have been often burnt by the fermentation of the materials which they contained. Galen informs us that the dung of a pigeon is sufficient to set fire to a house, and he assures us that he has often seen it take fire when it had become rotten. Casati likewise relates on good authority, that the fire which consumed the great church of Pisa was occasioned by the dung of pigeons that had for centuries built their nests under its roof.

Among the substances subject to spontaneous combustion, pulverized or finely-powdered charcoal is one of the most remarkable. During the last thirty years no fewer than four cases of the spontaneous inflammation of powdered charcoal have taken place in France. When charcoal is triturated in tuns with bronze bruisers it is reduced into the state of the finest powder. In this condition it has the appearance of an unctuous fluid, and it occupies a space three times less than it does in rods of about six inches long. In this state of extreme division it absorbs air much more readily than it does when in rods. This absorption, which is so slow as to require several days for its completion, is accompanied with a disengagement of heat, which rises from 340° to 360° nearly of Fahrenheit, and which is the true cause of the spontaneous inflammation. The inflammation commences near the centre of the mass, at the depth of five or six inches beneath its surface, and at this spot the temperature is always higher than at any other. Black charcoal strongly distilled heats and inflames more easily than the orange, or that which is little distilled, or than the charcoal made in boilers. The most inflammable charcoal must have a mass of at least 66 lbs. avoirdupois, in order that it may be susceptible of spontaneous inflammation. With the

2 B

other less inflammable varieties, the inflammation takes place only in larger masses.

The inflammation of powdered charcoal is more active in proportion to the shortness of the interval between its carbonization and trituration. The free admission of air to the surface of the charcoal is also indispensable to its spontaneous combustion.

Colonel Aubert, to whom we owe these interesting results, likewise found that when sulphur and saltpetre are added to the charcoal, it loses its power of inflaming spontaneously. But as there is still an absorption of air and a generation of heat, he is of opinion that it would not be prudent to leave these mixtures in too large masses after trituration.*

A species of spontaneous combustion, perfectly analogous to that now described, but produced almost instantaneously, was discovered by Professor Dobereiner of Jena in 1824. He found that when a jet of hydrogen gas was thrown upon recently-prepared spongy platinum, the metal became almost instantly red hot, and set fire to the gas. In this case the minutely-divided platinum acted upon the hydrogen gas, in the same manner as the minutely-divided charcoal acted upon common air. Heat and combustion were produced by the absorption of both gases, though in the one case the effect was instantaneous, and in the other was the result of a prolonged absorption.

This beautiful property of spongy platinum was happily applied to the construction of lamps for producing an instantaneous light. The form given to the lamp by Mr. Garden of London is shown in the annexed figure, where A B is a globe of glass, fitting tightly into another glass globe C D by a ground shoulder *m n*. The globe A B terminates in a hollow tapering neck *m n o p*, on the

---

* See *Edinburgh Journal of Science*, New Series, No. viii. p. 274.

lower end of which is placed a small cylinder of zinc *o p*.
A brass tube *a b c* is fitted at *a* into the neck of the globe
C D, and through this tube, which is furnished with a
stop-cock *d*, the gas can escape at the small aperture *c*.
A brass pin *c f*, carrying a brass box P, is made to slide
through a hole *h*, so that the brass box P, in which the
spongy platinum is placed, can be set at any required
distance from the aperture *c*. If sulphuric acid diluted

Fig. 73.

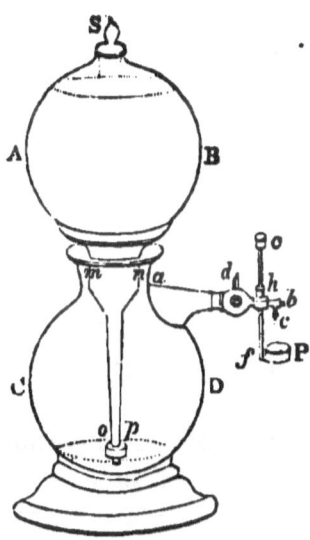

with an equal quantity of water is now poured into the
vessel A B by its mouth at S, now closed with a stopper,
the fluid will descend through the tube *m n o p*, and if·the
cock *d* is shut, it will compress the air contained in C D.
The dilute acid thus introduced into C D will act upon
the ring of zinc *o p*, and generate hydrogen gas, which
after the atmospheric air in C D is let off, will gradually
fill the vessel C D, the diluted acid being forced up the
tube *o p m n*, into the glass globe A B. The ring of zinc
o p floats on a piece of cork, so that when C D is full of

hydrogen, the diluted acid does not touch the zinc, and consequently is prevented from producing any more gas. The instant, however, that any gas is let off at c, the pressure of the fluid in the globe A B, and tube $m\,n\,o\,p$, overcomes the elasticity of the remaining gas in C D, and forces the diluted acid up to the zinc $o\,p$, so as to enable it to produce more gas to supply what has been used.

The lamp being supplied with hydrogen in the manner now described, it is used in the following manner: The spongy platinum in P being brought near c, the cock d is turned, and the gas is thrown upon the platinum. An intense heat is immediately produced, the platinum becomes red hot, and the hydrogen inflames. A taper is then lighted at the flame, and the cock d is shut. Professor Cumming of Cambridge found it necessary to cover up the platinum with a cap after every experiment. This ingenious chemist likewise found that, with platinum foil the 9000dth part of an inch thick kept in a close tube, the hydrogen was inflamed; but when the foil was only the 6000dth of an inch thick, it was necessary to raise it previously to a red heat.

Spontaneous combustion is a phenomenon which occurs very frequently, and often to a great extent, within the bowels of the earth. The heat by which it is occasioned is produced by the decomposition of mineral bodies, and other causes. This heat increases in intensity till it is capable of melting the solid materials which are exposed to it. Gases and aqueous vapours of powerful elasticity are generated, new fluids of expansive energy imprisoned in cavities under great pressure are set free, and these tremendous agents, acting under the repressing forces of the superincumbent strata, exhibit their power in desolating earthquakes; or, forcing their way through the superficial crust of the globe, they waste their fury in volcanic eruptions.

When the phenomena of spontaneous combustion take place near the surface of the earth, its effects are of a less dangerous character, though they frequently give birth to permanent conflagrations, which no power can extinguish. An example of this milder species of spontaneous combustion has been recently exhibited in the burning cliff at Weymouth; and a still more interesting one exists at this moment near the village of Bradley, in Staffordshire. The earth is here on fire, and this fire has continued for nearly sixty years, and has resisted every attempt that has been made to extinguish it. This fire, which has reduced many acres of land to a mere calx, arises from a burning stratum of coal about four feet thick and eight or ten yards deep, to which the air has free access, in consequence of the main coal having been dug from beneath it. The surface of the ground is sometimes covered for many yards with such quantities of sulphur that it can be easily gathered. The calx has been found to be an excellent material for the roads, and the workmen who collect it often find large beds of alum of an excellent quality.

A singular species of invisible combustion, or of combustion without flame, has been frequently noticed. I have observed this phenomenon in the small green wax tapers in common use. When the flame is blown out, the wick will continue red hot for many hours, and if the taper were regularly and carefully uncoiled, and the room kept free from currents of air, the wick would burn on in this way till the whole of the taper was consumed. The same effects are not produced when the colour of the wax is red. In this experiment the wick, after the flame is blown out, has sufficient heat to convert the wax into vapour, and this vapour, being consumed without flame, keeps the wick at its red heat. A very disagreeable vapour is produced during this imperfect combustion of the wax.

Professor Dobereiner of Jena observed, that when the alcohol in a spirit of wine lamp was nearly exhausted, the wick became carbonized, and though the flame disappeared, the carbonized part of the wick became red hot, and continued so while a drop of alcohol remained, and provided the air in the room was undisturbed. On one occasion the wick continued red hot for twenty-four hours, and a very disagreeable acid vapour was formed.

On these principles depend the *lamp without flame* which was originally constructed by Mr. Ellis. It is shown in the annexed figure, where A B is the lamp, and *h* a cylindrical coil of platinum wire, the hundredth part

Fig. 74.

of an inch in diameter. This spiral is so placed that four or five of the twelve coils of which the cylinder consists are upon the wick, and the other seven or eight above it. If the lamp is lighted, and continues burning till the cylindrical coil is red hot, then if the flame is blown out, the vapour which arises from the alcohol will by its combustion keep the coils above the wick red hot, and this red heat will in its turn keep up the vaporisation of the alcohol till the whole of the alcohol is consumed. The heat of the wire is always sufficient to kindle a piece of German fungus or saltpetre paper, so that a sulphur match may at any time be lighted. Mr. Gill found that a wick composed of twelve threads of the cotton yarn commonly used for lamps will require half an ounce of alcohol to keep the wire red hot for eight hours. This lamp has been kept burning for sixty hours ; but it can scarcely be recommended for a bed-room, as an acid vapour is disengaged during the burning of the alcohol. When perfumes are dissolved in the alcohol, they are diffused through the apartment during the slow combustion of the vapour.

A species of combustion without flame, and analogous to that which has been described, is exhibited in the extraordinary phenomena of the spontaneous combustion of living bodies. That animal bodies are liable to internal combustion is a fact which was well known to the ancients. Many cases which have been adduced as examples of spontaneous combustion are merely cases of individuals who were highly susceptible of strong electrical excitation. In one of these cases, however, Peter Bovisteau asserts, that the sparks of fire thus produced reduced to ashes the hair of a young man ; and John De Viana informs us, that the wife of Dr. Freilas, physician to the Cardinal de Royas, Archbishop of Toledo, emitted by perspiration an inflammable matter of such a nature, that when the ribbon which she wore over her shift was taken from her and exposed to the cold air, it instantly took fire, and shot forth like grains of gunpowder. Peter Borelli has recorded a fact of the very same kind respecting a peasant whose linen took fire, whether it was laid up in a box when wet, or hung up in the open air. The same author speaks of a woman who, when at the point of death, vomited flames ; and Thomas Bartholin mentions this phenomenon as having often happened to persons who were great drinkers of wine or brandy. Ezekiel de Castro mentions the singular case of Alexandrinus Megetius, a physician, from one of whose vertebræ there issued a fire which scorched the eyes of the beholders ; and Krantzius relates, that during the wars of Godfrey of

Boulogne, certain people of the territory of Nivers were burning with invisible fire, and that some of them cut off a foot or a hand where the burning began, in order to arrest the calamity. Nor have these effects been confined to man. In the time of the Roman consuls Gracchus and Juventius, a flame is said to have issued from the mouth of a bull without doing any injury to the animal.

The reader will judge of the decree of credit which may belong to these narrations when he examines the effects of a similar kind which have taken place in less fabulous ages, and nearer our own times. John Henry Cohausen informs us, that a Polish gentleman in the time of the Queen Bona Sforza, having drunk two dishes of a liquor called brandy-wine, vomited flames, and was burned by them, and Thomas Bartholin* thus describes a similar accident: "A poor woman at Paris used to drink spirit of wine plentifully for the space of three years, so as to take nothing else. Her body contracted such a combustible disposition, that one night, when she lay down on a straw couch, she was all burned to ashes except her skull and the extremities of her fingers." John Christ Sturmius informs us in the German Ephemerides, that in the northern countries of Europe flames often evaporate from the stomachs of those who are addicted to the drinking of strong liquors; and he adds, "that seventeen years before, three noblemen of Courland drank by emulation strong liquors, and two of them died scorched and suffocated by a flame which issued from their stomach."

One of the most remarkable cases of spontaneous combustion is that of the Countess Cornelia Zangari and Bandi of Cesena, which has been minutely described by the Reverend Joseph Bianchini, a prebend in the city of

---

* *Acta Medica et Philosophica Hafniensia,* 1673

Verona. This lady, who was in the sixty-second year of her age, retired to bed in her usual health. Here she spent above three hours in familiar conversation with her maid and in saying her prayers; and having at last fallen asleep, the door of her chamber was shut. As her maid was not summoned at the usual hour, she went into the bed-room to wake her mistress; but receiving no answer she opened the window, and saw her corpse on the floor in the most dreadful condition. At the distance of four feet from the bed there was a heap of ashes. Her legs, with the stockings on, remained untouched, and the head, half-burned, lay between them. Nearly all the rest of the body was reduced to ashes. The air in the room was charged with floating soot. A small oil lamp on the floor was covered with ashes, but had no oil in it; and in two candlesticks, which stood upright upon a table, the cotton wick of both the candles was left, and the tallow of both had disappeared. The bed was not injured, and the blankets and sheets were raised on one side as if a person had risen up from it. From an examination of all the circumstances of this case, it has been generally supposed that an internal combustion had taken place; that the lady had risen from her bed to cool herself, and that, in her way to open the window, the combustion had overpowered her, and consumed her body by a process in which no flame was produced which could set fire to the furniture or the floor. The Marquis Scipio Maffei was informed by an Italian nobleman who passed through Cesena a few days after this event, that he heard it stated in that town, that the Countess Zangari was in the habit, when she felt herself indisposed, of washing all her body with camphorated spirit of wine.

So recently as 1744 a similar example of spontaneous combustion occurred in our own country at Ipswich. A fisherman's wife of the name of Grace Pett, of the parish

of St. Clements, had been in the habit for several years of
going down stairs every night after she was half-undressed
to smoke a pipe. She did this on the evening of the 9th
of April, 1744. Her daughter, who lay in the same bed
with her, had fallen asleep, and did not miss her mother
till she awaked early in the morning. Upon dressing
herself, and going down stairs, she found her mother's
body lying on the right side with her head against the
grate, and extended over the hearth with her legs on the
deal floor, and appearing like a block of wood burning
with a glowing fire without flame. Upon quenching the
fire with two bowls of water, the neighbours, whom the
cries of the daughter had brought in, were almost stifled
with the smell. The trunk of the unfortunate woman
was almost burned to ashes, and appeared like a heap of
charcoal covered with white ashes. The head, arms, legs,
and thighs, were also much burned. There was no fire
whatever in the grate, and the candle was burned out in
the socket of the candlestick, which stood by her. The
clothes of a child on one side of her, and a paper screen
on the other, were untouched; and the deal floor was
neither singed nor discoloured. It was said that the woman
had drunk plentifully of gin overnight in welcoming a
daughter who had recently returned from Gibraltar.

Among the phenomena of the natural world which are
related to those of spontaneous combustion, are what have
been called the natural fire temples of the Guebres, and
the igneous phenomena which are seen in their vicinity.
The ancient sect of the Guebres or Parsees, distinguished
from all other sects as the worshippers of fire, had their
origin in Persia; but, being scattered by persecution,
they sought an asylum on the shores of India. Those
who refused to expatriate themselves continued to inhabit
the shores of the Caspian Sea, and the cities of Ispahan,
Yezd, and Kerman. Their great fire temple called Attush

Kudda stands in the vicinity of Badku, one of the largest and most commodious ports in the Caspian. In the neighbourhood of this town the earth is impregnated with naphtha, an inflammable mineral oil, and the inhabitants have no other fuel, and no other light, but what is derived from this substance.

The remains of the ancient fire temples of the Guebres are still visible about ten miles to the north-east of the town. The temple in which the Deity is worshipped under the form of fire is a space about thirty yards square, surrounded with a low wall, and containing many apartments. In each of these a small volcano of sulphureous fire issues from the ground through a furnace or funnel in the shape of a Hindoo altar. On closing the funnel the fire is instantly extinguished, and by placing the ear at the aperture a hollow sound is heard, accompanied with a strong current of cold air, which may be lighted at pleasure by holding to it any burning substance. The flame is of a pale clear colour, without any perceptible smoke, and emits a highly-sulphureous vapour, which impedes respiration, unless when the mouth is kept beneath the level of the furnace. This action on the lungs gives the Guebres a wan and emaciated appearance, and oppresses them with a hectic cough, which strangers also feel while breathing this insalubrious atmosphere.

For about two miles in circumference, round the principal fire, the whole ground, when scraped to the depth of two or three inches, has the singular property of being inflamed by a burning coal. In this case, however, it does not communicate fire to the adjacent ground; but if the earth is dug up with a spade, and a torch brought near it, an extensive, but instantaneous conflagration takes place, in which houses have often been destroyed, and the lives of the people exposed to imminent danger.

When the sky is clear and the weather serene, the springs in their ebullition do not rise higher than two or three feet; but in gloomy weather, and during the prevalence of stormy clouds, the springs are in a state of the greatest ebullition, and the naphtha, which often takes fire spontaneously at the earth's surface, flows ·burning in great quantities to the sea, which is frequently covered with it, in a state of flame, to the distance of several leagues from the shore.

Besides the fires in the temple there is a large one which springs from a natural cliff in an open situation, and which continually burns. The general space in which this volcanic fire is most abundant is somewhat less than a mile in circuit. It forms a low flat hill sloping to the sea, the soil of which is a sandy earth mixed with stones. Mr. Forster did not observe any violent eruption of flame in the country around the Attush Kudda; but Kinneir informs us, that the whole country round Badku has at times the appearance of being enveloped in flames. "It often seems," he adds, "as if the fire rolled down from the mountains in large masses, and with incredible velocity; and during the clear moonshine nights of November and December, a bright blue light is observed at times to cover the whole western range. The fire does not consume, and if a person finds himself in the middle of it no warmth is felt."

The inhabitants apply these natural fires to domestic purposes, by sinking a hollow cane or merely a tube of paper, about two inches in the ground, and by blowing upon a burning coal held near the orifice of the tube, there issues a slight flame, which neither burns the cane nor the paper. By means of these canes or paper tubes, from which the fire issues, the inhabitants boil the water in their coffee-urns, and even cook different articles of food. The flame is put out by merely plugging up the orifice. The same tubes are employed for illuminating houses that are not paved. The smell of naphtha is of course diffused through the house, but after any person is accustomed to it it ceases to be disagreeable. The inhabitants also employ this natural fire in calcining lime. The quantity of naphtha procured in the plain to the south-east of Badku is enormous. It is drawn from wells, some of which yield from 1000 to 1500 lbs. per day. As soon as these wells are emptied, they fill again till the naphtha rises to its original level. *

Inflammable gases issuing from the earth have been used both in the old and the new world for domestic purposes. In the salt mine of Gottesgabe at Rheims, in the county of Fccklenburg, there is a pit called the *Pit of the Wind,* from which a constant current of inflammable gas has issued for sixty years. M. Roeder, the inspector of the mines, has used this gas for two years not only as a light, but for all the purposes of domestic economy. In the pits which are not worked he collects the gas and conveys it in tubes to his house. It burns with a white and brilliant flame, has a density of about 0·66, and contains traces of carbonic acid gas and sulphuretted hydrogen.†

Near the village of Fredonia in North America, on the shores of Lake Erie, are a number of burning springs as they are called. The inflammable gas which issues from these springs is conveyed in pipes to the village, which is actually lighted by them.‡

In the year 1828, a copious spring of inflammable gas was discovered in Scotland in the bed of a rivulet which crosses the north road between Glasgow and Edinburgh, a little to the east of the seventh mile-stone from Glasgow

* See *Forster's Travels,* and *Kinneir's Geog. Memoir.*
† *Edinburgh Journal of Science,* No. xv. p. 183.
‡ *Id. Id.*

and only a few hundred yards from the house of Bedlay. The gas is said to issue for more than half a mile along the banks of the rivulet. Dr. Thomson, who has analysed the gas, saw it issuing only within a space about fifty yards in length, and about half as much in breadth. "The emission of gas was visible in a good many places along the declivity to the rivulet in the immediate neighbourhood of a small farm-house. The farmer had set the gas on fire in one place about a yard square, out of which a great many small jets were issuing. It had burnt without interruption during five weeks, and the soil (which was clay) had assumed the appearance of pounded brick all around.

"The flame was yellow and strong, and resembled perfectly the appearance which *carburetted hydrogen gas* or *fire damp* presents when burnt in daylight. But the greatest issue of gas was in the rivulet itself, distant about twenty yards from the place where the gas was burning. The rivulet when I visited the place was swollen and muddy, so as to prevent its bottom from being seen. But the gas issued up through it in one place with great violence, as if it had been in a state of compression under the surface of the earth; and the thickness of the jet could not be less than two or three inches in diameter. We set the gas on fire as it issued through the water. It burnt for some time with a good deal of splendour; but as the rivulet was swollen and rushing along with great impetuosity, the regularity of the issue was necessarily disturbed, and the gas was extinguished." Dr. Thomson found this gas to consist of *two* volumes of hydrogen gas and *one* volume of vapour of carbon; and as its specific gravity was 0·555, and as it issues in great abundance, he remarks that it might be used for filling air-balloons. "Were we assured," he adds, "that it would continue to issue in as great abundance as at present, it might be employed in lighting the streets of Glasgow."*

A very curious natural phenomenon, called the *Lantern* or *Natural Lighthouse* of Maracaybo, has been witnessed in South America. A bright light is seen every night on a mountainous and uninhabited spot on the banks of the river Catatumbo, near its junction with the Sulia. It is easily distinguished at a greater distance than *forty* leagues, and as it is nearly in the meridian of the opening of the Lake of Maracaybo, navigators are guided by it as by a lighthouse. This phenomenon is not only seen from the sea-coast but also from the interior of the country,— at Merida, for example, where M. Palacios observed it for two years. Some persons have ascribed this remarkable phenomenon to a thunderstorm, or to electrical explosions, which might take place daily in a pass in the mountains ; and it has even been asserted that the rolling of thunder is heard by those who approach the spot. Others suppose it to be an air volcano, like those on the Caspian Sea, and that it is caused by asphaltic soils like those of Mena. It is more probable, however, that it is a sort of carburetted hydrogen, as hydrogen gas is disengaged from the ground in the same district.†

Grand as the chemical operations are which are going on in the great laboratory of Nature, and alarming as their effects appear when they are displayed in the terrors of the earthquake and the volcano, yet they are not more wonderful to the philosopher than the minute though analogous operations which are often at work near our own persons, unseen and unheeded. It is not merely in the bowels of the earth that highly-expansive elements are imprisoned and restrained, and occasionally called into tremendous action by the excitation of heat and other

---

* *Edinburgh Journal of Science*, No. i. New Series, pp. 71—75.

† *Humboldt's Personal Narrative*, Vol. iv. p. 254, note.

causes. Fluids and vapours of a similar character exist in the very gems and precious stones which science has contributed to luxury and to the arts.

In examining with the microscope the structure of mineral bodies, I discovered in the interior of many of the gems thousands of cavities of various forms and sizes. Some had the shape of hollow and regularly-formed crystals: others possessed the most irregular outline, and consisted of many cavities and branches united without order, but all communicating with each other. These cavities sometimes occurred singly, but most frequently in groups forming strata of cavities, at one time perfectly flat and at another time curved. Several such strata were often found in the same specimen, sometimes parallel to each other, at other times inclined, and forming all varieties of angles with the faces of the original crystal.

These cavities, which occurred in *sapphire, chrysoberyl, topaz, beryl, quartz, amethyst, peridot,* and other substances, were sometimes sufficiently large to be distinctly seen by the naked eye, but most frequently they were so small as to require a high magnifying power to be well seen, and often they were so exceedingly minute that the highest magnifying powers were unable to exhibit their outline.

The greater number of these cavities, whether large or small, contain two new fluids different from any hitherto known, and possessing remarkable physical properties. These two fluids are in general perfectly transparent and colourless, and they exist in the same cavity in actual contact, without mixing together in the slightest degree. One of them expands *thirty* times more than water; and at a temperature of about 80° of Fahrenheit it expands so as to fill up the vacuity in the cavity. This will be understood from the annexed figure, where A B C D is the cavity, *m n p o* the highly-expansible fluid in which at low temperatures there is always a vacuity V, like an air-bubble in common fluids, and A *m n*, C *o p*, the second fluid occupying the angles A and C. When heat such as that of the hand is applied to the specimen, the vacuity V gradually contracts in size, and wholly vanishes at a temperature of about 80°, as shown in Fig. 76. The fluids are shaded, as in these two figures, when they are seen by light reflected from their surfaces. .

Fig. 75.

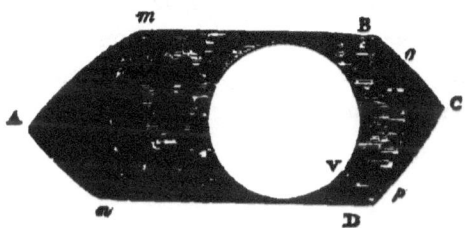

When the cavities are large, as in Fig. 77, compared with the quantity of expansible fluid *m n p o*, the heat converts the fluid into vapour, an effect which is shown by the circular cavity V becoming larger and larger till it fills the whole space *m n o p*.

Fig. 76.

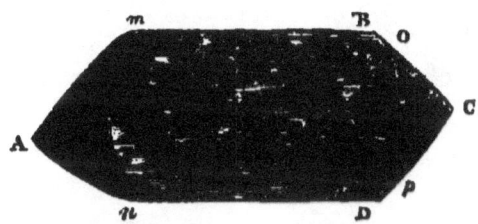

When any of these cavities, whether they are filled with fluid or with vapour, is allowed to cool, the vacuity V reappears at a certain temperature. In the fluid cavities the fluid contracts, and the small vacuity appears, which grows larger and larger till it resumes its original size. When the cavities are large several small vacuities make their appearance and gradually unite into one, though they sometimes remain separate. In deep cavities a very remarkable phenomenon accompanies the reappearance of the vacuity. At the instant that the fluid has acquired the temperature at which it quits the sides of the cavity, an effervescence or rapid ebullition takes place, and the transparent cavity is for a moment opaque, with an infinite number of minute vacuities, which instantly unite into one that goes on enlarging as the temperature diminishes. In the vapour cavities the vapour is reconverted by the cold into fluid, and the vacuity V, Fig. 77, gradually contracts till all the vapour has been precipitated. It is curious to

Fig. 77.

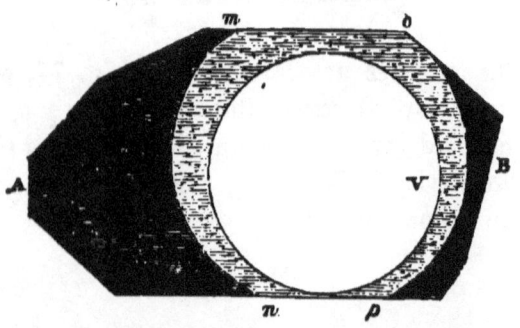

observe, when a great number of cavities are seen at once in the field of the microscope, that the vacuities all disappear and reappear at the same instant.

While all these changes are going on in the expansible fluid, the other denser fluid at A and C, Figs. 75, 76, remains unchanged either in its form or magnitude. On this account I experienced considerable difficulty in proving that it was a fluid. The improbability of two fluids existing in a transparent state in absolute contact, without mixing in the slightest degree, or acting upon each other, induced many persons to whom I showed the phenomenon to consider the lines *m n o p*, Figs. 75, 76, as a partition in the cavity, or the spaces A *m n*, C *o p*, either as filled with solid matter, or as corners into which the expanding fluid would not penetrate. The regular curvature, however, of the boundary line *m n o p*, and other facts, rendered these suppositions untenable.

This difficulty was at last entirely removed by the discovery of a cavity of the form shown in the annexed figure, where A, B, and C are three portions of the expansible fluid separated by the interposition of the second fluid D E F. The first portion A of the expansible fluid had four vacuities V, X, Y, Z, while the other two portions B, C had no vacuity. In order to determine if the vacuities of the portions B, C had passed over to A, I

Fig. 78.

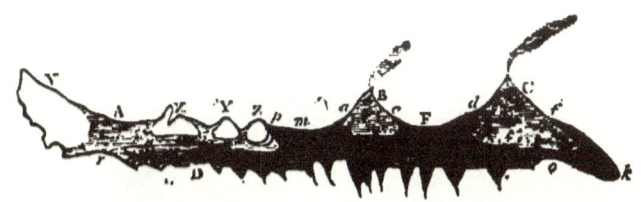

took an accurate drawing of the appearances at a temperature of 50°, as shown in the figure, and I watched the changes which took place in raising the temperature to 83°. The portion A gradually expanded itself till it filled up all the four vacuities V, X, Y, and Z; but as the portions B, C had no vacuities, they could expand themselves only by pushing back the supposed second fluid D E F. This effect actually took place. The dense fluid quitted the side of the cavity at F. The two portions B, C of the expansible fluid instantly united, and the dense fluid having retreated to the limit *m n n o*, its other limit advanced to *p q r*, thus proving it to be a real fluid. This experiment, which I have often shown to others, involves one of those rare combinations of circum-

stances which nature sometimes presents to us in order to
illustrate her most mysterious operations. Had the portions B, C been accompanied, as is usual, with their
vacuities, the interposed fluid would have remained
immoveable between the two equal and opposite expansions ; but owing to the accidental circumstance of these
vacuities having passed over into the other branch A of
the cavity, the fluid yielded to the difference of the
expansive forces between which it lay, and thus exhibited
its fluid character to the eye.

Fig. 79.

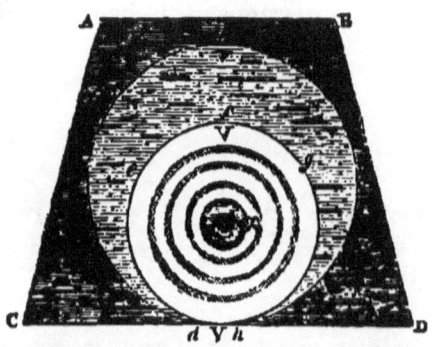

When we examine these cavities narrowly, we find that
they are actually little laboratories, in which chemical operations are constantly going on, and beautiful optical phenomena continually displaying themselves. Let A B D C,
for example, be the summit of a crystallized cavity in
topaz, S S representing the dense, N N the expansible
fluid, bounded by a circular line $a\,b\,c\,d$, and V V the
vacuity in the new fluid, bounded by the circle $e\,f\,g\,h$.
If the face A B D C is placed under a compound microscope, so that light may be reflected at an angle
less than that of total reflection, and if the observer now
looks through the microscope, the temperature of the
room being 50°, he will see the second fluid S S shining

with a very feeble reflected light, the dense fluid N N with a light perceptibly brighter, and the vacuity V V with a light of considerable brilliancy. The boundaries *a b c d, e f g h* are marked by a well-defined outline, and also by the concentric coloured rings of thin plates produced by the extreme thinness of each of the fluids at their edges.

If the temperature of the room is raised slowly to 58°, a brown spot will appear at *x* in the centre of the vacuity V V. This spot indicates the commencement of evaporation from the expansible fluid below, and arises from the partial precipitation of the vapour in the roof of the cavity. As the heat increases, the brown spot enlarges and becomes very dark. It is then succeeded by a white spot, and one or more coloured rings rise in the centre of the vacuity. The vapour then seems to form a drop, and all the rings disappear by retiring to the centre, but only to reappear with new lustre. During the application of heat, the circle *e f g h* contracts and dilates like the pupil of the eye. When the vaporization is so feeble as to produce only a single ring of one or two tints of the second order, they vanish instantly by breathing upon the crystal, but when the slight heat of the breath reaches the fluid, it throws off fresh vapour, and the rings again appear.

If a drop of ether is put upon the crystal when the rings are in a state of rapid play, the cold produced by its evaporation causes them to disappear, till the temperature again rises. When the temperature is perfectly uniform, the rings are stationary, as shown between V and V in Fig. 79; and it is interesting to observe the first ring produced by the vapour swelling out to meet the first ring at the margin of the fluid, and sometimes coming so near it that the darkest parts of both form a broad black band. As the heat increases, the vacuity V V diminishes, and disappears at 79°, exhibiting many curious phenomena which we have not room to describe.

Having fallen upon a method of opening the cavities, and looking at the fluids, I was able to examine their properties with more attention. When the expansible fluid first rises from the cavity upon the surface of the topaz, it neither remains still like the fixed oils, nor disappears like evaporable fluids. Under the influence, no doubt, of heat and moisture it is in a state of constant motion, now spreading itself on a thin plate over a large surface, and now contracting itself into a deeper and much less extended drop. These contractions and extensions are marked by very beautiful optical phenomena. When the fluid has stretched itself out into a thin plate, it ceases to reflect light like the thinnest part of the soap-bubble, and when it is again accumulated into a thicker drop, it is covered with the coloured rings of thin plates.

After performing these motions, which sometimes last for ten minutes, the fluid suddenly disappears, and leaves behind it a sort of granular residue. When examining this with a single microscope, it again started into a fluid state, and extended and contracted itself as before. This was owing to the humidity of the hand which held the microscope, and I have been able to restore by moisture the fluidity of these grains twenty days after they were formed from the fluid. This portion was shown to the Reverend Dr. Fleming, who remarked that, had he observed it accidentally, he would have ascribed its apparent vitality to the movements of some of the animals of the genus Planaria.

After the cavity has remained open for a day or two, the dense fluid comes out and quickly hardens into a transparent and yellowish resinous-looking substance, which absorbs moisture, though with less avidity than the other. It is not volatilized by heat, and is insoluble in water and alcohol. It readily dissolves, however, with effervescence in the sulphuric, nitric, and muriatic acids. The residue of the expansible fluid is volatilized by heat, and is dissolved, but without effervescence, in the above-mentioned acids. The refractive power of the dense fluid is about 1·295, and of the expansible one 1·131.

The particles of the dense fluid have a very powerful attraction for each other and for the mineral which contains them, while those of the expansible fluid have a very slight attraction for one another, and also for the substance of the mineral. Hence the two fluids never mix, the dense fluid being attracted to the angles of angular cavities, or filling the narrow necks by which two cavities communicate. The expansible fluid, on the other hand, fills the wide parts of the cavities, and in deep and round cavities it lies above the dense fluid.

When the dense fluid occupies the necks which join two cavities, it performs the singular function of a fluid valve, opening and shutting itself according to the expansions or contractions of the other fluid. The *fluid valves* thus exhibited in action may suggest some useful hints to the mechanic and the philosopher, while they afford ground of curious speculation in reference to the functions of animal and vegetable bodies. In the larger organizations of ordinary animals, where gravity must in general overpower, or at least modify, the influence of capillary attraction, such a mechanism is neither necessary nor appropriate; but, in the lesser functions of the same animals, and in almost all the microscopic structures of the lower world, where the force of gravity is entirely subjected to the more powerful energy of capillary forces, it is extremely probable that the mechanism of immiscible fluids and fluid valves is generally adopted.

In several cavities in minerals I have found crystallised and other bodies, sometimes transparent crystals, sometimes black spicular crystals, and sometimes black spheres, all of which are moveable within the cavity. In some cavities the two new fluids occur in an indurated state, and others I have found to be lined with a powdery matter. This last class of cavities occurred in topaz, and they were distinguished from all others by the extraordinary beauty and symmetry of their form. One of these cavities represented a finely-ornamented sceptre, and, what is still more singular, the different parts of which it is composed lay in different planes.

When the gem which contains the highly-expansive fluid is strong, and the cavity not near the surface, heat may be applied to it without danger; but in the course of my experiments on this subject, the mineral has often burst with a tremendous explosion, and in one case wounded me on the brow. An accident of the same kind occurred to a gentleman, who put a crystal into his mouth for the purpose of expanding the fluid. The specimen burst with great force and cut his mouth, and the fluid which was discharged from the cavity had a very disagreeable taste.

In the gems which are peculiarly appropriated for female ornaments, cavities containing the expansible fluid frequently occur, and if these cavities should happen to be very near the surface or the edge of the stone, the fever heat of the body might be sufficient to burst them with an alarming and even dangerous explosion. I have never heard of any such accident having occurred; but if it has, or if it ever shall occur, and if its. naturally marvellous character shall be heightened by any calamitous results, the phenomena described in the preceding pages will strip it of its wonder.

There are no facts in chemistry more interesting than those which relate to the changes of colour which are produced by the mixture of fluids, and to the creation of brilliant colours by the combination of bodies in which no colouring matter is visible. Feats of this kind are too common and too generally known to require to be noticed in a work like this. The art of producing such changes was known to some of the early impostors, who endeavoured to obtain a miraculous sanction to their particular dogmas. Marcos, the head of one of the sects that wished to engraft paganism upon Christianity, is said to have filled three transparent glasses with white wine, and while he prayed, the wine in one of the glasses became red like blood, that in another became purple, and that in the third sky-blue. Such transformations present no difficulty to the chemist. There are several fluids, such as some of the coloured juices of plants, which change their colour rapidly and without any additional ingredient; and in other cases, there would be no difficulty in making additions to fluids, which should produce a change of colour at any required instant.

A very remarkable experiment of an analogous nature has been publicly exhibited in modern times. Professor Beyruss, who lived at the court of the Duke of Brunswick, one day pronounced to his highness that the dress which he wore should during dinner become red; and the change actually took place to the astonishment of the prince and the rest of his guests. M. Vogel, who has recorded this curious fact, has not divulged the secret of the German chemist; but he observes, that, if we pour lime-water into the juice of beet-root, we shall obtain a colourless liquid; and that a piece of white cloth dipped in this liquid and dried rapidly will in a few hours become red by the mere contact of air. M. Vogel is also of opinion that this singular effect would be accelerated in an apartment where champagne or other fluids charged with carbonic acid are poured out in abundance.

Among the wonders of chemistry we must number the remarkable effects produced upon the human frame by the inhalation of *paradise* or *intoxicating gas*, as it has been called. This gas is known to chemists by the name of the *nitrous oxide*, or the *gaseous oxide of azote*, or the *protoxide of nitrogen*. It differs from atmospheric air only in the proportion of its ingredients, atmospheric air being composed of twenty-seven parts of oxygen and seventy-three of nitrogen, while the nitrous oxide consists of thirty-seven parts of oxygen and sixty-seven of nitrogen. The most convenient way of procuring the gas is to expose nitrate of ammonia in a tubulated glass retort to the heat of an argand's lamp between 400° and 500° of Fahrenheit. The salt first melts; bubbles of gas begin to rise from the mass, and in a short time a brisk effervescence takes place, which continues till all the salt has disappeared. The products of this operation are the nitrous oxide and water, the watery vapour being condensed in the neck of the retort while the gas is received over water. The gas thus obtained is generally white, and hence, when it is to be used for the purposes of respiration, it should remain at least an hour over water, which will absorb the small quantity of acid and of nitrate of ammonia which adhere to it. A pound of the nitrate of ammonia will in this way yield five cubic feet of gas fit for the purpose of inhalation.

It was discovered by Sir Humphry Davy, that this gas could be safely taken into the lungs, and that it was capable of supporting respiration for a few minutes. In making this experiment he was surprised to find that it produced a singular species of intoxication, which he thus describes : " I breathed," says he, " three quarts of oxide from and into a silk bag for more than half a minute without previously closing my nose or exhausting my lungs. The first inspiration caused a slight degree of giddiness. This was succeeded by an uncommon sense of fulness in the head, accompanied with loss of distinct sensation and voluntary power, a feeling analogous to that produced in the first stage of intoxication, but unattended by pleasurable sensations." In describing the effects of another experiment, he says, "Having previously closed my nostrils and exhausted my lungs, I breathed four quarts of nitrous oxide from and into a silk bag. The first feelings were similar to those produced in the last experiment, but in less than half a minute, the respiration being continued, they diminished gradually, and were succeeded by a highly-pleasurable thrilling, particularly in the chest and the extremities. The objects around me became dazzling, and my hearing more acute. Towards the last respiration the thrilling increased, the sense of muscular power became greater, and at last an irresistible propensity to action was indulged in. I recollect but indistinctly what followed; I knew that my motions were varied and violent. These effects very rarely ceased after respiration. In ten minutes I had recovered my natural state of mind. The thrilling in the extremities continued longer than the other sensations. This experiment was made in the morning; no languor or exhaustion was consequent, my feelings through the day were as usual, and I passed the night in undisturbed repose."

In giving an account of another experiment with this gas, Sir Humphry thus describes his feelings : " Immediately after my return from a long journey, being fatigued, I respired nine quarts of nitrous oxide, having been precisely thirty-three days without breathing any. The feelings were different from those I had experienced on former experiments. After the first six or seven respirations, I gradually began to lose the perception of external things, and a vivid and intense recollection of some former experiments passed through my mind, so that I called out, ' what an annoying concatenation of ideas.' "

Another experiment made by the same distinguished chemist was attended by still more remarkable results. He was shut up in an air-tight breathing box, having a capacity of about nine and a-half cubic feet, and he allowed himself to be habituated to the excitement of the gas, which was gradually introduced. After having undergone this operation for an hour and a quarter, during which eighty quarts of gas were thrown in, he came out of the box and began to respire twenty quarts of unmingled nitrous oxide. " A thrilling," says he, " extending from the chest to the extremities, was almost immediately produced. I felt a sense of tangible extension, highly pleasurable in every kind, my visible impressions were dazzling, and apparently magnified. I heard distinctly every sound in the room, and was perfectly aware of my situation. By degrees, as the pleasurable sensation increased, I lost all connection with external things ; trains of vivid visible images rapidly passed through my mind, and were connected with words in such a manner as to produce perceptions perfectly novel. I existed in a world of newly connected and newly modified ideas. When I was awakened from this same delirious trance by Dr. Kinglake, who took the bag from my mouth, indignation and pride were the first feelings produced by the sight of the persons about me. My emotions were enthusiastic and sublime, and for a moment I walked round the room, perfectly regardless of what was said to me. As I recovered my former state of mind, I felt an inclination to communicate the discoveries I had made during the experiment. I endeavoured to recal the ideas ; they were feeble and indistinct. One recollection of terms, however, presented itself, and with the most intense belief and prophetic manner I exclaimed to Dr. Kinglake, ' nothing exists but thoughts ; the universe is composed of impressions, ideas, pleasures, and pains.' "

These remarkable properties induced several persons to repeat the experiment of breathing this exhilarating medicine. Its effects were, as might have been expected, various in different individuals ; but its general effect was to produce in the gravest and most phlegmatic the highest degree of exhilaration and happiness, unaccompanied with languor or depression. In some it created an irresistible disposition to laugh, and in others a propensity to muscular exertion. In some it impaired the intellectual functions, and in several it had no sensible effect, even when it was breathed in the purest state and in considerable quantities. It would be an inquiry of no slight interest to ascertain the influence of this gas over persons of various bodily temperaments, and upon minds varying in their intellectual and moral character.

Although Sir Humphry Davy experienced no unpleasant effects from the inhalation of the nitrous oxide, yet such effects are undoubtedly produced ; and there is reason to believe that even permanent changes in the constitution may be induced by the operation of this remarkable stimulant. Two very interesting cases of this kind presented themselves to Professor Silliman of Yale College, when the nitrous oxide was administered to some of his pupils. The students had been in the habit for several years of preparing this gas and administering it to one another, and these two cases were the only remarkable ones which deserved to be recorded. We shall describe them in Professor Silliman's own words :—

"A gentleman about nineteen years of age, of a sanguine temperament, and cheerful temper, and in the most perfect health, inhaled the usual quantity of the nitrous oxide when prepared in the ordinary manner. Imme·diately his feelings were uncommonly elevated, so that, as he expressed it, he could not refrain from dancing and shouting. Indeed to such a degree was he excited, that

he was thrown into a frightful fit of delirium, and his
exertions became so violent, that after a while he sunk to
the earth exhausted, and there remained, until having by
quiet in some degree recovered his strength, he again
arose only to renew the most convulsive muscular efforts,
and the most piercing screams and cries; within a few
moments, overpowered by the intensity of the paroxysm,
he again fell to the ground apparently senseless and pant-
ing vehemently. The long continuance and violence of
· the affection alarmed his companions, and they ran for
professional assistance. They were, however, encouraged
by the person to whom they applied to hope that he would
come out of his trance without injury, but for the space
of two hours these symptoms continued; he was perfectly
unconscious of what he was doing, and was in every
respect like a maniac. He states, however, that his *feelings*
vibrated between perfect happiness and the most consum-
mate misery. In the course of the afternoon, and after
the first violent effects had subsided, he was compelled to
lie down two or three times, from excessive fatigue,
although he was immediately aroused upon any one's
entering the room. The effects remained in a degree for
three or four days, accompanied by a hoarseness, which he
attributed to the exertion made while under the immediate
influence of the gas. This case should produce a degree
of caution, especially in persons of a sanguine temperament, whom, much more frequently than others, we have
been painfully and even alarmingly affected." ·

The · other case described by Professor Silliman was
that of a man of mature age, and of a grave and respectable
character. " For nearly two years previous to his taking
the gas his health had been very delicate, and his mind
frequently gloomy and depressed. This was peculiarly
the case for a few days immediately preceding that time,
and his general state of health was such that he was

obliged almost entirely to discontinue his studies, and was about to have recourse to medical assistance. In this state of bodily and mental debility he inspired about three quarts of nitrous oxide. The consequences were, an astonishing invigoration of his whole system, and the most exquisite perceptions of delight. These were manifested by an uncommon disposition for pleasantry and mirth, and by extraordinary muscular power. The effects of the gas were felt without diminution for at least thirty hours, and in a greater or less degree for more than a week.

" But the most remarkable effect was that *upon the organs of taste*. Antecedently to taking the gas, he exhibited no peculiar choice in the articles of food, but immediately subsequent to that event, he *manifested a taste for such things only as were sweet*, and for several days *ate nothing but sweet cake*. Indeed this singular taste was carried to such excess, that he used *sugar and molasses not only upon his bread and butter and lighter food, but upon his meat and vegetables*. This he continues to do even at the present time, and although eight weeks have elapsed since he inspired the gas, he is still found *pouring molasses over beef, fish, poultry, potatoes, cabbage, or whatever animal or vegetable food is placed before him*.

" His health and spirits since that time have been uniformly good, and he attributes the restoration of his strength and mental energy to the influence of the nitrous oxide. He is entirely regular in his mind, and now experiences no uncommon exhilaration, but is habitually cheerful, while before he was as habitually grave, and even to a degree gloomy."

Such is a brief and a general account of the principal phenomena of Nature, and the most remarkable deductions of science, to which the name of Natural Magic has been applied. If those who have not hitherto sought for instruction and amusement in the study of the material world shall have found a portion of either in the preceding pages, they will not fail to extend their inquiries to other popular departments of science, even if they are less marked with the attributes of the marvellous. In every region of space, from the infinitely distant recesses of the heavens to the "dark unfathomed caves of ocean," the Almighty has erected monuments of miraculous grandeur, which proclaim the power, the wisdom, and the beneficence of their author. The inscriptions which they bear—the handwriting which shines upon their walls—appeal to the understanding and to the affections, and demand the admiration and the gratitude of every rational being. To remain willingly ignorant of these revelations of the Divine Power is a crime next to that of rejecting the revelation of the Divine will. Knowledge, indeed, is at once the handmaid and the companion of true religion. They mutually adorn and support each other; and beyond the immediate circle of our secular duties, they are the only objects of rational ambition. While the calm deductions of reason regulate the ardour of Christian zeal, the warmth of a holy enthusiasm gives a fixed brightness to the glimmering lights of knowledge.

It is one of the darkest spots in the history of man that these noble gifts have been so seldom combined. In the young mind alone can the two kindred seeds be effectually sown; and among the improvements which some of our public institutions require, we yet hope to witness a national system of instruction, in which the volumes of Nature and of Revelation shall be simultaneously perused.

D. BREWSTER.

ADDITIONAL PHENOMENA

OF

NATURAL MAGIC.

CHAPTER I.

*Optical illusions—The Mirage of the desert—Belzoni's description—
Quintus Curtius's account—Probable cause—Apathy of the Arabs
and neglect of the example of the patriarchs—Prospect of a
remedy—Optical illusion of Mr. W. G. S.—Association of ideas
—Cause of vividness of such phenomena—And of dreams over
ordinary events — Magic lantern improved by photography
and the improvements in artificial light, &c.—Professor Pepper's
ghost—The decapitated head speaking—Floating cherubs—The
automatic Leotard—The high merits of these Polytechnic inventions—Herr Frikel's "Masks and Faces"—Aurora Borealis
—Sensitive flames—Shadow pantomime.*

ON the subject of optical illusions little falls to be added
to the preceding Letters, beyond what Sir David Brewster
has already so fully written. The mirage in the Arctic
regions has been considerably dilated on in more recent
voyages than those Sir David has referred to, but
nothing has been added to the interest of this phenomenon
which would be regarded as more than mere amplification
of details in the present volume. The following, on
what is called the mirage in the desert, however, possesses
sufficiently distinctive features to justify notice. M.
Belzoni, writing of the desert in Upper Egypt, on the
western side of the Red Sea, which he crossed, and which

2 D

is parallel with the great desert on the eastern side, the scene of the wanderings of the Israelites, says : " Generally speaking, in a desert there are few springs of water : some of them at the distance of four, six, and eight days' journey from one another, and not all of sweet water : on the contrary, it is generally salt or bitter, so that if the thirsty traveller drinks it, it increases his thirst, and he suffers more than before. But when the calamity happens that when the next well, which is so anxiously sought for, is found dry, the misery of such a situation cannot be well described. The camels, which afford the only means of escape, are so thirsty that they cannot proceed to another well; and if the travellers kill them, to extract the little liquid which remains in their stomachs, they themselves cannot advance any further. The situation must be dreadful, and admits of no resource. Many perish victims of the most horrible thirst. It is then that the value of a cup of water is really felt. He that has a zenzabra of it is the richest of all. In such a case there is no distinction. If the master has none the servant will not give it to him ; for very few are the instances where a man will voluntarily lose his life to save that of another, particularly in a caravan in the desert, where people are strangers to each other. What a situation for a man, though a rich one, perhaps the owner of all the caravans! He is dying for a cup of water—no one gives it to him : he offers all he possesses —no one hears him : they are all dying—though by walking a.few hours further they might be saved. If the camels are lying down, and cannot be made to rise, no one has strength to walk. Only he that has a glass of that precious liquor lives to walk a mile further, and perhaps dies too. * * * In short, to be thirsty in the desert without water, exposed to the burning sun without shelter, and no hopes of finding either, is the most terrible situation that a man can be placed in, and one of the greatest sufferings that a human being can sustain : the eyes grow inflamed, the tongue and lips swell, a hollow sound is heard in the ears, which brings on deafness, and the brain appears to grow thick and inflamed. All these feelings arise from the want of a little water. *In the midst of all this misery, the deceitful morasses appear before the traveller at no great distance—something like a lake or river of clear fresh water. If, perchance, a traveller is not undeceived he hastens his pace to reach it sooner : the more he advances towards it the more it recedes from him, till at last it vanishes entirely, and the deluded passenger often asks where is the water he saw at no great distance ? He can scarcely believe that he was so deceived ; he protests that he saw the waves running before the wind, and the reflection of the high rocks in the water.*" Elsewhere M. Belzoni gives the following further particulars of this desert mirage : " It generally appears like a still lake, so unmoved by the wind that everything above is to be seen most distinctly reflected by it. If the wind agitate any of the plants that rise above the horizon of the mirage the motion is seen perfectly at a great distance. If the traveller stands elevated much above the mirage the apparent water seems less united and less deep ; for as the eyes look down upon it, there is not thickness enough in the vapour on the surface of the ground to conceal the earth from the sight ; but if the traveller be on a level with the horizon of the mirage he cannot see through it, so that it appears to him clear water. By putting my head first to the ground, and then mounting a camel, the height of which from the ground might have been about ten feet at the most, I found a great difference in the appearance of the mirage. On approaching it, it becomes thinner, and appears as if agitated by the wind, like a field of ripe corn. It gradually vanishes as the traveller approaches, and at last entirely disappears when he is on the spot."—*Belzoni's Narrative*, pp. 341 343, and p. 196. This description substantially coincides with that of Quintus Curtius, who, in detailing the passage of Alexander the Great and his army through the deserts of Sogdiana, says : "Amidst a dearth of water, despair of obtaining any created thirst before it was excited by nature. Throughout four hundred stadia not a drop of water springs. As soon as the summer heat pervades the sand everything is dried up as in a burning kiln. Steaming from the fervid expanse, *which appears like a surface of sea*, a cloudy vapour darkens the day," &c.—*Quint. Curt.*, lib. vii. c. 5. The phenomenon described by these writers is supposed to be produced by a decrease in the density of the stratum of the atmosphere in immediate contact with the ground, arising from the intense heat of the sun upon the sand; but there is probably also a small amount of vapour or steam at the high temperature of invisibility along with it, and which would in that state rather increase the inconvenience of the traveller, and even aid to blister his skin, as Curtius further remarks, than modify the heat and drought, or help him ; for more recent travellers seem to indicate from their observations that there is water at no very great depth below the sand. And, indeed, it is a remarkable fact that the Arabs, with the well-remembered examples of the patriarchs before them, whose Artesian works remain, and are pointed out by them to this day, should not have dug wells at convenient distances for their caravan journeys, and established caravansaries at them, to prevent the horrors Belzoni has described, and with the fatal features of which they have had grim familiarity down through all the ages of their history. The desire for short routes and railway communication will probably come to their aid at last, and accomplish this object by the sinking of Artesian wells and the dissemination of streams of water along the surface of the ground by means of steam pumps, which would soon be sheltered by vegetation if water were steadily supplied, for it is astonishing how rapidly the desert blooms and becomes covered with verdure whenever plants find moisture to support them. And there appears little reason to doubt that these deserts are great basins full of water, but only fuller still of sand. Dean Stanley, in his "Sinai and Palestine," speaking of the general characteristics of the wadys or valleys, says: "There is nearly everywhere a thin, it might almost be said a transparent coating of vegetation."

Allied to the class of optical illusions mentioned in Sir David's third Letter, the following, communicated to the editor by the gentleman by whom it was experienced, is sufficiently distinctive to deserve notice. One day, not many years since, Mr. W. G. S., the gentleman in question, was after an interval of years walking along a picturesque country road in the neighbourhood of Edinburgh, when reaching a certain point he was suddenly, and without any previous preparation for such a spectacle, surprised by the appearance of a magnificent cavalcade of knights and dames on horseback arrayed in the costume of the Middle Ages, accompanied with a suitable following of squires and other attendants, with hounds and hawks: many of the ladies with falcons on their wrists, as if the party were bent on hunting. The cavalcade consisted of a numerous company, and defiled with gay but graceful dignity, passed him and disappeared in a woodland path. The gentleman stood riveted in surprise for some moments after the spectacle had disappeared; for, convinced it was only an illusion, he was astonished at its vivid magnificence and complete details. At length, overcoming his wonder, he proceeded on his walk, still ruminating on the pageant

he had seen, and striving to explain it to himself, when he
at last recollected that in his boyhood, many years before,
when he had given himself up to the reading of romance-
literature, at the period when it was most in fashion, he
had been in the habit of identifying himself with the subjects he had read; and being of a peculiarly intense
character, with a highly-picturesque imagination, had on
many occasions during his solitary country rambles abandoned himself to the enthusiasm of the time and imagined
himself one of the characters in just such chivalrous and
romantic pageants; and he then felt fully satisfied that
some peculiarity in the appearance of the road at the
point where he had just beheld the spectacle mentioned
had recalled the whole association of ideas connected with
a past visit to the spot, and revived in this vivid form a
day-dream of his youth.

The mere vividness, however, of such an incident was
its only peculiarity. The association of ideas is so strong
and so well known, that we can scarce hear certain subjects
mentioned, or look upon certain articles, without having at
once a long train of the past suggested to the mind's eye,
and the intensity with which the subject presents itself
often passes unnoticed on account of its being expected
and a matter of course. Thus the presence of an article
of furniture such as an old chair will set the fancy into a
trance of contemplation as to some departed and venerable
occupant, and the whole thought in connection with it will
be pictured by the mind, for it is a mistake to say we
think in language only; we think in pictures also, just as
much as we dream in pictures, and the only reason why
such pictures do not strike us with surprise is that they
are, if not pictures resulting from direct volition, at all
events pictures tacitly acquiesced in, and therefore such as
we are mentally prepared for. It is in fact only when we
think without the will or consent that the imagery of the

mind, unfamiliar under that aspect, is more than usually vivid from the effect of surprise. Indeed, reality is in much the same condition with us. We meet friends day by day who have been the associates of our lives, and we scarce realize the fact that they have been with us. A familiar face may appear, a familiar step enter the study while we are busily engaged, and pass out again without our recognition, and scarcely with our consciousness that they have been with us. But should any friend long absent appear suddenly and unexpectedly in the same way, surprise and the intensity of special recognition will be evoked at once, and a vividness of the whole incident impressed upon the mind which will produce the strongest impression at the moment, and leave elements for permanent reflection afterwards when things common have been long forgotten. The vividness of dreams is very much, if not wholly, attributable to the same cause. The will in our mental life to a certain extent directs and controls the current of ideas under ordinary circumstances, and with regard to real incidents, we are in contact with a series of causes, all the associations and results of which are regarded as matter of course, calculated on and looked for. They are therefore looked forward to before they take place, or so far foreknown as to have their interest and novelty exhausted before they occur; but dreams are things out of the list of anticipation, for they never are, when vivid or impressive, what we expected them to be; hence the impression of their novelty is not and cannot be forestalled, and they strike us with as much vividness as any surprising or unexpected incident in the eventualities of life.

Among artificial illusions many ingenious novelties have appeared of late years. The ingenious suggestions of Sir David Brewster, before mentioned, for the improvement of the magic lantern have been all more or less exceeded by the great progress of recent discovery. Photography has given accuracy of detail and life-like intensity to the subjects displayed by the lantern, while improvements in the mechanism, together with lime ball, magnesium, and other powerful means of illumination, have been successfully applied to produce almost a daylight clearness on the screen compared with the darkness in which the audience sits in viewing such objects. How far Sir David had anticipated some of the most advanced improvements by his suggestions however will appear from the following passage in a recent publication compared with his letter on this subject :—

"An ingenious experimentalist, desirous of showing various chemical phenomena by means of the magic lantern, makes a glass tank, into which different liquids or solutions may be poured, which will illustrate the effect of refraction on light and other phenomena. If a pipette be skilfully used to introduce some of the solutions into the water in the tank, the appearance thrown on the screen is that of a submarine volcano, pouring forth clouds of smoke and torrents of lava, which, however, are soon absorbed in the surrounding ocean. A solution of cochineal in alcohol, similarly introduced, produces the effect of a magnificent crimson fountain : a solution of litmus appears as a delicate blue sky ; a few drops of acid being let fall into this give a variety of forms and combinations, as of clouds seen in a sunset sky. Black, stormy clouds may be produced by dropping into the water a small quantity of sulphate of copper in solution and weak ammonia ; and with dilute sulphuric acid and ferrocyanide of potassium, other cloud-effects can be represented which have a most impressive appearance on the screen. It is possible also to show the changes in colour produced by chemical reaction, the decomposition of water by a galvanic current, and the convection of heat by liquids; and to exhibit all these operations to a large number of persons at once, opens a new application of the magic lantern which clever operators will no doubt turn to account; any one familiar with the manipulation of apparatus will know how to contrive the tanks for the different purposes."

The eminently-ingenious Professor Pepper also, in conjunction with the other talented gentlemen forming the staff of the Royal Polytechnic Institution of London, has distinguished himself by great success not only in showing all the illusions practised by charlatans who claim a higher authority than mere skill and dexterity for their séances, but in the forestalling by their inventive genius discoveries which otherwise might have been used in course of time to deceive and operate upon the superstitious by vile and unprincipled pretenders to the supernatural.

Among other novelties, Professor Pepper's ghost, the speaking head, floating cherubs, automatic Leotard, &c., deserve special mention and the highest praise. The ghost is got up in a very simple yet remarkably effective way, and suggests the idea that the Professor must have caught sight of his own image in a plate-glass window more than once before he engaged in spirit-making. This illusion is easily accomplished by placing a large sheet of plate glass E F on the stage before a dark-green cloth under a subdued light, and throwing the reflection of a person acting the ghost upon it by having him placed in front in such a position as to cause his image to appear at the point desired. For this purpose the person acting the ghost must be placed with a screen of dark-green cloth behind him, as shown in the following diagram. In this way the reflection of the dark-green cloth A B behind the figure will not appear, but will blend with the colour of the dark-green cloth C D behind the sheet of plate glass, while the figure will appear reflected alone. The light being kept more subdued upon the stage than upon the figure to be reflected, the presence of any real actor upon the stage will appear less vivid under the subdued light than that of the ghost. If the plate glass be so arranged that the actor on the stage in approaching or passing the shadow can go behind or in front of the plate glass at pleasure, the illusion of passing through the shadow or appearing to strike, stab, or grasp it in vain, will be very perfectly shown. The distance between the figure and its reflection at E F is necessarily circumscribed by the limits of our space. The angularity of the glass to the audience, so as to throw the image of the ghost only toward them, and all other reflection on it in other directions, is easily arranged.

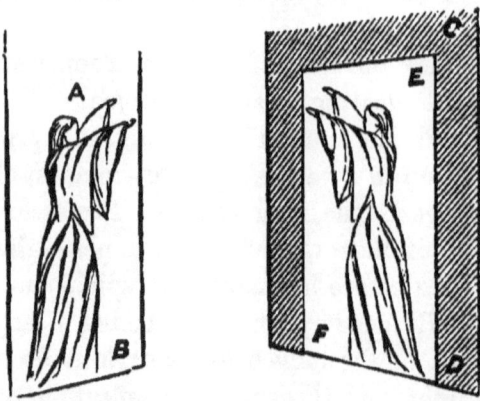

The speaking head, floating cherubs, &c., are accomplished by similar arrangements of plate glass and dark background. But in these cases the figures seen may, or may not be in shadow or reflection, at the option of the conductor. When not reflections, the arrangement may be accomplished by having the plate glass divided into pieces. Thus a half sheet from the bottom of the stage, with a screen of green cloth in front of the performer, will conceal the whole body but the head, which may appear to be resting on a pole or narrow pedestal in front of the glass. In this way Blue Beard places the carefully-embalmed head of a deceased wife, the victim of his cruelty, upon the pedestal to look at. This head, if an excellent wax likeness of some lady performer of the establishment, is easily put out of the way when being placed on the pedestal and represented by the lady performer herself, who appears from behind, showing only so much of her head as replaces and represents the wax likeness. Blue Beard then retires to smoke and contemplate, when to his astonishment and horror the dead head addresses him, opens its eyes, &c. This illusion is very ingenious and perfect. Cherubs may be made to float about by representing heads of children or young performers in the same way, their bodies being concealed by a screen of green cloth in front of the floating stage on which they stand. The great advantage of the dark-green cloth groundwork in blending, though in separate pieces, as if it were only one continuous background, is of great importance, together with such a subdued and appropriate arrangement of the light as prevents the plate glass from glancing and becoming apparent to the audience, and the ingenious invention is capable of far higher dramatic effects than it has yet been applied to. Professor Pepper's ghosts, like those of Shakespeare, are almost too refined and gentlemanly for any but those delicate and metaphysical qualities of mind which appreciate the characteristics of propriety and logical connection in everything. The white sheet horror is more suited to the modern sensational drama. But there really is some defect in the representation of Shakespeare's grand ghost scenes, which modern science might surely apply itself to remedy. The ghost of Hamlet's father and others want a glistering, phosphorescent and self-lighted aspect to distinguish their spectral character vividly from the living actors with whom they mingle, and doubtless Shakespeare's own ideal was something of this kind, though the resources of the time did not afford very satisfactory means of realising it. The innocuous allotropic phosphorus now in use, with perhaps some other chemical appliances, might afford means of overcoming this difficulty.

The automatic Leotard is another of those admirably-achieved Polytechnic illusions which may be said to surpass in some respects even the living prototype. This figure is admirably formed, and its possible motions, with their swing, are well kept within the range of easy physical action in the natural joints. To the close observer it becomes at once apparent, from the want of bend in the elbow-joints and the complete circles performed by the shoulders of the figure, that the hands and inflexible arms are permanently fixed to the cross-bar of the trapeze, which is made to revolve in any direction by means of rods and wheels connected with its ends and set in motion from above, the rods being concealed by what appear to be the cords by which the whole is suspended, which also have a manifest inflexibility and an otherwise unnecessary thickness. These peculiarities, however, are far from detracting from the merit of this admirable Polytechnic invention. Professor Pepper manfully disavows the power to work impossibilities. He only aims at accomplishing apparent impossibilities by the most skilful and graceful application of possible means, and assuredly these are of them. To what infamous purposes, by contrast, the ancient statecrafts and priestcrafts would have turned these meritorious and honourable ingenuities, had they known them, many a passage in the preceding Letters of Sir David Brewster will abundantly suggest.

The illusion as to the direction of sight and the expression of faces, mentioned in one of the preceding Letters, has been further and most successfully illustrated lately by the "Masks and Faces" of the talented and ingenious Herr Frikel, who by the mere arrangement of head-gear and appropriate accessories has shown how readily the same face may be made to realise our typical ideas of the European and Asiatic, Hindoo, Chinese, Turk, or Tartar, &c., as well as the masculine or feminine expression and countenance. Indeed our attention or inattention to facts, which perhaps do or do not strongly affect us, is apt to make us imagine there are greater differences in some cases and less differences in others than really exist. The man who would never doubt, until confronted with one of Herr Frikel's trans- formations, that he could at once tell, by the aspect of the countenance, the difference between a German and a Chinaman would be apt to deny the possibility of a shepherd being able to distinguish every individual sheep of a numerous flock which has been for a short time under his care. Yet any one who takes the trouble to look carefully at a flock of sheep driven through the streets will be able to see that, even in the shape of the nose, sheep are as much distinguished from each other in- dividually by all the varieties of Roman, Greek, and snub nose as human beings are, and that all the other features are equally marked by individual identity. Indeed, the aphorism "as like as two peas" is by no means so very close or proximate a resemblance as the expression appears to assume. We doubt if there ever were two peas exactly alike since the creation of the world, any more than two kinds or specimens of handwriting. Nay, much as identity in this latter respect is distinctively recog- nisable, we doubt if any man ever wrote his own signature exactly alike twice in the whole course of his life; and yet a man with perfect integrity and justifiability swears to his own handwriting, and others acquainted with it do so also, in the perfect and conscientious certainty of the fact.

One of the subjects which it appears justifiable to introduce here, along with the associated subject of the mirage which has been so interestingly treated by Sir David Brewster, is the aurora borealis, which is displayed with remarkable brilliance within the Arctic circle during the prolonged winter darkness of that region, which is much indebted to this splendid phenomenon for the relief of its prolonged and inhospitable gloom. Those who observe this phenomenon attentively will find that its point of convergence, or the centre towards which its "streamers" point, is generally identical with, or very nearly approximate to, that point of the heavens which is opposite to the sun during the manifestation of the spectacle. It is a point, in fact, only seen in the northern and southern regions beyond the range of the ecliptic while the sun is within that plane, and on the opposite side of the earth, and everything conspires to show that while the atmosphere of the world acts like a sphere of glass enclosing the earth, by which the rays of the sun are refracted as if they were intercepted by a globular or double convex lens, these rays so refracted are converged on the opposite side of this atmospheric lens, from the edges of the terrestrial disc exposed to the sun, according to the greater or less purity of the atmosphere under that region forming the edge of the disc, and that the coloured rays seen to prevail sometimes are mere prolongations of the gorgeous tints of sunset or of dawn then prevailing at those points of the world's surface from which the re-fraction takes place. The rapidity with which the aurora darts its rays, and changes, is readily accounted for from the presence of intercepting clouds, projecting ice, and mountain ranges, and other inequalities along the circumference of the earth's disc exposed to the solar action, combined with the rapidity of the earth's motion (diurnal and orbitual) with reference to the sun; while the weather which such an appearance is held to presage is also accounted for by the atmospheric conditions necessary to enable the phenomenon to take place.

One of the remarkable discoveries of recent scientific inquiry is that of Mr. Barrett, late Assistant at the Royal Institution, with regard to what are called "sensitive flames." A metal pipe with an orifice of steatite, when emitting such an amount of gas as to afford that quantity of flame which a burner gives forth just before the flame "roars," as we are accustomed to hear it called, from the excessive pressure of the gas, furnishes a light which is exceedingly sensitive to certain sounds. A grave sound such as a low whistle will cause it to shoot out numerous tongues of flame, which subside when the sound is discontinued. By different arrangements of the burner this may be varied. An aperture supplying a column of flame of about two feet in length will cower and quiver under the influence of certain sibilant sounds. Words containing the letters, *s*, *x*, and *z*, especially the former, powerfully affect it even when pronounced at a considerable distance from it. And a variety of manifestations may be occasioned by certain notes of the pianoforte. Under one set of conditions the effect being produced by high, and under another by low notes. This peculiarity is manifestly the effect of vibration on highly-elastic elements, which may either be the gas forming the supporter of combustion, or the metallic orifice from which the flame proceeds. Indeed, every element known is more or less elastic, and it is quite possible to conceive that certain sounds, by the peculiarity of their vibration, could shiver solid bodies to pieces, and that the character of the sound, more than the power of the atmospheric concussion involved, might produce the most serious consequences. Who is not familiar with that most disagreeable of sounds, the sharpening of a saw with a file, to recall the very recollection of which is to conjure up a sensation of horror? It is not in such a case because our dislike is arbitrary and capricious that we hate the sensation produced, but because it is really disagreeable, and to some delicate constitutions has a positively injurious physical effect, that repugnance to it prevails, and the nerves shrink and quiver painfully beneath its action.

A very amusing novelty has recently been successfully exhibited at one of the London amphitheatres, which may be called "Shadow Pantomime." The body of the house or room being darkened, a white screen is interposed between the audience and the performers, with a light behind it, by means of which the shadows of the performers only are given projected on the screen. When a performer approaches near to the light at the back of the stage his shadow is greatly magnified and appears of gigantic proportions, while the other performers approaching nearer to the screen appear upon it by their shadows of nearly their natural size. The effect is highly striking and effective, as well as amusing, as the hand of an individual near the light will appear larger by its shadow on the screen than the whole body of an actor more remote from the light, and nearer to the screen. Jack the Giant Killer, and the adventures of Gulliver, admit of a highly effective and comic representation by means of this very ingenious adaptation of shadow, and the arrangements are so simple and easily made that the amusements of the nursery may be readily and greatly enhanced and illustrated by it at absolutely no expense, and scarcely any trouble.

CHAPTER II.

*Life and suspended animation, or asphyxia—Interment alive—Pheno-
mena of the grave—Coma, or extraordinarily long sleeps—Bears
—Toads found in rocks—Tadpoles: separated vitality—Polypes
—Annelides, or worms—Process of restoring severed parts—Suspended and restored animation—Rotifera—Reproductive powers
of animals and plants—Divisibility of matter—Facts beyond the
range of physics—Extraordinary divisibility of life—New fact in
philosophy—The philosophers of fixity—Superiority of a child s
logic—A fact of science for Unitarians—Conclusion.*

THE extraordinary circumstances under which life may
sometimes continue to exist has given rise to many
remarkable, and, in some instances, painful impressions
among mankind. The dormant condition of bears and
other animals during their winter's sleep of many months'
duration, and many well-authenticated instances of unusually long periods of sleep by human beings, who
during this condition have maintained their vitality without food and at a very low and all but suspended rate of
vital action, have doubtless given rise to those popularly-
recited cases of asphyxia, or suspended animation, under
which people have been said to be buried alive, and which
many living individuals have a horror may be their fate
if left to the charge of the careless and incautious at the
time of death. Many have felt this apprehension so
oppressive that they have desired that their interment
should not take place after apparent death under ordinary
circumstances, unless in addition some violence were done
to the physical organization, so as to prevent the possibility of their coming to life again after the earth had
been closed in upon them; and many have wished to do

2 E

away with interment altogether to avoid suffering the horror of suffocation in the tomb. This kind of death, it is idle to deny, has a character of horror for the human mind, the metaphysical associations of which invest it with an ideal, but not on that account the less a real agony, eminently beyond every other conceivable form of terminating our mortality. That instances well authenticated of people being buried alive under misapprehension have occurred cannot be gainsayed, and a circumstance was brought before public attention not many years ago which appeared to support the idea that this was much more common than was usually suspected, for it was found on opening many tombs for the purposes of subsequent interments in the same place that the faces of the parties previously interred were generally found turned downward. This was concluded to be evidence of the persons having awoke in the grave after their interment, and in their helpless and hopeless struggles for relief turning round upon their faces, and dying under these dark circumstances in despair. Fortunately a more careful investigation of the facts satisfactorily dispelled this truly horrible impression. It was found that, though the skull was face downward, it was not until decay had so far progressed as to effect separation of the vertebrae of the neck that it was so, and that the rest of the skeleton still remained upon its back. This fact was utterly at variance with the idea of the person having become alive in the tomb and afterwards dying of suffocation, because the position of the face downwards, and the body on its back, was impossible as a result of voluntary action—which any one may prove by attempting to turn the head round so as to see directly behind him while retaining the breast in the opposite direction; and a little further investigation showed that the skull when separated by decay from the neck could not balance itself on the back of the head, but invariably turned round on the face under the law of its own gravitation. But though this satisfactorily dispelled a most painful impression, it has neither fully dissipated the popular horror of being buried alive, nor disproved instances in which that has actually taken place : and a general belief prevails that there are cases of unusually long-suspended animation, or asphyxia, under which the same thing is continually liable to be repeated. That the medical profession have not been able to authenticate any such cases of long-continued asphyxia, or suspended animation, is however a very important fact. To suspect that highly honourable profession of any collusive suppression on the subject seems impossible ; but that the reader may fully understand the subject, and place the question beyond suspicion to his own intelligence, let him consider what the conditions of asphyxia, or suspended animation, are. Now a complete cessation of the pulse, and a consequently complete stoppage in the circulation of the blood, which cannot proceed without pulsation, are primary features of asphyxia ; and such conditions have not been found capable of continuing beyond a certain time without such a change taking place in the stagnated blood as utterly unfits it from resuming its circulation or retaining those elements of vitality which are necessary to the resumption of human life. The time usually allowed for this fatal change taking place in the condition of the blood is that ascribed to cases beyond which restoration from drowning, hanging, syncope or fainting, and suffocation, have never been known to take place, and is held by such experience not to exceed a few hours. On this subject an eminent authority, Mr. Smee, says : " Where one dies suddenly without a clear equivalent cause *which is irremediable*, the heat of the body should be maintained *at least twelve hours* by hot bottles, and artificial respiration should be at-

tempted as for drowning. Remember that the death may
be only apparent, and your care may be repaid by the
inexpressible delight of seeing life gradually resumed and
the party restored to his family." This excellent advice
cannot be too carefully adhered to, for there can be no
doubt that where people have been buried alive culpable
carelessness has had much to do with the matter. There
is a condition to which humanity is in extraordinary
instances liable, where, without absolute asphyxia or
complete stoppage of the circulation, the pulsation may
be so low that, though the person is only in a very profound state of prolonged sleep and low vitality, the
evidence of circulation in the blood and consequent
pulsation may escape ordinary attention, and the coldness
of the breath, from the temperature of the body being
allowed by those in attendance to get too low, may not
even mist a mirror held before the face. This, however,
which is only a state of coma, will not deceive the competent physician, who in all such cases will be able at
once to detect the difference between coma and asphyxia;
and the danger of interment alive to the sufferer will only
occur where medical aid has not been called. Instances
of coma being produced artificially are said to be known
to the Hindoos, who will allow themselves to be thrown
into it, and even buried alive, for short periods, in
shallow graves, where the porousness of the earth allows
sufficient air to reach them for the low rate of respiration
which takes place while they are in that state. More
astonishing instances occur among some of the other
animals—that of bears in the northern districts of Europe
and elsewhere, which has been already referred to, being
sufficiently well known. And those remarkable cases of
toads found in stones in the course of quarrying, and
other excavations of the earth's crust, where the animal
must to all appearance have remained imprisoned for

thousands of years, are instances of vitality supported under circumstances so abnormal as to excite the utmost wonder at its tenacity. Such cases are manifestly not asphyxia, and can hardly be said to be even coma. The toad, as is well known to naturalists, is a foul-blooded animal, and does not purify its blood perfectly at the lungs during circulation. It seems capable, there-fore, of living under similar circumstances to those under which thick-leaved plants exist in hermetically-closed conservatories without renewed air or water, and is able sufficiently to purify the air around it for the purposes of its own respiration. It can, therefore, live in a less quantity of air, and with a less degree of absolute purity in the atmosphere by which it is surrounded, than would be possible for a pure-blooded animal, or one which, as an essential of its health, required to purify its blood perfectly at the lungs. But it is well known that the toad possesses remarkable powers of vitality in the earlier stages of its existence, i.e., when in the tadpole state, in which, with gills like a fish, it may be seen in our slow running streams and stagnant pools during the period of its development as a small black comet-shaped creature, consisting of a round nucleus or head, and a tail. In this state, if separated from the head, the tail will continue to live, and even grow for many days; while, in the mean-while, the head grows a new tail for itself, repairing the injury and restoring the completeness of the animal. But this power of vitality in animals, as well as in plants, is in many instances more remarkable than the above. In plants, as is well known, propagation by slips and off shoots is easily effected, and inversion of the whole direction of vitality may be accomplished, for trees and shrubs capable of being propagated by cuttings seem generally to possess this remarkable peculiarity—that either end of the cutting may be inserted into the ground

or into the stock in grafting, and the cutting will reverse
the action of its fluids, and throw out its branches with a
downward, instead of an upward tendency, such as we see
in that plant now so much cultivated, the weeping, or
drooping ash, which is a tree grafted on this principle.
Among animals the polypes seem to possess still more
wonderful powers of vitality.   They are tube-like forms,
and if turned inside out the outer coating will become a
stomach, and the stomach an outer skin.   They can be
cut into pieces, and each piece will continue to live and
become a perfect polype.   If punctured, the punctured
part will shoot forth a young polype, which may be cut
off and separated from the parent, and cut into pieces, and
each piece become an independent and perfect polype.   The
annelides, or earth-worms (*Lumbricidæ*), seem possessed of
similar vital energies.   These worms, like the leeches, are
hermaphrodites (*Monoicous*), the one end being male and
the other female.   If cut in two both ends will become
separate individuals, and will grow into perfect worms by
reproducing the ends of which they are deprived. Nothing
is more common in turning up soil than to see worms
with a thick and a thin end.   These are worms which
have been severed by the spade or other cause, the thick
end being one of the halves of the original worm, and the
thin end being a reproduction of the severed part.   In
such cases it might be said that the hermaphrodite is two
animals joined together, but capable of separate existence,
and possessed of distinct and separable vitalities; and so
of plants capable of being propagated by cuttings,
and of polypes—that they are a combination of many
distinct and separable vitalities, and capable, when
severed from each other, of self-restoring powers : the
plant restoring itself by reproducing the severed root,
and the animal by reproducing the severed member.   In
both plant and animal the hermaphrodite peculiarity in

such cases prevails. The animal and the plant are equally capable of reproducing in the ordinary way, as well as by cuttings, and the long period during which vitality may be entirely dormant in plant life, as well as in some animals, bears a very close analogy. In plants we have the example of the mummy wheat, representing thousands of years of dormant life; but it is also found, not only that seeds may be kept for many years without injury to their vegetating power, but that even the pollen or yellow dust from the anthers of flowers may be kept for years, and afterwards used in hybridizing and in producing seed. While in animal life, that of the toad, which we have already referred to, might be supplemented by many instances of the prolonged dormancy of eggs or ova, and also by the remarkable experiments by Spallanzani, Davaine, Gavarret, and others with the Tardigrades and Rotifera, or Wheel Animalculæ, which it has been found can be dried and moistened, or killed and revived as it was at one time considered, and the experiment repeated with them many times after intervals of years. At one time it was supposed these animalculæ could bear to be perfectly desiccated, but more careful observation has shown that, unless a small essential quantity of moisture remains in them, replacing them in water will fail to restore their vitality. Of course their vitality is never actually gone, it is merely in a state of suspension or dormancy.

But these remarks are introduced less because they are conclusions, than because they form the threshold, and merely the threshold, of an exceedingly great and interesting and, at the same time, utterly incomprehensible subject—the great life chain of reality. Take up any link of this wonderful subject and examine it carefully, and we will find that, instead of being within the range of intelligible and natural laws, we are altogether thrown out of our logic into a region for which nature has no law, but which is not the less a vivid reality, most deeply and permanently concerning ourselves. We have many wonderful statements in scientific works on the subject of matter and its divisibility. It is stated, for example, that there are more animals in the milt of a single codfish than there are men on the whole earth, and that a single grain of sand is larger than four millions of these animals. But let us take a moderate estimate of this fact, far within the limits of truth, and therefore free from all hyperbole, for the purpose of reaching a deeper and more interesting region of reality beyond it. Let us, for example, content ourselves with assuming that there are only ten millions of those animals in a single codfish, it follows that this single codfish was but one of ten millions in the milt of its progenitor, and that progenitor but one of ten millions in the milt of its parent, and so on backward until you reach the three-hundredth ancestor in a direct line of reproduction; and here you find the fact utterly surpassing all our possible investigation into its physical reality, but not the less a fact on that account, that this three-hundredth ancestor must at that stage of his existence when he was in the milt of his parent, and only, say, a millionth part the size of a grain of sand—for we are speaking of the progeny in the milt, not in the roe— this animal in this minute condition, we say, must have had within him in turn a progeny whose numbers in the three-hundredth generation after him would be so numerous that, were we to begin at the top of this page with the number ten millions, we should have to add as many ciphers as there is space for types in the whole page to note them down. Taking the page, then, at thirty-six lines of three inches long, we should have for this number a line of figures, of the size of the present type, three yards long. Carrying this curious calculation back to the time of Cæsar

Augustus, the product would fill six pages of this work; and if extended in a single line of figures as large as our type would form a sum eighteen yards long : carried back to the founding of the Chinese Empire, according to some historians, it would fill thirteen of our pages, and give a single line of figures thirty-nine yards long, as any of our readers may satisfy himself by multiplying the first ten millions by ten millions for the succeeding year, and so on, and observing that each year adds seven ciphers to the product. He has therefore merely to take the number of years and add seven ciphers for each. And yet this extraordinary result is probably as far within the mark as it may at first sight appear hyperbolical and excessive, for we have not merely assumed, within our limits, that the cod milt contains only ten millions, instead of more nearly eight or ten hundred millions, but that each fish reproduces its species only once a year, and once in a life-time. At the same time it is not essential to our calculation, or its object, that these animals do not all reach full development and maturity ; it is enough for what we are about to observe on the subject that they exist even for only an instant at any stage of their vitality. Now we do not state this for the purpose of illustrating the infinitesi-mal divisibility of matter, nor the extent of its practicable divisibility in the hands of its great Maker and Master ; for while we freely and reverently acknowledge God's per-fectly illimitable omnipotence in this as in all directions, we do not believe that He *has* chosen to subdivide matter to this degree, and we venture to think that various chemical facts are inconsistent with such a hypothesis. We think, on the contrary, that we are on the verge of a new dis-covery, and a discovery with which we cannot hope to laurel ourselves, for it will only, we fear, reveal to us how little we know—how little of palpable and unchallengeable fact and reality we ever here can hope to know. In editing

Joyce's Scientific Dialogues for Mr. Tegg, the present writer ventured, at p. 324 of that work, to say that, while it was impossible to conceive of any body or particle of matter so small as not to have two surfaces, the one of which must be capable of physical separation from the other, had we means sufficiently fine to accomplish the separation, "yet there is reason to believe that the subdivision of matter stops short of this infinitesimal reducibility of parts in a definite and ultimate molecular form, very minute indeed, but beyond which material elements never are divided, though it is of course impossible to conceive that these molecules or atoms of matter are incapable of being divided still further had we the means; only if further divided they would cease to be molecules, and would only be fragments of molecules. Chemistry, from the proportions in which different elements chemically combine, has long pointed to, and now absolutely demands, this solution of the structure of matter." The view above stated we find no good ground for qualifying here, even in the presence of the extraordinary fact as to reproduction in the codfish which has just been set forth, and which is greatly exceeded in the reproductive history of many other animals and in many plants. What we maintain is, that the subdivision we have set forth in this case of animated nature is far beyond the molecular, and very, very far beyond the possible organic subdivision of matter, taking nature as it is—that the hundredth progeny or descendant of a codfish has, consequently, no physical or organic existence whatever in its hundredth ancestor or progenitor, and that its connection with its ancestor during the earlier stages of that ancestor's existence and development *is not and cannot be a physical one.* We do not at the same time deny that the connection exists, or existed at that stage; on the contrary, we affirm that it did then exist, and was in the parent as essentially as the parent's own life and reproductive powers were in it. But then it must have been in it only in the condition of life—in that mysterious yet real, but utterly incomprehensible state of dormant vitality, of which nature's laws—which hazy philosophies make the absolute and dominant rule of everything in these days—can give us not the very slightest knowledge, and material criteria not the vestige of available measurement.

⊢ There is certainly little corroboration to be derived from facts like the preceding in behalf of the *ex nihilo nihil fit* philosophy. It is a remarkable circumstance that all who have ventured to state these absolute and ultimate propositions have had but a very limited knowledge of scientific fact, even while claiming to be exclusively scientific men. In the age in which these philosophies sprang up all the science known, even had it been all comprehended in one mind, was, as compared with that of our own age, limited and imperfect. Among modern philosophers who have ventured to reproduce these propositions we have never found one who had a wide and comprehensive knowledge of comparative science—who was more than distinguished in some particular department within which his knowledge was respectable enough and worthy of being received as authority, but beyond which it was all but contemptible and feebler than that of a child, as well as more erring because more confident—who ever could draw a wider analogy than that which his own limited department of study afforded, or look upon the illimitable range of general philosophy save with a monochromatic vision coloured exclusively by the light pervading his own point of view. If all scientific knowledge when these propositions were first dogmatised was inadequate as a basis for ultimate and absolute conclusions, how much less can the professor distinguished by merely one branch of study now be justified in rearing up his solitary testimony in behalf of them when reproduced in an age like this, in which we are only beginning to feel fully the littleness of achievement, the feebleness of human capacity, and the inexhaustible harvest of eternal discovery and expansion before us ? " Through the EVIDENCE—conviction, manifestation, demonstration, Ελεγχος—OF THINGS NOT SEEN" (for that is the apostolic and authoritative meaning of Christian FAITH, which those who do not know it call credulity), "we understand that the worlds were framed by the word of God, so that things that are seen were not made of things which do appear." How far such a fact reaches through and beyond the uttermost depths of present scientific achievement, even when we deal with the subject of Matter only! What, for example, do we really know or explain of any portion of matter by saying, in the ultimatum of scientific language, It is a primary element? "What is gold made of?" a child will ask of a philosopher. "Gold! why gold is gold—it is a primary element, my dear—it is nothing but gold :" so replies the scientific sage. "Yes, but what is it made of?" insists the pertinacious child ; for a child is a healthy inquirer, and has not learned to be silenced with an unsatisfactory answer. "What can it be made of but gold?" says the stultified philosopher; "chemistry can reduce it into nothing else — gold is gold." But the child is not answered. He is not yet acquainted with Mammon's fluctuating, but on the whole approximately satisfactory solution of its value ; he is not questioning his broker, and is innocent of the ways of 'Change, so he pecks another fathom deep into the wisdom of the vexed philosopher, and spits him through his shallows with the broad and startlingly assertive proposition, "But gold *must* be made of *something;*" and then, petulantly reiterative, adds "What is it made of?" The philosopher, remembering when he also had such a question suggested by his own mind, feels that he is on the verge of a primeval headache, and seeing the vivacious child attracted by some new subject, waits till his attention is fairly tackled, and quietly leaves the throne of philosophy vacant.

But the child is right after all, and how clearly and confidently he knows it! Gold *is* made of something. It has a molecular structure of some kind, apart from which and its chemical ratios it would cease to be gold, chemically and monetarily. Its ultimate molecule, whether we are right in all we have said of its structure in Joyce's Scientific Dialogues, p. 324, or not, is divisible into something else could we but reach it, and its molecular structure once divided its whole chemical ratios and combinations would be destroyed. The philosopher may be satisfied with the fact that gold is gold, but the unso phisticated child will reason straight up to his Maker, and be satisfied with no explanation short of that which satisfies all his awed and deep-felt consciousness that He who could make himself could also make gold, whatever lesser ultimatum science may proclaim on the basis of primary and hypothetically *irresoluble elements*. This is not quite intuition in a child, it is the honest energy of unvitiated dialectics penetrating to the legitimate ultimatum of all causation : the only possible source of those things not seen which the apostle and our own experience alike demonstrate to us have their evidence in the metaphysical existence and consciousness of us all. The child knows he has been but recently brought into existence himself, and by a competent Power which he perceives by analogy to be competent to bring anything else into existence. In mathematical language, the first of these facts is an axiom, the second is its corollary ; and both, if not explanatory, are at least irresistibly convincing. But the proposition that gold is self-existent is a hypothesis not based on any axiomatic premise. Gold, we know, has a structure which we find can be chemically acted on. But structure implies construction, and therefore gold must have been constructed. We also know that self-existence must reside, not in the thing constructed, but in the primary constructor; and thus we analytically prove the superiority of a child's logic over that of a philosopher. It may be asked, why does man as he grows up lose this originally high and clear reasoning power reaching to absolute conclusions? The answer is, that as man grows up he acquires bias, and starts favourite theories and hypotheses *within* the limits of his powers. It is the unvitiated candour of a child that constitutes its superiority and its conclusiveness—reaching to the utmost penetrable limits.

Here in a department then of distinctly demonstrable and experienced scientific fact we have as it were the evidence that from the Creator's vital energy all conscious existence has been produced, in that He has conferred upon vitality a reproductive power which would be almost as wonderful as his own, were it, like his, exerted by an absolute, conscious, and fully enlightened volition.

What a marvellous essence then is this intrinsic element of us all called life! An element whose association with physical nature is merely factitious, not inherent—which requires no physical space for its accommodation, and does not disturb the quiescence, nor displace the juxta-position or volume of matter while traversing through or touching it. Matter may touch matter, and cause motion or action in it; but while life may also touch matter, and by its presence endow it with vital powers, it is not, save when associated with feeling, as in animals—but not in plants—conscious of its contact with the matter in which it exists, any more than a stone is conscious of contact with a stone, where the contact is not the less real that consciousness does not perceive it. Life may indeed cause motion in matter, but not by direct but only by secondary agency—it must use matter to act on matter. We may place the hand on an object, and vainly by force of will endeavour, because our vital power is placed in simple contact with it, to make that object move. We must use the physical power of the hand to compel the motion we require ; so that the will, without the physical agency, is practically nothing. But in such a case as the reproduction of animal forms which has just been referred to, how divisible must this vital principle Life be, which yet itself requires no physical space to contain it! The divisibility of matter is a fact obvious and apparent, but this divisibility of life, associated as it is in man with an equally extensive and incomprehensible divisibility of mind and feeling, is a metaphysical phenomenon—inherently all that importantly and essentially constitutes ourselves—before which the facts of natural magic within their physical limits dwarf into insignificance, and which makes us, even in this life, denizens of a reality wholly beyond their range.

The philosophers of fixity would tell us that two and two cannot make any other number than four; that it is impossible they can make any other number even with God, and that Omnipotence itself has here a limit. How would such theorists of the abstract-absolute explain that demonstration of Omnipotence in the concrete, by which life in the Polypes and Annelides is capable of being subdivided from one life into many distinct and independent lives? Even accepting the theory that a polype may be a combination of many lives in one, this explanation, if it could be substantiated in that case, would not apply to a worm to the same extent. For even assuming that a worm as a hermaphrodite is a duplex animal, or two animals in one, that fact would not explain how by being cut in halves it became two such duplex animals instead of one, or four animals instead of two. We can understand the separation of the material part or body of the animal, for the matter of the one is not the matter of the other, but we cannot so easily understand the division of one life into two lives, or two lives into four, for that is changing an identity into more than one. Perhaps the Unitarians, who have so long denied the existence of the Trinity, on the ground of its absolute impossibility, will aid us with their logical taper here.

Some of our readers will possibly think the *argumentum ad hominem* might be applied to us on this subject, on the ground of what we have said ourselves in a preceding page as to the fixity of truth, but it must be borne in mind that we have never—with the inherent consciousness of our own purely contingent and dependent existence—ventured to assert, or been able to find any ground for asserting, the essential fixity and unchangeableness of anything, as being positive, eternal, or superior to Omnipotence, and we have nowhere found science able to demonstrate anything of the kind. Manifestly nothing is absolutely fixed in this life but by the choice of Omnipotence, and only during the pleasure of that Great Power; and scientific men may ridicule miracles, and talk of impossibility as they will, while they cannot demonstrate to themselves, or to any one else, the primary law of their own existence, or the permanency of it, or that what *is*— what they are most sure about, viz., their own lives—*may not cease to be.* If this, then, be all the certainty of what men are most sure of, what becomes of other realities on the argument of analogy? Change is everywhere, and something more than change—in the mysterious region of vitality creation and extinction, increase and diminution, numerical as well as quantitative, are everywhere.

CHATTO & WINDUS'S
LIST OF BOOKS.

*** For NOVELS, see pp. 19-25.

Beautifully bound in a novel style, small 4to, 16s.

THE LADY OF THE LAKE. By Sir WALTER

SCOTT. With numerous fine Illustrations.

" The Lady of the Lake" has been chosen as a subject for illustration, not only for its picturesque features, which invite in an unusual degree the sympathetic treatment of the artist, but also for the romantic personal interest which the story inspires, and which gives it a close hold on the affections of all readers. So thorough is the verisimilitude of the poem, and so accurate are its descriptions of scenery, that the events which it describes are accepted as absolute history in the region where the scene is laid; and no true Highlander looks with tolerance on anyone who ventures to doubt their actual occurrence. It has happened, therefore, that the romantic poem in which the genius of Scott has united and harmonised the legends of Loch Katrine and the Trosachs has become the best Handbook to the Scottish Lake-region. It is believed that the present Illustrated Edition will be a welcome souvenir to thousands of travellers who have visited that beautiful region.

In order to secure accuracy as well as freshness of treatment, the Publishers commissioned Mr. A. V. S. ANTHONY, under whose supervision this Edition has been executed, to visit the Scottish Highlands and make sketches on the spot. Nearly every scene of the poem was personally visited and sketched by him, and these Sketches have afforded the basis of the landscapes offered in this book. These landscapes, for obvious reasons, depict the Scenery as it is at the present time; while the Costumes, Weapons, and other accessories of the figure-pieces are of the period of the action of the poem, being carefully studied from contemporary pictures and descriptions, or from later authoritative works.

Crown 8vo, Coloured Frontispiece and Illustrations, cloth gilt, 7s. 6d.

Advertising, A History of,

From the Earliest Times. Illustrated by Anecdotes, Curious Specimens, and Notices of Successful Advertisers. By HENRY SAMPSON.

Allen (Grant), Works by:

Colin Clout's Calendar. Crown 8vo, cloth extra, 6s.
The Evolutionist at Large. Crown 8vo, cloth extra, 6s.
Vignettes from Nature. Crown 8vo, cloth extra, 6s.

" One of the best specimens of popular scientific exposition that we have ever had the good fortune to fall in with."—LEEDS MERCURY.

Crown 8vo, cloth extra, with 639 Illustrations, 7s. 6d.

Architectural Styles, A Handbook of.

From the German of A. ROSENGARTEN, by W. COLLETT-SANDARS.

Artemus Ward:

Artemus Ward's Works: The Works of CHARLES FARRER BROWNE, better known as ARTEMUS WARD. Crown 8vo, with Portrait and Facsimile, cloth extra, 7s. 6d.

Artemus Ward's Lecture on the Mormons. With 32 Illustrations. Edited, with Preface, by EDWARD P. HINGSTON. 6d.

Ashton (John), Works by:

A History of the Chap-Books of the Eighteenth Century. By JOHN ASHTON. With nearly 400 Illustrations, engraved in facsimile of the originals. Crown 8vo, cloth extra, 7s. 6d.

Social Life in the Reign of Queen Anne. Taken from Original Sources. By JOHN ASHTON. With nearly One Hundred Illustrations. Two Vols., demy 8vo, cloth extra, 28s.

Crown 8vo, cloth extra, 7s. 6d.

Bankers, A Handbook of London;

Together with Lists of Bankers from 1677. By F. G. HILTON PRICE.

Bardsley (Rev. C. W.), Works by:

English Surnames: Their Sources and Significations. By the Rev. C. W. BARDSLEY, M.A. Crown 8vo, cloth extra, 7s. 6d.

Curiosities of Puritan Nomenclature. By the Rev. C. W. BARDSLEY, M.A. Crown 8vo, cloth extra, 7s. 6d.

Crown 8vo, cloth extra, Illustrated, 7s. 6d.

Bartholomew Fair, Memoirs of.

By HENRY MORLEY. New Edition, with One Hundred Illustrations.

Imperial 4to, cloth extra, gilt and gilt edges, 21s. per volume.

Beautiful Pictures by British Artists:

A Gathering of Favourites from our Picture Galleries. In Two Series. All engraved on Steel in the highest style of Art. Edited, with Notices of the Artists, by SYDNEY ARMYTAGE, M.A.

Small 4to, green and gold, 6s. 6d.; gilt edges, 7s. 6d.

Bechstein's As Pretty as Seven,

And other German Stories. Collected by LUDWIG BECHSTEIN. With Additional Tales by the Brothers GRIMM, and 100 Illustrations by RICHTER.

One Shilling Monthly, Illustrated.

Belgravia for 1883.

"Maid of Athens," JUSTIN MCCARTHY'S New Serial Story, Illustrated by FRED. BARNARD, is begun in the JANUARY Number of BELGRAVIA, which Number contains also the First Portion of a Story in Three Parts, by OUIDA, entitled "Frescoes;" the continuation of WILKIE COLLINS's Novel, "Heart and Science;" a further instalment of Mrs. ALEXANDER's Novel, "The Admiral's Ward;" and other Matters of Interest.

Belgravia Annual.

With Stories by WALTER BESANT, JULIAN HAWTHORNE, F. W. ROBINSON, DUTTON COOK, JUSTIN H. MCCARTHY, J. ARBUTHNOT WILSON, HENRY W. LUCY, JAMES PAYN, and others. Demy 8vo, with Illustrations, 1s.

Belgravia Holiday Number,

Written by the well-known Authors who have been so long associated with the Magazine, will be published as usual in July.

Demy 8vo, Illustrated, uniform in size for binding.

Blackburn's (Henry) Art Handbooks:

Academy Notes, 1875. With 40 Illustrations. 1s.
Academy Notes, 1876. With 107 Illustrations. 1s.
Academy Notes, 1877. With 143 Illustrations. 1s.
Academy Notes, 1878. With 150 Illustrations. 1s.
Academy Notes, 1879. With 146 Illustrations. 1s.
Academy Notes, 1880. With 126 Illustrations. 1s.
Academy Notes, 1881. With 128 Illustrations. 1s.
Academy Notes, 1882. With 130 Illustrations. 1s.
Grosvenor Notes, 1878. With 68 Illustrations. 1s.
Grosvenor Notes, 1879. With 60 Illustrations. 1s.
Grosvenor Notes, 1880. With 56 Illustrations. 1s.
Grosvenor Notes, 1881. With 74 Illustrations. 1s.
Grosvenor Notes, 1882. With 74 Illustrations. 1s.
Pictures at the Paris Exhibition, 1878. 80 Illustrations. 1s.
Pictures at South Kensington. With 70 Illustrations. 1s.
The English Pictures at the National Gallery. 114 Illusts. 1s.
The Old Masters at the National Gallery. 128 Illusts. 1s. 6d.
Academy Notes, 1875-79. Complete in One Volume, with nearly 600 Illustrations in Facsimile. Demy 8vo, cloth limp, 6s.
Grosvenor Notes, 1877-1882. A Complete Catalogue of Exhibitions at the Grosvenor Gallery since the Commencement. With upwards of 300 Illustrations. Demy 8vo, cloth limp, 6s.
A Complete Illustrated Catalogue to the National Gallery. With Notes by H. BLACKBURN, and 242 Illusts. Demy 8vo, cloth limp, 3s.

UNIFORM WITH "ACADEMY NOTES."

The Art Annual for 1882-3. Edited by F. G. DUMAS. With 250 full-page Illustrations. Demy 8vo, French grey cover, 3s. 6d.
Royal Scottish Academy Notes, 1878. 117 Illustrations. 1s.
Royal Scottish Academy Notes, 1879. 125 Illustrations. 1s.
Royal Scottish Academy Notes, 1880. 114 Illustrations. 1s.
Royal Scottish Academy Notes, 1881. 104 Illustrations. 1s.
Royal Scottish Academy Notes, 1882. 114 Illustrations. 1s.
Glasgow Institute of Fine Arts Notes, 1878. 95 Illusts. 1s.
Glasgow Institute of Fine Arts Notes, 1879. 100 Illusts. 1s.
Glasgow Institute of Fine Arts Notes, 1880. 120 Illusts. 1s.
Glasgow Institute of Fine Arts Notes, 1881. |108 Illusts. 1s.
Glasgow Institute of Fine Arts Notes, 1882. 102 Illusts. 1s.
Walker Art Gallery Notes, Liverpool, 1878. 112 Illusts. 1s.
Walker Art Gallery Notes, Liverpool, 1879. 100 Illusts. 1s.
Walker Art Gallery Notes, Liverpool, 1880. 100 Illusts. 1s.
Royal Manchester Institution Notes, 1878. 88 Illustrations. 1s.
Society of Artists Notes, Birmingham, 1878. 95 Illusts. 1s.
Children of the Great City. By F. W. LAWSON. 1s.

Folio, half-bound boards, India Proofs, 21s.

Blake (William) :

Etchings from his Works.   By W. B. SCOTT.   With descriptive Text.

In Illuminated Cover, crown 4to, 6s.

Birthday Flowers: Their Language and Legends.

By W. J. GORDON. Illust. in Colours by VIOLA BOUGHTON. [*Shortly.*

This sumptuous and elegant Birthday Book is the first in which our floral treasures have been laid under really effective contribution. It has been produced at immense cost, and in it we have one of the most accurate and beautiful Masterpieces of Chromo-lithography yet issued from the press. Within its sixty-four fully-coloured pages, each lithographed in fourteen printings, we have a noble Series of lovely Bouquets, depicting in all their wealth of grace and beauty the most famous of our field and garden jewels; as a different flower is taken for every day in the year, there are no fewer than three hundred and sixty-six separate selections. The legends and the sentiments ascribed to each of the chosen blossoms have formed the theme of some fifteen hundred lines of Original Verse, and there is thus given one of the fullest "Languages of Flowers" in existence, and the only one which is free from duplicates. An unusual amount of thought and labour has been expended on the work, and the publishers congratulate themselves that in a literary and artistic sense the result has been fully commensurate thereto. Such a collection of flowers, so complete and compact, has never before been offered. As a Book of Birthdays and Family Records it is unsurpassed. The addition of the scientific names to the minutely accurate delineations of plants renders its pages invaluable to the botanist and every lover of leaf and bloom. The legends which form the burden of its verse will delight the scholar and archæologist and all students of song and folk-lore; while the copious floral meanings, completer than in any other "language of flowers" yet available, will render it the constant companion and most treasured gift of a much more numerous section of the community—the whole world of Sweethearts of the English-speaking nations.

Crown 8vo, cloth extra, gilt, with Illustrations, 7s. 6d.

Boccaccio's Decameron ;

or, Ten Days' Entertainment.   Translated into English, with an Introduction by THOMAS WRIGHT, Esq., M.A., F.S.A.   With Portrait, and STOTHARD's beautiful Copperplates.

Bowers' (G.) Hunting Sketches :

Canters in Crampshire. By G. BOWERS.   I. Gallops from Gorseborough.   II. Scrambles with Scratch Packs.   III. Studies with Stag Hounds.   Oblong 4to, half-bound boards, 21s.

Leaves from a Hunting Journal. By G. BOWERS.   Coloured in facsimile of the originals.   Oblong 4to, half-bound, 21s.

Crown 8vo, cloth extra, gilt, with numerous Illustrations, 7s. 6d.

Brand's Observations on Popular Antiquities,

chiefly Illustrating the Origin of our Vulgar Customs, Ceremonies, and Superstitions.   With the Additions of Sir HENRY ELLIS.

Brewster (Sir David), Works by :

More Worlds than One: The Creed of the Philosopher and the Hope of the Christian. By Sir DAVID BREWSTER. With Plates. Post 8vo, cloth extra, 4s. 6d.

The Martyrs of Science: Lives of GALILEO, TYCHO BRAHE, and KEPLER. By Sir DAVID BREWSTER. With Portraits. Post 8vo, cloth extra, 4s. 6d.

Bret Harte, Works by:

Bret Harte's Collected Works. Arranged and Revised by the Author. Complete in Five Vols., crown 8vo, cloth extra, 6s. each.

Vol. I. COMPLETE POETICAL AND DRAMATIC WORKS. With Steel Plate Portrait, and an Introduction by the Author.

Vol. II. EARLIER PAPERS—LUCK OF ROARING CAMP, and other Sketches —BOHEMIAN PAPERS—SPANISH AND AMERICAN LEGENDS.

Vol. III. TALES OF THE ARGONAUTS—EASTERN SKETCHES.

Vol. IV. GABRIEL CONROY.

Vol. V. STORIES—CONDENSED NOVELS, &c.

The Select Works of Bret Harte, in Prose and Poetry. With Introductory Essay by J. M. BELLEW, Portrait of the Author, and 50 Illustrations. Crown 8vo, cloth extra, 7s. 6d.

Gabriel Conroy: A Novel. Post 8vo, illustrated boards, 2s.

An Heiress of Red Dog, and other Stories. Post 8vo, illustrated boards, 2s.; cloth limp, 2s. 6d.

The Twins of Table Mountain. Fcap. 8vo, picture cover, 1s.; crown 8vo, cloth extra, 3s. 6d.

The Luck of Roaring Camp, and other Sketches. Post 8vo, illustrated boards, 2s.

Jeff Briggs's Love Story. Fcap. 8vo, picture cover, 1s.; cloth extra, 2s. 6d.

Flip. Post 8vo, illustrated boards, 2s.; cloth limp, 2s. 6d.

Buchanan's (Robert) Works:

Ballads of Life, Love, and Humour. With a Frontispiece by ARTHUR HUGHES. Crown 8vo, cloth extra, 6s.

Selected Poems of Robert Buchanan. With Frontispiece by THOS. DALZIEL. Crown 8vo, cloth extra, 6s.

Undertones. Crown 8vo, cloth extra, 6s.

London Poems. Crown 8vo, cloth extra, 6s.

The Book of Orm. Crown 8vo, cloth extra, 6s.

Idyls and Legends of Inverburn. Crown 8vo, cloth extra, 6s.

St. Abe and his Seven Wives: A Tale of Salt Lake City. With a Frontispiece by A. B. HOUGHTON. Crown 8vo, cloth extra, 5s.

White Rose and Red: A Love Story. Crown 8vo, cloth extra, 6s.

The Hebrid Isles: Wanderings in the Land of Lorne and the Outer Hebrides. With Frontispiece by W. SMALL. Crown 8vo, cloth extra, 6s.

** See also Novels, pp. 19, 21, 22, 25.

Demy 8vo, cloth extra, 7s. 6d.

Burton's Anatomy of Melancholy.

A New Edition, Complete, corrected and enriched by Translations of the Classical Extracts.

** Also an Abridgment in " The Mayfair Library," under the title " Melancholy Anatomised," post 8vo, cloth limp, 2s. 6d.

Burton (Captain), Works by:

The Book of the Sword: Being a History of the Sword and its Use in all Countries, from the Earliest Times. By RICHARD F. BURTON. With over 400 Illustrations. Crown 8vo, cloth extra, 25s. [*In preparation.*

To the Gold Coast for Gold: A Personal Narrative. By RICHARD F. BURTON and VERNEY LOVETT CAMERON. With Maps and Frontispiece. Two Vols., crown 8vo, 21s.

THE STOTHARD BUNYAN.—Crown 8vo, cloth extra, gilt, 7s. 6d.

Bunyan's Pilgrim's Progress.

Edited by Rev. T. SCOTT. With 17 beautiful Steel Plates by STOT-
HARD, engraved by GOODALL; and numerous Woodcuts.

Crown 8vo, cloth extra, gilt, with Illustrations, 7s. 6d.

Byron's Letters and Journals.

With Notices of his Life. By THOMAS MOORE. A Reprint of the
Original Edition, newly revised, with Twelve full-page Plates.

Two Vols., crown 8vo, cloth extra, 21s.

Cameron (Commander) and Captain Burton.

To the Gold Coast for Gold: A Personal Narrative. By RICHARD
F. BURTON and VERNEY LOVETT CAMERON. With Frontispiece and
Maps.

Demy 8vo, cloth extra, 14s.

Campbell.—White and Black:

Travels in the United States. By Sir GEORGE CAMPBELL, M.P.

Carlyle (Thomas):

Thomas Carlyle: Letters and Recollections. By MONCURE D.
CONWAY, M.A. Crown 8vo, cloth extra, with Illustrations, 6s.

On the Choice of Books. With a Life of the Author by R. H.
SHEPHERD. New and Revised Edition, post 8vo, cloth extra, Illustrated,
1s. 6d.

The Correspondence of Thomas Carlyle and Ralph Waldo
Emerson, 1834 to 1872. Edited by CHARLES ELIOT NORTON. Two Vols.
crown 8vo, cloth extra, 24s. [*Shortly.*

These letters, extending over a period of nearly forty years, were, by the com-
mon consent and direction of the illustrious writers, long since placed in Mr.
Norton's hands with the fullest powers for editing and publication. It is not
too much to claim that the correspondence will be found to form the most valu-
able and entertaining work of the kind ever issued.

Crown 8vo, cloth extra, 7s. 6d.

Century (A) of Dishonour:

A Sketch of the United States Government's Dealings with some of
the Indian Tribes.

Large 4to, half-bound, profusely Illustrated, 28s.

Chatto and Jackson.—A Treatise on Wood

Engraving; Historical and Practical. By WILLIAM ANDREW CHATTO
and JOHN JACKSON. With an Additional Chapter by HENRY G.
BOHN; and 450 fine Illustrations. A reprint of the last Revised Edition.

Chaucer:

Chaucer for Children: A Golden Key. By Mrs. H. R. HAWEIS.
With Eight Coloured Pictures and numerous Woodcuts by the Author.
New Edition, small 4to, cloth extra, 6s.

Chaucer for Schools. By Mrs. H. R. HAWEIS. Demy 8vo, cloth
limp, 2s. 6d.

Crown 8vo, cloth extra, gilt, 7s. 6d.

Colman's Humorous Works :

'' Broad Grins,'' '' My Nightgown and Slippers, ' and other Humorous Works, Prose and Poetical, of GEORGE COLMAN. With Life by G. B. BUCKSTONE, and Frontispiece by HOGARTH.

Post 8vo, cloth limp, 2s. 6d.

Convalescent Cookery :

A Family Handbook. By CATHERINE RYAN.
'' Full of sound sense and useful hints.''—SATURDAY REVIEW.

Conway (Moncure D.), Works by :

Demonology and Devil-Lore. Two Vols., royal 8vo, with 65 Illustrations, 28s.

A Necklace of Stories. Illustrated by W. J. HENNESSY. Square 8vo, cloth extra, 6s.

The Wandering Jew. Crown 8vo, cloth extra, 6s.

Thomas Carlyle : Letters and Recollections. With Illustrations. Crown 8vo, cloth extra, 6s.

Cook (Dutton), Works by :

Hours with the Players. With a Steel Plate Frontispiece. New and Cheaper Edition, crown 8vo, cloth extra, 6s.

Nights at the Play. Two Vols., crown 8vo, cloth, 21s. [*In the press.*

Post 8vo, cloth limp, 2s. 6d.

Copyright.—A Handbook of English and

Foreign Copyright in Literary and Dramatic Works. By SIDNEY JERROLD, of the Middle Temple, Esq., Barrister-at-Law.
'' Till the time arrives when copyright shall be so simple and so uniform that it can be generally understood and enjoyed, such a handbook as this will prove of great value. It is correct as well as concise, and gives just the kind and quantity of information desired by persons who are ignorant of the subject, and turn to it for information and guidance.''—ATHENÆUM.

Crown 8vo, cloth extra, 7s. 6d.

Cornwall.—Popular Romances of the West

of England; or, The Drolls, Traditions, and Superstitions of Old Cornwall. Collected and Edited by ROBERT HUNT, F.R.S. New and Revised Edition, with Additions, and Two Steel-plate Illustrations by GEORGE CRUIKSHANK.

Crown 8vo, cloth extra, gilt, with 13 Portraits, 7s. 6d.

Creasy's Memoirs of Eminent Etonians ;

With Notices of the Early History of Eton College. By Sir EDWARD CREASY, Author of '' The Fifteen Decisive Battles of the World.''

Crown 8vo, cloth extra, with Etched Frontispiece, 7s. 6d.

Credulities, Past and Present.

By WILLIAM JONES, F.S.A., Author of '' Finger-Ring Lore,'' &c.

Crown 8vo, cloth extra, 6s.

Crimes and Punishments.

Including a New Translation of Beccaria's '' De Delitti e delle Pene.'' By JAMES ANSON FARRER.

Cruikshank, George:

The Comic Almanack. Complete in TWO SERIES: The FIRST from 1835 to 1843; the SECOND from 1844 to 1853. A Gathering of the BEST HUMOUR of THACKERAY, HOOD, MAYHEW, ALBERT SMITH, A BECKETT, ROBERT BROUGH, &c. With 2,000 Woodcuts and Steel Engravings by CRUIKSHANK, HINE, LANDELLS, &c. Crown 8vo, cloth gilt, two very thick volumes, 7s. 6d. each.

The Life of George Cruikshank. By BLANCHARD JERROLD, Author of "The Life of Napoleon III.," &c. With numerous Illustrations and a List of his Works. Two Vols., crown 8vo, cloth extra, 24s.

Crown 8vo, cloth extra, 7s. 6d.

Cussans.—Handbook of Heraldry;

with Instructions for Tracing Pedigrees and Deciphering Ancient MSS., &c. By JOHN E. CUSSANS. Entirely New and 'Revised Edition. Illustrated with over 400 Woodcuts and Coloured Plates.

Post 8vo, cloth limp, 2s. 6d.

Davenant.—What shall my Son be?

Hints for Parents on the Choice of a Profession or Trade for their Sons. By FRANCIS DAVENANT, M.A.

New and Cheaper Edition, crown 8vo, cloth extra, Illustrated, 7s. 6d.

Doran.—Memories of our Great Towns.

With Anecdotic Gleanings concerning their Worthies and their Oddities. By Dr. JOHN DORAN, F.S.A. With 38 Illustrations.

Crown 8vo, half-bound, 12s. 6d.

Drama, A Dictionary of the.

Being a comprehensive Guide to the Plays, Playwrights, Players, and Playhouses of the United Kingdom and America, from the Earliest to the Present Times. By W. DAVENPORT ADAMS. (Uniform with BREWER's " Reader's Handbook.")   *[In preparation.*

Crown 8vo, cloth extra, 6s.

Dyer.—The Folk-Lore of Plants.

By T. F. THISELTON DYER, M.A.   *[In preparation.*

Among the subjects treated of will be the following:—1. Primitive and Savage Notions respecting Plants — 2. Plant-Worship—3. Plant-Life — 4. Lightning Plants—5. Legendary Origin of Plants—6. Mystic Plants—7. Plant Nomenclature—8. Ceremonial Use of Plants—9. The Doctrine of Signatures—10. Plants in Folk-Medicine—11. Plants in Folk-Tales—12. Plants in Demonology and Witchcraft—13. Wishing-Plants—14. Sacred Plants—15. Luck-Plants.

Crown 8vo, cloth boards, 6s. per Volume.

Early English Poets.

Edited, with Introductions and Annotations, by Rev. A. B. GROSART.

1. **Fletcher's (Giles, B.D.) Complete Poems.** One Vol.

   Davies' (Sir John) Complete Poetical Works. Two Vols.

3. **Herrick's (Robert) Complete Collected Poems.** Three Vols.

4. **Sidney's (Sir Philip) Complete Poetical Works.** Three Vols.

Crown 8vo, cloth extra, gilt, with Illustrations, 6s.

Emanuel.—On ·Diamonds ·and Precious

Stones; their History, Value, and Properties; with Simple Tests for ascertaining their Reality. By HARRY EMANUEL, F.R.G.S. With numerous Illustrations, Tinted and Plain.

Crown 8vo, cloth extra, with Illustrations, 7s. 6d.

Englishman's House, The:

A Practical Guide to all interested in Selecting or Building a House, with full Estimates of Cost, Quantities, &c. By C. J. RICHARDSON. Third Edition. With nearly 600 Illustrations.

Ewald (Alex. Charles, F.S.A.), Works by:

Stories from the State Papers. With an Autotype Facsimile. Crown 8vo, cloth extra, 6s.

The Life and Times of Prince Charles Stuart, commonly called the Young Pretender. New and Cheaper Edition, with Portraits, crown 8vo, cloth extra, 6s.

Crown 8vo, cloth extra, with Illustrations, 6s.

Fairholt.—Tobacco:

Its History and Associations; with an Account of the Plant and its Manufacture, and its Modes of Use in all Ages and Countries. By F. W. FAIRHOLT, F.S.A. With Coloured Frontispiece and upwards of 100 Illustrations by the Author.

Demy 8vo, cloth extra, 7s. 6d.

Familiar Allusions:

A Handbook of Miscellaneous Information; including the Names of Celebrated Statues, Paintings, Palaces, Country Seats, Ruins, Churches, Ships, Streets, Clubs, Natural Curiosities, and the like. By WILLIAM A. WHEELER, Author of " Noted Names of Fiction ; " and CHARLES G. WHEELER.

Faraday (Michael), Works by:

The Chemical History of a Candle: Lectures delivered before a Juvenile Audience at the Royal Institution. Edited by WILLIAM CROOKES, F.C.S. Post 8vo, cloth extra, with numerous Illustrations, 4s. 6d.

On the Various Forces of Nature, and their Relations to each other: Lectures delivered before a Juvenile Audience at the Royal Institution. Edited by WILLIAM CROOKES, F.C.S. Post 8vo, cloth extra, with numerous Illustrations, 4s. 6d.

Crown 8vo, cloth extra, with Illustrations, 7s. 6d.

Finger-Ring Lore:

Historical, Legendary, and Anecdotal. By WM. JONES, F.S.A. With Hundreds of Illustrations of Curious Rings of all Ages and Countries.

"*One of those gossiping books which are as full of amusement as of instruction.*" —ATHENÆUM.

New and Cheaper Edition, crown 8vo, cloth extra, 6s.

Fitzgerald.—Recreations of a Literary Man;

or, Does Writing Pay? With Recollections of some Literary Men, and a View of a Literary Man's Working Life. By PERCY FITZGERALD.

Gardening Books:

A Year's Work in Garden and Greenhouse: ·Practical Advice to Amateur Gardeners as to the Management of the Flower, Fruit, and Frame Garden. By GEORGE GLENNY. Post 8vo, cloth limp, 2s. 6d.

Our Kitchen Garden: The Plants we Grow, and How we Cook Them. By TOM JERROLD, Author of "The Garden that Paid the Rent," &c. Post 8vo, cloth limp, 2s. 6d.

Household Horticulture: A Gossip about Flowers. By TOM and JANE JERROLD. Illustrated. Post 8vo, cloth limp, 2s. 6d.

The Garden that Paid the Rent. By TOM JERROLD. Fcap. 8vo, illustrated cover, 1s.; cloth limp, 1s. 6d.

My Garden Wild, and What I Grew there. By FRANCIS GEORGE HEATH. Crown 8vo, cloth extra, 5s.

One Shilling Monthly.

Gentleman's Magazine (The) for 1883.

"**The New Abelard,**" ROBERT BUCHANAN'S New Serial Story, is begun in the JANUARY Number of THE GENTLEMAN'S MAGAZINE. This Number contains many other interesting Articles, and the continuation of "**Science Notes,**" by W. MATTIEU WILLIAMS, F.R.A.S.

** Now ready, the Volume for JULY to DECEMBER, 1882, cloth extra, price 8s. 6d.; and Cases for binding, price 2s. each.

Gentleman's Annual (The).

Containing Complete Novels by R. E. FRANCILLON, the Author of "Miss Molly," FRED. BOYLE, and F. ABELL. Demy 8vo, illuminated cover, 1s.

THE RUSKIN GRIMM.—Square 8vo, cl. ex., 6s. 6d.; gilt edges, 7s. 6d.

German Popular Stories.

Collected by the Brothers GRIMM, and Translated by EDGAR TAYLOR. Edited with an Introduction by JOHN RUSKIN. With 22 Illustrations on Steel by GEORGE CRUIKSHANK. Both Series Complete.

"*The illustrations of this volume . . . are of quite sterling and admirable art, of a class precisely parallel in elevation to the character of the tales which they illustrate; and the original etchings, as I have before said in the Appendix to my 'Elements of Drawing,' were unrivalled in masterfulness of touch since Rembrandt (in some qualities of delineation, unrivalled even by him). . . . To make somewhat enlarged copies of them, looking at them through a magnifying glass, and never putting two lines where Cruikshank has put only one, would be an exercise in decision and severe drawing which would leave afterwards little to be learnt in schools.*"—*Extract from Introduction by JOHN RUSKIN.*

Post 8vo, cloth limp, 2s. 6d.

Glenny.—A Year's Work in Garden and

Greenhouse: Practical Advice to Amateur Gardeners as to the Management of the Flower, Fruit, and Frame Garden. By GEORGE GLENNY.

"*A great deal of valuable information, conveyed in very simple language. The amateur need not wish for a better guide.*"—LEEDS MERCURY.

Crown 8vo, cloth gilt and gilt edges, 7s. 6d.

Golden Treasury of Thought, The:

An ENCYCLOPÆDIA OF QUOTATIONS from Writers of all Times and Countries. Selected and Edited by THEODORE TAYLOR.

Square 16mo (Tauchnitz size), cloth extra, 2s. per volume.

Golden Library, The:

Ballad History of England. By W. C. BENNETT.

Bayard Taylor's Diversions of the Echo Club.

Byron's Don Juan.

Emerson's Letters and Social Aims.

Godwin's (William) Lives of the Necromancers.

Holmes's Autocrat of the Breakfast Table. With an Introduction by G. A. SALA.

Holmes's Professor at the Breakfast Table.

Hood's Whims and Oddities. Complete. With all the original Illustrations.

Irving's (Washington) Tales of a Traveller.

Irving's (Washington) Tales of the Alhambra.

Jesse's (Edward) Scenes and Occupations of Country Life.

Lamb's Essays of Elia. Both Series Complete in One Vol.

Leigh Hunt's Essays: A Tale for a Chimney Corner, and other Pieces. With Portrait, and Introduction by EDMUND OLLIER.

Mallory's (Sir Thomas) Mort d'Arthur: The Stories of King Arthur and of the Knights of the Round Table. Edited by B. MONTGOMERIE RANKING.

Pascal's Provincial Letters. A New Translation, with Historical Introduction and Notes, by T. M'CRIE, D.D.

Pope's Poetical Works. Complete.

Rochefoucauld's Maxims and Moral Reflections. With Notes, and an Introductory Essay by SAINTE-BEUVE.

St. Pierre's Paul and Virginia, and The Indian Cottage. Edited, with Life, by the Rev. E. CLARKE.

Shelley's Early Poems, and Queen Mab, with Essay by LEIGH HUNT.

Shelley's Later Poems: Laon and Cythna, &c.

Shelley's Posthumous Poems, the Shelley Papers, &c.

Shelley's Prose Works, including A Refutation of Deism, Zastrozzi, St. Irvyne, &c.

White's Natural History of Sel- borne. Edited, with Additions, by THOMAS BROWN, F.L.S.

New and Cheaper Edition, demy 8vo, cloth extra, with Illustrations, 7s. 6d.

Greeks and Romans, The Life of the,

Described from Antique Monuments. By ERNST GUHL and W. KONER. Translated from the Third German Edition, and Edited by Dr. F. HUEFFER. With 545 Illustrations.

" *Must find a place, not only upon the scholar's shelves, but in every well-chosen library of art.*"—DAILY NEWS.

Crown 8vo, cloth extra, gilt, with Illustrations, 4s. 6d.

Guyot.—The Earth and Man;

or, Physical Geography in its relation to the History of Mankind. By ARNOLD GUYOT. With Additions by Professors AGASSIZ, PIERCE, and GRAY; 12 Maps and Engravings on Steel, some Coloured, and copious Index.

Crown 8vo, 1s.; cloth, 1s. 6d.

Hair (The) : Its Treatment in Health, Weak-

ness, and Disease. Translated from the German of Dr. J. PINCUS.

Hake (Dr. Thomas Gordon), Poems by :

Maiden Ecstasy. Small 4to, cloth extra, 8s.
New Symbols. Crown 8vo, cloth extra, 6s.
Legends of the Morrow. Crown 8vo, cloth extra, 6s.
The Serpent Play. Crown 8vo, cloth extra, 6s.

Two Vols., crown 8vo, cloth extra, 12s.

Half-Hours with Foreign Novelists.

With Notices of their Lives and Writings. By HELEN and ALICE ZIMMERN. A New Edition.

Medium 8vo, cloth extra, gilt, with Illustrations, 7s. 6d.

Hall.—Sketches of Irish Character. By Mrs.

S. C. HALL. With numerous Illustrations on Steel and Wood by MACLISE, GILBERT, HARVEY, and G. CRUIKSHANK.

"The Irish Sketches of this lady resemble Miss Mitford's beautiful English sketches in 'Our Village,' but they are far more vigorous and picturesque and bright."—BLACKWOOD'S MAGAZINE.

Haweis (Mrs.), Works by:

The Art of Dress. By Mrs. H. R. HAWEIS. Illustrated by the Author. Small 8vo, illustrated cover, 1s.; cloth limp, 1s. 6d.

"A well-considered attempt to apply canons of good taste to the costumes of ladies of our time. . . . . Mrs. Haweis writes frankly and to the point; she does not mince matters, but boldly remonstrates with her own sex on the follies they indulge in. . . . . We may recommend the book to the ladies whom it concerns."—ATHENÆUM.

The Art of Beauty. By Mrs. H. R. HAWEIS. Square 8vo, cloth extra, gilt, gilt edges, with Coloured Frontispiece and nearly 100 Illustrations, 10s. 6d.

The Art of Decoration. By Mrs. H. R. HAWEIS. Square 8vo, handsomely bound and profusely Illustrated, 10s. 6d.

*** See also CHAUCER, p. 6 of this Catalogue.

Crown 8vo, cloth extra, 6s.

Haweis (Rev. H. R.).—American Humorists.

Including WASHINGTON IRVING, OLIVER WENDELL HOLMES, JAMES RUSSELL LOWELL, ARTEMUS WARD, MARK TWAIN, and BRET HARTE. By the Rev. H. R. HAWEIS, M.A.

Crown 8vo, cloth extra, 5s.

Heath (F. G.)—My Garden Wild,

And What I Grew there. By FRANCIS GEORGE HEATH, Author of "The Fern World," &c.

"If gardens of wild flowers do not begin at once to spring up over half the little patches of back yard within fifty miles of London it will not be Mr. Heath's fault, for a more exquisite picture of the felicity of horticulture has seldom been drawn for us by so charming and graphic a word-painter as the writer of this pleasant little volume."—GRANT ALLEN, in THE ACADEMY.

SPECIMENS OF MODERN POETS.—Crown 8vo, cloth extra, 6s.

Heptalogia (The); or, The Seven against Sense.

A Cap with Seven Bells.

"The merits of the book cannot be fairly estimated by means of a few extracts; should be read at length to be appreciated properly, and in our opinion its merits entitle it to be very widely read indeed."—ST. JAMES'S GAZETTE.

Cr.8vo, bound in parchment, 8s. ; Large-Paper copies (only 50 printed), 15s.

Herbert.—The Poems of Lord Herbert of

Cherbury. Edited, with an Introduction, by J. CHURTON COLLINS.

Crown 8vo, cloth limp, with Illustrations, 2s. 6d.

Holmes.—The Science of Voice Production

and Voice Preservation : A Popular Manual for the Use of Speakers
and Singers. By GORDON HOLMES, M.D.
"*The advice the author gives, coming as it does from one having authority, is
most valuable.*"—NATURE.

Crown 8vo, cloth extra, gilt, 7s. 6d.

Hood's (Thomas) Choice Works,

In Prose and Verse. Including the CREAM OF THE COMIC ANNUALS.
With Life of the Author, Portrait, and Two Hundred Illustrations. .

Square crown 8vo, cloth extra, gilt edges, 6s.

Hood's (Tom) From Nowhere to the North

Pole : A Noah's Arkæological Narrative. With 25 Illustrations by
W. BRUNTON and E. C. BARNES.

Crown 8vo, cloth extra, gilt, 7s. 6d.

Hook's (Theodore) Choice Humorous Works,

including his Ludicrous Adventures, Bons-mots, Puns and Hoaxes.
With a new Life of the Author, Portraits, Facsimiles and Illustrations.

Tenth Edition, crown 8vo, cloth extra, 7s.

Horne.—Orion :

An Epic Poem, in Three Books. By RICHARD HENGIST HORNE.
With Photographic Portrait from a Medallion by SUMMERS.

Crown 8vo, cloth extra, 7s. 6d.

Howell.—Conflicts of Capital and Labour

Historically and Economically considered. Being a History and
Review of the Trade Unions of Great Britain, showing their Origin,
Progress, Constitution, and Objects, in their Political, Social, Eco-
nomical, and Industrial Aspects. By GEORGE HOWELL.
"*This book is an attempt, and on the whole a successful attempt, to place the
work of trade unions in the past, and their objects in the future, fairly before the
public from the working man's point of view.*"—PALL MALL GAZETTE.

Demy 8vo, cloth extra, 12s. 6d.

Hueffer.—The Troubadours :

A History of Provençal Life and Literature in the Middle Ages. By
FRANCIS HUEFFER.

Crown 8vo, cloth extra, 6s.

Ireland under the Land Act :

Letters to the *Standard* during the Crisis. Containing the most
recent Information about the State of the Country, the Popular
Leaders, the League, the Working of the Sub-Commissions, &c.
With Leading Cases under the Act, giving the Evidence in full ;
Judicial Dicta, &c. By E. CANT-WALL.

Crown 8vo, cloth extra, 6s.

Janvier.—Practical Keramics for Students.

By CATHERINE A. JANVIER.
"*Will be found a useful handbook by those who wish to try the manufacture or
decoration of pottery, and may be studied by all who desire to know something of
the art.*"—MORNING POST.

A New Edition, crown 8vo, cloth extra, Illustrated, 7s. 6d.

Jennings.—The Rosicrucians :

Their Rites and Mysteries. With Chapters on the Ancient Fire and
Serpent Worshippers. By HARGRAVE JENNINGS. With Five full-
page Plates and upwards of 300 Illustrations.

Jerrold (Tom), Works by :

The Garden that Paid the Rent. By TOM JERROLD. Fcap. 8vo,
illustrated cover, 1s.; cloth limp, 1s. 6d

Household Horticulture: A Gossip about Flowers. By TOM and
JANE JERROLD. Illustrated. Post 8vo, cloth limp, 2s. 6d.

Our Kitchen Garden: The Plants we Grow, and How we Cook
Them. By TOM JERROLD, Author of "The Garden that Paid the Rent,"
&c. Post 8vo, cloth limp, 2s. 6d.

*"The combination of hints on cookery with gardening has been very cleverly
carried out, and the result is an interesting and highly instructive little work. Mr.
Jerrold is correct in saying that English people do not make half the use of vegetables they might; and by showing how easily they can be grown, and so obtained
fresh, he is doing a great deal to make them more popular."—DAILY CHRONICLE.*

Two Vols. 8vo, with 52 Illustrations and Maps, cloth extra, gilt, 14s.

Josephus, The Complete Works of.

Translated by WHISTON. Containing both "The Antiquities of the
Jews" and "The Wars of the Jews."

Small 8vo, cloth, full gilt, gilt edges, with Illustrations, 6s.

Kavanagh.—The Pearl Fountain,

And other Fairy Stories. By BRIDGET and JULIA KAVANAGH.
With Thirty Illustrations by J. MOYR SMITH.

*"Genuine new fairy stories of the old type, some of them as delightful as the
best of Grimm's ' German Popular Stories.' . . . . For the most part the stories
are downright, thorough-going fairy stories of the most admirable kind. . . . .
Mr. Moyr Smith's illustrations, too, are admirable."—SPECTATOR.*

Square 8vo, cloth extra, with Illustrations, 6s.

Knight (The) and the Dwarf.

By CHARLES MILLS. With Illustrations by THOMAS LINDSAY.

Crown 8vo, illustrated boards, with numerous Plates, 2s. 6d.

Lace (Old Point), and How to Copy and

Imitate it. By DAISY WATERHOUSE HAWKINS. With 17 Illustrations by the Author.

Lane's Arabian Nights, &c. :

The Thousand and One Nights: Commonly called, in England,
"THE ARABIAN NIGHTS' ENTERTAINMENTS." A New Translation from
the Arabic, with copious Notes, by EDWARD WILLIAM LANE. Illustrated
by many hundred Engravings on Wood, from Original Designs by
WILLIAM HARVEY. A New Edition, from a Copy annotated by the
Translator, edited by his Nephew, EDWARD STANLEY POOLE. With a
Preface by STANLEY LANE-POOLE. Three Vols., demy 8vo, cloth extra,
7s. 6d. each.

Arabian Society in the Middle Ages: Studies from " The Thousand and One Nights." By EDWARD WILLIAM LANE, Author of "The
Modern Egyptians," &c. Edited by STANLEY LANE-POOLE. Crown 8vo,
cloth extra, 6s.

Lamb (Charles):

Mary and Charles Lamb: Their Poems, Letters, and Remains. With Reminiscences and Notes by W. CAREW HAZLITT. With Hancock's Portrait of the Essayist, Facsimiles of the Title-pages of the rare First Editions of Lamb's and Coleridge's Works, and numerous Illustrations. Crown 8vo, cloth extra, 10s. 6d.

Lamb's Complete Works, in Prose and Verse, reprinted from the Original Editions, with many Pieces hitherto unpublished. Edited, with Notes and Introduction, by R. H. SHEPHERD. With Two Portraits and Facsimile of a Page of the "Essay on Roast Pig." Crown 8vo, cloth extra, 7s. 6d.

" *A complete edition of Lamb's writings, in prose and verse, has long been wanted, and is now supplied. The editor appears to have taken great pains to bring together Lamb's scattered contributions, and his collection contains a number of pieces which are now reproduced for the first time since their original appearance in various old periodicals.*"—SATURDAY REVIEW.

Poetry for Children, and Prince Dorus. By CHARLES LAMB. Carefully Reprinted from unique copies. Small 8vo, cloth extra, 5s.

"*The quaint and delightful little book, over the recovery of which all the hearts of his lovers are yet warm with rejoicing.*"—A. C. SWINBURNE.

Crown 8vo, cloth extra, 6s.

Lares and Penates;

Or, The Background of Life. By FLORENCE CADDY.

" *The whole book is well worth reading, for it is full of practical suggestions. We hope nobody will be deterred from taking up a book which teaches a good deal about sweetening poor lives as well as giving grace to wealthy ones.*"—GRAPHIC.

Crown 8vo, cloth extra, with Illustrations, 7s. 6d.

Life in London;

or, The History of Jerry Hawthorn and Corinthian Tom. With the whole of CRUIKSHANK'S Illustrations, in Colours, after the Originals.

Crown 8vo, cloth extra, 6s.

Lights on the Way:

Some Tales within a Tale. By the late J H. ALEXANDER, B.A. Edited, with an Explanatory Note, by H. A. PAGE, Author of "Thoreau: A Study."

Longfellow:

Longfellow's Complete Prose Works. Including "Outre Mer," "Hyperion," "Kavanagh," "The Poets and Poetry of Europe," and "Driftwood." With Portrait and Illustrations by VALENTINE BROMLEY. Crown 8vo, cloth extra, 7s. 6d.

Longfellow's Poetical Works. Carefully Reprinted from the Original Editions. With numerous fine Illustrations on Steel and Wood. Crown 8vo, cloth extra, 7s. 6d.

Crown 8vo, cloth extra, 5s.

Lunatic Asylum, My Experiences in a.

By A SANE PATIENT.

" *The story is clever and interesting, sad beyond measure though the subject be. There is no personal bitterness, and no violence or anger. Whatever may have been the evidence for our author's madness when he was consigned to an asylum, nothing can be clearer than his sanity when he wrote this book; it is bright, calm, and to the point.*"—SPECTATOR.

Demy 8vo, with Fourteen full-page Plates, cloth boards, 18s.

Lusiad (The) of Camoens.

Translated into English Spenserian Verse by ROBERT FFRENCH DUFF.

McCarthy (Justin), Works by:

History of Our Own Times, from the Accession of Queen Victoria to the General Election of 1880. By JUSTIN McCARTHY, M.P. Four Vols., demy 8vo, cloth extra. 12s. each.—Also a POPULAR EDITION, in Four Vols., crown 8vo, cloth extra, 6s. each.

"*Criticism is disarmed before a composition which provokes little but approval. This is a really good book on a really interesting subject, and words piled on words could say no more for it.*"—SATURDAY REVIEW.

History of the Four Georges. By JUSTIN McCARTHY, M.P. Four Vols., demy 8vo, cloth extra. 12s. each.   [*In preparation.*
   ** For Mr. McCarthy's Novels, see pp. 21, 24.

McCarthy (Justin H.)—An Outline of Irish

History, from the Earliest Times to the Present Day. Crown 8vo, cloth extra, 1s.; cloth, 1s. 6d.

MacDonald (George, LL.D.), Works by:

The Princess and Curdie. With 11 Illustrations by JAMES ALLEN. Small crown 8vo, cloth extra, 5s.

Gutta-Percha Willie, the Working Genius. With 9 Illustrations by ARTHUR HUGHES. Square 8vo, cloth extra, 3s. 6d.
   ** For George Macdonald's Novels, see pp. 22, 25.

Crown 8vo, cloth extra, 7s. 6d.

Maclise Gallery (The) of Illustrious Literary

Characters: 85 fine Portraits, with Descriptive Text, Anecdotal and Biographical, by WILLIAM BATES, B.A.   [*In preparation.*

Macquoid (Mrs.), Works by:

In the Ardennes. By KATHARINE S. MACQUOID. With 50 fine Illustrations by THOMAS R. MACQUOID. Square 8vo, cloth extra, 10s. 6d.

Pictures and Legends from Normandy and Brittany. By KATHARINE S. MACQUOID. With numerous Illustrations by THOMAS R. MACQUOID. Square 8vo, cloth gilt, 10s. 6d.

Through Normandy. By KATHARINE S. MACQUOID. With 90 Illustrations by T. R. MACQUOID. Square 8vo, cloth extra, 7s. 6d.

Through Brittany. By KATHARINE S. MACQUOID. With numerous Illustrations by T. R. MACQUOID. Sq. 8vo, cloth extra, 7s. 6d.

About Yorkshire. By KATHARINE S. MACQUOID. With about 70 Illustrations by THOMAS R. MACQUOID, Engraved by SWAIN. Square 8vo, cloth extra, 10s. 6d.   [*In preparation.*

Mallock (W. H.), Works by:

Is Life Worth Living? Crown 8vo, cloth extra, 6s.

The New Republic; or, Culture, Faith, and Philosophy in an English Country House. Post 8vo, cloth limp, 2s. 6d.

The New Paul and Virginia; or, Positivism on an Island. Post 8vo, cloth limp, 2s. 6d.

Poems. Small 4to, bound in parchment, 8s.

A Romance of the Nineteenth Century. Second Edition, with a Preface. Two Vols., crown 8vo, 21s.

Handsomely printed in facsimile, price **5s.**

Magna Charta.

An exact Facsimile of the Original Document in the British Museum, printed on fine plate paper, nearly 3 feet long by 2 feet wide, with the Arms and Seals emblazoned in Gold and Colours.

Mark Twain, Works by:

The Choice Works of Mark Twain. Revised and Corrected throughout by the Author. With Life, Portrait, and numerous Illustrations. Crown 8vo, cloth extra, 7s. 6d.

The Adventures of Tom Sawyer. With 100 Illustrations. Small 8vo, cloth extra, 7s. 6d. CHEAP EDITION, illustrated boards, 2s.

An Idle Excursion, and other Sketches. Post 8vo, illustrated boards, 2s.

The Prince and the Pauper. With nearly 200 Illustrations. Crown 8vo, cloth extra, 7s. 6d.

The Innocents Abroad; or, The New Pilgrim's Progress: Being some Account of the Steamship "Quaker City's" Pleasure Excursion to Europe and the Holy Land. With 234 Illustrations. Crown 8vo, cloth extra, 7s. 6d. CHEAP EDITION, post 8vo, illustrated boards, 2s.

The Stolen White Elephant, &c. Crown 8vo, cloth extra, 6s.

Mississippi Sketches. With about 300 Original Illustrations. Crown 8vo, cloth extra, 7s. 6d. [*In preparation.*

A Tramp Abroad. With 314 Illustrations. Crown 8vo, cloth extra, 7s. 6d.

"*The fun and tenderness of the conception, of which no living man but Mark Twain is capable, its grace and fantasy and slyness, the wonderful feeling for animals that is manifest in every line, make of all this episode of Jim Baker and his jays a piece of work that is not only delightful as mere reading, but also of a high degree of merit as literature. . . . The book is full of good things, and contains passages and episodes that are equal to the funniest of those that have gone before.*"—ATHENÆUM.

Small 8vo, cloth limp, with Illustrations, 2s. 6d.

Miller.—Physiology for the Young;

Or, The House of Life: Human Physiology, with its application to the Preservation of Health. For use in Classes and Popular Reading. With numerous Illustrations. By Mrs. F. FENWICK MILLER.

"*An admirable introduction to a subject which all who value health and enjoy life should have at their fingers' ends.*"—ECHO.

Milton (J. L.), Works by:

The Hygiene of the Skin. A Concise Set of Rules for the Management of the Skin; with Directions for Diet, Wines, Soaps, Baths, &c. Small 8vo, 1s. cloth extra, 1s. 6d.

The Bath in Diseases of the Skin. Small 8vo, 1s.; cloth extra, 1s. 6d.

The Laws of Life, and their Relation to Diseases of the Skin. Small 8vo, 1s.; cloth extra, 1s. 6d.

Post 8vo, cloth limp, 2s. 6d. per volume.

Mayfair Library, The:

A Journey Round My Room. By XAVIER DE MAISTRE. Translated by HENRY ATTWELL.

Latter-Day Lyrics. Edited by W. DAVENPORT ADAMS.

Quips and Quiddities. Selected by W. DAVENPORT ADAMS.

The Agony Column of "The Times," from 1800 to 1870. Edited, with an Introduction, by ALICE CLAY.

Balzac's "Comédie Humaine" and its Author. With Translations by H. H. WALKER.

Melancholy Anatomised: A Popular Abridgment of "Burton's Anatomy of Melancholy."

Gastronomy as a Fine Art. By BRILLAT-SAVARIN.

The Speeches of Charles DICKENS.

Literary Frivolities, Fancies, Follies, and Frolics. W. T. DOBSON.

Poetical Ingenuities andEccentricities. Selected and Edited by W. T. DOBSON.

The Cupboard Papers. By FIN-BEC.

Original Plays by W. S. GILBERT. FIRST SERIES. Containing: The Wicked World—Pygmalion and Galatea—Charity—The Princess—The Palace of Truth—Trial by Jury.

Original Plays by W. S. GILBERT. SECOND SERIES. Containing: Broken Hearts—Engaged—Sweethearts—Gretchen—Dan'l Druce—Tom Cobb—H.M.S. Pinafore—The Sorcerer—The Pirates of Penzance.

Animals and their Masters. By Sir ARTHUR HELPS.

Curiosities of Criticism. By HENRY J. JENNINGS.

The Autocrat of the Breakfast-Table. By O. WENDELL HOLMES. Illustrated by J. GORDON THOMSON.

Pencil and Palette. By ROBERT KEMPT.

Clerical Anecdotes. By JACOB LARWOOD.

Forensic Anecdotes; or, Humour and Curiosities of the Law and Men of Law. By JACOB LARWOOD.

Theatrical Anecdotes. By JACOB LARWOOD.

Carols of Cockayne. By HENRY S. LEIGH.

Jeux d'Esprit. Edited by ditto.

The True History of Joshua Davidson. By E. LYNN LINTON.

Witch Stories. By E. L. LINTON.

Pastimes and Players. By ROBERT MACGREGOR.

The New Paul and Virginia. By W. H. MALLOCK.

The New Republic. By ditto.

Muses of Mayfair. Edited by H. CHOLMONDELEY-PENNELL.

Thoreau: His Life and Aims By H. A. PAGE.

Puck on Pegasus. By H. CHOLMONDELEY-PENNELL.

Puniana. By the Hon. HUGH ROWLEY.

More Puniana. By ditto.

The Philosophy of Handwriting. DON FELIX DE SALAMANCA.

By Stream and Sea. By WILLIAM SENIOR.

Old Stories Re-told. By WALTER THORNBURY.

Leaves from a Naturalist's Note-Book. By Dr. ANDREW WILSON.

Large 4to, bound in buckram, 21s.

Moncrieff.—The Abdication; or, Time Tries All.

An Historical Drama. By W. D. SCOTT-MONCRIEFF. With Seven Etchings by JOHN PETTIE, R.A., W. Q. ORCHARDSON, R.A., J. MAC WHIRTER, A.R.A., COLIN HUNTER, R. MACBETH and TOM GRAHAM.

Square 8vo, cloth extra, with numerous Illustrations, 7s.6d.

North Italian Folk.

By Mrs. COMYNS CARR. Illustrated by RANDOLPH CALDECOTT.

"*A delightful book, of a kind which is far too rare. If anyone wants to really know the North Italian folk, we can honestly advise him to omit the journey, and read Mrs. Carr's pages instead. . . Description with Mrs. Carr is a real gift . It is rarely that a book is so happily illustrated.*"—CONTEMPORARY REVIEW.

New Novels:

SABRAN. By OUIDA. 3 vols., crown 8vo. [Shortly.
WOMEN ARE STRANGE, &c. By F. W. ROBINSON, Author of "Grandmother's Money." 3 vols., crown 8vo.
THE CAPTAINS' ROOM, &c. By WALTER BESANT, Author of "All Sorts and Conditions of Men," &c. 3 vols., crown 8vo.
OF HIGH DEGREE. By CHARLES GIBBON, Author of "Robin Gray," "The Golden Shaft," &c. 3 vols., crown 8vo. [Shortly.
SELF-CONDEMNED. By Mrs. ALFRED HUNT. 3 vols., crown 8vo. [Shortly.
KIT: A Memory. By JAMES PAYN. 3 vols., crown 8vo.
VAL STRANGE: A Story of the Primrose Way. By DAVID CHRISTIE MURRAY. 3 vols., crown 8vo.
REGIMENTAL LEGENDS. By J. S. WINTER, Author of "Cavalry Life," &c. 3 vols., crown 8vo.
THE GOLDEN SHAFT. By CHARLES GIBBON, Author of "Robin Gray," &c. 3 vols., crown 8vo.
GIDEON FLEYCE. By HENRY W. LUCY. 3 vols., crown 8vo.
KEPT IN THE DARK. By ANTHONY TROLLOPE. With a Frontispiece by J. E. MILLAIS, R.A. 2 vols., post 8vo, 12s.
FOXGLOVE MANOR. By ROBERT BUCHANAN, Author of "God and the Man," &c. 3 vols., crown 8vo. [Shortly.
DUST: A Story. By JULIAN HAWTHORNE, Author of "Garth," "Sebastian Strome," &c. 3 vols., crown 8vo. [Shortly.
BEAUTY AND THE BEAST. By SARAH TYTLER. 3 vols., crown 8vo. [Shortly.
HEART AND SCIENCE: A Story of the Present Day. By WILKIE COLLINS. 3 vols., crown 8vo. [Shortly.
A NEW COLLECTION of STORIES by CHARLES READE is now in preparation, in 3 vols., crown 8vo.

Post 8vo, cloth extra, Illustrated, 5s.

Number Nip (Stories about),
The Spirit of the Giant Mountains. Retold for Children by WALTER GRAHAME. With Illustrations by J. MOYR SMITH.

O'Shaughnessy (Arthur), Works by:
Songs of a Worker. Fcap. 8vo, cloth extra, 7s. 6d.
Music and Moonlight. Fcap. 8vo, cloth extra, 7s. 6d.
Lays of France. Crown 8vo, cloth extra, 10s. 6d.

Crown 8vo, red cloth extra, 5s. each.

Ouida's Novels.—Library Edition.

Held in Bondage.	Pascarel.
Strathmore.	Two Little Wooden Shoes,
Chandos.	Signa.
Under Two Flags.	In a Winter City,
Idalia.	Ariadne.
Cecil Castlemaine's Gage.	Friendship.
Tricotrin.	Moths.
Puck.	Pipistrello.
Folle Farine.	A Village Commune.
A Dog of Flanders.	In Maremma.

*** Also a Cheap Edition of all but the last, post 8vo, illustrated boards, 2s. each.
OUIDA'S NEW STORIES.—Sq. 8vo, cloth gilt, cinnamon edges, 7s. 6d.
BIMBI: Stories for Children. By OUIDA.

Crown 8vo, cloth extra, with Vignette Portraits, price 6s. per Vol.

Old Dramatists, The:

Ben Jonson's Works.
With Notes Critical and Explanatory, and a Biographical Memoir by WIL-LIAM GIFFORD. Edited by Colonel CUNNINGHAM. Three Vols.

Chapman's Works.
Complete in Three Vols. Vol. I. contains the Plays complete, including the doubtful ones; Vol. II. the Poems and Minor Translations, with an Introductory Essay by ALGERNON

CHARLES SWINBURNE; Vol. III. the Translations of the Iliad and Odyssey.

Marlowe's Works.
Including his Translations. Edited, with Notes and Introduction, by Col. CUNNINGHAM. One Vol.

Massinger's Plays.
From the Text of WILLIAM GIFFORD. Edited by Col. CUNNINGHAM. One Vol.

Post 8vo, cloth limp, 1s. 6d.

Parliamentary Procedure, A Popular Handbook of. By HENRY W. LUCY.

Crown 8vo, cloth extra, 6s.

Payn.—Some Private Views:

Being Essays contributed to *The Nineteenth Century* and to *The Times*. By JAMES PAYN, Author of " Lost Sir Massingberd," &c.

⁎ For Mr. PAYN's *Novels, see* pp. 22, 24, 25.

Two Vols. 8vo, cloth extra, with Portraits, 10s. 6d.

Plutarch's Lives of Illustrious Men.

Translated from the Greek, with Notes Critical and Historical, and a Life of Plutarch, by JOHN and WILLIAM LANGHORNE.

Proctor (Richard A.), Works by:

Flowers of the Sky. With 55 Illustrations. Small crown 8vo, cloth extra, 4s. 6d.

Easy Star Lessons. With Star Maps for Every Night in the Year, Drawings of the Constellations, &c. Crown 8vo, cloth extra, 6s.

Familiar Science Studies. Crown 8vo, cloth extra, 7s. 6d.

Myths and Marvels of Astronomy. Crown 8vo, cloth extra, 6s.

Pleasant Ways in Science. Crown 8vo, cloth extra, 6s.

Rough Ways made Smooth: A Series of Familiar Essays on Scientific Subjects. Crown 8vo, cloth extra, 6s.

Our Place among Infinities: A Series of Essays contrasting our Little Abode in Space and Time with the Infinities Around us. Crown 8vo, cloth extra, 6s.

The Expanse of Heaven: A Series of Essays on the Wonders of the Firmament. Crown 8vo, cloth extra, 6s.

Saturn and its System. New and Revised Edition, with 13 Steel Plates. Demy 8vo, cloth extra, 10s. 6d.

The Great Pyramid: Observatory, Tomb, and Temple. With Illustrations. Crown 8vo, cloth extra, 6s.

Mysteries of Time and Space. With Illustrations. Crown 8vo, cloth extra, 7s. 6d. [In preparation.

Wages and Wants of Science Workers. Crown 8vo, 1s. 6d.

" *Mr. Proctor, of all writers of our time, best conforms to Matthew Arnold's conception of a man of culture, in that he strives to humanise knowledge and divest it of whatever is harsh, crude, or technical, and so makes it a source of happiness and brightness for all.*"—WESTMINSTER REVIEW.

LIBRARY EDITIONS, many Illustrated, crown 8vo, cloth extra, 3s. 6d. each.

Piccadilly Novels, The.

Popular Stories by the Best Authors.

BY MRS. ALEXANDER.
Maid, Wife, or Widow?

BY W. BESANT & JAMES RICE.
Ready-Money Mortiboy.
My Little Girl.
The Case of Mr. Lucraft.
This Son of Vulcan.
With Harp and Crown.
The Golden Butterfly.
By Celia's Arbour.
The Monks of Thelema.
'Twas in Trafalgar's Bay.
The Seamy Side.
The Ten Years' Tenant.
The Chaplain of the Fleet.

BY ROBERT BUCHANAN.
A Child of Nature.
God and the Man.

BY MRS. H. LOVETT CAMERON.
Deceivers Ever.
Juliet's Guardian.

BY WILKIE COLLINS.
Antonina. | Basil.
Hide and Seek.
The Dead Secret.
Queen of Hearts.
My Miscellanies.
The Woman in White.
The Moonstone.
Man and Wife.
Poor Miss Finch.
Miss or Mrs?
The New Magdalen.
The Frozen Deep.
The Law and the Lady.
The Two Destinies.
The Haunted Hotel.
The Fallen Leaves.
Jezebel's Daughter.
The Black Robe.

BY M. BETHAM-EDWARDS.
Felicia.

BY MRS. ANNIE EDWARDES.
Archie Lovell.

BY R. E. FRANCILLON.
Olympia. | Queen Cophetua.

BY EDWARD GARRETT.
The Capel Girls.

BY CHARLES GIBBON.
Robin Gray.
For Lack of Gold.
In Love and War.
What will the World Say?
For the King.
In Honour Bound.
Queen of the Meadow.
In Pastures Green.
The Flower of the Forest.
A Heart's Problem.

BY THOMAS HARDY.
Under the Greenwood Tree.

BY JULIAN HAWTHORNE.
Garth.
Ellice Quentin.
Sebastian Strome.

BY MRS ALFRED HUNT.
Thornicroft's Model.
The Leaden Casket.

BY JEAN INGELOW.
Fated to be Free.

BY HENRY JAMES, Jun.
Confidence.

BY HARRIETT JAY.
The Queen of Connaught.
The Dark Colleen.

BY HENRY KINGSLEY.
Number Seventeen.
Oakshott Castle.

BY E. LYNN LINTON.
Patricia Kemball.
Atonement of Leam Dundas.
The World Well Lost.
Under which Lord?
With a Silken Thread.
The Rebel of the Family.
"My Love!"

BY JUSTIN McCARTHY, M.P.
The Waterdale Neighbours.
My Enemy's Daughter.
Linley Rochford.
A Fair Saxon.
Dear Lady Disdain.
Miss Misanthrope.
Donna Quixote.
The Comet of a Season.

PICCADILLY NOVELS—*continued.*

BY *KATHARINE S. MACQUOID.*

Lost Rose. | The Evil Eye.

BY *FLORENCE MARRYAT.*

Open! Sesame!
Written in Fire.

BY *JEAN MIDDLEMASS.*

Touch and Go.

BY *D. CHRISTIE MURRAY.*

A Life's Atonement.
Joseph's Coat.

BY *MRS. OLIPHANT.*

Whiteladies.

BY *JAMES PAYN.*

Lost Sir Massingberd.
The Best of Husbands.
Fallen Fortunes. | Halves.
Walter's Word
What He Cost Her.
Less Black than We're Painted.
By Proxy. | Under One Roof.
High Spirits. | Carlyon's Year.
A Confidential Agent.
From Exile.

BY *CHARLES READE, D.C.L.*

It is Never Too Late to Mend.
Hard Cash. | Peg Woffington.
Christie Johnstone.
Griffith Gaunt.
The Double Marriage.
Love Me Little, Love Me Long.

By CHARLES READE—*continued.*

Foul Play.
The Cloister and the Hearth.
The Course of True Love.
The Autobiography of a Thief.
Put Yourself in His Place.
A Terrible Temptation.
The Wandering Heir.
A Simpleton.
A Woman-Hater. | Readiana.

BY *MRS. J. H. RIDDELL.*

Her Mother's Darling.

BY *JOHN SAUNDERS.*

Bound to the Wheel.
Guy Waterman.
One Against the World.
The Lion in the Path.
The Two Dreamers.

BY *BERTHA THOMAS.*

Proud Maisie. | Cressida.
The Violin-Player.

BY *ANTHONY TROLLOPE.*

The Way we Live Now.
The American Senator.

BY *T. A. TROLLOPE.*

Diamond Cut Diamond.

BY *SARAH TYTLER.*

What She Came Through.
The Bride's Pass.

BY *J. S. WINTER.*

Cavalry Life.

NEW VOLUMES OF THE PICCADILLY NOVELS IN THE PRESS.

All Sorts and Conditions of Men. By WALTER BESANT. Illustrated by FRED. BARNARD.
The Shadow of the Sword. By ROBERT BUCHANAN.
The Martyrdom of Madeline. By ROBERT BUCHANAN.
Love Me for Ever. By ROBERT BUCHANAN. Front. by P. MACNAB.
Sweet Anne Page. By MORTIMER COLLINS.
Transmigration. Ditto.
Blacksmith and Scholar. Ditto.
From Midnight to Midnight. Do.
The Village Comedy. Ditto.
You Play me False. Ditto.
Hearts of Gold. By WM. CYPLES.
One by One. R. E. FRANCILLON.
The Braes of Yarrow. By CHARLES GIBBON.
Prince Saroni's Wife. By JULIAN HAWTHORNE.

Ivan de Biron. By Sir ARTHUR HELPS.
Paul Faber, Surgeon. By GEO. MACDONALD, LL.D. With a Frontispiece by J. E. MILLAIS, R.A.
Thomas Wingfold, Curate. By GEORGE MACDONALD, LL.D. With a Frontispiece by C. J. STANILAND.
Coals of Fire. By D. CHRISTIE MURRAY. Illust.by ARTHUR HOPKINS, G. L. SEYMOUR, and D. T. WHITE.
A Grape from a Thorn. By JAMES PAYN. Illust. by W. SMALL.
For Cash Only. By JAMES PAYN.
Valentina. By E. C. PRICE.
The Prince of Wales's Garden-Party. By Mrs. J. H. RIDDELL.
The Mysteries of Heron Dyke. By T. W. SPEIGHT.
Frau Frohmann. By ANTHONY TROLLOPE.
Marion Fay. By A. TROLLOPE.

Post 8vo, illustrated boards, 2s. each.

Popular Novels, Cheap Editions of.

[WILKIE COLLINS'S NOVELS and BESANT and RICE'S NOVELS may also be had in cloth limp at 2s. 6d. See, too, the PICCADILLY NOVELS, for Library Editions.]

BY EDMOND ABOUT.
The Fellah.

BY HAMILTON AÏDÉ.
Confidences.
Carr of Carrlyon.

BY MRS. ALEXANDER.
Maid, Wife, or Widow?

BY W. BESANT & JAMES RICE.
Ready-Money Mortiboy.
With Harp and Crown.
This Son of Vulcan.
My Little Girl.
The Case of Mr. Lucraft.
The Golden Butterfly.
By Celia's Arbour.
The Monks of Thelema.
'Twas in Trafalgar's Bay.
The Seamy Side.
The Ten Years' Tenant.

BY SHELSLEY BEAUCHAMP.
Grantley Grange

BY FREDERICK BOYLE.
Camp Notes. | Savage Life.

BY BRET HARTE.
An Heiress of Red Dog.
The Luck of Roaring Camp.
Gabriel Conroy. | Flip.

BY MRS. BURNETT.
Surly Tim.

BY MRS. H. LOVETT CAMERON.
Deceivers Ever.
Juliet's Guardian.

BY MACLAREN COBBAN.
The Cure of Souls.

BY C. ALLSTON COLLINS.
The Bar Sinister.

BY WILKIE COLLINS.
Antonina. | Basil.
Hide and Seek.
The Dead Secret.
The Queen of Hearts.
My Miscellanies.
The Woman in White.
The Moonstone.
Man and Wife.
Poor Miss Finch.
Miss or Mrs.?
The New Magdalen.
The Frozen Deep.
The Law and the Lady.

By WILKIE COLLINS—*cont.*
The Two Destinies.
The Haunted Hotel.
Fallen Leaves.
Jezebel's Daughter.

BY DUTTON COOK.
Leo.

BY MRS. ANNIE EDWARDES.
A Point of Honour.
Archie Lovell.

BY M. BETHAM-EDWARDS.
Felicia.

BY EDWARD EGGLESTON.
Roxy.

BY PERCY FITZGERALD.
Polly. | Bella Donna.
Never Forgotten.
The Second Mrs. Tillotson.
Seventy-five Brooke Street.

BY ALBANY DE FONBLANQUE
Filthy Lucre.

BY R. E. FRANCILLON.
Olympia. | Queen Cophetua.

BY EDWARD GARRETT.
The Capel Girls.

BY CHARLES GIBBON.
Robin Gray.
For Lack of Gold.
What will the World Say?
In Honour Bound.
The Dead Heart.
In Love and War.
For the King.
Queen of the Meadow.
In Pastures Green.

BY JAMES GREENWOOD.
Dick Temple.

BY ANDREW HALLIDAY.
Every-day Papers.

BY LADY DUFFUS HARDY.
Paul Wynter's Sacrifice.

BY THOMAS HARDY.
Under the Greenwood Tree.

BY JULIAN HAWTHORNE.
Garth. | Ellice Quentin.

BY TOM HOOD.
A Golden Heart.

BY VICTOR HUGO.
The Hunchback of Notre Dame.

POPULAR NOVELS—*continued.*

BY MRS. ALFRED HUNT.
Thornicroft's Model.

BY JEAN INGELOW.
Fated to be Free.

BY HENRY JAMES, Jun.
Confidence.

BY HARRIETT JAY.
The Queen of Connaught.
The Dark Colleen.

BY HENRY KINGSLEY.
Number Seventeen.
Oakshott Castle.

BY E. LYNN LINTON.
Patricia Kemball.
Atonement of Leam Dundas.
The World Well Lost.
Under which Lord?
With a Silken Thread.

BY JUSTIN McCARTHY, M.P.
The Waterdale Neighbours.
Dear Lady Disdain.
My Enemy's Daughter.
A Fair Saxon.
Linley Rochford.
Miss Misanthrope.
Donna Quixote.

BY AGNES MACDONELL.
Quaker Cousins.

BY KATHARINE S. MACQUOID.
The Evil Eye. | Lost Rose.

BY FLORENCE MARRYAT.
Open! Sesame!
A Harvest of Wild Oats.
A Little Stepson.
Fighting the Air.
Written in Fire.

BY JEAN MIDDLEMASS.
Touch and Go.
Mr. Dorillion.

BY D. CHRISTIE MURRAY.
A Life's Atonement.

BY MRS. OLIPHANT.
Whiteladies.

BY OUIDA.
Held in Bondage.
Strathmore. | Chandos.
Under Two Flags.
Idalia.
Cecil Castlemaine's Gage.
Tricotrin
Puck. | Folle Farine.

By OUIDA—*cont.*
A Dog of Flanders.
Pascarel.
Two Little Wooden Shoes.
Signa.
In a Winter City.
Ariadne. | Friendship.
Moths. | Pipistrello.
A Village Commune.

BY JAMES PAYN.
Lost Sir Massingberd.
A Perfect Treasure.
Bentinck's Tutor.
Murphy's Master.
A County Family.
At Her Mercy.
A Woman's Vengeance.
Cecil's Tryst.
The Clyffards of Clyffe.
The Family Scapegrace.
The Foster Brothers.
Found Dead.
Gwendoline's Harvest.
Humorous Stories.
Like Father, Like Son.
A Marine Residence.
Married Beneath Him.
Mirk Abbey.
Not Wooed, but Won.
Two Hundred Pounds Reward.
The Best of Husbands.
Walter's Word. | Halves.
Fallen Fortunes.
What He Cost Her.
Less Black than we're Painted.
By Proxy.
Under One Roof.
High Spirits.
A Confidential Agent.
Carlyon's Year.

BY EDGAR A. POE.
The Mystery of Marie Roget.

BY CHARLES READE, D.C.L.
It is Never Too Late to Mend.
Hard Cash.
Peg Woffington.
Christie Johnstone.
Griffith Gaunt.
The Double Marriage.
Love Me Little, Love Me Long.
Foul Play.
The Cloister and the Hearth.
The Course of True Love.
The Autobiography of a Thief.
Put Yourself in his Place.

POPULAR NOVELS—*continued.*

BY MRS. J. H. RIDDELL.
Her Mother's Darling.

BY GEORGE AUGUSTUS SALA.
Gaslight and Daylight.

BY JOHN SAUNDERS.
Bound to the Wheel.
Guy Waterman.
One Against the World.
The Lion in the Path.

BY ARTHUR SKETCHLEY.
A Match in the Dark.

BY WALTER THORNBURY.
Tales for the Marines.

BY ANTHONY TROLLOPE.
The Way we Live Now.
The American Senator.

BY T. ADOLPHUS TROLLOPE
Diamond Cut Diamond.

BY MARK TWAIN.
A Pleasure Trip in Europe.
Tom Sawyer.
An Idle Excursion.

BY LADY WOOD.
Sabina.

BY EDMUND YATES.
Castaway.
Forlorn Hope.
Land at Last.

ANONYMOUS.
Paul Ferroll.
Why P. Ferroll Killed his Wife.

NEW TWO-SHILLING NOVELS IN THE PRESS.

The Chaplain of the Fleet. By BESANT and RICE.
The Shadow of the Sword. By ROBERT BUCHANAN.
A Child of Nature. R. BUCHANAN.
Sweet Anne Page. By MORTIMER COLLINS.
Transmigration. Ditto.
Frances. Ditto.
Sweet and Twenty. Ditto.
Blacksmith and Scholar. Ditto.
From Midnight to Midnight. Do.
A Fight with Fortune. Ditto.
The Village Comedy. Ditto.
You Play me False. Ditto.
The Black Robe. By WILKIE COLLINS.
One by One. R. E. FRANCILLON.
Dr. Austin's Guests. W. GILBERT.
The Wizard of the Mountain. By WILLIAM GILBERT.
James Duke. By WM. GILBERT.
Sebastian Strome. By JULIAN HAWTHORNE.
Ivan de Biron. By Sir A. HELPS.

The Leaden Casket. By Mrs. ALFRED HUNT.
The Rebel of the Family. By Mrs. LYNN LINTON.
"My Love!" E. LYNN LINTON.
Paul Faber, Surgeon. By GEO. MACDONALD, LL.D.
Thomas Wingfold, Curate. Do.
New Republic. W. H. MALLOCK.
Phœbe's Fortunes. By Mrs. ROBERT O'REILLY.
From Exile. By JAMES PAYN.
Some Private Views. Ditto.
Valentina. By E. C. PRICE.
A Levantine Family. By BAYLE ST. JOHN.
The Two Dreamers. By JOHN SAUNDERS.
The Mysteries of Heron Dyke. By T. W. SPEIGHT.
Cressida. By BERTHA THOMAS.
Proud Maisie. BERTHA THOMAS.
The Violin-Player. Ditto.
What She Came Through. By SARAH TYTLER.

Fcap. 8vo, picture covers, 1s. each.

Jeff Briggs's Love Story. By BRET HARTE.
The Twins of Table Mountain. By BRET HARTE.
Mrs. Gainsborough's Diamonds. By JULIAN HAWTHORNE.
Kathleen Mavourneen. By the Author of "That Lass o' Lowrie's."
Lindsay's Luck. By the Author of "That Lass o' Lowrie's."
Pretty Polly Pemberton. By the Author of "That Lass o' Lowrie's."
Trooping with Crows. By Mrs. PIRKIS.
The Professor's Wife. By LEONARD GRAHAM.
A Double Bond. By LINDA VILLARI.
Esther's Glove. By R. E. FRANCILLON.
The Garden that Paid the Rent. By TOM JERROLD.

Planché (J. R.), Works by:

The Cyclopædia of Costume; or, A Dictionary of Dress—Regal, Ecclesiastical, Civil, and Military—from the Earliest Period in England to the Reign of George the Third. Including Notices of Contemporaneous Fashions on the Continent, and a General History of the Costumes of the Principal Countries of Europe. By J. R. PLANCHÉ, Somerset Herald. Two Vols. demy 4to, half morocco, profusely Illustrated with Coloured and Plain Plates and Woodcuts, £7 7s. The Volumes may also be had *separately* (each complete in itself) at £3 13s. 6d. each: Vol. I. THE DICTIONARY. Vol. II. A GENERAL HISTORY OF COSTUME IN EUROPE.

The Pursuivant of Arms; or, Heraldry Founded upon Facts. By J. R. PLANCHÉ. With Coloured Frontispiece and 200 Illustrations. Crown 8vo, cloth extra, 7s. 6d.

Songs and Poems, from 1819 to 1879. By J. R. PLANCHÉ. Edited, with an Introduction, by his Daughter, Mrs. MACKARNESS. Crown 8vo, cloth extra, 6s.

Crown 8vo, cloth extra, with Portrait and Illustrations, 7s. 6d.

Poe's Choice Prose and Poetical Works.

With BAUDELAIRE'S Essay on his Life and Writings.

Small 8vo, cloth extra, with 130 Illustrations, 3s. 6d.

Prince of Argolis, The:

A Story of the Old Greek Fairy Time. By J. MOYR SMITH.

Crown 8vo, cloth extra, with Illustrations, 7s. 6d.

Rabelais' Works.

Faithfully Translated from the French, with variorum Notes, and numerous characteristic Illustrations by GUSTAVE DORÉ.

Crown 8vo, cloth gilt, with numerous Illustrations, and a beautifully executed Chart of the various Spectra, 7s. 6d.

Rambosson.—Popular Astronomy.

By J. RAMBOSSON, Laureate of the Institute of France. Translated by C. B. PITMAN. Profusely Illustrated.

Entirely New Edition, Revised, crown 8vo, 1,400 pages, cloth extra, 7s. 6d.

Reader's Handbook (The) of Allusions, References, Plots, and Stories. By the Rev. Dr. BREWER. Third Edition, revised throughout, with a New Appendix, containing a COMPLETE ENGLISH BIBLIOGRAPHY.

Crown 8vo, cloth extra, 6s.

Richardson. — A Ministry of Health, and

other Papers. By BENJAMIN WARD RICHARDSON, M.D., &c.

Rimmer (Alfred), Works by:

Our Old Country Towns. By ALFRED RIMMER. With over 50 Illustrations by the Author. Square 8vo, cloth extra, gilt. 10s. 6d.

Rambles Round Eton and Harrow. By ALFRED RIMMER. With 50 Illustrations by the Author. Square 8vo, cloth gilt, 10s. 6d.

About England with Dickens. With Illustrations by ALFRED RIMMER and C. A. VANDERHOOF. Sq. 8vo, cl. gilt, 10s. 6d. [*In preparation.*

Crown 8vo, cloth extra, 7s. 6d.

Robinson.—The Poets' Birds.

By PHIL. ROBINSON, Author of " Noah's Ark," &c. [*In the press.*

Handsomely printed, price 5s.

Roll of Battle Abbey, The;

or, A List of the Principal Warriors who came over from Normandy with William the Conqueror, and Settled in this Country, A.D. 1066–7. With the principal Arms emblazoned in Gold and Colours.

Crown 8vo, cloth extra, profusely Illustrated, 4s. 6d. each.

" Secret Out " Series, The :

The Pyrotechnist's Treasury; or, Complete Art of Making Fire-works. By THOMAS KENTISH. With numerous Illustrations.

The Art of Amusing : A Collection of Graceful Arts, Games, Tricks, Puzzles, and Charades. By FRANK BELLEW. 300 Illustrations.

Hanky-Panky : Very Easy Tricks, Very Difficult Tricks, White Magic, Sleight of Hand. Edited by W. H. CREMER. 200 Illusts.

The Merry Circle : A Book of New Intellectual Games and Amusements. By CLARA BEL-LEW. Many Illustrations.

Magician's Own Book : Performances with Cups and Balls, Eggs, Hats, Handkerchiefs, &c. All from actual Experience. Edited by W. H. CREMER. 200 Illustrations.

Magic No Mystery : Tricks with Cards, Dice, Balls, &c., with fully descriptive Directions; the Art of Secret Writing; Training of Performing Animals, &c. Coloured Frontispiece and many Illustrations.

The Secret Out : One Thousand Tricks with Cards, and other Recreations; with Enter-taining Experiments in Drawing-room or "White Magic." By W. H. CREMER. 300 Engravings.

Crown 8vo, cloth extra, 6s.

Senior.—Travel and Trout in the Antipodes.

An Angler's Sketches in Tasmania and New Zealand. By WILLIAM SENIOR (" Red-Spinner "), Author of " By Stream and Sea."

Shakespeare :

The First Folio Shakespeare.— MR. WILLIAM SHAKESPEARE'S Comedies, Histories, and Tragedies. Published according to the true Originall Copies. London, Printed by ISAAC IAGGARD and ED. BLOUNT. 1623.—A Reproduction of the extremely rare original, in reduced facsimile by a photographic process—ensuring the strictest accuracy in every detail. Small 8vo, half-Roxburghe, 7s. 6d.

The Lansdowne Shakespeare. Beautifully printed in red and black, in small but very clear type. With engraved facsimile of DROESHOUT'S Portrait. Post 8vo, cloth extra, 7s. 6d.

Shakespeare for Children : Tales from Shakespeare. By CHARLES and MARY LAMB. With numerous Illustrations, coloured and plain, by J. MOYR SMITH. Crown 4to, cloth gilt, 6s.

The Handbook of Shakespeare Music. Being an Account of 350 Pieces of Music, set to Words taken from the Plays and Poems of Shakespeare, the compositions ranging from the Elizabethan Age to the Present Time. By ALFRED ROFFE. 4to, half-Roxburghe, 7s.

A Study of Shakespeare. By ALGERNON CHARLES SWINBURNE. Crown 8vo, cloth extra, 8s.

Crown 8vo, cloth extra, gilt, with 10 full-page Tinted Illustrations, 7s. 6d.

Sheridan's Complete Works,

with Life and Anecdotes. Including his Dramatic Writings, printed from the Original Editions, his Works in Prose and Poetry, Transla-tions, Speeches, Jokes, Puns, &c. With a Collection of Sheridaniana.

Crown 8vo, cloth extra, with 100 Illustrations, 7s. 6d.

Signboards:
Their History. With Anecdotes of Famous Taverns and Remarkable Characters. By JACOB LARWOOD and JOHN CAMDEN HOTTEN.

Crown 8vo, cloth extra, gilt, 6s. 6d.

Slang Dictionary, The:
Etymological, Historical, and Anecdotal.

Exquisitely printed in miniature, cloth extra, gilt edges, 2s. 6d.

Smoker's Text-Book, The.
By J. HAMER, F.R.S.L.

Demy 8vo, cloth extra, Illustrated, 14s.

South-West, The New:
Travelling Sketches from Kansas, New Mexico, Arizona, and Northern Mexico. By ERNST VON HESSE-WARTEGG. With 100 fine Illustrations and 3 Maps. [In preparation.

Crown 8vo, cloth extra, 5s.

Spalding.—Elizabethan Demonology:
An Essay in Illustration of the Belief in the Existence of Devils, and the Powers possessed by them. By T. ALFRED SPALDING, LL.B.

Crown 4to, with Coloured Illustrations, cloth gilt, 6s.

Spenser for Children.
By M. H. TOWRY. With Illustrations by WALTER J. MORGAN.

A New Edition, small crown 8vo, cloth extra, 5s.

Staunton.—Laws and Practice of Chess;
Together with an Analysis of the Openings, and a Treatise on End Games. By HOWARD STAUNTON. Edited by ROBERT B. WORMALD.

Crown 8vo, cloth extra, 9s.

Stedman.—Victorian Poets:
Critical Essays. By EDMUND CLARENCE STEDMAN.

Stevenson (R. Louis), Works by:
Familiar Studies of Men and Books. By R. LOUIS STEVENSON. Crown 8vo, cloth extra, 6s.

New Arabian Nights. By R. LOUIS STEVENSON. New and Cheaper Edition. Crown 8vo, cloth extra, 6s.

" We must place the 'New Arabian Nights' very high indeed, almost hors concours, among the fiction of the present day."—PALL MALL GAZETTE.

Two Vols., crown 8vo, with numerous Portraits and Illustrations, 24s.

Strahan.—Twenty Years of a Publisher's
Life. By ALEXANDER STRAHAN. [In preparation.

Crown 8vo, cloth extra, with Illustrations, 7s. 6d.

Strutt's Sports and Pastimes of the People of
England; including the Rural and Domestic Recreations, May Games, Mummeries, Shows, Processions, Pageants, and Pompous Spectacles, from the Earliest Period to the Present Time. With 140 Illustrations. Edited by WILLIAM HONE.

Crown 8vo, with a Map of Suburban London, cloth extra, 7s. 6d.

Suburban Homes (The) of London:

A Residential Guide to Favourite London Localities, their Society, Celebrities, and Associations. With Notes on their Rental, Rates, and House Accommodation.

Crown 8vo, cloth extra, with Illustrations, 7s. 6d.

Swift's Choice Works,

In Prose and Verse. With Memoir, Portrait, and Facsimiles of the Maps in the Original Edition of "Gulliver's Travels."

Swinburne's (Algernon C.) Works:

The Queen Mother and Rosa-mond. Fcap. 8vo, 5s.

Atalanta in Calydon.
A New Edition. Crown 8vo, 6s.

Chastelard.
A Tragedy. Crown 8vo, 7s.

Poems and Ballads.
FIRST SERIES. Fcap. 8vo, 9s. Also in crown 8vo, at same price.

Poems and Ballads.
SECOND SERIES. Fcap. 8vo, 9s. Also in crown 8vo, at same price.

Notes on Poems and Reviews.
8vo, 1s.

William Blake:
A Critical Essay. With Facsimile Paintings. Demy 8vo, 16s.

Songs before Sunrise.
Crown 8vo, 10s. 6d.

Bothwell:
A Tragedy. Crown 8vo, 12s. 6d.

George Chapman:
An Essay. Crown 8vo, 7s.

Songs of Two Nations.
Crown 8vo, 6s.

Essays and Studies.
Crown 8vo, 12s.

Erechtheus:
A Tragedy. Crown 8vo, 6s.

Note of an English Republican
on the Muscovite Crusade. 8vo, 1s.

A Note on Charlotte Bronte.
Crown 8vo, 6s.

A Study of Shakespeare.
Crown 8vo, 8s.

Songs of the Springtides.
Crown 8vo, 6s.

Studies in Song.
Crown 8vo, 7s.

Mary Stuart:
A Tragedy. Crown 8vo, 8s.

Tristram of Lyonesse, and other
Poems. Crown 8vo, 9s.

Medium 8vo, cloth extra, with Illustrations, 7s. 6d.

Syntax's (Dr.) Three Tours,

In Search of the Picturesque, in Search of Consolation, and in Search of a Wife. With the whole of ROWLANDSON'S droll page Illustrations in Colours, and a Life of the Author by J. C. HOTTEN.

Four Vols. small 8vo, cloth boards, 30s.

Taine's History of English Literature.

Translated by HENRY VAN LAUN.

. Also a POPULAR EDITION, in Two Vols. crown 8vo, cloth extra, 15s.

Crown 8vo, cloth gilt, profusely Illustrated, 6s.

Tales of Old Thule.

Collected and Illustrated by J. MOYR SMITH.

One Vol., crown 8vo, cloth extra, 7s. 6d.

Taylor's (Tom) Historical Dramas:

"Clancarty," " Jeanne Darc," " 'Twixt Axe and Crown," " The Fool's Revenge," " Arkwright's Wife," " Anne Boleyn," " Plot and Passion."
*** The Plays may also be had separately, at 1s. each.

Crown 8vo, cloth extra, with numerous Illustrations, 7s. 6d.

Thackerayana:

Notes and Anecdotes. Illustrated by a profusion of Sketches by WILLIAM MAKEPEACE THACKERAY, depicting Humorous Incidents in his School-life, and Favourite Characters in the books of his every-day reading. With Coloured Frontispiece and Hundreds of Wood Engravings, facsimiled from Mr. Thackeray's Original Drawings.

Crown 8vo, cloth extra, gilt edges, with Illustrations, 7s. 6d.

Thomson's Seasons and Castle of Indolence.

With a Biographical and Critical Introduction by ALLAN CUNNING-HAM, and over 50 fine Illustrations on Steel and Wood.

Thornbury (Walter), Works by:

Haunted London. Edited by EDWARD WALFORD, M.A. With Illustrations by F. W. FAIRHOLT, F.S.A. Crown 8vo, cloth extra, 7s. 6d.
The Life and Correspondence of J. M. W. Turner. Founded upon Letters and Papers furnished by his Friends and fellow Academicians. With numerous Illustrations in Colours, facsimiled from Turner's Original Drawings. Crown 8vo, cloth extra, 7s. 6d.

Timbs (John), Works by:

Clubs and Club Life in London. With Anecdotes of its Famous Coffee-houses, Hostelries, and Taverns. With numerous Illustrations. Crown 8vo, cloth extra, 7s. 6d.
English Eccentrics and Eccentricities: Stories of Wealth and Fashion, Delusions, Impostures, and Fanatic Missions, Strange Sights and Sporting Scenes, Eccentric Artists, Theatrical Folks, Men of Letters, &c. With nearly 50 Illustrations. Crown 8vo, cloth extra, 7s. 6d.

Demy 8vo, cloth extra, 14s.

Torrens.—The Marquess Wellesley,

Architect of Empire. An Historic Portrait. *Forming Vol. I. of* PRO-CONSUL and TRIBUNE: WELLESLEY and O'CONNELL: Historic Portraits. By W. M. TORRENS, M.P. In Two Vols.

Large folio, handsomely bound, 31s. 6d.

Turner's Rivers of England:

Sixteen Drawings by J. M. W. TURNER, R.A., and Three by THOMAS GIRTIN, Mezzotinted by THOMAS LUPTON, CHARLES TURNER, and other Engravers. With Descriptions by Mrs. HOFLAND. A New Edition, reproduced by Heliograph. Edited by W. COSMO MONK-HOUSE, Author of "The Life of Turner" in the "Great Artists" Series. [*Shortly.*

Two Vols., crown 8vo, cloth extra, with Map and Ground-Plans, 14s.

Walcott.—Church Work and Life in English

Minsters; and the English Student's Monasticon. By the Rev. MACKENZIE E. C. WALCOTT, B.D.

The Twenty-third Annual Edition, for 1883, cloth, full gilt, 50s.

Walford.—The County Families of the United

Kingdom. By EDWARD WALFORD, M.A. Containing Notices of the Descent, Birth, Marriage, Education, &c., of more than 12,000 distinguished Heads of Families, their Heirs Apparent or Presumptive, the Offices they hold or have held, their Town and Country Addresses, Clubs, &c.

Large crown 8vo, cloth antique, with Illustrations, 7s. 6d.

Walton and Cotton's Complete Angler;

or, The Contemplative Man's Recreation; being a Discourse of Rivers, Fishponds, Fish and Fishing, written by IZAAK WALTON; and Instructions how to Angle for a Trout or Grayling in a clear Stream, by CHARLES COTTON. With Original Memoirs and Notes by Sir HARRIS NICOLAS, and 61 Copperplate Illustrations.

Crown 8vo, cloth extra, 3s. 6d. per volume.

Wanderer's Library, The:

Wanderings in Patagonia; or, Life among the Ostrich Hunters. By JULIUS BEERBOHM. Illustrated.

Camp Notes: Stories of Sport and Adventure in Asia, Africa, and America. By FREDERICK BOYLE.

Savage Life. By FREDERICK BOYLE.

Merrie England in the Olden Time. By GEORGE DANIEL. With Illustrations by ROBT. CRUIKSHANK.

The World Behind the Scenes. By PERCY FITZGERALD.

Circus Life and Circus Celebrities. By THOMAS FROST.

The Lives of the Conjurers. By THOMAS FROST.

The Old Showmen and the Old London Fairs. By THOMAS FROST.

Low-Life Deeps. An Account of the Strange Fish to be found there. By JAMES GREENWOOD.

The Wilds of London. By JAMES GREENWOOD.

Tunis: The Land and the People. By the Chevalier de HESSE-WARTEGG. With 22 Illustrations.

The Life and Adventures of a Cheap Jack. By One of the Fraternity. Edited by CHARLES HINDLEY.

Tavern Anecdotes and Sayings: Including the Origin of Signs, and Reminiscences connected with Taverns, Coffee Houses, Clubs, &c. By CHARLES HINDLEY. With Illusts.

The Genial Showman: Life and Adventures of Artemus Ward. By E. P. HINGSTON. Frontispiece.

The Story of the London Parks. By JACOB LARWOOD. With Illusts.

London Characters. By HENRY MAYHEW. Illustrated.

Seven Generations of Executioners: Memoirs of the Sanson Family (1688 to 1847). Edited by HENRY SANSON.

Summer Cruising in the South Seas. By CHARLES WARREN STODDARD. Illust. by CHARLES MACKAY.

Carefully printed on paper to imitate the Original, 22 in. by 14 in., 2s.

Warrant to Execute Charles I.

An exact Facsimile of this important Document, with the Fifty-nine Signatures of the Regicides, and corresponding Seals.

Beautifully printed on paper to imitate the Original MS., price 2s.

Warrant to Execute Mary Queen of Scots.

An exact Facsimile, including the Signature of Queen Elizabeth, and a Facsimile of the Great Seal.

Crown 8vo, cloth limp, with numerous Illustrations, 4s. 6d.

Westropp.—Handbook of Pottery and Porce-

lain ; or, History of those Arts from the Earliest Period. By HODDER M. WESTROPP. With numerous Illustrations, and a List of Marks.

SEVENTH EDITION. Square 8vo, 1s.

Whistler v. Ruskin : Art and Art Critics.

By J. A. MACNEILL WHISTLER.

Williams (Mattieu), Works by :

Science in Short Chapters. By W. MATTIEU WILLIAMS, F.R.A.S., F.C.S. Crown 8vo, cloth extra, 7s. 6d.

A Simple Treatise on Heat. By W. MATTIEU WILLIAMS F.R.A.S., F.C.S. Crown 8vo, cloth limp, with Illustrations, 2s. 6d.

Wilson (Dr. Andrew), Works by :

Chapters on Evolution : A Popular History of the Darwinian and Allied Theories of Development. By ANDREW WILSON, Ph.D., F.R.S.E. Crown 8vo, cloth extra, with 259 Illustrations, 7s. 6d.

Leaves from a Naturalist's Note-book. By ANDREW WILSON, Ph.D., F.R.S.E. (A Volume of "The Mayfair Library.") Post 8vo. cloth limp, 2s. 6d.

Leisure - Time Studies, chiefly Biological. By ANDREW WILSON, Ph.D., F.R.S.E. Second Edition. Crown 8vo, cloth extra, with Illustrations, 6s.

"It is well when we can take up the work of a really qualified investigator. who in the intervals of his more serious professional labours sets himself to impart knowledge in such a simple and elementary form as may attract and instruct with no danger of misleading the tyro in natural science. Such a work is this little volume, made up of essays and addresses written and delivered by Dr. Andrew Wilson, lecturer and examiner in Science at Edinburgh and Glasgow, at leisure intervals in a busy professional life. . . . Dr. Wilson's pages teem with matter stimulating to a healthy love of science and a reverence for the truths of nature."—SATURDAY REVIEW.

Small 8vo, cloth extra, Illustrated, 6s.

Wooing (The) of the Water Witch :

A Northern Oddity. By EVAN DALDORNE. Illust. by J. MOYR SMITH.

Crown 8vo, half-bound, 12s. 6d.

Words, Facts, and Phrases :

A Dictionary of Curious, Quaint, and Out-of-the-Way Matters. By ELIEZER EDWARDS.

Wright (Thomas), Works by :

Caricature History of the Georges. (The House of Hanover.) With 400 Pictures, Caricatures, Squibs, Broadsides, Window Pictures, &c. By THOMAS WRIGHT, F.S.A. Crown 8vo, cloth extra, 7s. 6d.

History of Caricature and of the Grotesque in Art, Literature, Sculpture, and Painting. By THOMAS WRIGHT, F.S.A. Profusely Illustrated by F. W. FAIRHOLT, F.S.A. Large post 8vo, cloth extra, 7s. 6d.

J. OGDEN AND CO., PRINTERS, 172, ST. JOHN STREET. E.C.